SUSPENDED SENTENCES:
FICTIONS OF ATONEMENT

For Amparo, Ana and Philip

and for
my aunt Margaret McWatt, the real
story-teller of the family, whose
stories, told to us as children,
are still vivid in my memory.

SUSPENDED SENTENCES:
FICTIONS OF ATONEMENT

MARK MCWATT

PEEPAL TREE

First published in Great Britain in 2005
Peepal Tree Press Ltd
17 King's Avenue
Leeds LS6 1QS
England

ISBN 1 84523 001 9

Peepal Tree gratefully acknowledges Arts Council support

PREFACE

The idea of writing a book of short stories, purportedly by different authors and within a narrative frame, first occurred to me in 1989, when I remember discussing it briefly with David Dabydeen, who thought that it would prove too difficult to maintain distinctions between the styles/voices of the story-tellers. He was (is) probably right, but I wasn't concerned too much with that, I just wanted to try it if/when I got the chance. A brief (and very immature) version of one of the stories existed since 1969, but the writing of the collection really began in the summer of 1999 in Toronto, when I wrote the first draft of 'Uncle Umberto's Slippers'. That story and two others, plus a draft of a fourth, were completed during the month of June, 2000, which I spent as a guest in the small Benedictine Monastery overlooking the Mazaruni river in Guyana. It rained incessantly and I am eternally grateful to Brother Paschal and the other monks for providing me with the time and atmosphere (and that wonderful room looking out on the river) perfect for writing. Over the next two years the plan of the collection was worked out in detail, including the names and personalities of the story-tellers (many modelled loosely on my own college classmates from the mid-sixties) but, although I tinkered a bit with the stories already written, I could not find enough time to write the rest of them until I took sabbatical leave in 2002-03. Two more stories were completed in Toronto before Christmas of 2002 and all the others were written (and the whole book revised) in a little staff flat at the University of Warwick, where I was a Visiting Fellow at the Centre for Caribbean Studies from January to July, 2003. I'm very grateful to the Centre and the

University for the opportunity to work on several writing projects, prominently including this one.

I was told by a literary agent in London (to whom I had sent the typescript) that, although he personally enjoyed the book of stories, collections of short fiction were not at the time commercially marketable, and I would have to try a small publisher somewhere. I'm not so sure about 'small', but Peepal Tree Press – in the person of Jeremy Poynting – agreed to read the book and decided to publish it. For this I am very grateful.

I should thank Joanne Davis, whose delight with the stories she read and whose e-mailed demands for more helped me to keep working on them in the little flat at Warwick. My wife Amparo and my children Ana and Philip also read many of the stories as I finished them, and offered valuable – and sometimes mischievous – comments. I must mention too Margaret McWatt, Wayne McWatt, Ronnie Ramsay, Paschal Jordan, Al Creighton, Hazel Simmons-McDonald and, especially, Gloria Lyn, who all commented usefully on some or all of the stories. David Dabydeen was kind enough to read the completed typescript at a time when he was busy with the finishing touches to his own latest novel. To all these, and any whom I have omitted, I am extremely grateful for the time you took to read my work, for your kind encouragement and your valuable critical comments.

Mark McWatt

CONTENTS

INTRODUCTION

This collection of stories is a project I inherited from my cousin Victor Nunes, who disappeared somewhere in the Pomeroon in 1991. His mother, my aunt Margot, sent a message to me to come and see her urgently about something important when I visited Guyana in 1994, and she handed me a battered grey box-file which contained versions of six of the stories and several pages of Victor's notes and drafts; she told me that he had considered it an important project and a serious obligation, although several of 'the others' (and she gave me an accusing look), didn't seem to share his concern... It was true that I had put off the business of finishing my own story for the collection, in part because I was not convinced that there was ever any legal obligation to do so, but also because Victor had always insisted that mine be the last story in the collection, and that it must tell the tale of what happened on the night of the 'celebration' which had resulted in the 'court case' and the imposed sentence of writing stories for and about our (at the time) newly independent Guyana. On the other hand, I'd always considered it a good pretext for getting a collection of short stories published, and had never entirely abandoned my part in the project.

I told Aunt Margot – in fact she made me promise solemnly – that I would take over and complete the business of collecting, editing and publishing the stories, if only that they might serve, as she put it, as a fitting memorial to her son who had disappeared overboard in the Pomeroon river and was presumed drowned. The more I read of the material in the box-file (and the more stories and revisions I was able to wring out of the scattered members of the gang), the more enthusiastic I became about seeing the project concluded, but I have not really had the time both to pester the delinquent contributors and to work steadily at the editing, and it is only now, in the third year of a new millennium that I've managed to complete the task – some two years after, I might add, the demise of my aunt Margot.

For the rest of this introduction I make use of Victor Nunes' drafts and jottings (in italics – as opposed to my own interpolations, which are in normal script, and between square brackets). The stories themselves are roughly in the order he had devised, although four of the six stories that he would have read have been revised by their authors at my invitation.

THE GANG
[written in August, 1966]

The authors of these stories were members of a gang of sixth-formers at St. Stanislaus College, most of whom completed their A-level exams in 1966, a month after Guyana achieved independence. It was not a gang in the sense that we had a specific purpose or aim, but rather a group people thrown together by time and circumstance who chose to spend their spare time together, whether it be to study or to lime. I suppose I was leader of the gang by default, as it were, and because I took the trouble to do what minimal organizing was necessary for our various study and other sessions... St. Stanislaus [was in those days] of course a boys' school, but there were a couple of convent girls eagerly conscripted into our gang, since they attended our sixth form for classes in subjects not taught at the convent. In addition, one of our members was from the lower sixth (principally, I believe, because he happened to be a cousin of mine and tended to hang around with me (us). There was also one member of the gang who was a fifth-former, but was permitted to take A-level Art (at which he was brilliant) and simply assumed that he was entitled thereby to be a member of the gang. Here are brief descriptions of the members of the gang (and therefore the authors of the stories):

[**Victor Vibert Nunes** – Head boy of the College, leader of the group: serious and scholarly with strong organizational and planning skills; his birth certificate describes him as a 'mixed native of Guyana' and he claims that a measure of Amerindian blood is part of that mix. Good at languages which he took at A-level.]

Desmond Stewart Arthur – *Desi lives for literature, at which he excels; has written plays which have been performed at college; sensitive, loyal and probably homosexual. He's like a brother to Hilary Sutton and is specially fond of Nickie Calistro.*

Geoffrey Anselm deMattis – *Of Portuguese extraction but with dark brown skin; mischievous, inclined to be chubby and brilliant at the sciences. With a surname like his it was in the nature of our Catholic high-school wit to nickname him 'Nunc' deMattis. Nunc is an only*

11

child with wealthy parents who have more-or-less adopted the gang which is always over at his house.

Hilary Augusta Sutton – 'High brown', upper middle-class convent girl from an old Georgetown family which lives in a large wooden house with a tower. She tends to be touchy about class and propriety. She did Maths and Physics in our science sixth.

Jamila Muneshwar – Indian with smooth, beautiful, very dark skin (almost purple, like a jamoon, which is her nickname). She is the daughter of a prominent surgeon and did History and Geography in our sixth form.

Hilton Aubrey Llewellyn Seaforth – Called 'Prince Hal' because of his initials; deputy head-boy, tall and dark with stately, aristocratic bearing. Aloof and monumentally calm, Hal is the son of a head-teacher and afraid of no-one. Brilliant at History and Languages and is expected to win a scholarship.

Valmiki Madramootoo – Indian, son of a wealthy businessman who owns several cinemas and nightclubs. Light-skinned, grey-eyed, handsome and epicurean, Val is our expert on films, food and fashion. He did Literature and Modern Languages.

Terrence Gregory Wong – Known as 'Tennis Roll' because of his predilection for tennis rolls with cheese. Short, porcupine-haired, Chinese, T. Roll is playful and somewhat naive, though brilliant at Maths and Physics. He is impulsive and always falling in love.

Mark Andrew McWatt – First cousin to V.V. Nunes, Mac is in the lower sixth. The son of a District Commissioner, he knows a lot about the interior and the rivers of Guyana and has been writing poems about these. He is taking Literature, Latin and History.

Alexander Joseph Fonseca – Still a fifth-former, he's the baby of the group and diminutive to boot (hence his nickname: 'Smallie'). He makes up for his small stature by being loud and assertive; he's a prodigious and gifted artist with a foul tongue and a vocation to the priesthood.

John Dominic Calistro *– Came into our Sixth form from a school in the interior. During term-time he boards in the home of V.V. Nunes, his cousin, since his parents live in the interior. He's known as 'Nickie' and is always telling stories about his large, half-Amerindian family: parents, uncles, cousins, all of whom live in one huge house. Superstitious, fun-loving and illogical, Nickie did English, Geography and History. The smallest amount of alcohol puts him into a deep sleep.*

[I was tempted, at this distance from the sixties, to alter the above brief 'portraits' by removing the ethnic references which now seem at least gauche (by most standards, though mild perhaps, in terms of the rampant racial polarization in contemporary Guyana), but I decided that they help date the document and give, I think, an accurate indication of the preoccupations of Georgetown society at the time. Also, I did not want to appear to be quarrelling petulantly with Victor's descriptions.]

THE COURT CASE
[written in March–April, 1967]

Rather than recount at length the events that took place at the Sports club of the Imperial Bank on Friday 9th July, just over a month after independence, I have asked my cousin Mark McWatt to make his story a narrative of that evening's happenings and this will be the last 'story' in the collection. The reasons for my choice of the author and the position of this story will become evident at the end of the book. [I have no idea what Victor meant by this remark: I did not write my assigned 'story' until five years after he had disappeared and I often wonder what he imagined I would say in it]. *Suffice it to say that the gang of students listed above met at the club to celebrate both the end of A-level exams and the country's independence which they could not properly celebrate at the actual time because they were busy studying for the exams – and, due in part to an excess of alcohol and high spirits, they vandalized the club, defacing walls and destroying property. Nine members of the gang were charged with wilful damage of the Bank's property, although the Bank declined to press charges and it appeared as though a number of parents were involved in 'arranging' for the court case that followed a week later.* [I was surprised to find that Victor had written this last sentence, because he had always insisted that the court case was genuine and our obligations were clear, while most of the rest of us were convinced, even at that time, that the whole thing was a charade cooked up by some parents and their friends in the judiciary and legal profession to throw a scare into us and to teach us a lesson]

On Saturday morning (17th July) we all turned up in the courtroom of Mr. Justice Chanderband [this was, of course, long before he became Sir Ronald and ascended to his sinecure in the Hague], *along with Willow, our Literature teacher and Aubrey Chase, a lawyer and cousin of Hilary Sutton. There was also the police sergeant who went to the club on the night of the vandalism and who served as prosecutor. The judge began by making us all recite our names and addresses, including Mac and Smallie, although they had not been charged since they had gone home early, before any damage was done. Then the charges were read and the sergeant was asked by the judge to expand on the actual damage done:*

'This graffiti, the defacement of the upstairs wall... Can you tell the court, Sergeant, exactly what was written – or rather painted?'

'Yes, Milord,' and he opened his notebook and read: 'There was a two-line sentence as follows: 'Sir Eustace is an anachronism and Lady Dowding is a tight-assed termagant' (Sir Eustace, as your lordship is no doubt aware, is the English manager of the Imperial Bank); this was followed by a single word, 'latifundia' and then another sentence 'Don't pick the blue hibiscus'; finally there was a large blue hibiscus painted on the wall.'

'Anachronism', 'termagant', 'latifundia': were these words correctly spelt, Sergeant?'

'I believe so, Milord.'

'Not your run-of-the-mill graffiti artists, eh Sergeant? At least this new country can boast of literate vandals...' and the sergeant chuckled politely.

All of our other misdeeds that night were recounted in detail: the emptying of over forty bottles of whiskey and other spirits from the bar into the swimming pool, the tipping of a large concrete planter, full of soil and red geraniums, into the pool and the tying up and gagging of the barman, Mr. Dornford and the caretaker/watchman, Mr. Ramkisoon. Judge Chanderband had wonderfully expressive eyebrows and with each item related he managed to contort them into an expression of ever-increasing horror and disbelief. After telling us that these were very serious offences, he asked if any of us had anything to say. We all said, in mournful demeanour and suitably contrite tones, that we had had too much to drink, pointing out that Sir Rupert Dowding himself had generously told the barman to give us whatever we wanted to drink. Val, Nickie and Desmond also made the point that we were carried away by the euphoria of having completed our A-level examinations. The judge wore a tired smile through all this and seemed totally unimpressed. Aubrey Chase then spoke on our behalf, pointing out that we had all admitted our guilt and drunkenness and misbehaviour.

'Although your lordship might want to consider whether it was not even greater misbehaviour – or at least poor judgment – to give a gang of teenagers the freedom of drinking whatever they wanted from the bar... We should consider, too, the fact that the premises were officially closed for renovations at the time: furniture was covered with tarpaulins, the walls were primed, there were pots of paint lying around and *there was an atmosphere of chaos and confusion at the club – which is why there was no adult member present that evening who might have restrained these reckless young people…'*

Judge Chanderband gave poor Aubrey a withering look and proceeded to tear his arguments to shreds, pointing out that those charged were all adults, and highly intelligent and educated adults at that, and must take full responsibility for their behaviour since the same would be expected of a bunch of vagrants off the street whose entire lives might be 'chaos and confusion'. Sir Rupert's generosity might have been misguided, but could never be blamed for the criminal acts committed by this group of delinquents who certainly knew that what they were doing was wrong… If, my dear Mr. Chase, that kind of crippled argument is the best you can do in defence of these boys, I suggest that it would be better if you said nothing… I understand that there's a teacher who would like to say something on their behalf?…'

[As I recall it, both judge Chanderband and Aubrey Chase were laughing during this entire exchange, and that contributed to our perception that the entire proceedings were not to be taken seriously]

At this point Willow spoke, supposedly on our behalf, but he began by tearing into us, saying how disappointed he and the other masters were in us and that he felt it as a personal failure. He outlined our past academic achievements as well as the expectations the school had of each of us in the exams, concluding in each case with a version of the following: 'Of course all that's now up in the air; it's anybody's guess what he will achieve in the exams if he is capable of deviating so widely from the kind of behaviour we had every right to expect of him…' In fact it was a brilliant performance: he seemed at various points angry, deeply disappointed, shocked and saddened almost to the point of tears by what we had done, while saying at the same time what we were capable of doing and how great a contribution we could have been expected to make to our newly independent country, if only we had not spoiled everything that night by 'behaving worse than a class of unsupervised second-formers.' Then, having stolen much of the judge's thunder, he even managed to suggest what might be imposed on us by way of punishment.

'I do not plead for them to be excused or pardoned. What they did deserves punishment, and I'm sure, My Lord, that you will not hesitate to impose it; for my part, whatever you do decide on in the way of

punishment, I would wish, if possible to add to that the kind of punishment that will force them to realize some of the potential that they seem to have abandoned or negated in one night of drunken recklessness. I know what they are capable of: they are all bright, creative individuals with wonderful imaginations and, instead of defiling their new country by their actions, I'd like to see them being forced to help build it up in an important area, such as it's creative literature. I'd make each of them write a short story for or about their country and will not consider their debt to their country discharged until the collection of stories (which I feel could be a wonderful collection if they take it seriously) is published and available to their fellow Guyanese...'

Well, we were all in deep shock. [No argument here, Willow's performance was the one genuine moment of the 'trial' and we were all amazed and filled with shame and remorse by what he said; I've often thought that those who hastened to write their stories, did so for the English master and not for the judge or the so called court sentence.] *The Judge then tried to crush us with sarcasm and anger, but his fulminations were negated by the fact that we were still reeling from Willow's tirade and, in any case, judge Chanderband just couldn't match, in our minds, the sense of our unjust defilement of the confidence placed in us by our English master. He 'sentenced' us each to two weeks in prison and suspended the sentences for two years on condition that we keep the peace and avoid further trouble **and** that we each write a short story within that time that could be collected and published in an anthology of nine Guyanese short stories. He said that I, as head boy and leader of the gang, must undertake to collect and edit the stories.* [Actually he tried to get Willow to do it, but the teacher insisted that the entire project should be undertaken by the students themselves and it was he who suggested that Victor be made responsible for collecting and editing the stories.] *Willow said it should be eleven and not nine short stories, since Mac and Smallie were members of gang and it was 'accidental' that they were absent when the mischief took place. The judge replied that he had no objection to the two extra stories, although he could not impose this on the other two as part of a sentence.*

That is the origin of this project, therefore, and of my responsibility as editor. Thus far only two stories have been submitted and I am working on my own... [I now think that Victor needed to believe,

17

or to pretend to believe, in the sentences in order to continue collecting the stories; to several of us it was clear that there was no genuine court case, and Hilary told us that Aubrey Chase admitted as much, a few months after. Besides, Nunc overheard his mother telling someone on the phone: 'Anyway, my dear, we got Ronnie Chanderband to put the fear of God into them in what they think is a real court case – suspended sentences and all...' When it became my task to extract the remaining stories and revisions from members of the gang after all the years, I did not pretend that it was in order to fulfil a long forgotten sentence, but rather to honour the memory of our leader Victor Nunes, now presumed dead, and to make some contribution to the literature of Guyana, a country which most of us have abandoned and which seems in worse shape now than it was at independence.]

Victor Nunes/Mark McWatt

UNCLE UMBERTO'S SLIPPERS

by Dominic Calistro

Uncle Umberto was my father's eldest brother and he was well known for two things: the stories he told about ghosts and strange things that happened to him, and his slippers, which were remarkable because of their size. Uncle Umberto had the most enormous feet and could never get them into any shoe that a store would sell. When I was a small boy I remember him trying to wear the ubiquitous rubber flip-flops that we all wore. Uncle Umberto would wear the largest size he could find, but when he stood in them nothing could be seen of the soles, for his large feet completely covered them – only the two tight and straining coloured straps could be seen, emerging from beneath the calloused edges of his flat feet and disappearing between his toes. They never lasted very long and the story goes that Aunt Teresa, his wife, used to buy six pairs at a time, trying to get them all of the same colour so people would not realize how quickly Uncle Umberto's feet could destroy a pair.

But all that was before Uncle Umberto got his famous slippers. It is said that, on a rare trip to the city, Uncle Umberto stood a whole day by a leather craft stall in the big market and watched a Rasta man make slippers out of bits of car tire and lengths of rawhide strap. When he came home from this trip, Uncle set about making his own unique pair of slippers. It seems that no car tire was wide enough for the sole, so Uncle went foraging in the yard of the Public Works Depot in the town and came up with a Firestone truck tire that seemed in fairly good shape, with lots of deeply grooved treads on it – he claimed he 'signalled' to the

19

watchman that he was taking it and the watchman waved him through the gate. This he cut up for the soles of his slippers. Because they had to be so long they did not sit flat on the floor, but curled up somewhat at heel and toe, keeping the curved shape of the tire – this was of course when they did not contain Uncle's vast feet. Each of these soles had three thick, parallel strips of rawhide curving across the front and these kept Uncle Umberto's feet in the slippers. There were no straps around the heel. Uncle made these slippers to last the rest of his life: they were twenty-two inches long, eight inches wide and nearly two inches thick. The grooves in the treads on the sole were one and a quarter inches deep when I measured them about four years before he died – when I was twelve, and beginning to get interested in my family and its wonderful characters and oddities.

The other detail to be mentioned about the slippers is that Uncle Umberto took the trouble to cut or drill his initials into the thick soles, carving H.I.C., Humberto Ignatius Calistro – the central 'I' being about twice the height of the other two letters (he always wrote his name with the 'H', but was unreasonably upset if anyone dared to pronounce it. To be on the safe side, we children decided to abandon the H even in the written form of his name, and he seemed quite happy with this). These incised initials always struck me as being completely unnecessary, if their purpose was to indicate ownership, for there could never be another such pair of quarry barges masquerading as footwear anywhere else in the world.

These then became Uncle's famous badge of recognition – one tended to see the slippers first, and *then* become aware of his presence. Quite often one didn't actually have to see them: a muddy tire print on the bridge into Arjune's rumshop told us that Uncle was in there 'relaxing with the boys'. At home (we all live together in the huge house my grandmother built over the last thirty years of her life) my father would suddenly say, 'Umberto coming, you all start dishing up the food'. When we looked enquiringly at him he would shrug and say, 'I can hear the Firestones coming up the hill', and soon after we would all hear the wooden stairs protesting unmistakably under the weight of Uncle Umberto's footfalls.

My grandfather, whom I never knew, was a seaman; as a youngster he had worked on the government river ferries and coastal steamers, but then, after he'd had two children, and had started quarrelling with my grandmother, he took to going further away on larger ships. Often he would not return for a year or more, but whenever he did he would get my grandmother pregnant and they would start quarrelling and he would be off again, until, in his memory, their painful discord had mellowed into a romantic lovers' tiff – at which point he would return to start all over again. When he returned after the fourth child, it was supposed to be for good, and he actually married my grandmother as a statement of this intention, but when the fifth child was visible in my grandmother's stomach, he became so miserable (she said) and looked so trapped and forlorn, that for his own good she threw him out and told him not to come back until he remembered how to be a real man again. In this way their relationship ebbed and flowed like the great rivers that had ruled their lives and fortunes. They had nine children, although it pleased God, as Grandmother said, to reclaim two of them within their first few years of life.

The cycle of Grandfather's going and coming (and of my grandmother's pregnancies) was broken when he got into a quarrel in some foreign port and some bad men robbed him of his money, beat him up and left him to die on one of those dark and desperate docklands streets that I was readily able to picture, thanks to my mild addiction to American gangster movies. At least this is the version of the story of his death that they told me when I was a boy. As I grew into a teenager and my ears became more attuned to adult conversations – especially those that are whispered – I began to overhear other versions: that yes, the men had killed him, but it was because he had cheated in a card game and won all their money; that he had really died in a brothel in New Orleans, in bed with a woman of stunning beauty called Lucinda – shot by a jealous rival; even that he had been caught on a ship that was smuggling narcotics into the United States, and was thrown to the sharks by federal agents who boarded the vessel at sea... At any rate he was still quite a young man when he died.

My grandmother mourned her husband for thirty years by embarking on a building project of huge proportions – the house we now lived in. She decided she would move her family out of the unhealthy capital city on the coast and build them a home on a hill overlooking the wide river and the small riverside mining town in which she herself was born. The first section of the house ('the first Bata shoe box', as my father puts it) was built by a carpenter friend of my grandmother's who had hopes of replacing my grandfather in her affections, and ultimately in the home he was building for her. My grandmother allegedly teased and strung him along, like Penelope, until the new house was habitable; then, becoming her own Ulysses, she quarrelled with him in public and sent him packing. The next section of the house was built when Uncle Umberto, the eldest boy, was old enough to build it for her, and for the next twenty years he periodically added on another 'shoe box', until the house became as I now know it – a huge two-story structure with labyrinthine corridors and innumerable bedrooms and bathrooms (none of which has ever been completely finished) and the four 'tower' rooms, one at each corner, projecting above the other roofs and affording wonderful views of the town, river and surrounding forest. It is to one of these towers – the one we call 'the bookroom' – that I have retreated to write this story.

When Uncle Umberto began to clear the land to lay the foundation for the third 'shoe box' (in the year of the great drought), he said one night he saw a light, like someone waving a flashlight, coming from one of the sandbanks that had appeared out of the much diminished river. Next morning he saw a small boy apparently stranded on the bank and he went down to the river, got into the corrial and paddled across. When he got close to the bank he realized that it was not a boy, but a naked old man, scarcely four feet tall, with a wispy beard and an enormous, crooked penis. This man gesticulated furiously to Uncle, indicating first that he should paddle closer to the sandbank and then, when the bow of the corrial had grated on the sand, that he should come no further. Uncle swears that the little man held him paralysed in the stern of the boat and spoke to him at length in a language he did not understand, although somehow he knew that

22

the man was telling him not to build the extension to the house, because an Indian chief had been buried in that spot long ago.

My grandmother, who had lived the first fifteen years of her life aboard her father's sloop and had seen everything there is to be seen along these coasts and rivers, did not believe in ghosts and walking spirits and she would have none of it when Uncle Umberto suggested they abandon the second extension to the house. To satisfy Uncle she allowed him to dig up the entire rectangle of land and when no bones were found, she said: 'O.K. Umberto, you've had your fun, now get serious and build on the few rooms we need so your brother Leonard could marry the woman he living in sin with and move her in with the rest of the family. It's more important to avoid giving offence to God than to worry about some old-time Indian chief who probably wasn't even a Christian anyway.'

So Uncle built the shoe box despite his misgivings, but the day before his brother Leonard was to be married, there was an accident at the sawmill where he worked and a tumbling greenheart log jammed him onto the spinning blade and his body was cut in two just below the breastbone. Everyone agreed it was an accident, but Uncle Umberto knew why it had happened. Aunt Irene, Uncle Leonard's bride, who was visibly pregnant at the time, moved into the new extension nevertheless and she and my big cousin Lennie have been part of the household ever since. Uncle Umberto, who never had children of his own, became like a father to Lennie and took special care of him, claiming that, from infancy, the boy had the identical crooked, oversized penis that the old man on the sandbank had flaunted. Uncle Umberto also saw from time to time in that part of the house apparitions of both his brother Leonard and the Indian chief, the latter arrayed in plumed headdress and beaded loincloth and sitting awkwardly on the bed or on the edge of Aunt Irene's mahogany bureau.

The others now living in the big house were my own family – Papi, Mami, my sister Mac, my two brothers and I – my uncle John, the lawyer, and his wife Aunt Monica, my uncle 'Phonso and the four children that my aunt Carmen had for four different men before she decided to get serious about life and move to the States, where she now works in a factory that builds aeroplanes and lives with an ex-monk who can't stand children. My father's other sister has also lived in the States from as far back as I can remember.

Actually, my Uncle 'Phonso doesn't really live with us either – he is the youngest and, it is said, the most like his father, both in terms of his skill as a seaman and his restlessness and rebellious spirit. He took over the running of my grandmother's sloop (which plies up and down the rivers, coasts and nearby islands, as it always has, engaged equally in a little trading and a little harmless smuggling), and always claimed he could never live under the same roof with 'the old witch' (his mother). So he spends most of his life on the sloop. On every long trip he takes a different female companion ('...just to grieve me and to force me to spend all my time praying and burning candles for his wicked soul,' my grandmother said). Once a year the sloop would be hauled up onto the river bank below our house for four or five weeks, so that Uncle Umberto could replace rotten planks and timbers and caulk and paint it. During this time Uncle 'Phonso would have his annual holiday in his section of the family home.

Uncle John, the lawyer, was the most serious of my father's brothers – though he was not really a lawyer. From as long as I can remember he has worked in the district administrator's office and has been 'preparing' to be a lawyer by wearing pin-striped shirts and conservative ties and dark suits and highly polished black shoes. His apprenticeship to the profession became an eternal dress rehearsal. Packages of books and papers would arrive for him from overseas (though less frequently in recent years) and we would all be impressed at this evidence of his scholarly intent, but as far as I know he has never sat an exam. He and Aunt Monica live very comfortably off his salary as a clerk in the district office, but they have agreed not to have any children until he is qualified. In the early years of their marriage the couple was cruelly teased about not having children. Papi would say, 'Hey, Johnno, you sure is Monica Suarez you married, and not Rima Valenzuela?' Rima Valenzuela was a beautiful and warm-hearted woman in town notorious for her childlessness. Since she was a teenager she has longed for children and tried to conceive with the aid of an ever-lengthening list of men (including, it was rumoured, one or two of my uncles). She was said to be close to forty now, and was beginning despairingly to accept what people had been telling her for years – that she was barren.

Every new-year's day after mass people would say to Uncle John, 'Well, Johnno, this is the year; don't forget to invite me to the celebrations when they call you to the bar.' But no one really believes any more that he will actually become a lawyer. One year Uncle 'Phonso patted him on the back and said consolingly, 'Never mind, brother John, there's a big sand bar two-three miles down river; I can take you there in the sloop any time you want, and you can tell all these idiots that you've been called to the bar, you didn't like the look of it and you changed your mind.'

In a way, Aunt Monica was as strangely obsessive as Uncle John. Papi said it was because she had no children to occupy her and bring her to her senses. She seemed to dedicate her life to neatness and cleanliness, not only making sure that Uncle John's lawyerly apparel was always impeccable, but every piece of cloth in their section of the house, from handkerchief to bed-sheet to window-blind, was more than regularly washed and – above all – ironed. Aunt Monica spent at least three or four hours every day making sure that every item of cloth she possessed was clean and smooth and shiny. She had ironing boards that folded out from the wall in each of the three rooms she and Uncle John occupied and kept urging the other branches of the family to install similar contraptions in their rooms. Once when my grandmother re-marked: 'All these children! The house beginning to feel crowded again. Umberto, we best think about adding on a few more rooms,' Papi quipped: 'Why? Just so that Monica could put in more fold-out ironing boards?' – and everyone laughed.

★   ★   ★

One morning as we were all at the kitchen table, dressed for work and school and finishing breakfast, Uncle Umberto came into the room in his sleeping attire (short pants and an old singlet) looking restless and confused. We all looked at him, but before anyone could ask, he said: 'You all, I didn't sleep at all last night, because I was studying something funny that happened to me last evening.' Everyone sensed one of his ghost stories coming and we waited

25

expectantly. I had got up from the table to go and do some quick revision before leaving for school, but I stood my ground to listen.

'Just as the sun was going down yesterday I went for my usual walk along the path overlooking the river – you know I does like to watch the sunset on the river and the small boats with people going home up-river from work in town. Suddenly, just as I reach that big rock overhanging the river at Mora Point, this white woman appear from nowhere on top the rock. Is like if she float up or fly up from the river and light on the rock. She was wearing a bright blue dress, shiny like one of them big blue butterflies...'

' Morpho,' interrupted my brother Patrick, the know-it-all. And Papi also had to put in his little bit.

'Shiny blue dress, eh? Take care is not Monica starch and press it for her.' But they were both told to be quiet and let Uncle Umberto get on with his story.

'She beckon me to come up on the rock, so I climb up and stand up there next to her and she start to ask me a whole set of questions – all kind of thing about age and occupation and how long I live in these parts and if I ever travel overseas – and she got a funny squarish black box or bag in her hand. Well, first of all, because she was white I expect her to talk foreign, like somebody from England or America, but she sound just like one of we.' He paused and looked around. 'Then after she had me talking for about ten or fifteen minutes, I venture to ask her about where *she* come from, but she laugh and say: "Oh, that's not important, *you're* the interesting subject under discussion here" – meaning me –' and Uncle Umberto tapped his breastbone twice. 'Then like she sensed that I start to feel a little uneasy, and she say: "Sorry, there's no need to keep you any longer, you can continue your walk." By then like she had me hypnotized, and I climb down from the rock onto the path and start walking away.'

'Eh-eh, when I catch myself, two, three seconds later and look back, the woman done disappear! I hurry back up the rock and I can't see her anywhere. I look up and down the path, I look down at the river, but no sign of her – just a big blue butterfly fluttering about the bushes on the cliff-side...'

It was vintage Umberto. Uncle John said: 'Boy, you still got the gift – you does tell some real good ones.'

'I swear to God,' Umberto said, 'I telling you *exactly* what happen. This isn't no make-up story.'

Still musing about Uncle Umberto's experience, we were all beginning to move off to resume our preparations for school and work, when Aunt Teresa began to speak in an uncharacteristically troubled voice.

'Umberto, I don't know who it is you see, or you think you see, but you got to be careful how you deal with strange women who want to ask a lot of questions – you say she had you hypnotized, well many a man end up losing his mind – not to mention his soul – over women like that. The day you decide to have anything personal to do with this woman, you better forget about me, because I ent having no dealings with devil women...'

This was certainly strange for Aunt Teresa, who usually shrugged off her husband's idiosyncrasies and strange 'experiences' with a knowing smile and a wink at the rest of us. Aunt Teresa's agitation seemed to be contagious among the women of the household. I noticed that Mami seemed suddenly very serious and, as Aunt Teresa continued to speak, Aunt Monica, preoccupied and fidgety, came and stood by the fridge next to me and began to unbutton my school shirt. As she reached the last button and began to pull the shirt-tails out of my pants, the talking stopped and everyone was looking at us.

Too shocked or uncertain to react to this divestiture before, I now smiled nervously and said: 'Hey, Aunty, I'm not too sure what we're supposed to be doing here, but should we be doing it in front of all these others?'

There was a general uproar of laughter and Aunt Monica removed her hands from my shirt as if stung; but she quickly recovered, gave me a swift slap on the cheek, and said, 'Don't fool around with me, boy, I could be your mother. Besides, everybody knows that I'm just taking off this crushed-up excuse for a school shirt to give it a quick press with the steam iron and see if I can't get you to look a little more decent. If your mother can't make sure you all children go to school looking present-able (and you, Mr. Nickie, are the worst of the lot), then somebody else will have to do it, for the sake of the good name of the family you represent...' By the time she'd finished saying this, she was traipsing out of the kitchen waving my shirt behind her like a flag.

We did not realize it at the time, but Uncle Umberto's story was the beginning of a strange sequence of events that was to befall him and to haunt the rest of us for a very long time.

No one was surprised when he revealed, a few days later, that he had met the woman again, and that she had walked up and down the riverside path with him, but the mystery of the woman was solved for me when she came into my classroom at school one day, along with our teacher, Mr. Fitzpatrick, who introduced her as Miss Pauline Vyfhuis, a graduate student who was doing fieldwork for her thesis in Applied Linguistics. She carried a tape-recorder in a black leather case and told us that Professor Rickford at the university had sent her up here to record the people's speech for her research. When I went home and announced this to the family, they all accepted that Miss Vyfhuis must be Uncle Umberto's blue butterfly lady – all except Uncle Umberto himself; he claimed to have spoken at length to his lady and she'd confirmed that she could appear and disappear at will; that she could fly or float in the air and that one day he (Uncle Umberto) would be able to accompany her – floating off the cliff to places unimagined by the rest of us.

'Umberto, before you go floating off over the river,' Papi interjected, 'just make sure you take off them two four-wheel drives 'pon your feet, in case they weight you down and cause you to crash into the river and drown.'

Ignoring Papi, Uncle Umberto went on to tell us that, besides all he'd just said, he had *also* met Miss Vyfhuis, outside Arjune's rumshop, and had even condescended to say a few words into her microphone. She was nothing like his butterfly lady; she was small and mousey-looking, and anyone could see that she could never fly. Also, her tape-recorder was twice the size of the magic black box carried by *his* lady... We shrugged – no one could take away one of Uncle's prized fantasies.

A few months after this my grandmother died one night in her sleep. The family was not overwhelmed with grief; the old lady was eighty-nine years old, and although her death was unexpected, everyone said that it was a good thing that it was not

28

preceded by a long or painful illness. 'She herself would have chosen to go in that way,' Mami said. Uncle Umberto seemed the one most deeply affected by the old lady's passing; he seemed not so much grief-stricken as bewildered. It was as though the event had caught him at a particularly inconvenient time and for days he walked about the house and the streets mumbling and distracted. Uncle Umberto should have become the head of our household, and I suppose he was, in a way, but he seemed to abdicate all responsibility in favour of Aunt Teresa, his wife, who took on the role of making the big decisions and giving orders. Umberto's slippers took their increasingly distracted occupant more and more frequently to the path above the river and he could be seen there not only in the evenings, but now also first thing in the morning and sometimes again in the heat of the day. None of us who saw him ever saw the butterfly woman – nor anyone else, for that matter – walking with him, although there were times when he seemed to be gesticulating to an invisible companion. Mostly he just walked. He haunted the riverside path like a Dutchman's ghost and we all began to worry about him.

One evening not long after this, Uncle Umberto came home dishevelled and distraught, a wild look in his eyes.

'She going,' he said. 'She say is time to go and she want me go with her.'

'Go where?' Aunt Teresa snapped. 'Just look at yourself, Umberto, look at the state you have yourself in over this imaginary creature.'

'I keep telling you,' Umberto pleaded, 'she's not imaginary – I see her for true, swear-to-god, although it seem nobody else can see her. Now she say she going away, and I must go with her – or else follow her later.'

'Tell her you will follow her, man Umberto,' Papi said. 'You know like how a husband or a wife does go off to America and then send later for the other partner and the children. Tell her to go and send for you when she ready. No need to throw yourself off the cliff behind her.'

I was sure Papi was joking, and there was a little nervous laughter in the room, but surprisingly, Umberto thought it was a great idea. His face cleared of its deep frown and he said simply: 'Thank you,

29

Ernesto, I will tell her that and see what she say,' and he went off to his room, followed by his visibly uncomfortable wife.

Two days later Umberto reported that the lady had agreed to the plan; they had said their goodbyes early that morning and she floated off the rock where she had first appeared, and was enveloped in the mist above the river. Umberto seemed in very good spirits and the family breathed a collective sigh of relief. In the weeks immediately following he appeared to be his old self again – having a drink or two with the boys in Arjune's rumshop, joking with the rest of us and talking of replacing the north roof of the house, which had begun to leak again. He never spoke of the butterfly lady.

In just over six weeks, however, Uncle Umberto was dead. He announced one morning that he was taking a walk into town to order galvanize, stepped into his famous slippers and disappeared down the road. It seemed like only minutes later (we hadn't left for school yet) that we heard shouting outside and looked down the road to see Imtiaz, Mr. Wardle from the drug store and even old Lall at the forefront of a crowd of people running up the hill, waving and shouting. The only thing that we could make out in the hubbub was the word 'Umberto'.

It seems Umberto had stopped at the edge of town to chat with a small group of friends when he suddenly looked up, shouted 'Oh God! Child, look out!' and leapt right in front of one of the big quarry trucks that was speeding down the hill. He died where he had landed after the impact, his rib-cage and one arm badly smashed and his face cut above the left eye. The slippers were still on his feet. There was no child – nor anyone else – near to the truck.

Well, you can guess what everyone said: the butterfly woman appeared to him and led him to his death – just when we all thought he was rid of her. The family was devastated. Unlike my grandmother's, Uncle Umberto's funeral was an extremely sad and painful occasion – not least because we saw Umberto's feet, for the first time ever, in a pair of highly polished black shoes. The shoes were large, but not as large as we thought they needed to be to contain Uncle's feet. The thought that the people at the funeral parlour had mutilated his feet and crammed them into those shoes was too much to bear. We all wept, and scarcely anyone looked at Umberto's face as he lay in the coffin – all eyes were on the extraordinary and deeply disturbing sight at its other end. At home, after the burial, we all turned on poor Aunt Teresa – how could she permit the undertakers to mutilate Uncle's feet? My cousin Lennie, his favourite, said tearfully that not even God would recognize Uncle Umberto in those shoes.

'You should have buried him in his slippers; those were his trademark.'

'Trademark, yes,' Aunt Teresa spat, her eyes bright with tears, 'and they made him a laughing-stock – everybody always laughing and making fun of him and his big feet. I wanted that he could have in death the dignity he was never allowed in life, what with Ernesto and John and you and Nickie and the children always making cruel jokes about the feet and the slippers. God knows he used to encourage you all with his antics, it's true, but it always hurt me to hear him ridiculed...'

At that point my brother Patti appeared in the room with the slippers in his hands, saying 'These are fantastic, just amazing – nobody else in the world – just look at them!' And he held them up, tears streaming down his face.

'Give me those!' Aunt Teresa shouted, flying into a rage, 'He only been buried two hours and already you parading these ridiculous things and making fun of the dead. At least you could have a little respect for *my* feelings.'

As she snatched the slippers from Patti I couldn't help noticing with awe that they still had the deep grooves of the tire tread and seemed to be hardly worn. At another time I might have re-marked: 'They look as though they have less than a hundred miles on them' (that is, if Papi didn't beat me to it), but now, with Aunty raging, we all kept silent and watched her disappear into her room, clutching the offending footwear.

★   ★   ★

You might think that the story is now ended, but in fact there is a little more to tell. You must remember that this is not the story of Uncle Umberto, but of his slippers. Several months later, when Aunt Teresa returned from a visit to her sister in Trinidad and seemed to be in a good mood, someone – Lennie, perhaps – casually asked her what had become of Uncle Umberto's slippers. Her face clouded over, but only for an instant. She smiled and said: 'Oh, those things – don't worry, I didn't burn them, only buried them away in the bottom of my trunk. I don't think I'm ready to see them again yet,' and the conversation moved on to other topics.

About a year later, when the house was in general upheaval – because Mr. Moses was replacing the rotten north roof at last; because Aunt Lina (one of my father's sisters) was visiting from New Jersey and because my cousin Lennie had just disgraced us all by getting Rima Valenzuela pregnant (and him barely nineteen!) – Aunt Teresa came into the kitchen one night and announced that Uncle Umberto's slippers had disappeared. 'What you mean "disappeared", Aunty?' Lennie said. 'Remember you told us that you had put them in the bottom of your trunk?'

'Yes,' Aunt Teresa said, 'in this big blue plastic bag; but when I was looking for them just now to show Lina, I find the bag empty. Look, you can still see the print of the truck tire where it press against the plastic for so long under the weight of the things in the trunk.' And she held up the bag for us to see.

'But it's impossible for them to just disappear,' Lennie insisted.

Aunt Teresa gave him a look: 'Just like how it's impossible for Rima Valenzuela to make baby, eh? You proud to admit that you responsible for that miracle; for all I know you may be to blame for this one as well.'

'Ow, Auntie,' I pleaded, 'don't start picking on him again.' I was feeling for Lennie, who had taken a lot of flack from the women in the family (and had become something of an underground hero to the men and boys!).

'OK. Look,' Teresa said, 'I don't know who removed the slippers. I would have said it has to be one of you, but I always lock the trunk, as you know, and walk everywhere with the key – in this menagerie of a house that is the only way I can have a little privacy and be able to call my few possessions my own. The disappearance of the slippers is a real mystery to me, but you could go and search for yourself if you want.' And she flung the bunch of keys at us, shaking her head. We did search – the trunk, the wardrobe, the chest of drawers, under the bed, everywhere, but there was no sign of the slippers. It was a mystery in truth.

Eventually the slippers became a dim memory for most of us. Life moved on; we children continued 'to grow like weeds', as my Aunt Monica would say. I went to board with cousins in the city during term-time, so that I could attend sixth form at college, and I found that my life changed, to the point where all that remained of Uncle Umberto and his slippers were memories, dim and fading memories. But.

After I wrote my last A-level exam – just days ago – I returned home at once to spend some time with my family and to prepare to leave them again in a few months, for I had already received provisional acceptance from the University of Toronto. The day after I returned home, about mid-morning, Aunt Teresa ran into the house in a state of shock; in her hands were Uncle Umberto's slippers. She had taken to walking along the path above the river, almost as regularly as Uncle Umberto had in the years before his death – perhaps she did it in memory of Uncle – but that morning, as she passed the large rock on the cliff at Mora point, she saw on the path, just at the base of the rock, Uncle Umberto's slippers. They were placed neatly, one beside the other, as though some-one had just stepped out of them to climb the rock. There was no one in sight. Aunt Teresa had almost fainted. The rest of us were in shock as well, at seeing the slippers again, and you can well imagine the wild surmises about how they got to be on the path that day.

But the strangest thing was that the slippers, while undoubt-edly Uncle Umberto's (portions of the incised initials were still discernible), had soles that were worn until the thickest parts were less than half as thick as they were when Uncle died; on the sections between instep and the tip of the toe the tire tread was worn away entirely and the rubber was smooth and black. In two and a half years someone – or something – had put ten thousand miles on Uncle Umberto's old Firestones!

The next day I came up here, to the bookroom tower, and began writing this story.

33

TWO BOYS NAMED BASIL

by Hilary Augusta Sutton

Basil Raatgever and Basil Ross were born three days apart in the month of November, 1939. Basil Ross was the elder. From the beginning their lives seem to have been curiously and profoundly interrelated. They were both born to middle-class Guyanese parents of mixed race and their skins were of almost exactly the same hue of brown. They were not related and although their parents knew of each other – as was inevitable in a small society like Georgetown at the time – there was no opportunity for them to meet as young children, because Mr. Ross was a Government dispenser who was posted from time to time to various coastal and interior districts, while the Raatgevers lived in Georgetown, where Mr. Raatgever was some kind of senior clerical functionary in the Transport and Harbours Department.

The two boys met at the age of ten, when Basil Ross began attending the 'scholarship class' in the same primary school in Georgetown which Basil Raatgever had attended from the age of six. Basil Ross had been sent to the city to live with his maternal grandparents so that he could have two years of special preparation in order to sit the Government scholarship examinations. The two Basils found themselves seated next to each other in the classroom and from that moment on their lives and fortunes became intertwined. Before the scholarship class neither child showed any particular scholarly aptitude. They both did well enough to get by, but the fourth standard teacher had already warned Mr. Raatgever not to hope for too much of Basil in the scholarship exams; he was restless and easily distracted, though he seemed to have the ability to do fairly well. Basil Ross, on the

34

other hand, possessed great powers of concentration and could occupy himself enthusiastically and obsessively with a number of demanding hobbies, but for him school work was a chore unworthy of his attention, to be done with haste and little care, so that he could return to his more interesting pursuits.

From the time they were placed together in the same class, however, all this changed. Whether this was due to their awakening to the pleasures and possibilities of scholarship – or simply the instinct to compete, to see which Basil was better – in a strange symbiosis they seemed to draw energy and inspiration from each other. At the end of the first term in scholarship class, Basil Ross was first in class, beating Basil Raatgever into second by a mere four marks. At the end of the second term, the positions were the same but the margin was only two marks, and after the third term – at the end of the first year – Basil Raatgever was first in class, beating Basil Ross by a single mark. And so they continued. The change in both boys was great and the marks they achieved were so astonishing that their teacher, Mr. Francis Greaves, remarked to the Headmistress that they seemed like two halves of a single personality – feeding off each other and challenging each other to achieve more and more.

They both easily won Government scholarships to the high school of their parents' choice, and although the ranking was never publicly announced, rumour had it that Basil Raatgever had scored the highest mark ever achieved in the scholarship examinations and this was two marks higher than Basil Ross's mark. The scholarships they won, in fact, nearly put paid to their remarkable joint development and achievement, for Basil Ross was a Roman Catholic and opted to attend St. Stanislaus college, whereas Basil Raatgever's family, though nominally Anglican, did not practice any religion, and wanted Basil to attend Queen's College, as his father had done. This proved to be a major crisis for the two boys who, at this time, were the best of friends and almost literally inseparable. The two families met and discussed the problem with the boys' teacher, Mr. Greaves. He reminded everyone that the boys' remarkable development as scholars began only when they were placed together at adjoining desks, and continued as a result of their strong friendship and preoccupation with each other. He offered the opinion that to send them to separate schools might cause them to revert to the under-achievement that had characterized their earlier classroom efforts. In the end it was reasoned that, although Queen's College was considered to have the edge academically, the difference was small and the boys seemed to need each other more than they needed top quality teaching. So, since religion was of no conse-quence to the Raatgevers, but of great importance to the Ross family, the boys would go to St. Stanislaus college.

In the first two years at high school, the boys continued taking turns at placing first and second in class; but their strange competitiveness and hunger for achievement began to manifest itself in other spheres, notably on the sports field. Despite their inseparability and the similarity of their accomplishments, the boys were not physically similar. Basil Raatgever was tall for his age and very thin, while Basil Ross had a somewhat shorter, more muscular build. This difference became more evident as the boys grew older, so that when they took to sports they had to settle for achieving equal prowess, but in different spheres. In cricket, for example, Basil Raatgever was a tall and elegant opening batsman, while Basil Ross used his more muscular physique to good effect as a fast bowler and a useful slugger and scrambler for runs in the lower order. In athletics, there was no one in their age-group who could beat Basil Ross in the sprint events and no one who could jump higher than Basil Raatgever. In this way the boys' symbiotic relationship, their friendship and their remarkable dominance in all the areas in which they chose to compete, continued for the first few years at St. Stanislaus college.

Their schoolmates always spoke of them in the same breath - 'Ratty-and-Ross' – as though they were a single person, and boasted to outsiders about their achievements.

It was in the third form that the trouble between the two Basils began. It started, as always, with little things, such as the fact that Raatgever was the first to manifest the onset of puberty. After a brief period of dramatic squeaks and tonal shifts in his voice, especially when chosen to read in class, Basil Raatgever soon acquired a remarkably deep and rich baritone, which seemed all the more incongruous coming from such a slender body. Basil

Ross's voice took longer to change, and in any case did not 'break' dramatically like that of his namesake, but deepened slightly over time, so that by the end of that school year it was different, but still high and somewhat squeaky, compared to Raatgever's. The other boys began to call them 'Ratty-and-Mouse'.

Then religion played a part in dividing the two Basils. They both did equally well in religious studies and Raatgever, although not a Catholic, attended weekly Benediction and Mass on special occasions with the other boys. But in the third form, Basil Ross was trained as an altar-boy, and, on one or two mornings a week he got up early and rode down to the Cathedral to serve at 7:00 o'clock mass. On those days he went straight on to college afterwards and did not cycle to school with Raatgever as they had done since the first day of first form.

Basil Raatgever pretended to take it in his stride – he knew he was not a Catholic and could not serve Mass, and he discovered that he did not really want to, but at the same time he was resentful that Ross had found a sphere of activity from which he was excluded. Basil Raatgever sulked, and in small and subtle ways he began to be mean to Basil Ross in revenge. On one of the days when he knew that Ross would pass by for him, unfasten the front gate, cycle right under the house and whistle for him, Raatgever 'forgot' to chain the dog early in the morning as he always did. The result was that Skip attacked Ross, forcing him to throw down his bike and school books and clamber onto one of the gateposts, putting a small tear in his school pants. Raatgever came down and berated the dog and apologized, but Ross had heard, above the noise of the falling bike and barking dog, muffled laughter coming from the gallery above.

There were other such pranks and, as with everything they did, Basil Ross tried to outdo his friend in this area as well. By the end of that year, when promotion exams were in the offing, each boy ostentatiously cultivated his own circle of friends and the two factions waged continuous verbal warfare.

Then one day Raatgever said: 'Ross now that we're no longer friends, I hope I won't find your name under mine when the exam results are put up – try and come fifth and give me a little breathing space.'

Ross had replied: 'Ha, you wish! You know I'll be coming first in class and I'm certain you'll be swinging on my shirt tails with a close second as usual – but believe me, nothing would please me more than to put a dozen places between us – even if I have to throw away marks to do it.'

Immediately he had said this, both boys were determined to show that their friendship and equality were at an end. The profoundly shocking result was that Basil Ross and Basil Raatgever were ranked a joint 10th in class in the promotion examinations! Even when they were deliberately determined to do badly, each did so to exactly the same extent – in fact they got identical overall marks – and of course, none of their teachers were fooled as they had lost marks with silly, obvious 'mistakes'. They were both sent in to see the headmaster and letters were sent to their parents along with their reports.

This incident had the effect of making both boys more irritated with each other and, at the same time, more certain that there was some uncanny chemistry going on between them that prevented them from breaking free of each other. They began to feel stifled, trapped in their relationship.

Then there was Alison Cossou. She was a bright, vivacious convent girl who boarded with relatives in the house next door to the Raatgever's, because her parents lived in Berbice. Basil Raatgever had known her for years and had found her quite pleasant and easy to talk to, but never had any amorous feelings towards her. Basil Ross too had known her casually, as his friend's next-door neighbour, but when Alison began attending seven o'clock mass at the cathedral and Ross, serving mass, saw her in a different context, he developed a serious crush on her. He would make sure that he touched her chin with the communion plate; this made her eyelids flicker and she would smile and Basil Ross would thrill to a sudden tightness about his heart. Then they took to chatting on the north stairs after mass. When he began stopping outside her gate and chatting with her in full view of the other Basil, the latter felt that he was being outmanoeuvred on his own doorstep and became incensed. So Basil Raatgever launched a campaign to woo and win Alison Cossou from Basil Ross and this new rivalry intensified the bitterness between them, as well as the hopeless sense that their lives would always be intertwined

This situation continued throughout fourth and fifth forms and the boys' mutual hostility and constant sniping at each other began to irk the teachers as well as their classmates. They were still considered inseparable and still spoken of in the same breath, but now their fellows adjusted their joint nickname, so that 'Ratty- and-Ross' became, derisively, 'Batty-and-Rass'. Even so, they continued to draw energy and competitive zeal from each other, so that St. Stanislaus won all the interschool sports events in those years as the two friends/enemies swept all before them.

A month before the O-level exams began, one of the Jesuit masters at the college – one whom all the students respected – had several sessions with them of what, at a later period, would be called 'counselling'. He sat them down, spoke to them as adults and reasoned with them. He listened carefully to all the recriminations and made them see that their main problem was a sense of entrapment – their fear that they did not seem to have the freedom to be separate and authentic persons, but must always in some way, feed on each other in order to survive and to achieve.

The priest told them it was indeed a serious situation but their bitterness towards each other was a natural reaction as they grew towards the self-assertion of adulthood. He told them that the problem was that they did not know how to deal with their dilemma and with each other, but if they promised him to try, he would help them devise strategies to either extricate themselves from, or survive, the suffocating relationship in which they had been for so long.

O-levels were thus written under a truce and in the sixth form, with the help of the Jesuit father, their relationship steadily improved. Alison Cossou and two other girls from the convent joined them in the sixth form since the subjects that they wanted to do were not available at their school. The girls had a calming effect on the class, especially on the two Basils, who outdid each other in being courteous and pleasant. In the sixth form too, the Basils discovered parties and dancing and it didn't take long for everyone to observe with wonder that there was no equality of achievement between the boys in that sphere. Basil Raatgever was a natural dancer – he was self-confident and stylish on the floor and could improvise wonderfully in order to flatter the abilities of all the girls.

The girls were enchanted by him – especially Alison Cossou, who declared one day: 'The man that will marry me must be able to dance up a storm, because I love to dance.'

Basil Ross heard this with dismay but he admitted defeat to himself and considered that Raatgever had won her – for now. It was not that Basil Ross couldn't dance – he made all the correct movements and had a fair sense of rhythm, but he did not attract attention as a dancer the way his friend did, and even he loved to watch the sinuous perfection of his friend Raatgever on the dance floor.

No one will ever know how the relationship might have developed after school, for, just after writing A-levels, there occurred a shocking and mysterious event which is still unexplained and which claimed the life of one of the boys and altered irreparably that of the other.

★   ★   ★

The priest who taught Religious Knowledge and Latin to the sixth forms, Father De Montfort – the same priest who had counselled the two Basils earlier – accompanied the entire final-year sixth on a trip to Bartica to unwind after the A-level exams. The year was 1957, the third consecutive year that such a trip was arranged, the previous two having been very successful and much talked about at the college. No one guessed that this year's trip would be the last. There were eight boys, the three convent girls and Father De Montfort himself and they stayed in the presbytery next to the little St. Anthony parish church in Front Street. The girls shared a room upstairs and the boys slept rough on the floor in the large front room downstairs, stowing away their bedding before Mass each morning so that the place could revert to its regular daytime uses.

On their second night in Bartica it was full moon and the young people from Georgetown went walking along Front Street, past the police station and the stelling, around the curve at the top of the street, ending up at the Bernard's Croft Hotel overlooking the confluence of the rivers. There they ordered soft drinks and bottles of the still new Banks beer from the bar and chatted loudly, imagining that they were behaving like adults. They fed the jukebox near the bar and it wasn't long before dancing started. Basil Ross, who had enjoyed the trip so far, began to feel uncomfortable; he knew that soon everyone would be admiring and applauding Basil Raatgever as he glided across the floor with one or other of the girls. He told himself it was silly to be jealous, especially now, when, on this trip, he and Raatgever were on good terms again and everyone was in high spirits, after the long slog of preparing for A-levels. Ross told the others he was feeling hot and would take a walk along the river wall to get some air; if he didn't see them when he returned, he would make his own way back to the presbytery.

The moonlight was brilliant and quite beautiful on the water. Basil Ross walked slowly along the wall, breathing deeply and remembering places in the interior where he had lived and gone to school as a child, and where he had later spent his school holidays with his parents. He sat on the wall not far from the little Public Works jetty and looked at the river and willed himself to be happy. He thought how good it was to have got through the exams feeling confident of his results and slowly his irritation eased. He was happy to be at that spot, pleased that his troubled relationship with Raatgever was resolved. While Ratty might be in love with dancing and the girls, he, Ross, was in love with the whole world, especially the part of it in front of him, touched magically by the silvery moonlight. He sat on the wall for a long time, deciding to say his night prayers and his rosary right there. Then he got up and headed back to the hotel. The jukebox still played, at lower volume, and there were a few men at the bar, but no sign of any of his classmates, so he made his way back to the presbytery. There people were unfolding bedding and getting ready to sleep, so he did the same. Then he noticed that Raatgever was not there. 'He and Alison went off walking somewhere with a couple of Bartica fellows we met at the hotel,' someone told him, and he began to feel uneasy again.

The others had gone to sleep but he was still awake, waiting.

Some time around two o'clock Basil Raatgever and Alison Cossou came in. They seemed to Basil Ross so mature and self-confident; he felt a pang as they moved carefully about in the almost-dark room. At the foot of the stairs he heard Raatgever whisper: 'See you tomorrow.' Alison tiptoed upstairs, but Ross could not help noticing, despite the dim light, that Raatgever had given her a gentle tap on her bottom as she ascended. Ross felt another pang.

When Raatgever was settled in his sleeping bag next to him, Ross pretended to wake up and asked where they had been. Raatgever told him that there had been a dance somewhere in Fourth Avenue and they were invited by two local fellows. The music was good, and Alison wanted to dance, which they did for a while, but most of the men seemed intent on getting drunk and the women looked fed up and uninteresting, so he and Alison had left, walked back to the hotel, sat on the wall and chatted for over an hour in the moonlight. Raatgever did not ask how Ross how he had spent the evening.

*　　*　　*

The next day they left early by boat to visit a small waterfall in the lower Mazaruni, where they would bathe and picnic for the day. The boat pulled into a section of riverbank near a small, forested island where the students noticed the beginning of an overgrown trail. It opened out a bit as they got further into it but, although quite distinct, it had evidently not been cleared for some time. The trail crossed a swift-flowing creek by means of a half-submerged log and they began to hear the sound of the waterfall.

When they emerged into a small clearing, Father De Montfort announced: 'This is it, Baracara Falls'. There the creek cascaded over a stone ledge about twenty feet above their heads and tumbled, foaming and splashing over a heap of large boulders and into a pool whose edges were covered in cream-coloured foam. The boys thought the waterfall was small, but quite impressive, and the water looked cool and refreshing. While their classmates put down baskets and haversacks and prepared to strip and stand or sit on the boulders and let the falling water cool them down after their brief hike, the two Basils, already in swimming trunks, were climbing the falls, one on either side.

Father De Montfort shook his head and smiled and one of the others remarked: 'Look at Ratty-and-Ross climbing the fall – trust them to make a contest out of it.' It was not difficult to climb, despite the volume of descending water, as there were many ledges and handholds among the boulders. It seemed as though Ross reached the top first, but soon both boys were standing on the ledge looking down on the others, the water curving high about their calves. After a while those below saw them turn and walk along the rocky ledge away from the lip and along the creek-bed, disappearing into the trees and bushes behind the waterfall. Ross was in front and Raatgever behind him. That was the last anyone ever saw of Raatgever – even Ross, if you believe his story.

The rest of the party bathed in the cold, falling water or in the little pool at its base; a few of the other boys eventually climbed to the ledge as the two Basils had done, but did not venture far along the creek in pursuit of them. All accepted that Ross and Raatgever were extraordinary people and at times it was best to leave them to pursue their own joint agenda. The group had arrived at Baracara Falls just after 10:00 a.m. At 12:30 they had lunch, making sure to leave some for the two Basils. Just before one o'clock Ross appeared on the lip of the waterfall looking troubled.

'Did Ratty come back?' he shouted. When they told him that he had not, Ross seemed more agitated.

'We thought he was with you. We saw him follow you into the bush,' Father De Montfort said.

'I thought he was behind me all the time, but when I turned around he'd disappeared. I'm going back to find him.'

And that, essentially, is the story. Pretty soon everybody was topside the falls looking for Raatgever, except the rather corpulent Tony D'Andrade and two of the girls. Alison Cossou had sprinted up the falls quicker than most of the boys. Ross took them to the spot where he said he had turned around for the first time to say something to Raatgever, only to discover that he had vanished. The others were surprised how far they'd gone along the creek; it was quite difficult going in places – there were swampy patches and places that were quite deep and other spots that seemed particularly gloomy and sinister. They could not understand why the two Basils would want to trudge through all that – it was hardly anyone's idea of fun. Ross said that he and Raatgever had spoken to each other from time to time and that he'd heard Ratty's footsteps splashing behind him – although when he turned around it was partly because he had not heard anything from Raatgever for a while.

The whole story sounded improbable and one of the other boys said, 'The two of you concocted this whole thing to play a trick on us – it's just the kind of thing you two would do. I'm sure Ratty's hiding in the bush somewhere, or else he's back at the falls by now, sharing the joke with fat D'Andrade and the girls.'

This immediately seemed plausible to all, including the priest, and they were ready to abandon the search and return to the waterfall, but it was hard not to believe Ross, who was by now visibly disturbed and swore that it was no trick. For more than an hour they shouted Raatgever's name and searched up and down the creek for him, making forays into the bush wherever there was an opening in the undergrowth through which he could have walked off into the surrounding forest. There was no response and no signs that Raatgever had been there.

The group assembled back at the falls at 4:30 p.m.. By then the three who had remained at the foot of the falls had grown concerned at all the distant shouting and thrashing around they had heard – and at the passage of time. The boatman then came along the path from the river to discover why the group was not waiting on the riverbank at 4:15 as planned, and there was a moment of pandemonium with everyone speaking and shouting at the same time. All were silenced by a loud and desperate shout of 'Ratt-a-a-a-y!' from Alison Cossou, who then burst into tears. At that point a profound gloom settled on the group. Led by the Jesuit Father, they prayed that they would find Raatgever – or that he would find them – and then they prayed for his family and the repose of his soul if anything tragic had happened to him.

When it began to get dark and they prepared to leave, Basil Ross announced that he was not going – he would spend the night there and wait for his friend. 'He would do the same for me,' he said firmly, and could not be persuaded to leave and return in the morning with the search party. In the end Father De Montfort decided to stay with him. Next morning the others, along with a large and curious group from Bartica, arrived at first light to find Ross and the priest wet and hungry, and miserable because there was still no sign of the missing boy.

For two days searches were made of the forest around the creek and far beyond; then a party of policemen arrived from town with dogs and they spent two days combing the area, but there was no sign of Raatgever. The speculation was that he had wandered far into the forest, got lost and been eaten by a jaguar or had fallen into a bottomless pit. Some said that if he knew how to survive he could wander around the Mazaruni-Potaro jungle for months.

All this was decades ago, and there has never been a satisfactory explanation of the mystery. There were those who harboured the suspicion that Ross had somehow done away with Raatgever – those who remembered their intense rivalry of a few years before; but no one could provide a plausible account of how he might have accomplished this without leaving some trace of this presumed crime.

But what of Ross himself? What did he think? On that harrowing night spent at the foot of Baracara falls, Ross had told the Father that he felt responsible for Raatgever's disappearance. It crossed the priest's mind that Ross might be about to confess to having done some harm to Raatgever, and he blessed himself quietly and asked the boy if he felt he needed to go to confession. Ross replied that he didn't know; he claimed that he had been quarrelling with Raatgever as they walked single file up the bed of the stream. He'd been jealous and angry that his friend and Alison Cossou seemed to be in love with each other and then he'd been annoyed with himself for having these feelings. At the top of the falls that morning Ross had been irritated anew over the fact that he and Raatgever couldn't seem to get away from each other, that it had occurred to Raatgever to climb the waterfall at the same time that he'd begun ascending the rocks. Then Raatgever had followed him up the stream. After they had walked some distance he had told Raatgever that he was fed up with him and he claimed that his friend had replied tauntingly, saying: 'You'll never be rid of me, I'm your doppelgänger. Wherever you go, I will follow, like Ruth in the bible.' This had made him more angry and he refused to look back at Raatgever, although the latter eventually began to plead with him.

'I'm only joking, Ross. Look at me, I'm your best friend, I always was and always will be.'

'I wish you'd disappear for good,' Ross had told him.

'You would suffer most if I did,' was the reply from behind him. 'Hasn't it occurred to you yet that we are nothing without each other? It's your wonderful Catholic religion, Ross, that makes it impossible for you to accept the truth: we are two halves of a single soul. Please Ross, forgive me whatever it is that I've done to wrong you: forgive me and accept me – accept yourself.'

'I wish to God you'd disappear, just *disappear!* Vanish!' Ross had heard himself insist in a terrible, hissing voice.

Then, he told Father De Montfort, there was a long silence before he thought he heard Raatgever say, very quietly: 'All right.'

After that he didn't hear any sounds from behind him, and after this silence seemed to have lasted several minutes, he looked back. There was no sign of Raatgever and he'd turned and walked further up the stream, convinced that Raatgever was hiding somewhere to make fun of him. Some time later he'd turned back, looking carefully along both banks of the creek, but refusing to call his friend's name, thinking that Raatgever meant to teach him a lesson by remaining hidden. He'd then returned to the top of the falls. He told Father De Montfort that he still expected Ratty to show up triumphantly, perhaps early next morning, and that his friend was doing this to punish him – adding after a pause that he (Ross) deserved to be punished for what he had said.

But hours later that night, after it had rained and they had begun to hear the noises of bats and animals in the surrounding forest, Ross said to the priest, as though continuing a current conversation: 'Unless he really disappeared, Father – unless I made him disappear...'

'And how could you have done that, child? How does one make a human being disappear?'

'I don't know, Father.' And Ross began to weep.

Father De Montfort tried to comfort Ross and, at the boy's insistence, gave him absolution for the sin of being angry with his friend and wishing for his disappearance. Father De Montfort tried to convince him that, if he was telling the truth, it was illogical to feel guilty, since it was not possible to make a human being disappear simply by wishing it. The priest also advised him not to repeat the story, since it would feed the superstitions of the ungodly and, in any case, was unlikely to lead to the recovery of his friend.

★ ★ ★

In August that year it was announced that Basil Raatgever had achieved the top marks in the A-level examinations and would have been awarded the scholarship to do university studies. Ross was named proxime, having achieved the second best results in the country and in the absence of Raatgever was offered the scholarship. He accepted it, reflecting sorrowfully that he and his achievements still seemed tied to his vanished friend. Ross studied law in England, returning to Guyana after four years. He worked for a while in the Public Prosecutor's office then, in the mid-1960s, he was appointed a legal officer in the Attorney General's office, and has remained there to the present.

By all accounts, Basil Ross became a taciturn, solitary individual; he played no games, never competed with anyone and neither married nor pursued the opposite sex. He seemed to live for his job, gaining a reputation as an excellent drafter of complex legislation and legal opinion, though by virtue of his position his name was never formally associated with the work he authored. One can guess that this struck Ross as peculiarly appropriate: Raatgever had disappeared because of him, and he might have felt comforted by the thought that there was no identification of self or personality in the work he did; that he, Basil Ross, had disappeared almost as completely as Basil Raatgever. He refused appointments to other, more prominent positions in government service and while his superiors relied more and more on his knowledge and experience, there were others happy to claim the prominence he eschewed.

Ross, in turn, relied on his secretary, Miss Morgan – an efficient, old-fashioned civil service spinster – to keep the office running smoothly and to shield him from public exposure. The country had long forgotten the mystery of Raatgever's disappearance, although on one or two occasions, not long after his return from England, Ross had permitted himself to be interviewed about the incident. He had hoped vaguely that the interviewer might have some new angle to explore; he knew that he had nothing useful to add to all that had been said before. He had been disappointed on each occasion, and decided he would not subject himself to any more journalistic probing.

People who knew him said that Basil Ross had changed physically after the incident: that he had become thin and ascetic-looking and, as the years passed, his physique began to resemble that of his vanished friend. He lived a life of careful routine – home to office, office to home. He visited his close relatives occasionally, but said very little and seemed to find casual conversation difficult. He remained devout in the practice of his religion and he was careful, through those oppressive years, to keep himself strictly above politics.

That might have been the end of the story, but then, in the mid-1990s, Basil Ross had a revelation. A number of eco-tourism companies had opened resorts in the Essequibo-Mazaruni area and one of these had rediscovered the Baracara falls, cleared the path and constructed a bridge over the little creek. A bathe in the 'therapeutic waters' of the falls was advertised in their brochure as one of the attractions of their tour package. This brochure had caught Basil Ross's attention. This was in 1996. On the brochure there was a small picture of Baracara falls with a few tourists in swimsuits arranged on the top ledge of the falls and on the boulders. Behind the veil of falling water next to the vertical edge of one of these boulders, Basil Ross thought he saw a face. Rationally, he knew it could not be a real face, but he was struck by the fact that it was the first thing he noticed when he looked at the photograph. He visited the office of the tour company, spoke to the proprietor's son and then the proprietor himself, found out who had taken the photograph and, with some difficulty and expense, managed to locate the negative and have a large blow-up made. This confirmed his belief that the face behind the veil of water was that of Basil Raatgever – the face of his classmate of 1957: the large forehead, the eyes, the wide mouth, the shadow of a moustache. Raatgever, Ross saw, was smiling.

No one else could see the face, though some agreed that there was a suggestion, in the pattern of water falling over rock, of eyes and a mouth – but only after Ross had pointed these out to them. The fact that no one else saw what he saw did not surprise or discourage him. He saw the face quite clearly and had no trouble recognizing it. He had the enlarged photograph framed and hung on the wall of his bedroom and a smaller version stood on his desk at work. He became convinced that the face of his lost friend had been made visible to him to free him from his years of guilt and sorrow, and he felt truly liberated. Basil Raatgever was *there* after all – had been *there* all along, there in the falls. He had reappeared in the place where he had made himself disappear in response to his (Ross's) angry wish.

At the office they noticed that Mr. Ross was more relaxed and approachable. He smiled with uncharacteristic frequency and seemed more inclined to stop and chat with his fellow workers. Some surmised that he was mellowing with age and perhaps looking forward to his retirement in a few years.

One day, Basil Ross stopped before the desk of his faithful secretary. 'Miss Morgan, I don't quite know how to say this, but... Well... The fact is that I find myself in possession of two tickets for something called an "Old Time Dance". I understand that there will be music that was popular in the fifties and sixties and refreshments of some sort. I was wondering if you...'

'Oh, yes, OK, Mr. Ross, I'll take them off you – you know I can't pass up a good dance. I'll get one of the friends in my little group to go with me. You're giving me the tickets, or do I have to pay?'

'Well... You see, Miss Morgan...'

But Miss Morgan didn't see... She couldn't see why Mr. Ross was making such a fuss and seemed so awkward. He had passed on many such tickets to her over the years. She couldn't help thinking that by now people should have realized that Mr. Ross didn't go to public events of that kind.

'Well, the truth is, Miss Morgan,' Basil Ross continued, 'I thought I would rather like to go myself – for a change, you know... to remind me of my youth, so to speak... Oh, I don't know, but I was wondering if you would do me the honour of allowing me to escort you.'

49

Miss Morgan opened her mouth, but no sound came from it. She was stunned. *The honour of allowing me to escort you...* The words rang in her head for a long time before she worked out that Mr. Ross was in fact asking her out to a dance, and it took her still longer to recover the power of speech and respond.

★　★　★

The evening at the dance was a revelation to Miss Morgan. She had never associated Mr. Ross with any social skills or with activities engaged in simply for pleasure. She had thought that she would have to humour him and be embarrassed on his behalf for his awkwardness, but would cheerfully endure this while savouring the novelty of the situation. But Mr. Ross danced like a man possessed. He was lively and fluent in the quicker numbers; he twirled her around and pulled her towards him with the utmost grace and perfect timing, but it was the slow, soulful hits of the sixties he seemed to like best. As the music sobbed rhythmically, Mr. Ross swayed and glided, his hips and shoulders drifting effortlessly with the waves of sound, and his feet hardly seemed to touch the floor. It took all of Miss Morgan's considerable skills to keep up with him and she noticed, with genuine pleasure, that they had begun to attract quite a lot of attention. Several couples, indeed, had stopped dancing to watch them. Mr. Basil Ross was entirely oblivious – he was floating, he was free. It was as if a long lost dimension of self had reawakened within him and was asserting its presence and its hunger for pleasures long denied. One or two of the older folk at the dance thought they remembered seeing someone dance like that before – a youngster, long, long ago.

SKY
by Desmond Arthur

*'No matter how wide and clear the sky, there's always a human
shadow between its purity and your own desire.'*
– Patamona proverb

Flight

When I board the plane at Gatwick I feel so tired and emotionally
drained that I fully expect to go to sleep at once and not wake up
for the entire journey. Instead, as the large jet ascends into the
cold morning air above Southern England, I find myself looking
out the window, not at the bleak grey land below, but at the swiftly
changing patterns of light and darkness in the clouds we are
climbing through; at patches of blue as we begin to leave the cloud
layer below us. Then a flood of cool blue light fills the oval
window. Turning my head to look directly out at it, I weep.

I am surprised at first: why now? Then I realize that it is my
first chance to think – or perhaps to feel – my first stretch of time
not filled with meeting people, arranging things, driving up and
down the wet roads, and sleeping briefly with the aid of a pill. I try
hard not to let my shoulders – my body – shake with the release
of this pent-up grief. The tears flow hot but quiet and I take out
my handkerchief to wipe them and blow my nose in one action.

Later, with my seat reclined, I tell the flight attendant that I
want nothing to eat or drink and I decline the earphones as well.
I think about Maggie – not the Maggie in the hospital bed, not the
Maggie in the coffin who seemed, with her stiff, incongruous
smile, to belong more to the doctors and the undertakers, and the

curious viewers filing past the coffin than to me. I think about *my* Maggie – the sudden light in her eyes when she caught a joke or realized that I was pulling her leg; the slight tilt of her head which meant that she was considering what you were saying, but not sure she agreed with you; the dismissive toss of her hair when she strongly disagreed. I think of the mystery of her presence in my life: a stranger I had loved and married; and I think of the warmth of her body, its softness against my own. Strangely, I do not wonder at her going so young – the unfairness or the hurt of it – but wonder that we had lived together and loved so intensely for so long: twenty-three years. I find myself thinking that she never *belonged* to me – to the children, perhaps – that with me she always conveyed the idea of a separate, autonomous beautiful self, sharing herself with me time and time again, but not really as 'one flesh' or 'bone of my bone'. She was always wonderfully, mysteriously other than me. And with this thought the tears come again.

I suppose the worst pain was seeing her helpless, unable to assert the fierce independence that bewildered me even as I admired and respected it. Her helplessness at the end caused her eyes to retreat in my presence, as though ashamed of her sudden vulnerability and dependence. I tried not to take over her life completely and do everything for her – at least at the beginning – and I think she was grateful for that.

The children thought I was too cold, that I coped too well. Marion said it was as though I had thoroughly rehearsed Mummy's illness and death, and Jamie, his eyes constantly full of tears, said it was cruel of me not to cry. They both felt that I should go on a trip somewhere after the funeral, though neither thought that returning to Guyana was the best choice. 'Go to New York, or to the Far East – or even to one of the Caribbean islands with good beaches and comfortable hotels.' But I didn't want to be entirely on my own. I'd always been fond of my cousin Aileen and her family, and it seemed natural to me to head for the place I still consider home – to lick my wounds and distract myself with people and places that were prominent in my past.

I look out the window again at the wide sunlit sky with its cool blue relieved by drifting scrawls of cloud – parallel like lines of writing on a page. I feel comforted. For months I have not seen the sky. I have always been a lover of the sky, its endless promise, its insistence on distant horizons. I realize suddenly that I am in flight from the skyless gloom of England in the winter, from the hospital, from the graveyard, from what I had become in the last year or so.

★   ★   ★

Meeting

On the third evening after my arrival in Georgetown there is an overseas call for me. It's Marion: 'Dad? Is anything the matter? You said you'd call when you arrived and let us know how you'd got on...' I tell her that I've been busy, meeting lots of people, travelling about. Not to worry, I'm OK. Sorry I'd forgotten to call. How were she and Jamie coping? But the truth is that I'd slept for most of the three days – dead to the world in Bunny's and Aileen's little guest-room at the end of the corridor upstairs. It was quiet; I was half-aware, at times, of the children tiptoeing down the corridor, the door being quietly opened, then closed again. I went down for meals – sometimes – but Aileen insisted that I rest myself and get over the ordeal of the past months. I am grateful.

Now with Marion's phone call I awaken to a sense of time slipping away. My trip was for ten days – now just a week. The next few days I busy myself getting re-acquainted with the city, stumbling into changes and memories: the sea wall, the college, the botanical gardens. So many changes: old streets with new names, the small house in which I grew up grotesquely expanded and filling almost completely what I remembered to be a large plot of land, the trees of my childhood climbing gone.

Then there's the absence of people. People I grew up and went to school with, all left, living overseas. Sometimes I meet a younger brother of a former classmate – half-ashamed to be still here – hoping to leave soon for Toronto, London, anywhere big and foreign. 'Bernie left four years ago. He was in Miami for a year, but now he's got a job in Philadelphia. I was there for a few weeks... I remember you, though; I entered College the year before you and Bernie left... You know life in Guyana hard these days...' I hear the same tune everywhere I search for missing

53

friends and acquaintances. As far as Guyana is concerned, I'm a member of a lost generation – lost to migration, lost to a better life abroad. Life in Guyana hard these days...

I become quite despondent and wonder if the children weren't right: 'A waste of time, Daddy, going back to Guyana.' Even the few people who are still in Georgetown seem lost. I manage to track down Alan Ifil in a decrepit government office. I gather that he's in charge, but he seems strangely embarrassed. We chat for a while, then agree to meet for a drink at the Palm Court that evening. He's a little more relaxed there and when he smiles at some of the classroom incidents we recall, I can see the old Alan – looking back from the front row (he would always sit in the front of the class) with a huge enthusiastic grin on his face. But it's painful to discover how quickly we exhaust common memories – how much of what I remember he has difficulty recalling – as though our adolescent experience was a palimpsest overwritten by subsequent life in Guyana, leaving him adrift and anxious. I feel sorry for him, then angry with myself for feeling that way. We have perhaps three drinks before we shake hands and leave in opposite directions. I see that this visit has been an error of judgement, born of a misplaced and sentimental nostalgia.

I go home to Aileen and complain that this country is making people old before their time, shadows of their former selves. She says: 'Well, you see it for yourself; people overseas don't believe it when I write and tell them...' I decide to stop searching for old friends, just sit out the two days left, then be off home. Home. This decision gives me calm, and in this mood I begin to enjoy the city: the sea-wall, walking down city streets, wandering through the Water Street stores ...

On my penultimate night in Guyana I find myself back at the Palm Court. I'm taking Bunny, Aileen and the kids to dinner – small recompense for putting up with my tiredness and complaining over the last week or so. They seem to enjoy it and I'm happy. During dessert, a vaguely familiar figure strides in and looks around; we half-recognize each other at the same time. 'Wait,' he says, 'I know this face.' I get up saying, 'Robbie, Eddie Roberts.' (Aileen has whispered the name as he strides over and instantly I remember, with great pleasure, our class leader and clown.) 'I knew it had to be you, Desmond,' Robbie says, pumping my hand. 'Alan told me he saw you the other night and I said, 'No! How come Desmond in the country and I can't butt up with him?' He's even more big and strapping than he was at school. I gesture to introduce him to Aileen and Bunny but of course everybody knows everybody in Georgetown. They say hi to each other and Robbie pulls up a chair and orders drinks and we chat. Robbie it is who notices soon after that the kids and Aileen are getting restless.

'Look, Bunny, I know y'all got to get home with the kids – I really want to catch up with Desmond here – how 'bout if I bring him home later?'

And Robbie and I go over to the bar. We drink XM 10 year-old and talk about our lives since school. He's visibly moved when I tell him about Maggie, and expresses such sincere sorrow that I have to blink back the tears. Eddie Roberts – or 'Robbie' as we called him then – was as good and warm-hearted as ever; I am pleasantly impressed to see that life in Guyana has not affected him the way it has Alan Ifil. Then, when he tells me his story, I discover that he returned to Guyana only eight years ago. I remember hearing that he was in a seminary in Scotland trying out a vocation to the priesthood. 'Didn't work out,' he says simply, with his large smile. After a year in the seminary he left and went to university in Aberdeen, taught maths for a few years in London and then went back up to Scotland and learned to fly aeroplanes. He flew for a few years with a small Scottish regional airline and then returned to Guyana and started his own flying business which, a little later, had expanded into eco-tourism. *Guyana Sky Tours* is doing very well.

As I drink and talk to this big bear of a man: his presence and the memories we share begin to redeem this trip. I tell him, as he drives me home, how good it is to meet him again, and what a miserable time I'd been having until then.

'Man Desi, if you had known your boy Robbie was around, I know you would have looked me up and we could have done a lot of things together. But now you're leaving when?'

'Day after tomorrow.'

'Wait, I think I have a trip to the Mazaruni in the morning. I'll work it myself and you can come with me – see something of the old interior that we used to roam about with the scouts, remember?'

'You mean you're going to fly tomorrow – I mean later today – after drinking all that rum?'

But his huge laugh and his insistence that he does it all the time reassures me. When I get out of the car, he says he'll pick me up at nine o'clock, but I tell him to call me an hour before to make sure that I still feel up to it.

★   ★   ★

Plans

'Didn't I tell you?' Robbie says when he comes to collect me at nine o'clock, 'that XM ten year-old is so good, there's no possibility of headaches or hangovers in the morning.'

As I climb into the seat of the plane next to Robbie, I glance to the back and see that we are fully loaded: two large barrels, other smaller containers and some cardboard boxes, a huge coil of rope and a set of coloured plastic buckets nesting in each other – all covered with a tight orange netting to prevent the load from coming forward or shifting too much in flight.

'Supposed to be some team of engineers doing a study of hydroelectric potential in the upper Mazaruni – yet another study. They'll write a report and nothing will be done. Five or ten years from now, somebody will fund another study. Anyway, in the meantime, I have the contract to fly in supplies, so I shouldn't complain.'

We take off from the Ogle airstrip and bank steeply over the seawall and head across the southern tip of Georgetown to the Demerara River. We climb over the river for what seems a long time, then inch our way over the western bank. I can see the plane's shadow over to my right, crawling over light green swampland, then the uneven tufted dark-green carpet of the forest.

'Look at that sky,' I shout to Robbie. 'Good day for flying.'

'Marvellous,' he shouts back. 'For now. It won't last much beyond mid morning.' So, determined to enjoy it while it lasts, I look all around – through my window, the curved windshield,

Robbie's window – and take in the wonder of a blue never seen in England, at least not in the cities. There are a few white puffs of cloud far in the distance, helping to accentuate its pure perfection.

'I can see you're a sky person – like me,' Robbie says, and I save my response for later as we see the Essequibo in the distance.

I muse about the misfortune of not running into Robbie earlier, but then consider the good fortune of meeting him, when I'd heard he'd gone away.

After about an hour and twenty minutes we settle with a slight bump onto a small landing strip on the bank of the river. I wander around a bit while the plane is unloaded, delight in wading at the edge of the dark river, watching my toes turn red in the amber shallows and remembering many such rivers in my childhood – swimming across them, drinking their water from a white enamel cup, travelling on them in launches or speed boats or quietly, magically, paddling in a small corrial with an inch or two of freeboard, with the sound of the river against the paddle and in the branches and silted roots of the riverbank trees. I look out further into the river and spot a lone kingfisher gliding swiftly inches above the water, re-stitching the seam between river and sky. I note that there is now just one small patch of blue above – lots of high white clouds and heavy grey ones moving in below.

Men from the airstrip make their way down to the small boats at the water's edge, carrying the drums and packages we'd just flown in. I go back up to the plane. Robbie, with a pen and clipboard in his hand, is talking to a tall blond fellow. I watch him shake the fellow's hand and give a small wave. Then he strides over to the edge of the forest where a few Amerindian children are quietly watching the activity on the airstrip. He returns to the plane grinning, with his hands full. 'When last you eat cookerite, Desi?' he asks, emptying several into my cupped hands.

We take off into a slight drizzle and almost immediately climb into thick cloud. Thin straight lines of rainwater dance across the windscreen and windows and we bump around for a long time cocooned in a rain cloud. Robbie glances at the small green screen of the GPS, then smiles. He leans over and says: 'Where's your perfect blue sky now?' I shrug and he grins. Twenty minutes later we begin to see glimpses of the multi-channelled, island-strewn lower Mazaruni through breaks in the cloud. Soon we're flying under a tent of high white cloud with the forest and river clearly visible beneath. From this point the flight is smooth and as we cross the Demerara we can see Georgetown ahead bathed in strong sunshine.

After we land, and some of Robbie's boys push the plane towards a hangar with a long green roof on the other side of the runway, we get in the car and Robbie crosses the runway and arrives ahead of the plane.

'Let me give you a little tour,' he says, and under the hangar I see three other planes of the same type – twin-engined, high-winged Islanders – with the word '*Skytours*' printed in slanting green letters on the yellow fuselage, and the company's logo (a stylized bird racing past a small white cloud) on the tail. We go into an air-conditioned office where he chats briefly with a slim woman sitting at a computer screen, then he shows me a pleasant little room with large T.V. screen at the front and chairs arranged as in a small cinema.

'People assemble here for the tours,' he says. 'If they want they can have a cup of coffee and a pastry while they're waiting, and we run videotapes of our various resorts and destinations so they can have a preview.' I notice that even the mugs, yellow like the planes, have '*Skytours*' printed in green with the logo.

'A classy operation,' I say to Robbie. He beams. 'Well, you know how it is. Is plenty of us competing for the eco-tourism dollar.'

'I love the name Skytours,' I say.

'That's me,' he replies. 'The sky is the only place where I feel truly free. Some people like the beauty of the river and others the mystery of the forest, but for me nothing beats the sky.' By the door from the waiting room to the hangar, I notice a large aerial photo of sky and clouds with glimpses of cloud-stained forest below. On a poster next to it is part of A.J. Seymour's poem 'Over Guyana Clouds'. I stop and remind myself of the poem:

> *…And they go rushing across the country*
> *Staining the land with shadow as they pass.*
> *Closer than raiment to the naked skin, that shadow,*
> *Bringing a pause of sun over and across*
> *Black, noiseless rivers running out to sea…*

Outside I say to Robbie: 'You know where there's the best sky in Guyana?'

'The Pakaraimas?' he asks.

'Of course,' I say. 'I'll never forget the magical quality of the light along the narrow paths over those rounded, treeless hills. Remember our scout trip to Kurukabaru?'

'I could never forget it,' he says, getting excited as we drive towards the east-coast road. 'You know, the two of us are really alike.'

After a long silence he says: 'Hear, why you don't make plans to come back at Easter. I'll take a week or so of holiday and we'll spend it walking around the Pakaraimas. We could land at one of the airstrips, take our time and walk around the villages, go back to good old Kurukabaru, bathe in the creeks and arrange for a plane to pick us up at another strip at the end of the week – just the two of us. How about it?'

'Well…' I say, and hesitate because although it sounds wonderful, I'm not sure that I'll be able to get away again so soon.

'Look, don't decide now,' Robbie says. 'Let me work some more on the idea and I'll be in touch with you.'

'I should give you my address in England.'

'Don't bother with address.' He hands me a pocket-sized notebook. 'Just write down your phone number, and make sure you write down all those foolish English codes so I would just look at it and dial.' I do as he asks and give the notebook back to him.

'Plans, Desi,' he says. 'The boys making plans like in the old days.' And he slaps me on the shoulder with his left hand. 'You'll be hearing from me.'

★   ★   ★

Trails and Villages

Robbie does call, several times – often completely oblivious of the time difference – waking me up after midnight. In the end it's not too difficult to find ten days just after Easter, although I feel a little guilty about leaving again so soon – as though I'm running away. Both my children are studying hard for approaching exams at their respective universities and they tell me to go, remembering that I'd said how much I enjoyed the trip in January.

So I fly out of Gatwick on Easter Sunday, having attended the Easter Vigil mass the night before. In the plane I keep thinking about John Donne's 'Good Friday, Riding Westward', as though it applies to me, and have a momentary foreboding about heading away from Christ's rising – and perhaps from grace – towards some dark and remote space where I might receive the 'chastisement' that Donne mentions. I shiver in the cold, thin air of the plane, but then I remember the incomparable light of the Pakaraima sky and the moment quickly passes. I settle in for the protracted afternoon that the flight to the Caribbean would entail.

After a day of carefully selecting and packing our equipment – to the buzzing of hundreds of kites overhead in the holiday sky – we leave early next morning for Kurukabaru. There's Robbie, myself and Anand, one of his pilots, to bring back the plane. He's slightly-built and looks like a schoolboy – far too young to be flying planes.

After seeing Anand take off from the same curious uphill airstrip that I'd remembered from so many years ago, we shoulder our packs and head along the trail to the village. Robbie's pack weighs close to seventy pounds, but he is as buoyant as ever under it. I fear that I will struggle with mine, which weighs only thirty-eight, but I'm relieved to feel neither tired nor winded. 'You see, is a good thing I phoned and made you go to the gym over the past weeks; you have to be fit to walk about these mountains,' Robbie says. As we arrive at the crest of a long rise, I feel certain that the holiday will be an idyll of sun, sky and fresh mountain air.

The first two days live up to my expectations. We make good time over the mountain paths, rejoicing in the light, the clear skies, the villages shimmering in the distance. Robbie is instantly recognized whenever we stride into a village. There is much loud greeting and hand-shaking and I can't help thinking what a wonderful personality he possesses.

In the villages, because of Robbie, we enjoy Patamona hospitality – drinking casserie and eating wild meat and cassava bread. On the trails we consume the freeze-dried and canned foods we've taken with us, helping to lighten our loads. The tent we sleep in at night weighs only five and a half pounds, although it's really a three-man tent – and needs to be to accommodate Robbie, myself and the packs. We always pitch the tent close to one of the mountain streams, so we can bathe and have water to cook with. It's wonderful, after hiking all day, to feel the refreshing cold water against my skin – to lather briskly with soap under the empty sky and then descend again into the stream's luminous mirror. Then the fire and the meal and the restorative oblivion of the tent. We are so tired that we make little use of the cumbersome solar lamp which Robbie carries, strapped to the top of his pack, absorbing and storing the sun's energy as we walk.

It's surprising how little we speak, communicating mostly in gestures and monosyllables, both of us savouring the silent wonder of the place and not wanting to break its spell with the noise of our voices. When we do chat – usually at night by the cooking fire – it is in quiet tones and mostly about our reactions to this place – its openness, its feeling of timelessness, its closeness to the images and memories of the camping trips of our adolescence. England seems distant as the present overwhelms me with a kind of sensual fullness that makes experience and imagination indistinguishable. 'The Pakaraimas,' I hear myself telling Robbie, 'are perhaps just close enough to earthly perfection to arouse a sense of impending catastrophe.'

★   ★   ★

Waterfall

On our third afternoon, somewhere between Paramakatoi and Kato, we detour along a path that descends into a thickly forested defile. Robbie says there's a waterfall there we can bathe in. The fall turns out to be higher than I had expected – about fifty to seventy feet – and the water in its plunge-pool is a translucent, milky emerald colour. There are flat rocks beside the stream at the foot of the fall and some open spaces under the trees, so we decide to pitch the tent there for the night, hesitating only momentarily to wonder whether the noise of the fall might keep us from sleeping.

When the tent is up, looking strangely incongruous and vulnerable under the tall trees – the guy ropes tied to trunks and roots – we strip and ease into the pale green water. The plunge-pool is surprisingly deep and we are able to swim a few strokes between the sides of the pool and the rocks at the base of the fall. We climb onto these rocks and let the cold water beat against our bodies – a delicious, numbing sensation. If I keep my head under the water it brings a thunderous delirium that takes away all other sensuous awareness of the world – and eventually all thought itself – as I become a resonant drum thrumming to the falling water's rhythms.

We swim back to the flat stone at the edge of the pool where we've left our bars of soap and there, in the softening afternoon light, we lather our naked bodies and our hair. As we walk to the edge of the rock to plunge in, I scoop a handful of lather off my head and fling it at Robbie. It catches him on the side of his head, covering his right ear. I laugh and he looks at me with a wide grin: 'Well now you're in for it, Desi, I can't let you get away with that.' He lunges for my arm, but it's too slippery with soap and I wriggle free, stumbling across the rock and onto the path. Robbie follows, his heavy footfalls thumping behind me. I run along the path parallel to the stream, through a patch of soggy ground, then cut into the trees and double back towards the rock; he follows doggedly. I can hear his breath. He catches me some yards up the path to the fall from the savannah. He catches and loses me several times because of the soap, but by then I'm winded and stumble and fall on the path. Robbie pins me down and we wrestle – he uses a grip like iron to counter the slipperiness of our limbs. He pins my arms, but I struggle and manage to topple him over. We are both on the path, covered with soap, dirt, leaves, twigs and small stones. 'Enough!' I shout, but Robbie pays no attention. 'Fight! Wrestle! You started it!' he says with a laugh. I put up a struggle for a while longer, but I'm exhausted and let my body go limp.

He's on top of me, a knee on my thigh, his hands pinning my upper arms. I see a cloud pass over his face. He releases me quickly and gets up. He is annoyed.

'Why you had to do that?'

'What?'

'Let your body go slack like that. Like some fucking woman. I thought we were having some boyish sport.'

'We were, Robbie,' I pant, a little uneasy at his change of mood, 'but you're stronger and fitter than I am and I'm exhausted. I couldn't put up a struggle any longer.'

'That's what you say, but I know what that slackening of the muscles means. Let me tell you, Desi, I ain't no fucking anti-man.'

And he walks off in the direction of the pool. I follow him, troubled. I plunge into the pool behind him and we rinse our bodies in silence, my biceps red from where he's gripped and pinned my arms. I do not know what to make of his outburst and obvious anger, so for a long while I say nothing. We dress and kindle a fire in silence. He seems sullen.

Eventually I say to him, 'Robbie, I'm sorry – I apologize for whatever it is I've done to annoy you.' He says nothing and I continue: 'I know I started the horseplay, but I didn't mean anything by it. As for our wrestling match; I was really exhausted by then – I can't match you for strength and stamina, I just physically gave up. I didn't mean to embarrass you, or to tempt or provoke you'. He's stopped what he was doing and listens carefully. For a second he seems about to make a heated response, but, after a brief silence, he turns to me with a weak smile.

'You know, Desi, is best we forget all this – forget what I said, forget it ever happened – we can't let this spoil our adventure.'

'Agreed,' I say, with huge relief. The last thing I want is to spend the rest of the week in unavoidably close proximity to a sullen and disturbed Robbie. I still don't understand what his problem is, but decide to dismiss it in the interest of our friendship and our carefully planned holiday.

I realize later that I should have taken the whole incident much more seriously. As someone who teaches a module on semiology in one of my graduate courses, I should know about paying more attention to signs.

★   ★   ★

The Shadow

When we emerge next morning onto the open hillside, leaving the waterfall and the forest behind, it seems that all has returned

63

to normal. Robbie is his old, enthusiastic, grinning self; so much so that I put his behaviour of the previous evening down to the influence of some malevolent spirit of the place and make a mental note to avoid forested campsites during our last few days in the Pakaraimas.

That night we pitch the tent on a little sandstone ledge, the only almost flat spot on a slope that descends to a small stream about forty metres below. There's a solitary troolie palm between the tent and the stream and a few more right next to the stream. After supper we sit facing each other across the dying cooking fire. Robbie asks me about Maggie and whether I think I'll ever marry again. I tell him that I love Maggie very much and how surprised I was to discover that love does not die with the death of the person loved; and although people warned me not to be too definite about not marrying again, I couldn't imagine marrying anyone else and I was sure the children would be upset if I did.

'Your boy Robbie will never get married,' he says, smiling, but the tone of his voice seems sad. 'It's just not me – you know? Anyway it's too late; I'm too set in my ways. A woman would mess up my life, distract me from my business; I'd be lost...' Then it seems he feels he's said enough about himself. 'You're different, Desi,' he continues, 'you were always different. Remember that camp in the North-West when you and Jeff Carpenter got into trouble for interfering with one of the maids at the convent?'

'I remember very well the "trouble" we got into, and the allegations that caused it, but they just were not true. Jeff and I had been teasing her in mildly erotic language – you know, making a few suggestive remarks about what she got up to after work, but we never put our hands under her skirt and into her bodice as she claimed. I believe that her claims that we did were pure spite. We'd left the laundry shed long before Sister Rose found her "in a state of dishevelment". She certainly wasn't dishevelled when we left her – God knows what she'd been doing in the interim. The injustice of our punishment still rankles.'

'When the two of you were sent home early, you were heroes to the rest of us – men with experience compared to us boys.'

'A reputation entirely undeserved, I can assure you – it's always amazed me that nobody believed us, not even the rest of you.'

'Desi Arthur and Jeff Carpenter: sent home for feeling up Sister's maid in the laundry shed,' Robbie says, speaking to himself – a kind of awe in his voice as though he's still an eager teenager.

'Cut it out, Robbie,' I say. 'You know it wasn't true – anyway the fire's gone and I'm turning in.'

I leave him sitting by the dead fire and crawl into the tent. The ground feels very hard and I decide to sleep *on* my sleeping bag, instead of in it, covering my lower body with my towel and bush jacket. Although I'm still a little disturbed at the memories aroused by our recent conversation, I feel myself drifting off to sleep.

I wake with a sensation of something amiss and find, when my eyes get accustomed to the faint foreday light, that Robbie is bending over me, on his knees (one on either side of my thighs) his hands by my shoulders. He's naked. I think his eyes must be closed, for he doesn't seem to notice that mine are open – perhaps it's still too dark, although I can see the shape of his body outlined against the lightening fabric of the tent. A thousand thoughts swirled through my mind, prompted by what had happened the previous evening. I wonder if Robbie is some kind of psychopath and how best to deal with this situation, although I'm not completely sure that it is real. It occurs to me that it may be a trick of the light or of a half-dreaming consciousness. I don't know whether to cough or shout, to pretend to turn over in my sleep, to lie still and wait. Then he starts to sob quietly, though his whole body shakes. I keep trying to see if he has an erection – if this is a sexual thing and he's about to rape me or something, but I can't see that far down without raising my head and I don't want to betray the fact that I'm awake. Through almost shut eyes I observe him tensely for what seems like an age. He continues to whimper and suddenly he lowers his head until it's just above mine, and I think I hear him whisper: 'Forgive me!'

I become alarmed. I open my eyes, raise my head and shout, 'Oh God, Robbie, what are you doing? What's wrong with you?' He lunges at me and pins my arms and legs with the weight of his body. 'No!' he says in a strange, deep voice. 'No! Not this time. You mustn't! You can't!' I see him reach for something above my head – it's my yellow, waterproof flashlight – and I feel a sharp stab of pain as he brings it down on my mouth and nose. 'No!' he keeps shouting. 'No! No!' The front of the flashlight pops open and the batteries fly out. I feel blood in my mouth, I'm having trouble breathing. He slams the heel of his hand into my right eye and I yelp at the pain, incongruously thinking that it's a good thing I'm not wearing my glasses. I roll over and manage somehow to push him off. I struggle with the zipped flap of the tent and am halfway out when a knee or a foot smashes into my back, propelling me into an uncontrollable stumble and I land in a heap near the edge of the little ledge. I watch him emerge from the tent and approach me: he kicks me twice in my stomach and the pain makes me certain he's going to kill me. He reaches down and pulls me up by the arms. I see his strangely frightened face and scream: 'Robbie, please!' A spatter of blood from my burst mouth appears on his face and chest. Suddenly he begins to sob loudly and shout, 'No! No!' He pushes me away and I fall and hit my head; I think I lose consciousness for a while.

When I come to I find I'm lying in the same spot; there's a fat mushroom of clotted blood in my mouth, my nose aches with every breath, I can only see out of my left eye and my stomach is on fire. I look around, but there's no sign of Robbie. I think, 'I'm still alive, I'm still alive', and I try to move. Apart from my head and my stomach nowhere else seems to be injured, although my whole body hurts. I try crawling around, but have to rest after only a few yards. I lie still for a while. It's now quite bright and I let the sun come up above the slope to my left before I try moving again.

I decide I have to get down to the stream to revive myself with the cold water, to check my injuries and bathe them. I crawl to the flap of the tent and retrieve my machete, drag it and myself to the edge of the ledge and start to ease my legs over. It's then that I hear the sobbing and notice Robbie sitting with his back against the troolie palm halfway down to the stream. He's hugging himself, sobbing and shaking his head from side to side. I test my legs and find that I can stand but cannot straighten my body, so I decide it's safer to scramble down on all fours. When I get close to Robbie I discover that he's chanting under his breath: 'I can't take it any more, I want to die, I want to die…' over and over. He looks at me and says, 'Oh God, Oh God!' I shout, 'Robbie!' but it comes out as a weak croak. He looks up at me and says again 'Oh God, Oh God!'

'Look what you've done to me,' I say, although I'm not sure he can understand the distorted sounds that come from my injured mouth. I take my machete, which is still sheathed in its leather case, and fling it at him; it slides against his foot. 'Here,' I say, 'before you die you'd better finish the job of killing me, because if I ever get out of this alive the whole world is going to know what you've done to me.'

'Oh God, Desi, I didn't want to hurt you,' he wails, but by now I'm feeling strangely light-headed and I shuffle past him and down to the water. I let myself slip off the edge of stone into the freezing water. I feel a sharp pain as my face goes under and then numbness. I carefully wash my face, sapping water on my right eye, which is swollen shut, and clean inside my mouth with a finger. I spend only a short time in the stream, but almost an hour sitting on the rock above it splashing myself with water from time to time. As I begin to think of making my way back up the path, Robbie comes down. He does not have the machete with him. He jumps into the water; his eyes, in the bright morning sunshine, are red and puffy and he looks desolate. 'Desi,' he says, 'what's going to happen to me?' I want to say that it is I who should be asking that question, but I think of the pain that the effort to speak would cause and say nothing.

I drag my naked and battered body up the slope and back to the tent. I'm amazed at the amount of blood there is inside and outside the tent. 'I'm still alive,' my mind keeps insisting, as though dumbfounded by the realization. I manage to swallow a double dose of painkillers with water from my canteen and lie down on the bloody bedding and doze. I awaken sweating in the late morning heat. I'm hungry and eat a small bar of chocolate – painfully. I curse Robbie quietly, but feel a little stronger and feel the need to get to the bottom of this business. I need to know why I'm suffering, what is the cause, what I'd done. Walking bent over like a hunchback, I go down to the stream with the canvas bucket, telling myself that I need coffee. Robbie is sitting on the rock beside the stream, his feet in the water. I fill my bucket and turn to go. Then I look at him and say: 'As soon as you feel like talking, I'm ready to hear what all of this is about.' I walk away and leave him. I make coffee, cook scrambled eggs from powder and open a pack of biscuits; I leave half of everything covered for him. I then make my way up and around the curve of the slope, where there is a slight breeze and from where I can see into a distant valley. I sit and try to figure which way I'd have to go if I have to make my own way to a village or the airstrip. I know the general direction in which we are headed and can see the path we left yesterday. I feel I'm not quite lost – yet.

When I return to the tent Robbie is eating. He looks at me and his eyes fill with tears.

'Talk,' I tell him.

'This is the third time this has happened to me,' he says.

'My God, Robbie, you've been beating up people like this and no-one has put you in jail or come after you with a weapon?'

It turns out that this was the reason he was kicked out of the seminary in Scotland: he'd beaten up another young seminarian who'd awakened to find Robbie in bed with him. Then it had happened again when he and another teacher had taken a group of sixth-form students to Belgium on some kind of field trip.

'You're gay, Robbie,' I say, half-question, half-statement.

'That's what the doctors and others said, but I don't – I didn't – want to believe them. You remember, Desi, how we hated those anti-men at college – Dario D'Almada and Ricky Barnett and people like that. I can't bear to think that I'm one of them.'

'Don't be an ass, Robbie; we didn't hate them, we teased them because they were effeminate; that doesn't necessarily have anything to do with being gay. In fact D'Almada lives somewhere in Kent and has a wife and children – I run into him from time to time: there's very little left of the flamboyantly effeminate speech and gestures of his adolescence.'

'You could actually be friends with a person like that?' Robbie was incredulous. 'You who used to be our lady-conquering hero.'

'As I told you last night, Robbie, that reputation was undeserved. There were times when I enjoyed the notoriety – and times when I may have promoted it – but if you want to know the truth, I was a virgin until my final year at university.'

'Oh God, Desi,' and he's weeping again, 'that's just my problem – I'm *still* a virgin, and I'm forty-eight, same age as you. I keep thinking, if only I could lose my virginity, but I can't even think of making love to a woman and whenever I fantasize about making love to a man I become terrified about what he would know about me for the rest of our lives. I'm so sorry I hurt you, Desi, I'll always be sorry. I know you can't forgive me.'

At that point I feel the tears come to my own eyes, in part because the pain we both feel now seems so unnecessary. I tell myself that what I should do, if I wasn't in such pain, is make passionate love to this huge, troubled adolescent, if only to put him out of his misery. But I knew I couldn't do it, even if I weren't injured. We're all haunted by what we have to live with, by ruling images of self, which we fashion very carefully over the years and which are more implacable than any 'real' person or thing or God.

I don't tell Robbie that night that I have forgiven him. At the time I'm not too sure that I have. Instead I let him hold me. I lean against his massive frame and he leans against the two back-packs in front the fire. He puts one arm around my chest and we stay like that most of the night, not talking much, thinking of our hurts. I prayed. I prayed for my pain, I prayed for my children and my dead wife, I prayed for Robbie, for all the shadows that had suddenly appeared between us and the clear Pakaraima sky. I prayed for all the maimed and crippled of the world, especially those concealed in healthy, laughing bodies. The fire died. I felt my arms and legs slowly grow numb. My head nodded.

★ ★ ★

It's now nearly six months since that night. I still don't know how we managed to walk into Orinduik by three o'clock on the second day following and find Anand and the plane waiting. I don't know how we convinced everyone about my 'accident', falling down a rocky hillside. When I got back to England the children were still away at university and by the time they came home there wasn't much to see of my injuries, although they were still very concerned. I recently got a letter from Robbie: he says he's on medication, and he thinks he may have found a friend. I pray for both of them.

AFTERNOON WITHOUT TEARS*

by Victor Nunes

The Pomeroon was covered with exploding raindrops, like goose-pimples on a black hand, and dreary bands of discoloured water meandered into the distance, distinct from the eternal blackness of the river. Charity was miserable in the rain. The barefoot man on the stelling laughed loudly at me when I mentioned going through to Anna Regina.

'Is rainy season,' he said simply, as though that explained everything; 'you know is rainy season?'

I began to feel that profound feeling of frustration sweeping over me, a sensation I had not known during the past six weeks on the rivers. I was prepared to blame everything on Charity, this phantom outpost of civilization, linked by road and steamer to the city and yet so miserably isolated. Charity seemed to lie on some unfathomable boundary between reality and dream, and the almost opaque curtain of rain obscured even this tenuous link

---

* Readers will recognize, in Victor's story, a strong tribute to the novelist Wilson Harris – in language and style and in the name of the ghostly apparition. He greatly admired Harris and it was he who introduced me to Harris's novels. I still have the letter he wrote me in 1971 after he'd read *Ascent to Omai*; two pages of that letter still constitute for me the best criticism I've ever read on that work. [Mark McWatt]

with the comprehensible. It was as though Charity was floating down the Pomeroon like one of those ubiquitous little clumps of muck and weed, flourishing in the quick liquid fertility of the river, only to succumb to the salt rage of the sea at its journey's end. Charity had no end, unless it was the end of one existence and the beginning – of what?

The other man on the stelling, the one with long rubber boots, who had stood quietly by, now took it upon himself to explain the situation.

'Rainy season,' he said, and spat into the river. 'Every rainy season the road does wash out. This time he wash out bad. Tractor-self can't pass; he worse than rice-field. Nothing, nothing can't pass now.' He grinned at me, as though a spirit of humour had suddenly smitten him, arising from the conspiracy of elements – earth and water – like the ghosts that haunted my trip on the rivers. 'You got to stay here tonight and then take a small-boat tomorrow. Small-boat does go round the crick and meet up with the good road, and there' – he gestured triumphantly – 'you could ketch the bus.' He lapsed into a satisfied silence.

Anyone who travels in the interior of this country must be prepared for such things, I told myself. What does it matter – two days, two weeks, two years – what does it matter in the bush? And suddenly the word 'bush' became a new experience, something that I was encountering for the first time. As I repeated the word in my mind it became tactile, granular, abrasive, like sand. In the city 'He's gone up in the bush' was sufficient explanation for an absence of any length of time. For most people the 'bush' was that vast, semi-real expanse of country other than the eastern strip of coast. It was known for consuming people for long periods before casting them up again upon the coast of civilization and certainty. With an involuntary shudder, I suddenly discovered in the word 'bush' a whole purgatorial experience, a dangerous trial and judgment of self, which only fools undertake willingly – and yet not to undertake it seemed somehow less forgivable. After six weeks on the rivers of the North-West I was being forced to undergo the decisive test: an afternoon in the vague and terrifying liminal space that was Charity in the rain.

71

It was twenty past one when I got my bags transferred from the launch to a rather bare room in the Purple Heart Hotel: a clumsy, extravagant wooden building which dwarfed all the other little houses and cake-shops on that side of the road. On the other side were the school and the church. A light, inescapable dust and the smell of wood enveloped me as I changed my clothes, and they prodded at some indefinite, dreaming recollection which made me appreciate for the first time the frailty of my life on the river's black, reaching hand. I now embraced a phantom of substance and security (though equally frail and amazingly alien, as I still walked with the movement of the launch) in the wooden box of the hotel room, overlooking the unusable road.

From the window of my room I could also see a stretch of rain-swept river north of the stelling, and thought I could just discern the gloomy outline of the far bank – though that may just have been my mind insisting on reading into the picture what it knew to be there. I suddenly felt bereft of the river: cut off from the promise of its movement and flow and purpose – from the phantom presences it contained. I had always thought these terrifying in themselves, but now I was ambushed by the sudden realization that their subversion of the tyrannies of time and place was what I would miss more than anything. When I turned to the interior of the room, my eyes found little comfort there until they lighted on my soggy green bush-jacket hanging on a hammock hook in a corner; I had worn it through rain and sun on the rivers and had become ridiculously fond of the clumsy green garment. I found myself retreating through it into the vault of memory for some solace from this hunger and despair. I remembered the boat-hands cutting up a huge tree that had fallen across the Bara-Bara, blocking our way; I remembered the thousands of insects of curious and obscene shapes that rained down into the launch with every stroke of the axe on a particular limb: they seemed more terrifying in their silent profusion than any jaguar or bushmaster.

I remembered the faces of the women and children in the upper reaches of the Kaituma: blank and unfathomable as if life – or God himself – had denied them the capacity of expression. Or perhaps there was nothing to express, besides the shallow fact of existence, painted quickly into the eyes, and everything else merely functional – ears, nose, lips. I had difficulty imagining a circumstance that would inscribe joy or sorrow on those faces, and yet somehow they, and the memory of them, did not depress me as much as did Charity and the rain. It's strange that in comparison with myself and my labyrinthine relationship with the world around me, these other human beings were at first easy to cope with. Even though I may have tried to overcome it, I felt at first that they were easily dismissed as obscure tribal remnants, upon whose ancient shore and birthright had washed up, like flotsam, an unfathomable civilization. They were without hope or longing, doomed to die in every possible sense of the word. Yet I was fascinated by the sight and company of the dying community. With enormous hubris I saw them as a people without a secret; I could discern (in those early days) no complexity of thought or feeling in the *tabula rasa* of each face. They were like faces formed among clouds – vivid, perhaps for a spectacular, unexpected moment, and then gone, changed disconcertingly into flowing river-water, into trees and huts or the more amorphous features of the riparian landscapes they inhabited. Each face left a vague sameness of expression on the retina of memory. I remembered without feeling that I could not even lust after one of their women.

Carmen was the hostess (the euphemism was her own) at the Purple Heart Hotel. One accepted Carmen as one accepted the passage of time: she was part of the logic of the place – she was simply the woman who ran things. At first the colour of Carmen's skin puzzled me; in the dim indoor light of the hotel corridor it looked a dark olive green; then, in my room as she let me in, grey; then as she was making the bed, her hands against the white pillow were black – like the Pomeroon.

'We don't get so many guests here this time of year,' she said when I asked for a second pillow. 'You could have as much as you want – pillows.'

I found myself looking at her legs as she bent to straighten the sheet. It is curious that not even the dust of longing was present for me, in spite of what I sensed Carmen to be. There were nights on the river – there were days – when I would have given anything to embrace the phantom of a Carmen. I remembered how, with scandalized conscience, I began to experience a curious delight in the physical figure of Angelo, the teenage son and apprentice of our half-Amerindian engineer: how he would sometimes relieve the bowman and stand in the bow with the giant paddle in his slender arms as we forged up the smaller creeks and capillaries of the river system. He would be looking down at the water, as if brooding upon some silent channel or bloodstream of memory. It was Angelo who made me revise my first prejudiced judgment of the river-folk; he it was who opened for me the painful but urgent possibility of discovering, rather than imposing, meaning and relationship with regard to the river folk and myself. A deep and troubling kinship with the person of Angelo seemed to accompany this awareness. I made his body dance on the foredeck of the launch as he pulled the clumsy bow around the sharp turns. His dance, against the background of dark forest was alien and yet exciting, as I slouched half-dreaming in the gloomy interior of the launch. That was the first time it had happened: he had suddenly changed before my eyes, like some strange forest insect that becomes leaf, twig or petal. Angelo changed into a vision of someone young and yet very old, dancing a different historical time and place on the wooden planks of the launch's bow. His bare feet would seem suddenly to wear extraordinary old leather shoes, and his T-shirt and khaki shorts would appear coarse and stiff. Now he was an Elizabethan sailor or cabin-boy, with the bruised, thickened arms of an overworked apprentice. Then I would blink a few times and be relieved to discover it was only Angelo, a half-Amerindian teenage boy, learning to be a boat-hand, signalling the helmsman to slow or cut the engine at the sight of a fallen tree or a floating log. I had promised mentally that I would give Angelo my bush jacket and the old scout belt, which he had admired, but in the end I never did, as that conflagration of feelings I'd experienced on the rivers seemed to burn itself out with our approach to the borders of civilization in the soul-dampening season of rain. A long while after Carmen had turned and gone, I was still staring at her legs – as unmoved as the rain was unremitting. 'Charity,' I whispered, and I wondered if the name was not originally a forlorn plea to the hostile spirit of this strip of swamp at the end of the road.

★ ★ ★

I settled uneasily into a chair in the enormous lounge of the Purple Heart Hotel – one of those large basket chairs with a sloping back that force you to lie almost horizontal. I felt indescribably foolish, lying in this awkward position and gazing up at the mildew-spotted ceiling – until a young Indian couple came into the hotel and claimed my attention. They were both soaked: he was in a soggy felt hat and carrying a cheap brown valise, and she was wearing a lilac bodice of the sort of material that becomes transparent when wet. I could see the straps of her thin brassiere and I found myself undressing her mentally as she stood silent in the gloom of the lounge while the man talked with our hostess. Off came the wet bodice and the brassiere, then the wet skirt – like the layers of an onion. My mental construction of her nakedness was not a pleasant one. Her straight, black hair clinging wetly to her bare shoulders and her old-fashioned scarlet lipstick were somehow appealing, but I was unable to imagine a beautiful naked body. The one that insisted on presenting itself to my dreaming gaze was a squat, tribal body, too large around the middle and with misshapen legs. I was instinctively aware of the internal battle between ways of seeing – perhaps between modes of being – that had been precipitated, it seemed, by my entrapment on a borderline between worlds.

The woman followed the man and Carmen up the stairs, so I was forced to abandon my mental exercise. I speculated that, like myself, they were stopping over for the night until the next day's promised transportation to another world materialized (and this seemed far from certain at that moment). I hoped that all their clothes in the brown valise were also wet and they would have to stay in their room for the rest of the day.

I was still thinking about the woman some moments later when the man appeared beside my chair, dressed in crushed, but dry trousers and an offensive pink shirt. He hesitated a moment before speaking to me.

'You know if they sell cigarette in this place, boy?'

'Carmen,' I called, stopping her in mid-stride as she hurried towards the stairs with sheets and pillowcases draped over her arms.

'Yes, Sir,' she said, surprised, it seemed by something in my voice as I called her name.

'This fellow here would like some cigarettes,' I said. 'He got to wait till the bar open?'

'Nah,' she quickly replied, 'I goin' fix you up just now, Mr. Narine, I just going up stairs for a minute.' And I watched her lithe body ascend the stairs, two at a time. When Carmen was out of the room, Mr. Narine turned to me and said: 'You, hear that, boy? She goin' fix me up.' And he chuckled loudly.

I smiled as he sat in the chair next to mine and folded his arms. I thought that his conversation would at least keep me firmly anchored to the present, preventing the kind of slippage between worlds that had become a feature of my travels on the river and that seemed to have pursued me into the Purple Heart Hotel. Narine told me that he was from Leguan; they had been visiting his wife's people who lived lower down the Pomeroon. It was Mrs. Narine's first visit home since they were married some months ago: in fact they had made the trip to tell her folks that she was pregnant. Narine seemed ready to tell me the entire story of his marriage, his farm in Leguan and the trip, and I began to wonder, with horror, whether he expected me to tell him about myself in return. Fortunately Carmen materialized at that point and called him over to the bar for his cigarettes, whereupon I settled back into the depths of the chair and closed my eyes.

Immediately the sound of the rain outside grew louder and more insistent and its endless, droning tympani on the neighbouring zinc roofs precluded any possibility of mental tranquillity. It is a peculiar quality of rain that it is capable of stirring up memories and unburied skeletons of moods and events somehow associated with rain in the past, and of forcing the mind to grope – sometimes in absolute panic – after every tyrannical twist and nuance of these haunting recollections. Thus I saw clearly again the tiny old schoolhouse at Red Hill on the Barima. I saw the dwarf coconut trees and the rain-blasted hillside bleeding ochrous streams that discoloured the black river. I remembered that this was my first inexplicable feeling of security and abandonment on my travels through the rivers. The rain reduced and dwarfed everything to the limits of obscure vision – everything beyond the drawn curtain of falling water became unattainable, and therefore irrelevant. That night I slept in a vacuum of ease and mental comfort – however false – lulled by the falling rain.

But there were other storms. My dreaming recollection leapt to that overcast evening at Baramanni on the way back (just four days ago – though it seemed an age). I had taken a large corrial belonging to the caretaker of the rest house and paddled up the Waini for quite a distance, just to be alone for a while. I remembered thinking that I needed to sort out some of the thoughts and impressions that had besieged my feeble understanding concerning the folk on these rivers and their relationship to my own idea of world and home. I was determined not to turn back until I had made some decision about myself. This trip on the rivers, after all, would soon be ended. How would it affect (how has it affected) who I might be in the future? As if to thwart my pretensions of autonomy and control, the grey clouds seemed to lower themselves around me and the black skin of the river became wrinkled with the tracks of foreboding breezes, and it seemed that hosts of phantom presences moved in the air around me and in the water beneath the smooth hull of my frail craft and sole support. I felt strangely close to the Waini then, and yet still secure from its intestinal secrets as I refused to alter my course.

Then the rain came and it was just myself and the river. The grey-green foliage on either bank grew vague, then merged into the silver-grey obscurity of the falling rain. I ceased to paddle and tore off my T-shirt, which was already soaked, and flung it into the bow of the corrial. There was something enchanting at first about this grey night of rain, which had the power to change even the eternal blackness of the river into an indescribably luminous colour. Now the solitude that I had formerly courted – and considered my only true context and substance – began to alarm me. I became very conscious of the river: not merely as a stretch of water, but as a powerful presence, sharing a special moment with me. It was now the underside or palm of the river's black hand, not only supporting, but also caressing me. In the hugging gloom of such poor visibility, I felt uncomfortable about the closeness of the river – it was not so much the fear of any physical danger, but the strangest apprehension of *impropriety*, as though the river was trying to establish some sort of forbidden relationship with me. At the same time I was aware of reflecting ironically on this strange access of prudish anxiety: I saw myself as a ludicrous figure lost in a vastness I could not fathom, derided by feelings I did not sufficiently recognize, and in a time and place I could no longer describe with any certainty... I *saw myself*...

As I lay in the basket chair in the lounge of the Purple Heart Hotel, I began to recognize that these recollections of that afternoon on the Waini river were neither voluntary nor fortuitous; I was aware of trying to resist being swept into a vortex of images and memories that had been carefully preserved (I felt certain) in order to summon me to some kind of trial of self that had begun on the river that afternoon, but that had not yet been completed. I opened my eyes in panic and was relieved to find that the hotel was dark and quiet, except for the rain which droned on. I tried to relax. But somewhere in my mind I realized (and accepted with a kind of resignation) that I did see someone on the river – *I saw myself*. I had become the object of my own perception in that confused moment when I began to suspect the river (of what?), when I seemed to hear voices and it was as though someone danced on the river behind the curtain of rain, just beyond the bow of my corrial. It was, I knew, a species of entertainment, a show that was performed for my benefit and yet mocked me at the same time, that mocked my prudish response and the blood and shame it summoned in a timeless moment of anxiety that I prayed would pass. *How* it passed I could not remember, and this is what suddenly seemed crucial for the first time, and I squirmed uncomfortably in the basket chair. I remembered a time when the storm had subsided, when the rain was just a drizzle, when I could again see the banks of the river. I saw that I had drifted down-river, and there was the guest-house, silent in the gloom, the little landing jutting halfheartedly into the river, nudged gently by the launch at its side. Everything had seemed ordinary again and I had smiled at my previous anxieties. I remembered a sudden shiver of cold as I had pointed the corrial's bow towards the landing with a little flick of the paddle.

Angelo had met me on the landing with a grin: 'Ah thought you did loss away in the rain,' he said. 'Dinner cook long time, everybody done eat – except you...' He then took the paddle from me and slung my wet shirt on the handle like a flag and walked ahead of me along the jetty. As I watched his bare feet touch the smooth wet planks of the jetty, I had forcibly to dismiss the sudden intuition that here was my dancer... the sinuous form that moved behind the veil of rain. For a moment I actually became anxious again, disturbed at the profligacy of my own imagination. He looked back at me and smiled and I remembered thinking that there was always something excitingly mysterious about Angelo – I sensed that he could retreat centuries further back than I could into the purest secrets of primordial memory. This intuition had reawakened in me a feeling of uneasiness, as did the recollection of it in the lounge of the Purple Heart Hotel.

That night at Baramanni I had gone to sleep in a smug cocoon of mental ease, lulled by the rain. And that night I again saw Angelo, dressed as some kind of sailor, in a strange, disturbing dream. This Angelo stood on a riverside rock, looking forlornly at a departing boat, a small, ugly wooden thing with a useless sail and a few sets of oars. There were tears on his face, which was at the same time the face of a child and that of an older man (in the implausible manner of dreams). As he opened his mouth to shout something at the men in the departing boat, I woke up in the midnight darkness with my heart racing. The sound of the rain had ceased, but there was a loud chorus of night-creatures and a gentle snoring coming from the other end of the room where the crew slept.

Whether that is what happened, or simply what I chose (or was forced) to remember as I lounged in the basket chair, I cannot say for certain. What struck me all of a sudden was the conviction that somehow I could not yet be released from that vision on the Waini river that afternoon in the rain; it would continue to return to me until I chose to understand or interpret whatever it was trying to convey. Perhaps it was wrong to consider it as an 'incident' that took place on a particular afternoon in the recent past. It was more (I now knew) like an ongoing test or trial, and would not end until I agreed to conspire in an outcome or verdict, the consequences of which would either validate or destroy the world I struggled to inhabit and possess.

★ ★ ★

My reverie in the basket chair was suddenly interrupted by an unexpectedly familiar voice. There, walking towards me was the tall, gaunt figure of Adrian Gall, Jesuit priest and former French teacher at the college. Because of his name, height, slender build and white hair, he had rejoiced in the nickname of 'Gauling' – and here he was with a large umbrella flapping towards me.

'Well well. If it isn't Gabriel dos Santos; good to see you again,' he said, extending a skeletal hand.

'Father Gall…' I responded, bounding out of the chair, 'you're the last person I'd have expected to find in this Godforsaken place…'

'Well, not quite Godforsaken, my boy, though in the present circumstances I can see that you would consider it gloomy… As it happens – and for my sins – I'm now the parish priest here. Our little church is just across the road. I'd heard that there were visitors over at the hotel, and now I'm so glad I decided to pop over. Tell me now how is it that you happen to be here.'

'Well, for my sins, Father, I've just spent seven purgatorial weeks on the rivers of the North-West, supposedly doing a survey of Amerindian villages and settlements – Moruka, Waini, Barima and tributaries...'

We chatted about my work and his for about half an hour and it was a genuine pleasure and relief to re-enter, through him, the world of church and college: the distracting labyrinth of ritual and knowledge, the city spaces I longed for, familiar, and exorcized of all demons. In the end he invited me to turn up in church later that evening for benediction, and I readily agreed.

'That is, if you'd care to... and have nothing better to do,' he added, shooting me a glance which attempted to look into my soul and discover whether it was still as Catholic as it should be after only five years out of college.

'For the past year or two I haven't been in church much, Father

80

– wrestling with various monsters,' I admitted with a smile. 'But if you don't mind I'll be happy to come.'

He nodded, gave me another look and seemed about to say something further, but either thought better of it or deferred it for later that evening. He merely shook hands again.

'At six o'clock, then,' he said simply, as he disappeared through the door and into the rain.

After he left I felt rescued, somehow, from the dark brooding recollections of the rivers that had afflicted me in the basket chair. To maintain this comforting distraction I readily agreed to sit and have a few drinks with Narine and three local men who drifted in as soon as the bar opened at three o'clock. The rum was soothing and the conversation comfortingly familiar: about brands of local rum, about items in the radio news, about women...

At one point Narine leant across the table towards me in a conspiratorial manner and said, 'You na gat wife, boy – Lall here a tell me' – indicating the taciturn figure seated at his right. 'You could get fix up easy-easy with Carmen...' The ghost of a smile hovered around Lall's tight lips as he nodded at me... 'or one of she friends. Ah hear they have plenty good girls in this place dyin' for a little fun – they like to sleep in hotel...'

My smile turned into a low laugh, and they all started laughing. I was surprised how 'happy' I felt, and I knew it had nothing to do with the possibility of enjoying, later that evening, what Father Gall would refer to as 'the venereal pleasures', but simply with the comfortable prejudices we all shared in this situation: the immediate access of understanding, the laughter, the conspiratorial willingness to pursue this kind of conversation through the familiar maze of the rules that govern it. Behind Lall's ghost of a smile lay generations of habit and convention, and these bred in me a sense of ease and a capacity to cope. It had to do with perceiving and recognizing – being able to 'read' – the world outside myself; there was no danger here of 'seeing myself', of becoming the object of my own perception. I think I rejoiced in this conversation because, despite Narine's conspiratorial remark, I knew it really had nothing to do with me and in fact heralded a return to an idea of civilization that I had felt in danger of losing on the rivers.

That feeling of comfort, that I took to be a fortunate recovery of the straight path towards a familiar home, was not, however, to last. My own dark forest and rivers were too close to give me up without a further struggle. I knew I'd not had much to drink, but felt a strange light-headedness, a sensation of drifting above and away from the table with its bottles and glasses and jug of water. The droning conversation of the group, including my own contributions, had become like a current I could no longer resist or control. It bore me out, out... away from safety. I realized, too late, that the amber fluid of the rum had somehow become the amber spirit of the river-shallows, as I clutched desperately at the rocks of chair and table in an effort to right myself and to avoid being swept away.

Dully, and as though from a great distance, the voices of the other men came to me in snatches, as though borne on intermittent gusts in a storm.

'We young frien' gone... Can't take the strong stuff... Sleep it off... Long chair yonder... is best...'

And the tide of voices swept me once more into the basket chair. I tried to protest, but the sounds that I heard from my lips were not what I had intended to utter. I made a frantic effort but was swept against a rock or a log and felt myself go limp...

When next I became aware of myself, it seemed I was in the Waini river again, in the rainstorm and lying in the bottom of the corrial as in a coffin, spent and weary, my head wedged in the narrow sloping groove of the stern. And yet, at the same time, I was also aware that I lay in the basket chair – I tried to clutch the handles, but I could not move. I realized that this was the final unfolding of what happened on the river that day, and something in me assented to the ordeal I sensed was about to take place. Sitting on the frail centre thwart down at my feet was the Elizabethan cabin-boy and dancer, the tattered rags of his uniform wet and drooping and his hair plastered down on his cheeks. This made him look more like Angelo... in fact his appearance, I noticed, flickered, as if by some sort of cinematic trickery, and became a dance between Amerindian and European appearances – serial masks and costumes, all rain-drenched, or fished from the deepest river of memory and longing, to bear witness in a trial of self where I seemed to be reluctant prosecutor, judge and jury. Was this, after all, what was missing from my travels – what I had really set out to discover and accomplish?

'Michael,' the dancer said, as if in answer to a question, 'Michael Harris... Th'moment I saw th'pinnace disappear downstream with Bo'sun and t'others was the end of my life, the end of everything... I thought...'

It was very difficult to understand him as he had a thick, unfamiliar accent; everything about him – clothing, speech, gesture – appeared to be covered with a distorting patina, which seemed to me to be time itself.

''Tweren't nothing I done; they all liked me well enough – per'aps the spirit of this place, this river, which I later learnt carries the name of a country, reminding them of another country they called home. I was their sacrifice, so's they could get back home. My loss in th'forest, killed by savages, was to turn this into a bad place, a place to flee. My loss was their ticket home; much better than finding th'gold. Capt'n Kames and the others were already fed up with the heat and the wet and the sickness – ready to chuck it in...'

I think I realized that I was being confronted by a dead man, or perhaps by death itself... the idea of death, conjured by the river, and by my own apprehensions, into a shape and features I seemed to recognize... Was it my own death?

'I wanted to, but couldn't die – instead I lived with them...' – he swung his arm in a wide gesture – 'the people hereabout. Became one of their best men in time: at war, in the canoes, in the hunt... And the women fought over me: no fancy rules about marriage here! In all I reckon I had five and thirty children – though not all survived childhood – but that makes me a bloody patriarch, don't it?' He grinned widely. 'And I've watched them become more and more the children of my blood... That's the reason I stay – Angelo and his Dad are two of them... living children of my blood...'

In a flash I realized now what I had known intuitively all along: that Angelo had something to do with these visions and with the disturbed state of my own consciousness and imagination. All this must have taken place that day out on the river, though it was brewing within me for weeks, I reasoned, yet it was strange that I only now became aware of it. Now was possible the kind of understanding that had eluded me all those weeks on the rivers. It was as though I'd never lowered (or was it raised?) myself sufficiently to experience and acknowledge it. Now, in the bottom of the corrial, with the rainwater splashing against me, I was looking up at the body of a 'patriarch' a 'first mover' of sorts – ghostly and frail and wet and a little sad, but elevated finally into my field of vision – into my feeble, despairing, rain-and-rum-induced capacities of understanding and hope as I lay stupefied in the basket chair on a gloomy afternoon in Charity – elevated finally into my life of doubt and uncertainty. I longed for him to say that I, too, was one of the 'children of his blood', but he only smiled at me.

'It weren't a bad life... better than on board the wretched ship, and in the other country... before that. The hardest part came after I'd gone: those hundreds of years of disappearance, of looking for someone who could know... The children have my blood, my life, but no-one knew my story – till you... till I realized what I needed was not the bond of blood, but the gift of understanding...'

Then I realized that the words were being spoken, not by the wraith in front of me, but by myself. This, then was the 'understanding' he/I had alluded to, and this was why I kept having the conviction that I had seen *myself*. 'I am Angelo, I am Michael, I am Gabriel,' I heard myself say, and the figure at the centre of the corrial smiled and moved his lips. I realized then that he/I had just pronounced the verdict at the end of my purgatorial trial, and instantly, he began to fade – to drift into the thinning curtain of rain. He looked back once and I heard him say: 'You should eat something.' Then he disappeared. I was struck by the incongruity of his/my last remark and was wrestling with its probable sacramental implications when I became aware of Carmen, hovering over my prostrate form in the basket chair.

'You should eat something,' she said. 'Is because you were drinking rum on an empty stomach that you get so...'

I sat up and looked around: there was a strange quiet and I realized that the rain had abated. The three men had disappeared from the table by the bar ('They gone down the road to arrange for the small-boat that will take all-you round the creek tomorrow,' Carmen explained, as she turned to fetch the plate of dinner I'd agreed to order). I sat at the table and ate heartily, discovering that I was really hungry. Perhaps, I thought, it was hunger that made me light-headed and delusional... But I decided that it didn't matter: I could summon into the certainty of memory, every nuance and detail of my trial and ordeal on the Waini river – indeed all the weeks of travels and observations assumed a startling clarity and vivid pattern on the retina of my memory. I knew I would always be able to see not only the world, but myself in it and to understand the intricate, changing relationship between the two. I marvelled at the gift of peace this realization brought me, as all the burdens of my heart lifted. It was a gift (I realized) not only of understanding, but also of acceptance, or self-acceptance: a gift that made Angelo my brother, and the crew and also Narine and Lall and even Father Gall. Carmen, pouring a glass of water beside me, was my hitherto unacknowledged sister. And the rivers and forest and washed-out road were at last our home.

When Father Gall poked his head in the door just before six, I was ready. There were about thirty people in the little church when we entered, mostly older folk and children; there were a few men, but none my age. We sang the *Tantum Ergo* to the same tune I remembered from Wednesday afternoons at college and our voices rose and filled the incipient night. As the monstrance moved from side to side, glittering as it reflected the candlelight, God's blessing seemed real to me, and associated somehow with my emergence from the trial of self – from my trip on the rivers – with an acceptance of the fortuity of our faith(s) and understanding; of our origins, ancestry, births, arrivals; of the privilege of our mortality in a place that looks more and more like home.

There were tears on my cheeks, but it was already night. I had survived my long afternoon of despair. Besides, the tears were caused by a love that seemed limitless within and around me. As I rose to leave the church, I knew that the next morning, dawning on this our eldorado, would be golden under a sky of brightest blue: 'Tomorrow to fresh forests and rivers new'.

ALMA FORDYCE AND THE BAKOO
by Valmiki Madramootoo

The two brothers who owned and operated the Kashmir Bar and Restaurant on Middle Street could not have been more dissimilar. Ashoka, the elder, was a dreamy romantic: long-haired and bearded, he looked like a sage or holy man, his grey eyes frequently retracting to distant landscapes that only he could see. Romesh, the younger brother, was clean-shaven and practical; his eyes were dark and unexpressive – people said that he was the real businessman, the man of numbers, who did the accounts and kept the business running. He spent most of his time at his desk in the office. Ashoka was always at the bar, chatting with the customers; Romesh had few words for anyone he did not consider rich or important. In his opinion, Ashoka moved far too slowly for the world they lived in and wasted too much time being nice to people; there was no profit in being nice and Romesh was always expressing impatience or disapproval of his brother's fanciful ideas and lack of business sense.

In August 1988 the Kashmir Bar and Restaurant shrank to one small storeroom for three weeks while the place was renovated and enlarged. Romesh considered this a testimony to the success of the business – due, he was certain, to his own acumen. Ashoka, on the other hand, considered that their success sprang from the relaxing atmosphere and pleasant conversation which attracted customers and for which he, Ashoka, was largely responsible.

On the last Friday afternoon in August, while the workers were putting the finishing touches to the new décor and varnishing the impressively large purpleheart counter of the bar, Ashoka invited the dozen or so customers in the temporary room to have a preview of the new space. Romesh, who had been supervising the last tasks of the workers, did not conceal his annoyance when Ashoka marched in, followed by the customers. When eyes had adjusted to the reduced light in the new room everyone looked around and took in the innovations, remarking – in subdued tones because of Romesh's obvious annoyance – items that caught their attention. The bar proved to be a big hit – and the bar stools which had attractive little wickerwork arms and back rests, and which swivelled noiselessly atop fixed metal poles. Others commented on the highly polished floors, or the heavy window drapes.

'In here going be hot no ass,' one fellow asserted, as he took a swig from his bottle of Banks beer.

Romesh was quick with his rejoinder: 'The place not ready for customers yet, you fool; it have air conditioner which will be turned on when the restaurant is officially open. I ent know is who tell allyou to come in here criticizing.'

But in general the comments were sufficiently positive, especially after the exchange above, for even Romesh to relent and permit himself to bask in the praise heaped on his good taste and hard work. He especially appreciated the several assertions that the place would be packed with grateful customers once people had seen the renovations. In fact Romesh had all but forgiven Ashoka for the intrusion when the next discordant note came from the elder brother himself.

'I still think, you know,' he said stroking his beard, 'that the place need something – you know, something that would really stand out and grab your attention.'

'You always singing the same song,' Romesh said dismissively. 'You make we spend nuff money on these Himalayan paintings on the wall, and still you ent satisfy. Soomie and Leela sew a whole set of expensive tablecloths embroider with elephants and monkeys, and still you ent satisfy. The place got hidden lighting, two powerful speakers to blast the music and specially designed menu-cards, and still you ent satisfy – what more you want?'

'All that is good, boy Romesh, I ent criticizing nothing, is just that – when I look around – I get the feeling that the place call for something special: something people will talk about and want to come and see not once or two times, but over and over again.'

'You know I think Ashoka right.' This came from Lambert, one of their regulars, who always wore a sailor hat that had once been white. 'The place now got atmosphere; it make you feel a certain way and you have to try and find something that will go with the atmosphere.'

'Ah, you know the thing, Lambert man, that is just what I mean: the place have something strange about it – something mysterious.'

Romesh snorted, but before he could intervene with a sarcastic remark, Ashoka continued, 'We need something that would make it even more mysterious and exciting – so people will come for the t'rill and the excitement.'

'I one would be happy if they come for the liquor and the food,' said Romesh. 'This ent a haunted house nor jumbie playground – it is what the sign say, a "Bar and Restaurant". Is a place where people coming to relax, eat, drink and chat – I don't want nothing that will distract them from that.'

'But you see,' Ashoka persisted, 'even you notice the atmosphere: why you think you mention "jumbie" and "haunted house"? That is what I mean by atmosphere – if we had a ghost or two in the place, guarding a canister of Dutch money buried beneath the floor.'

'You's a mad ass Ashoka,' Romesh said 'I done give up on you.'

It was at this point that Chunilall intervened. He was an old fellow with wispy white hair who spent time in the Kashmir whenever he was in town. No one knew much about him; it was said that he lived somewhere on the Essequibo coast and came to town regularly on some mysterious 'business'. He always carried a black leather bag shaped like a box, out of which had emerged, on different occasions, the most unexpected objects: a large brass frog, a bowl of steaming rice and curried vegetables, a lady's straw hat, an intricate model of a Toyota minibus, a lighted candle in a brass candleholder, the largest iron key that anyone had ever seen and a folded piece of bright yellow silk that, when unfolded, was bigger than the entire floor area of the restaurant.

'If you want,' Chunilall said, 'I can get you a genuine Bakoo.' Everyone looked at him; it was not just what he said, but the fact that he had spoken at all. It was well known that Chunilall seldom spoke aloud, and now here he was promising to produce a resident Bakoo for the Kashmir Bar and Restaurant. Romesh was the first to recover – he threw back his head and laughed loudly.

'You right to make fun of them, Chunilall,' he said, 'them and their foolishness; they want atmosphere: you right – bring Bakoo, ghost, jumbie, anything that would give them the t'rill they looking for. One? – nah, man Chunilall, bring three-four Bakoos – we could put one in each corner – or better yet, if they could cook and serve food I would fire every motherass employee and got the Bakoos doing all the work in the place. Allyou see how it take old Chunilall to show you what fools you are.'

By then all the workmen, and several of the others were laughing as well.

'But I ent making no joke,' Chunilall said, hushing the hubbub, 'I mean what I say. I know a man with a Bakoo who will part with it for – maybe eight, twelve hundred dollars.'

'What! You must be crazy, old man,' Romesh said. 'Like you's a more hopeless case than Ashoka. Who would spend good money on a Bakoo – to frighten people and chase them away – if such a thing exist at all, or could be seen at all?'

But Chunilall was not to be put off. 'Look,' he said, 'don't make joke of what you don't know or can't understand. This Bakoo is in a big glass bottle, he can be seen, but he won't trouble anybody unless some fool open the bottle and let him out. You could put him on that shelf right there, over the bar and you'd be surprise how people would be interested to come and see him.'

Well, that was all Ashoka wanted to hear. 'Chunilall,' he said in an almost reverent whisper, 'if what you say is true then that is exactly what the place needs: something to make people talk – to make news of the place spread throughout Georgetown, up east coast and even across the river.'

'Conversation piece,' interjected Lambert.

'Perfect, perfect!' Ashoka continued. 'Chunilall, make all the arrangements and bring the Bakoo for me to see as soon as possible – we opening next week. I will pay anything up to one thousand dollars, once I am satisfied that the article is genuine.'

'As long as it is your thousand dollars, Ashoka,' Romesh said disdainfully. 'I know better than to waste my money on such foolishness. In any case – if it turn out to be some ugly, nasty thing in a bottle, is no way I'm allowing it in this restaurant – we could lose our license.'

'Wait till you see before you judge,' was the only thing Chunilall would say as he walked back into the adjoining room and resumed his seat in the corner.

The sneak preview of the new bar and restaurant was over; the workers resumed their work and Romesh went off to see what was happening in the kitchen. It was only Ashoka who stood transfixed, lost in happy surmise, looking at the little shelf on the wall behind the bar and wondering with a shiver of excitement what it would look like with Chunilall's promised Bakoo in it's bottle, gazing down on the room and all that was in it.

★ ★ ★

On Tuesday the following week, the 'new' Kashmir Bar and Restaurant opened with little fanfare. Ashoka wanted to wait for the arrival and installation of the Bakoo, but Romesh would have none of it.

'*If* Chunilall bring any Bakoo at all, and *if* it turn out to be something that the law, the customers and ordinary common sense would allow we to keep in the place – then we could always put it on the shelf and see how many new customers it will attract and how much 'atmosphere' it will add. But it don't make no sense to keep customers crammed up in the little storeroom when the place done finish, and to besides, you have no idea if and when Chunilall will deliver this thing.'

Ashoka had to accept the logic of this and indeed, in the first few days, the new place did very well; all the old customers flocked to see how the renovations had turned out and several of the new and curious came along as well. There was a small advertisement in the daily papers announcing the reopening (Romesh had to settle for this – and pay for it too – when he failed to persuade the editor of one paper to do a lavish centre-page spread on the refurbished establishment). All were satisfied except Ashoka who, throughout the second week, kept a lookout for Chunilall and inquired of other customers if they had seen or heard anything of him. But no one

90

knew anything about his goings and comings. By the third week Ashoka began to have real doubts – who could say whether Chunilall could, indeed, deliver the goods?

On the Friday of that week, when all but Ashoka had given up on Chunilall, the old man turned up – quietly as usual – just before midday, choosing the corner of the new restaurant that would become *his* corner on the days that he visited. He had taken his seat and put his leather case in the corner next to his chair, and was reaching for something in his trousers' pocket before Ashoka became aware of his presence. Ashoka sailed out from behind the bar and approached the old man with some anxiety. There was no evidence of a bottle of the size he expected and he was ready to remonstrate with the old man. As he approached the table, however, Chunilall gestured towards his bag. Ashoka felt both satisfaction and disappointment: satisfied that the old man had kept his word, but disappointed that the object of his expectations was contained in a leather case that was no more than eighteen inches long, ten inches wide and about a foot high. These last few weeks, in his mind's eye he had seen a large sphere of green-tinted glass at least fifteen inches in diameter, with a long narrow neck like a laboratory flask, with a red rubber stopper shutting in the contents. The contents he had failed to imagine – everything that came into his mind seemed impossible, so he focused his expectations on the bottle – and now he was being assured by Chunilall that this, with the Bakoo, was among the clutter in his case.

Ashoka sighed, 'Chunilall, you had me doubting and cussing you these last few days, but at least you come; let me see this little Bakoo thing you bring.'

Without a word, Chunilall reached down and opened the case. What emerged from it was a large brown paper bag containing a cylindrical object about eight inches in diameter and twelve inches high. When the paper bag was pushed down, Ashoka saw an ordinary round bottle, like a large sweetie-bottle, or the bottles people keep on their kitchen shelves with rice or pasta or pickles. It even had one of those heavy glass lids with a rubber ring to seal it and a heavy wire hinge with a little lever that one pressed down or lifted up to seal or open the bottle. As he took in the size and type of the bottle and the fact that it was plain glass without any

91

blue or green tint, Ashoka's disappointment persisted. When he focused on the contents, however, his demeanour quickly changed. The Bakoo was not a thin, twelve-inch high figure like a stretched Barbie Doll, but was, literally, a little man. It sat on the base of the bottle with its knees drawn up under its chin. It had a large head that was almost the diameter of the bottle, perfectly formed limbs with fingers, toes, fingernails and toenails. Its head was balding on top but it had quite a bushy grey beard. It was naked but its feet were positioned in such a way that they covered its genitals. Its skin was a sort of light brown or beige, somewhat like a house lizard, and its eyes, which were wide open and unblinking, were a striking green. Ashoka realized that if the creature were to stand upright it would be a perfect miniature man of about two feet in height. He was amazed, and after looking at it open-mouthed for over five minutes, he considered it impossible to doubt that the creature was real flesh and blood. He cast a quick, inquiring glance at Chunilall who sat impassive before the bottle.

'This thing is alive?'

'Alive, yes, but once the bottle remain cover down tight he can't really move or do anything,' Chunilall said.

'He dangerous?' Now it was Chunilall's turn to shoot a quick, suspicious glance at Ashoka.

'Not in the bottle – cause he can't do nothing once he in there – but if you was to open the bottle or break it and let him out, of course he dangerous: you never hear bout Bakoo? How they does pelt stone and break up things and get on real wild?'

Ashoka had heard but he had never seen a Bakoo before and had not taken seriously all the stories he had heard over the years. As he looked now at the small hands of the Bakoo he could indeed picture them grasping and throwing stones.

'So how much you want for him?' Ashoka asked.

'Well I tried to get him for you for twelve hundred dollar, but my friend say he can't take less than fifteen hundred. If you can't pay that I have to take him back.'

Ashoka hesitated only a minute; the truth was that he would have paid twice that amount if forced to. He made suitable whining and complaining noises, but he took out a wad of notes from his pocket and peeled off fifteen hundreds for the old man.

'Anything special we got to do…?' but Ashoka's question was lost in a loud exclamation behind him.

'What the ass!' This was from old Smithie, who was coming over to chat with Ashoka when he saw the bottle. His shout focused the attention of the entire room, and soon there was pushing and shouting and a stream of questions – to the point where Chunilall stood up with arms outstretched and shouted: 'Allyou take care! If you break this bottle today is hell on earth in here. This Bakoo been in the bottle for over twenty years, if he get out now he going be in his rickitiks an nuff of allyou will get hurt – don't mind he look so small and quiet.'

The crowd shrank back from the table and people even took turns in approaching, a few at a time, to inspect the bottle more carefully. All were impressed. Even Romesh, when he emerged from the office to see what was going on, had to admit that he'd never expected something quite so realistic. Of course he knew that it was some kind of elaborate doll (you couldn't fool him), but he had to concede that it was damn well made, and, for that reason alone, worth having in the restaurant. Indeed it was Romesh who took the bottle, climbed on a chair behind the bar and placed the Bakoo on the little shelf. One of the miniature spotlights, intended originally to illuminate popular brands of liquor on the shelves behind the bar, was adjusted to focus on the bottle, revealing its contents quite clearly to all who looked up at it.

That afternoon and evening the news spread rapidly and everyone who could dropped in to see the Bakoo, including several (especially women) who had never set foot in a bar before. One old Portuguese woman created a bit of a fuss by claiming loudly that the bottle was her old garlic pork bottle, stolen years ago from her kitchen, along with a large pot and a frying pan. No one paid her any mind and she left muttering to herself. Even Inspector Dalrymple, deputy head of the crime squad, came to inspect the Bakoo when he observed the crowd in and around the bar on his way home from work. Like Romesh, he regarded it as a cleverly contrived artefact, but admitted it was a good gimmick to attract customers.

The crowds continued for the next few days. Old Nana Shepherd, barely able to walk, got her niece to take her to see the

Bakoo, since she had claimed to have seen one before. She shuffled in and looked up at the bottle. After studying the creature for a while she became agitated and shouted: 'You! It's you, you brute! I thought I had seen the last of you, you miserable bastard. Is a good thing they got you lock up in that bottle. I pray God will take me before you get out of in there.'

When they had calmed her down, and someone had bought her a stiff gin-and-tonic to loosen her tongue ('with just a little squeeze of lemon, young fellow, if you please, and a dash of bitters for the throat'), she explained to them that she recognized the creature as the Sharples Bakoo of years ago. He had terrorized the Sharples family, for whom she worked as a maid at the time, and she had had several unfortunate encounters with 'that rascal', as she called him (shaking her fist at the bottle). She claimed that once he had even tried to put his hand under her skirt. When a few in her audience around the bar expressed scepticism, she said, 'It's him, I know it's him; I would never forget that face. But if you don't believe me, lift up the bottle and check and you will see that he has a big black mole like a watermelon seed on the left cheek of his backside.'

This caused some confusion, with several people offering to check it right away, but the barman insisted that Mr. Romesh would have to be called before anyone would be allowed to lift the bottle. When Romesh came and heard what was proposed, he was reluctant to indulge the ravings of this crazy old woman; but after ten minutes he was persuaded by the customers that there could be no harm in taking a quick look. When he got up on the chair and raised the bottle, the mole on the left cheek could clearly be seen and there was pandemonium for several minutes. Thus it was established that what the brothers had on their premises was not just *a* Bakoo, but *the* notorious Sharples Bakoo, of whom many in Georgetown had heard, even if only a few were familiar with the details of his legendary exploits.

The next day someone had painted a little plywood sign and fixed it beneath the larger sign with the name of the establishment, so that passers-by now read: 'Kashmir Bar and Restaurant – Home of the Sharples Bakoo.' The newspapers could no longer resist the story and several features on the Bakoo appeared, complete with photographs and interviews. Romesh was pleasantly surprised and entirely satisfied with this turn of events. The daily takings had more than doubled since the Bakoo arrived and he found himself feeling enormous gratitude to his brother and old Chunilall. They had been right.

★ ★ ★

Miss Alma Fordyce considered herself the last remnant of a venerable Queenstown family: she alone now occupied the family home on New Garden Street, which she did her best to upkeep, with the help of a faithful family maid, just a few years older than herself. People said that Agnes, the maid, continued to work for Alma Fordyce only out of respect for the family she had served since childhood, because Alma could pay her very little. Agnes treated Alma Fordyce like a spoiled younger sister whom it was best to humour and flatter, although she, Agnes, knew best what should be done in and around the house, and made sure that things were done *her* way. For years Alma Fordyce had worked part-time at the public library, riding to work at two-thirty each afternoon on her old-fashioned ladies bicycle, and riding back home again just after dark at six-thirty each night. She had long been a familiar figure on the streets of Georgetown, sitting bolt upright in the saddle, ringing her bell impatiently at jaywalkers and all those awful vendors who had taken over the verges of some city streets of late. She was not above supplementing the warning sounds of her bicycle bell with a few well chosen phrases of remonstration. Most people regarded her as a colourful but harmless anachronism, in keeping with her claim to be the last of the Queenstown Fordyces. This was not strictly accurate, for her sister Iris was very much alive and living with her second husband in Toronto, from where she wrote regularly to Alma and sent her a monthly remittance (to help pay for the upkeep of the family home), and the occasional barrel packed with necessities difficult to obtain (legally) in Guyana at the time. There was also a question mark concerning her elder brother Sedley, who had long been presumed dead after he disappeared somewhere in the interior trying to make his fortune as a porkknocker. No corpse was ever found, and there were times (less frequently nowadays)

95

when Alma Fordyce contemplated the possibility that Sedley was alive and living with a family of his own in a neighbouring country. In which case he was either the victim of amnesia or (though she dismissed this possibility) had deliberately absconded to avoid the consequences of twin scandals: a pregnant schoolgirl and some kind of financial fraud. Alma had heard rumours, but dismissed them as malicious fabrications and told any would-be informant that she preferred not to listen to gossip and mischief-making and that therefore they should 'kindly desist from mentioning such unsavoury matters' in her presence. Over time, her campaign to dismiss talk of Sedley's wrongdoing had so convinced herself that she let it be known that her brother had drowned while trying to rescue an Amerindian child from a river in spate 'somewhere near the Venezuelan border'. She found, with only faint surprise, that after a number of years, she firmly believed it herself and marvelled at the ability of the human mind to intuit the truth in circumstances where at first it might seem quite beyond reach. When Alma Fordyce said, therefore, that she was the last of the Queenstown Fordyces, what she meant was that she was the last one still residing in Guyana in the family home.

One morning, Agnes said to her, 'Eh Miss Alma, you hear about the Bakoo they have in a bottle up in Middle Street?'

'What Bakoo, Agnes? For heavens sake, where do you get all these stories?'

'But it all over the papers, Miss. You must be the only body in Georgetown who hasn't heard about it. I don't know why you bother to buy the papers if you don't read them.'

'I suppose I buy them so that *you* can read them and tell me if there's anything important. After all what are maids for? Besides, you know that I dislike the vulgarity of the local press, Agnes, and after what they wrote about my brother, I have never been able to trust them to tell the truth about anything. Now what is this business about a Bakoo?'

Agnes thrust Sunday's paper into her hand, open at the page where the large headline proclaimed: *'Bottled Bakoo finds home in bar'*. Alma Fordyce read the story quickly, finding herself more than usually irritated by the grammatical errors and the flippant journalese. Then she looked briefly at the fuzzy picture of the form in the bottle and sucked her teeth. She went through the house in quest of Agnes.

'This is a lot of old rubbish, Agnes,' she said. 'I remember Mama used to tell us stories about the Sharples Bakoo, but she never claimed to have seen it – it was all just idle gossip, surely. Now it appears that someone has perpetrated this hoax on the owners of the bar. Nice people too, if I'm not mistaken. I'm certain it was outside this very establishment that the chain of my bicycle slipped off and this very pleasant young Indian gentleman came out and put it back on for me so that I could get to work on time. His hands were quite black with grease when he was finished, but he nodded politely and said, 'You're welcome Miss Fordyce', when I thanked him. I'm surprised that he allowed himself to be duped by this Bakoo-in-a-bottle nonsense.'

'It look quite real to me, Miss Alma,' Agnes said; 'it even got fingernails and toenails and to besides…'

'You mean you've seen the wretched thing? Oh Agnes, you disappoint me – chasing after cheap thrills and nine-day wonders like a vulgar urchin – and at your age.'

'All I can say is that the thing look real to me, and everybody I know was going over there to take a look. In any case, I'm glad I went, because I never seen nothing like that before: I can tell my grandchildren I have seen…'

'Watch what you're doing, Agnes,' Alma interrupted (Agnes was ironing). 'That sleeve will be scorched if you keep the iron on one spot so long; then what will I wear to work today? Let me leave you to your work before all this Bakoo talk distracts you and you burn up my clothes, most of which come all the way from my sister Iris in Toronto.' And she stalked out of the room.

Alma Fordyce reflected that Agnes, poor thing, had never really grown up; she still laughed at schoolgirl jokes and covered her mouth with her hand whenever she heard anything shocking. She tended to believe whatever story she was told and was particularly susceptible to the flattery of men. After all, did she not have two children for two different fathers, neither of whom would marry her? How could she be expected to see through such a hoax? But, as things turned out, it was not long before Alma Fordyce herself was gazing at the little man in the bottle above the bar.

One afternoon, not long after Agnes had handed her a copy of the newspaper story about the Bakoo, Alma Fordyce was preparing to leave for work at the library, but was doing so with some apprehension. The sky had become quite dark and it seemed certain that it was soon going to rain and she remembered that two evenings before, she had reluctantly handed over her trusty umbrella to Miss Armogan at work so that Miss Armogan's brother, Taj, could repair it for her. She was still annoyed that she had put a small hole in the umbrella and bent a few of its spokes when she swung it at a particularly obnoxious mongrel who had taken to running after her bike and barking and snapping at her ankles whenever she approached Light Street corner. The howl of pain that the animal emitted when she connected was very satisfying, but she immediately regretted the damage done to her umbrella. She was further annoyed at herself for allowing Miss Armogan to persuade her to have her brother Taj fix it for her that day. After all, the umbrella still opened and would have kept the rain off her. Now she would probably be drenched on her way to work that afternoon.

Since there was no other umbrella in the house, Miss Fordyce decided there was nothing for it but to set out in the hope that the rain kept off for at least fifteen minutes. If it did fall, she would have to stop and shelter somewhere along the way. She pedalled briskly up Crown Street, noting with satisfaction that, for the second afternoon in a row, no cursed mongrel had accosted her as she approached Light Street. But it had begun to drizzle and, as she turned into Middle Street, it really bucketed down. She looked quickly around and headed for an overhanging roof she spotted on her left. It was only after she got off her bike and took out her handkerchief to wipe her face that she noticed that she had sought shelter under the roof which overhung the wide doorway of the Kashmir Bar and Restaurant, home of the Sharples Bakoo. She grimaced at the thought of the bottle over the bar, but had to think of other things as the rain came down in torrents and quite a bit of spray found it's way under the overhanging roof. She leaned her bicycle and flattened herself against the front wall of the building and was just wondering whether she dared seek shelter in the dim interior, when a voice in the doorway spoke her name.

'Oh, is Miss Fordyce! Good afternoon, Miss Fordyce – oh but you getting wet there. Please come inside, you can shelter as long as the rain lasts.'

She recognized the young man who had fixed her bicycle chain a few years ago. 'Are there many people inside?' she asked, 'I'm not sure I want to be seen inside a rum shop.'

Romesh wanted to correct her, let her know that the establishment was a 'Bar and Restaurant', but he smiled weakly and said, 'Well, you know, Miss Fordyce, there are always lots of people in the place these days, what with the Bakoo and all – but I can find you a quiet table in a corner.'

'Oh, I don't have time to sit down at a table. As soon as this rain eases up I have to be off to work – in fact I think it's falling less hard already. But,' she was surprised to hear herself say, 'as I'm here, let me just come in for a minute and see this famous Bakoo of yours.'

'Certainly, Miss Fordyce, come in nuh,' Romesh said, waving her inside. She went right up to the bar where a couple of regulars hopped off their stools and stood and nodded at her as she leaned on the counter.

'There it is,' said Romesh, 'up on the shelf – it look real, eh?' And Miss Fordyce saw the pale brown creature squatting in its bottle and was quite astonished.

'My gracious! He *is* an authentic looking fellow,' she said, 'beard and all – I wonder if it was made here in Guyana.'

'Made!' One of the fellows at the bar seemed quite outraged. 'It's not *made*, lady; this is a living creature – a little man with flesh and bones like me and you – only he's trapped in a bottle so he can't damage property and frighten people. Don't tell me you never hear bout Bakoo.'

Alma Fordyce was disposed to be quite indignant in the face of such an ignorant outburst, but she had kept looking at the Bakoo and found herself strangely fascinated. More than fascinated, in fact, for she found herself thinking that the little creature's face reminded her of someone.

'Well, it's certainly quite amazing,' she said weakly, smiling briefly at the man at the bar. 'I must come back and get a better look at it another time, but right now, I have to go to work. It sounds as though the rain is holding up.'

Romesh escorted her back to the door where she discovered that the rain had indeed stopped.

'Come back any time you want,' he said. 'You'd be surprised at the people who come here to see it – all kinds of people.'

By then Alma Fordyce had given a brief, almost dismissive wave of farewell and was pedalling up Middle Street at great pace. The light had changed after the rain, and everything, somehow, seemed different. In her mind Alma Fordyce associated this strangeness with the Bakoo, that homunculus squatting in the bottle with the enigmatic, familiar countenance. Yes, she thought, she must look at it again. She thought of the Bakoo all the way to the library and even as she entered the building. It was only when she saw Miss Armogan emerge from the room behind the desk, and she remembered that she must quarrel with her about having deprived her of the use of her umbrella, that the image of the Bakoo faded from her mind.

★ ★ ★

So obsessively had the Bakoo haunted the thoughts and imagination of Miss Fordyce, that on the very next Saturday, she found herself again at the Kashmir Bar and Restaurant. This time she was able to see the little man in the bottle from much closer range and to study him at greater length. When she entered the room the first thing she noticed was that the shelf above the bar was bare. A strange panic gripped her for a moment – like the morning after her mother's death, nine years ago, when she sat to breakfast at the dining table and realized her mother's place was empty. In the Kashmir that Saturday, the mystery of the missing bottle was solved when she noticed a corner table bathed in very bright light and surrounded by a lot of people. As she approached she could see the Bakoo in his bottle on the table, a powerful spotlight focused on him. There was a young man with a video camera and another with an ordinary camera and five or six other youngsters, plus an older fellow of very dark complexion with an almost bald head and a bushy, greying beard.

Ashoka hurried over to greet her. 'Miss Fordyce, eh, I don't have to ask to what we owe the pleasure of seeing you again so soon – I know you come back to see the Sharples Bakoo. Well, you will be able to see him good-good today, because we have some scientists from the University of Guyana doing some investigations.'

By this time they were at the table and the older, bearded fellow was looking in their direction with an expression of undisguised annoyance.

'Oh,' Ashoka said, 'Miss Fordyce, this is Professor Patrick De Florimonte from up at UG. Professor, this is Miss …'

'Yes, I'm acquainted with Miss Fordyce,' the professor interrupted. 'We met several years ago, in somewhat less pleasant circumstances – for me at any rate.'

'We did?' asked Alma Fordyce, looking at him closely. 'De Florimonte, De Florimonte – oh, yes, we did. Now I remember.'

'Well, if you'll just excuse us for a few minutes – you needn't leave – you can stand quietly and observe – we are about to conclude our work for today and you can have the Bakoo all to yourself.' And he turned back to the table, signalling the young students with the cameras to proceed with their filming. Afterwards other students took out callipers and rulers and started making measurements of the major bones as best as they could through the glass: femur, tibia, radius and ulna. The bottle was weighed in a balance and the professor asked if anyone knew where he could obtain a similar bottle that was empty. Then he asked the astonishing question, 'I don't suppose I can persuade you to let me lift the lid, just for a minute or two to take further measurements.'

'Sorry, Professor,' Ashoka said firmly, 'you know what they say will happen if we do that. We can't take any chances.'

While this was going on Alma Fordyce was reflecting on her previous encounter with this professor. It was a few years ago and he'd looked younger then, not quite as bald, with a trimmer beard, unstreaked with grey. He had not long been appointed Professor of Psychology and head of the University's Paranormal Phenomena Unit (PANPU). He was checking all possible sources of information concerning local superstitions and lore about supernatural creatures and had come to the library seeking to borrow a copy of A R. F. Webber's *Centenary History of Guyana* and some other titles that had seemed promising. Alma Fordyce particularly remembered the Webber book, because the only copy available was for overnight loan only. As she checked it out she instructed him that it had to be returned by 10:30am on Monday – no later. The unfortunate professor arrived with the book on Monday at 3:10 in the afternoon – during Miss Fordyce's shift – and she'd remonstrated loudly with him, calling him irresponsible and a dismal example to students and other young people, who were already inclined to be unmindful of rules and authority. When he had protested with some heat that he was a senior academic engaged in serious research and did not appreciate being spoken to in that manner, she had drawn herself up to her full height: 'All the more reason, sir, why you should be scrupulous about the rules.' She'd continued in this manner for several minutes, concluding that it was her duty to remind him of the rules whether he was 'a professor, a pan-boiler or the president himself.' When he had muttered something about 'not having to take this kind of abuse from some frustrated old spinster,' she had ostentatiously torn up his library card and let him know in a loud voice that his library privileges were being rescinded indefinitely.

And here was this same professor with his students photographing and measuring the Bakoo and even seeking to poke about in his bottle. Without knowing why, she instantly resented what they were doing, and scowled silently as the group completed its business, packed up their equipment and left. When Ashoka invited her to sit at the table with the Bakoo, she managed a defiant smile and transferred her attention to the thing in the bottle. She was amazed at how realistic the skin appeared, how human the creature seemed in every way, realizing with a sudden blush that it probably had miniature sexual organs obscured behind its feet. Her heart did a little flip. Such thoughts always brought to mind her brother Sedley. She remembered that when she was twelve and he was almost seventeen, he had asked her to let him touch her budding breasts, but when she had replied that she would have to ask their mother first, he'd quickly laughed and said it was all a joke. 'You silly little chicken, why would anyone want to touch those mosquito bites?' She remembered the hurt and the shame his words had awakened – and his eyes had seemed to penetrate and expose her – like the eyes of this Bakoo.

'That's it! It's him,' she said aloud.

'Who, Miss Fordyce,' Ashoka asked, 'who you talking about?'

She felt she had to tell him. She looked around and said in a low voice: 'The Bakoo – it's Sedley! My brother Sedley who's been missing for years. Somehow – I don't know how – he's returned as this Bakoo. It's his face, his eyes. I didn't recognize him at first because of the bald head and the grey beard but I just *know* it's him.'

'Take it easy, Miss Fordyce,' Ashoka said with some concern. 'This is the Sharples Bakoo – it's been around since the beginning of the century – it can't be your brother.'

'But I know it is,' Alma Fordyce insisted in a fierce whisper. 'I would recognize that look anywhere – those eyes.'

Ashoka shook his head sadly. 'I'm sorry to have to disappoint you, but we have proved that this is the Sharples Bakoo. An old servant who remembered the Bakoo made us check for a special mark which she said the Sharples Bakoo had – and she'd recognized the Bakoo in any case. When we checked, that mark was there. That's how we know for certain.'

'What kind of mark? Where? Show me,' Alma Fordyce said.

'Well it's a mole in a kind of private place…'

'Not a mole the size of a raisin on his left buttock, is it?' she asked, suddenly galvanized. 'Oh my God, can it be?' And without waiting for a reply she lifted up the bottle and looked through the glass underneath. 'Oh my God,' she repeated, 'this proves that it's him. It's my brother Sedley. I've only seen that mole once before, but I'd never forget it. Sedley!' And she looked imploringly at the bottled homunculus whose eyes continued to stare straight ahead with an impassivity that seemed to her fiercely defiant.

Ashoka became flustered. He did not know what to make of this poor lady and her claims – logically it was impossible for this creature to be her brother, but he had great respect for the powers of the imagination and already suspected that it was futile to argue with Alma Fordyce. He picked up the bottle, walked over to the bar and replaced it on its shelf.

Alma Fordyce followed him in a daze, her mind back in the past – the night, soon after he started working at the insurance company, when Sedley first came home drunk. Their father was already asleep but Mama had waited up for him, had heard his friends drag him up the steps and leave him on the landing outside the front door, after knocking softly. They were disappearing on their bicycles when she hurried to open the door and Sedley was leaning against the bannister swaying drunkenly. When a curious Alma Fordyce, fourteen years old at the time, came out to see what was going on, she found her mother struggling to manhandle Sedley into the house. 'Come,' she whispered to Alma, 'come and give me a hand. Let's get him into his bed before he wakes up your father. Your father will kill him if he sees him like this.' She and Mama had got Sedley into his bedroom with some difficulty. He was inclined to head for the kitchen and kept saying, 'I need a little drink.' They shut the bedroom door and urged him in loud whispers to get into bed, but he just held on to the bedpost and tottered.

'Perhaps he needs to do wee-wee,' Alma, ever practical, had suggested. Her mother had looked heavenwards.

'Oh lord, if we take him to the toilet he's bound to wake up your father.'

Sedley solved their problem by peeing in his pants; a large glistening puddle growing under his shoes at the foot of the bed. They took off his tie and shirt, Mrs. Fordyce loosened his pants and let them fall.

'OK, Alma dear,' Mama had said, 'you can go back to your room now – you shouldn't see him like this. It's not decent. I can manage from here,' and she turned to yank down his soggy white underpants.

Alma obediently headed for the bedroom door, but not before taking a last look at her drunken brother, seeing his underpants come down, and the startling black mole like a small beetle embossed on the left cheek of his pale backside. She had never forgotten that sight, and had always associated it with his earlier request to touch her breasts and, more generally, with the dangers and forbidden secrets of the flesh.

★　★　★

So it was that Alma Fordyce began to frequent the Kashmir Bar and Restaurant. When she discovered how indescribably awkward it felt just standing there at the bar, gazing up at the bottled Bakoo, she decided that the only thing to do was to order a drink and nurse it slowly for the thirty or forty-five minutes she usually spent on what she liked to think of as her visits to her brother. 'It's as though he's in jail,' she told herself, 'imprisoned for some serious crime.' She was doing her Christian duty – perhaps that's what all of this was about, the expiation of sin and guilt. She began to recall everything she could about her brother. The childhood memories were extraordinarily vivid and invariably positive, but as she traced the development of their relationship through her adolescence, there were more and more areas of darkness. There were memories that stirred powerful feelings within her that she would have preferred not to acknowledge – even to herself – such as the memory of his drunken incontinence on the night when she saw the mole on his behind.

She remembered that when, as an attractive young woman of twenty-one, she had rebuffed the amorous attentions of Philbert Granger at a dance, he had said: 'It must be true what they say: you're too much in love with your own brother to pay any attention to anyone else.' This remark had stung.

She remembered when Sedley Fordyce had run away to the bush and there were all those ugly rumours about embezzling his firm's money, and then that force-ripe Melinda Abinsetts' opportunistic claim that he had fathered the child with which she was pregnant. Alma Fordyce had taken the decision then to retire from society and to have nothing to do with men or 'romance'. Sedley's disappearance/death and her younger sister's disastrous first marriage confirmed her spinsterhood. She devoted herself to her parents in their declining years and, eventually, to her part-time job at the library.

The obsession with the Bakoo, then, represented a significant departure from her rigid and accustomed standards of behaviour and her aloofness from public places and occasions, but Alma Fordyce considered the chance to re-acquaint herself with her long lost brother (despite the re-awakening of long suppressed emotions and memories) was well worth the sacrifice. The whiskey and soda she drank in the Kashmir Bar helped to make it easier – so much so that the gossip column of one newspaper gleefully reported that Alma Fordyce, 'the virgin queen of Queenstown and well known terror of the public library', had become a regular at a certain Middle Street watering hole notorious as the home of the Sharples Bakoo: 'We hear that our prim and proper Miss Fordyce imagines this Bakoo to be none other than her long lost brother Sedley whom, older readers might recall, disappeared in the interior several years ago.' Alma Fordyce decided she could endure even this rude exposure. The only thing that she really disliked about her visits was the frequent presence in the bar of Professor De Florimonte – sometimes with his students and scientific equipment, sometimes without. The professor, like Alma Fordyce, could often be seen just gazing up at the bottle on the shelf. Though their reasons were different, without doubt, in all Georgetown, these were the two people most obsessed with the Sharples Bakoo.

There suddenly sprung up a rumour that the professor, to make a closer observation, had once opened the lid for a brief moment. It was Lambert, one of the regulars, who spread this rumour, but no one really believed him. The Bakoo, everyone knew, would have escaped the instant the bottle was opened, so Lambert, who in any case was not sure exactly what he'd seen, must have been mistaken. Nevertheless, Romesh decided that it would be a long time before he permitted the professor to take down the bottle again; and even then he would make sure that he supervised the entire operation. The next time Chunilall came into the Kashmir, Romesh made a point of having a chat with him.

'Hey Uncle,' he said with a broad smile, 'we haven't seen you for a few weeks – you weren't sick or anything?' The old man shook his head slowly and sipped his rum and water.

'Anyway, we had a little rumour last week that somebody opened the Bakoo bottle.'

Chunilall was instantly galvanized and he looked sharply up at the shelf above the bar.

'Nobody believe the idiot who spread this rumour,' Romesh assured him, 'because as you see, the Bakoo still inside and it would bound to have escaped if the bottle was opened in truth – right?'

Chunilall looked grave: 'All you fool around good – you don't know what it is you playing with, you hear! Once the bottle open the Bakoo will begin to wake up and when it ready nothing can

106

keep it inside. Even if you close back the bottle, it will get strong enough to break out sooner or later. You better hope is only a rumour for true.' Romesh was really worried at this and decided that at the first sign that anything was amiss with the Bakoo, he would get rid of it – though he was not sure how. For the moment he would observe it carefully and often.

After a few days Romesh relaxed somewhat; the Bakoo had not stirred. A few weeks later, the rumour was forgotten. The professor had not visited for some time and there even seemed to be a slight falling off in the daily takings, as the Bakoo seemed no longer the novelty it had been before Christmas. Then one mid-day Miss Fordyce, who was sitting at the bar and gazing up at her 'brother', gave a sudden shriek. Sedley/the Bakoo had winked at her.

Ashoka smiled indulgently and turned to the barman: 'What all you put in Miss Fordyce drink?' he asked with a wink, having glanced up to see that the Bakoo was staring straight ahead as impassively as ever. 'She beginning to see things.'

Miss Fordyce responded indignantly that she could hold her liquor better than any of them and that she was certainly not drunk. She insisted that the Bakoo had winked at her, although now he seemed to have returned to normal.

'He must have waited until you were the only one looking at him, miss,' someone at the bar said with a chuckle. 'He must be got a soft spot for you.' There was a ripple of laughter, but Alma Fordyce became convinced that this was in fact what had happened – Sedley had intended that only she should see it. This strengthened her conviction that somehow the creature in the bottle was her brother and he was trying to communicate with her, and she thought how difficult it must be for him to be under constant scrutiny, how lacking he was in privacy.

When she saw him wink at her a second time – a Saturday evening when the mood in the crowded bar was very festive – she started, but said nothing. It was after this second incident that Alma Fordyce approached Romesh.

'I just want you to know,' she told him, 'that I'm willing to buy the Bakoo from you whenever you're ready. As you know, I associate it with my lost brother and would like to spend more time with it in the privacy of my own home. I have some money saved and will pay you handsomely for it. After all, it won't remain a novelty attracting new customers for ever.'

Romesh told her that the Bakoo was not for sale, though after she left the office, he reflected that here was the answer to the problem of disposing of the Bakoo if it ever threatened to act up.

Then, a few days after Miss Fordyce had visited him in his office, people began to notice a change inside the bottle. Whereas the glass had always been crystal clear, it began to become slightly misted on the inside as if from the condensation of moisture.

'Is the Bakoo's breath clouding up the glass,' someone said. Romesh was only slightly concerned. It still looked much the same to him, though he thought that perhaps he should remind Miss Fordyce of her offer – just in case. By the next afternoon, the mistiness inside the bottle had increased and there was even a tiny track where a drop of moisture had run down the inside. For her part, Alma Fordyce was quite certain that something was happening. The Bakoo had winked at her four times and Romesh was less inclined to disbelieve her. He was, though, reluctant to part with the Bakoo just yet.

The following afternoon the Bakoo got an erection. Everyone had long assumed that the creature had its diminutive sexual organs carefully hidden behind it's feet, but now what could only be a tumescent penis began to appear, protruding between the insteps of the two feet. Spellbound patrons saw this thing touch the glass and crawl a good two inches up the front of the bottle. It struck everyone that this penis was certainly not in proportion to the rest of the creature's body parts – it was nearly an inch in diameter. The consensus was that the organ would not have disgraced an average adolescent boy soon after puberty and one of the waitresses, who rejoiced in the nickname 'Miss Pudding' – and everyone felt she should know – remarked that she knew a few 'big men' who would struggle to produce something that size when fully aroused.

Pandemonium broke out. In no time the place filled up and there was a large crowd jostling and shouting outside. Miss Fordyce, who had witnessed the Bakoo's shameful lack of control and had considered it an embarrassing personal and family scandal, had to be hustled into the office for her own safety as the curious crowded the bar and shrieked and laughed in the most vulgar manner. Ashoka climbed up on the bar and shouted at the people to get out, but no one moved. Just as he was beginning to feel desperate, he heard a commotion at the front entrance and saw the large wrought-iron security gates begin to slide together and close. This happened very slowly for there were hundreds of people jostling to squeeze inside. Eventually the gates were bolted and padlocked. This was the work of Romesh and some of the kitchen helpers. Forcing his way back through the crowd to the bar, Romesh stood on the counter and shouted that he was not putting up with any riot on his premises, that those inside could look at the Bakoo, then they would be let out in orderly fashion through the back. Those outside had better leave, because the place was closed and would not open until the next day. 'By which time,' he said, 'the Bakoo should be – back to normal.' A howl of protest broke out both in and outside the bar. Nevertheless, the place slowly emptied as people were hustled out the back. The crowd outside only dispersed when the police arrived and threatened, through a megaphone, the use of tear gas.

Later that evening, it was discovered that several bottles of ten-year-old rum and over fifty thousand dollars in cash were missing from behind the bar. An 'opportunistic crime', the police called it. Romesh called it something much worse and threatened to fire every employee. Meanwhile, all Ashoka could do was to think wistfully what a remarkable feat it was for such a small and seemingly bloodless creature to maintain an erection for so many hours!

Romesh was just beginning to recover his composure, and was about to leave the bar to go and talk business with Miss Fordyce, when a bottle of soda water narrowly missed his head and smashed on the wall to his left, leaving a hissing patch of foam glistening in the artificial light.

'What the ass!' he said, ducking and turning around at the same time. Only Ashoka or one of the two barmen could have thrown it, but all three were themselves diving for cover as another bottle detached itself from the shelf, sailed over the bar and detonated on the floor. Everyone headed for the kitchen at once, realizing that the Bakoo, though apparently still in his bottle, was indeed 'acting up'. Romesh quickly concluded a deal with Miss Fordyce, who had waited in the office for precisely that purpose. When they peeped into the bar, however, with the idea of handing over the bottle, they saw with sinking hearts that the bottle was empty, the room was quiet and the Bakoo was nowhere to be seen.

Early the next morning, Romesh and Ashoka were in the office trying to read the sensational story in the newspaper ('Sharples Bakoo Aroused: Causes Riot') but were constantly being interrupted by the telephone. Romesh had just spoken to an inspector of police, assuring him that he had already got rid of the Bakoo, so there should be no recurrence of the events of the previous evening. Ashoka had taken a call from a TV station and declined an offer of several thousand dollars to appear, with the Bakoo, on 'Talk Of The Town' that evening. Then there was a knock on the office door and in strode Professor De Florimonte. He was sorry to have missed the previous evening's adventures, but he was sure that the brothers now realized that the bar was not the place for a Bakoo. He proposed taking it to a lab at the University where its nature and its powers could be investigated scientifically. It was an opportunity for him and his students to make an important contribution to the world's knowledge about such phenomena and he was certain that he would eventually be able to offer the brothers a considerable sum in compensation from a generous research grant he was hoping to receive. If they agreed he would remove the creature at once, before it could do any further damage.

Romesh threw back his head and laughed and showed the professor the empty bottle. The poor man was deflated. He kept mumbling about his work having gone down the drain and seemed so desolate that Ashoka took pity on him.

'I tell you what, Professor, since the bottle empty it mean the Bakoo on the loose somewhere out there. You know he not going to keep quiet, he bound to cause ruction somewhere. You just have to listen out for news of some house getting pelt with stones or somebody girlchild getting interfere with by invisible hands and you will know where to locate the Bakoo again. Look on the bright side: since he know you well as the body who been measuring him up and shining all them bright lights in his face, he might even come looking for you up at the University.'

Professor De Florimonte's face registered alarm, but he quickly regained his composure and reflected that there was a lot in what Ashoka had said. He took his leave, determined to investigate any report that might indicate the presence of the Sharples Bakoo.

Thus the Kashmir Bar and Restaurant lost its edge of excitement. The sensation-mongers no longer frequented the place, the professor and his scientific paraphernalia were not seen again, and the presence of Miss Alma Fordyce, seated at the bar, knocking back whisky and soda, became a fading memory. To tell the truth, the brothers were not too disappointed: their regulars still came and the place prospered in a quieter, more ordinary manner – but that is not quite the end of the story.

$$\star \quad \star \quad \star$$

After several weeks had passed, Professor De Florimonte heard from one of his students that there was talk of Miss Alma Fordyce having lost her mind. She had, it was claimed, confined herself to her house where, many a night, she could be heard cackling in a loud and vulgar manner and smashing her possessions in fits of madness. Discreet inquiries by the professor confirmed that Miss Fordyce had unexpectedly requested early retirement from her post at the Public Library and had not been to work for weeks. While he was somewhat gratified by this news – long overdue recompense for his humiliation at her hands in the library – he also wondered how the Bakoo could have had such a strong effect upon a woman such as Miss Fordyce.

A month or so later, Professor De Florimonte was in his office when he was informed that someone called Agnes Butters wanted to see him about a Bakoo. The name rang no bell, but he was still very much on the lookout for news of what he considered *his* Bakoo and he told the secretary to show Miss Butters in.

'Excuse me for bothering you, Professor,' she began, 'but people tell me that you are studying Bakoos and suchlike supernaturals and I come to you because I am very worried about my mistress, Miss Alma Fordyce.'

From her long and rambling narrative, interrupted only by having to request his secretary to cancel his three o'clock class, Professor De Florimonte gathered that 'his' Bakoo had ended up as a guest in Miss Fordyce's New Garden Street residence. A week after the Bakoo had disappeared from the Kashmir Bar and Restaurant, it had turned up in New Garden Street one night, breaking a few glasses and throwing Miss Alma Fordyce heavily onto her bed. Agnes Butters had heard her mistress shouting: 'Sedley, is that you?' and 'Sedley, you mad brute, stop it at once or you will break all of Mama's expensive china! Behave yourself!' This went on for several nights and then nothing seemed to happen for a while. Then one morning she had found her mistress in a terrible state: her hair let down and tangled, her face swollen and bruised, her nightgown torn and she was weeping. She had told Agnes, by way of explanation, that her brother Sedley had tried to take advantage of her. Not long after that Miss Fordyce stopped going to work and Agnes heard her in her bedroom pleading with Sedley to leave her alone. The bedroom was locked. Then came the sound of breaking glass, a scream and later Miss Fordyce's voice in an uncharacteristic fit of giggling. Agnes had later discovered an empty whisky bottle in the bedroom. Miss Fordyce had made her promise not to tell anyone what was going on, but it was clear to Agnes that this Bakoo, or whatever it was, had seduced her mistress ('And if it was her own brother, what a terrible thing that was!') and was destroying all the breakable items in the house. In addition, they had now drunk all the liquor in the cabinet and Miss Fordyce had taken to sending Agnes to the shop at the corner to buy bottles of rum. The neighbours had begun to ask questions, particularly those with banana trees in their backyards. Their fruit was being plundered, presumably by the Bakoo. It had got so bad that Agnes had written to Miss Iris ('who is Mrs. Walters, you know, Miss Fordyce's sister in Canada'), who had phoned to tell Agnes that she would be in Guyana as soon as possible to look into the situation for herself. More recently, the Bakoo had taken to ringing the bell on her mistress's bicycle and Miss Fordyce could be heard shouting: 'No, Sedley, I told you I will not go riding with you – you are a drunkard and a libertine, and what would people say.' Agnes couldn't help reflecting that it was Miss Fordyce who looked really bad – dark, sunken eyes, unkempt hair and bruised features.

'I'll tell you something, Professor,' she said in a whisper, leaning across his desk to be close to his ear, 'that Bakoo is a beast and a sex maniac; he has poor Miss Alma in a state! If her parents only knew what was going on they would be turning in their graves.' Then she leaned back in her seat and said in a normal voice and with an air of finality: 'and *that* is why I come to you, to see if you can do anything.'

Professor De Florimonte was dubious about several of the details in the story, though not about the presence of the Bakoo in New Garden Street. At any rate the situation warranted investigation and he arranged with Agnes Butters to visit the house the following day and assess the situation for himself. He would prefer, he told the maid, if she said nothing to Miss Fordyce about his visit. She should meet him at the gate at nine o'clock and bring him up to date on the latest happenings, after which he would decide whether to confront her mistress and the Bakoo.

When Professor Patrick De Florimonte, with two of his students, turned the corner into New Garden Street at ten minutes to nine the following morning, it was immediately obvious that something big had happened. There was a large and noisy crowd outside the Fordyce home, two police cars parked nearby and neighbours at their windows or standing in groups in their front yards. The professor pulled over and parked several houses away and started making his way through the crowd. By the time he reached the gate he had picked up that there had been a terrible ruckus in the house from about five o'clock that morning: a constant noise of smashing glass and china and the shrieking of Miss Fordyce. Agnes had been forced to flee into the street in her nightgown shouting for help, and neighbours had called the police, who arrived nearly an hour later, when everything was quiet again. Miss Fordyce, it seemed, had disappeared.

When, at the insistence of the maid, the professor was admitted into the house, he found the floor littered with broken glass and china and the lighting fixtures and windowpanes all smashed, as were many of the chairs, tables, and other items of furniture.

'Oh Professor,' wailed Agnes, still in a flowered nightgown, with her hair frizzed out, 'you're too late – I left it too late to contact you. I blame myself…' and she sobbed loudly.

'Where is …'

'Miss Alma? Oh Professor, you are not going to believe, the police don't believe me either, but some of the neighbours see it with their own eyes too.'

'What? What happened? Try to settle down, Miss Butters, and tell me.'

'They gone,' said Agnes. 'Miss Alma and the Bakoo – after they had a big quarrel and everything get break up as you see here. I was out on the street, cause I thought the whole house would fall on top of me in my room downstairs. I was out in the street with neighbours and others – it was foreday and we hear the bicycle bell and I could just make out Miss Fordyce on the bicycle, and that shameless brute of a Bakoo sitting on the handle bars, naked as he born and she riding fast towards the gate, towards me and the others out in the street. Well! It was scatteration, cause nobody wanted to get lick down by a mad woman and a Bakoo on a bike. Eh-eh! When you hear the shout, the bike take off like airplane and they riding away fast-fast – up there, over the roof of Mr. Armstrong house, and the two of them disappear in the dark foreday sky. I couldn't do nothing – nothing – we were all so frighten.'

Miss Alma Fordyce was never seen again. Her sister Iris arrived two days after she disappeared, stayed for two weeks, hoping to have some word, but there was nothing, and she was not sure what to believe among the several dozen versions of the story that she heard. She arranged a memorial service for her sister and the church was packed.

About a month after the disappearance there was an item in one of the newspapers about a strange happening at Bunbury Hill, near Mabaruma in Region One. There the villagers heard a great commotion after midnight on the path outside the village, including the furious ringing of a bicycle bell. No one had dared to investigate, fearful of Kenaima or other spirits. Next morning they found an old-fashioned lady's bicycle abandoned in the bushes off the path. There was no sign of anyone. The newspaper story ended as follows: 'Very mysterious goings on, indeed. The mention of an old-fashioned lady's bicycle makes this reporter wonder whether it might not be the bicycle of Miss Alma Fordyce of New Garden Street, Queenstown, which, readers will remember, disappeared along with its owner and (so they say) the

114

Sharples Bakoo, late of the Kashmir Bar and Restaurant in Middle Street. I don't suppose we'll ever know for sure.'

Professor Patrick De Florimonte, head of the university's Paranormal Phenomena Unit (PANPU), disagreed sharply with the last sentence of this story. As soon as he finished reading it, he phoned his secretary and told her to book him a flight to Mabaruma.

THE VISITOR

by Terrence Wong

As he approached the Georgetown ferry stelling, Gerry was regretting having agreed to accompany two of his sixth-form classmates, Pompey and Ivan, to Uitvlugt, where they would spend the day at Pompey's uncle's farm. Pompey had complained that the Easter vacation had not seemed at all like a vacation, as they had been attending classes half-day and studying hard for their approaching A-level exams. They needed, he said, at least one day's break from books and from Georgetown, before school started again on Monday. It had seemed a good idea at the time, but as he rode into the bike-shed at college to leave his bike for the day, prior to walking over to the ferry stelling, Gerry recognized a sufficient number of the cycles there to realize that most of his classmates were beating their books upstairs in the classrooms, and he felt a twinge of guilt. Besides, he'd had a strangely vivid dream the night before which seemed somehow about the trip he was now undertaking. In the dream he was moving through a bizarre and vividly coloured urban landscape that he did not recognize. He seemed to be falling uncontrollably, but he was not falling *down*: he was falling horizontally – *along* a crowded road, unable to stop or even to notice properly his rapidly changing surroundings. He could see a dark tunnel at the end of the road, emitting a purple light, and he seemed to be speeding towards the entrance to the tunnel, although it didn't seem to be getting any nearer. In the manner of dreams, Gerry had sensed that there was some unspeakable danger inside the tunnel and that he must not enter it at any cost.

116

In the end he must have held out an arm to protect himself, for he had woken up when his right arm crashed into his bedside lamp, knocking it to the floor and waking the entire household. Members of his family were accustomed to his wild dreams and dismissed this one with knowing smiles and shrugs, but Gerry felt uneasy, suspecting that the dream was a warning about his trip.

'You supposed to be smart,' his father had said, 'writing A-levels in a few weeks – and it's 1969: people don't believe in dreams and such foolishness any more. Is probably all that black pudding you eat last night...'

As he approached the stelling, Gerry tried to shrug off his feelings of unease and was sure he would be alright as soon as he met Ivan and Pompey and bought his ticket. But at that point, the world seemed to go dark and Gerry found himself in strange surroundings. The first thing he became aware of was the smell: the air seemed dryer and smelled of electricity, the smell he associated with overheated or burnt-out electrical motors, and this was overlaid with the smell of some kind of essence – rose-water, perhaps – nothing overpowering, just noticeable. Then he saw that he was no longer approaching the ferry stelling, but some sort of multiple-gate structure. He could see the river beyond, but thronging all around him was an enormous crowd of people, strangely dressed and talking in an unfamiliar accent, though still speaking the 'Guyanese English' that was familiar to him. He tried to stop and get his bearings, but there was no stopping in that relentless press of people. It seemed strangely cool to Gerry, even for early morning. Who were these people? How did he get there in the middle of them, and why did they look so strange? They were clothed in loose robes down to their ankles and these robes shimmered or glowed with vivid colours. They seemed in celebratory mood, as if he were in the middle of a carnival band.

As he looked around at the people closest to him, he noticed an older man wearing very ornate robes, a rainbow-hewed skullcap and a large pectoral cross of some translucent substance like glass or perspex on a chain around his neck. The cross glowed with green and orange lights which seemed to flicker along wires and circuits. Gerry realized, with some apprehension, that the man had probably been watching him closely for some time.

'My cross interests you?' the stranger said. 'I think it's time to turn it off,' and he touched it near the bottom. Now it appeared to be made of opaque blue glass.

'I'm sorry,' Gerry said. 'I'm confused... I'm afraid I don't know where I am.'

'I realize that,' the man said. 'Don't worry, there's no danger to you here. Can I ask your name?'

'Gerry. Gerry Fung. Can you tell me where I am and what's going on?'

'I suspect it's not so much where as when,' the man said. 'This is the year 2070 and you're in the middle of the funeral procession of Archbishop Dilip Henderson, NCSJB.'

'Hold it! Hold it!' Gerry held up his hand. 'Did you say 2070?' He uttered an anxious, mirthless chuckle; 'That's ridiculous! That would make me a hundred and twenty years old.'

'Yes,' the stranger said, 'I suspected that you were a visitor.'

'A visitor! Look, I don't know what's going on, but I was headed for the ferry to meet some school friends for a trip across the river, and all of a sudden I find myself in the middle of... this...'

'I know, and I realize your predicament, but you must be patient and I'll try to explain things to you.'

By now the procession had passed through the gates and had narrowed somewhat as it swarmed onto an old steel structure that seemed to float on the river. At first Gerry thought it was some kind of barge or pontoon (which would surely sink, he reasoned, under the weight of such a vast throng), but as they continued moving he saw that it stretched way out into the river and must be some kind of bridge.

'It's the old Demerara Harbour Floating Bridge,' the man said. 'It's more convenient for our purpose than the skyway bridge,' and he pointed up river.

Gerry looked and saw a wonderful structure about a mile or two away: it was a slender, gracefully curving bridge, at least 200 feet above the river at its highest point, but it seemed almost unsupported, as all he could see were what looked like two slanting pencils of red light stretching from the underside of the bridge into the river at points about a hundred yards from each bank. A steady stream of vehicles was crossing in both directions. It was surely at least a mile long and supported only by those slender, luminous columns.

'Modern engineering and materials science,' the stranger told him. 'I doubt I'd be able to explain it satisfactorily for you, but these days all bridges are built like that. Those 'pencils of light', as you think of them, are columns about fifteen feet in diameter, made from special materials and surrounded by adjusting energy-fields which cause the red light. It's all very safe.'

'And what about the temperature here?' Gerry asked. 'The sun seems as bright as usual, yet it seems quite cool.'

'Oh, yes, these days temperature is controlled all over the world by energy fields – electromagnetic – or else there would have been a disastrous rise in the sea-level and unbearable heat.'

Gerry wanted to hear more, but as they reached the middle of the bridge it occurred to him that if he were separated from this man, he would not know where to turn, so he asked the man to tell him who he was.

'Certainly,' the man said. 'My name is Isaiah Valdman, and, as you can probably deduce from the cross, I'm a Church official.'

Here he extended his right hand and Gerry was about to shake it with his own, but instead, the man touched Gerry on the left side of his stomach and then slipped his hand back and down, cupping and jiggling the left cheek of his bum. Gerry stood open-mouthed, with his right hand still awkwardly extended.

'Ah, yes, of course! Forgive me,' the stranger said, 'the old *handshake,* I'd forgotten about that. What I just did is how we greet each other these days, but I'll shake your hand if you're more comfortable with that,' and he gripped Gerry's hand tightly. 'As I was saying, I'm a Papal Nuncio with the title of Monsignor, and I'm representing His Holiness Pope Aldrick II.'

'The Pope!' Gerry exclaimed. 'You came all the way from Rome to attend this funeral?'

'Not Rome,' said the Monsignor. 'I keep forgetting how much things have changed... What year is it where you came from?'

'1969... I think,' Gerry said, no longer certain about anything.

'Ah, well, a hundred years does make a big difference, I suppose... Where was I? Oh, yes. No, I'm not from Rome. There has been devolution in the church for nearly forty years now:

there are eleven regional Popes around the world, in addition to the one in Rome – twelve in all, the same number as the apostles. There are three in the Americas, one of which, our own Aldrick II, is regional Pontiff of the Caribbean. He's based in Vatican Caribbean, which is in Trinidad. It used to be a little town on the northeast tip of the island called Toco. Now it's a great centre of the arts and learning – and a place of pilgrimage, especially as two of our former Popes have been canonized. Our first Regional Pontiff, Selassie-I the first, is now a saint, and his uncorrupted body can be seen in a glass case in Vatican Caribbean: he's holding a spike of unwilted dendrobium orchid flowers that was placed there when he died in 2041, and if you look carefully at the petals of these flowers, you can discern the outlines of winged angels...'

This was proving a bit much for Gerry. He was obviously in Guyana, but a much altered Guyana. They were now in the middle of the floating bridge and he turned to his right to look at the city: it was much bigger and seemed further away than he'd expected and the skyline was very different – the Stabroek market tower was still there, but now the roof was a vivid, glowing red and dwarfed by high-rise buildings behind it, buildings of odd shapes and gaudy, brilliant colours, some of which seemed to emit a shimmering light like the supports of the bridge up river. Gerry began to wonder, with a sudden pang of anxiety, whether he were trapped forever in this age.

Monsignor Valdman must have guessed his thoughts, because he said: 'It's not so unusual, you know; sometimes we have visitors from other times' – he fingered his pectoral cross and seemed to Gerry to be avoiding his eyes – 'people who can sometimes help with some situation here. Usually they return as suddenly as they came. Relax: enjoy the experience and learn what you can about this world. No one here knows what a visitor will remember on his return.'

'Yours is a great country, and a rich one, these days,' he continued, 'the richest in the Caribbean...'

'Richer than Trinidad, with all its oil?'

'Oh dear, yes. Since the world stopped using oil in the thirties, Trinidad has declined sharply, I'm afraid. It's not a poor country, by any means – it's the administrative centre of the region – but it

120

does not produce wealth the way Guyana does... Oh, you must excuse me for a minute, my young friend, I see the Vicar Particular of Georgetown approaching, and I need to have a word with him.'

Gerry saw a youngish man working his way through the crowd towards them. He was in a bright yellow robe and wore a small silver cross. The Monsignor stepped forward and the two talked in low tones for a few minutes, before he heard him say: 'Come Barry, meet our visitor – Gerry Fung – he's from 1969. Gerry, this is Bharrat Fitzpatrick, Vicar Particular of Georgetown...'

Then it happened again: Gerry went to shake the man's hand and the next thing he knew the Prelate was jiggling his left buttock and waiting for him to reciprocate. Feeling thoroughly awkward, Gerry brushed his hand over the man's waist and bum and muttered a greeting.

'As you see,' the Monsignor said, 'the young visitor is unaccustomed to our form of greeting – still shaking hands in his time.'

'Ah,' said the Vicar Particular, 'we can forgive him that. I hope you enjoy your brief time with us, Mr. Fung. We're certainly happy to have you here...' and he moved off again into the crowd.

Gerry learnt that, in addition to the Vicar General, each dioceses had a Vicar Particular, who functioned as the personal aide to the bishop. At the moment, however, he was troubled by what this Vicar Particular had said.

'What did he mean about my "brief stay"?'

'Nothing, really. Visitors don't usually stay very long; in all likelihood you'll return at the end of the day, as soon as the ceremony is over.'

Again Gerry had the impression that the Monsignor had more to tell him. By now they had crossed the river and Gerry noticed that there was a solid crowd of people as far as he could see, both behind and ahead of him. The procession had turned right and was moving along the West Bank road towards the sea and towards Vreed-en-Hoop – or whatever it was called in 2070. In the distance he could see the western end of the new bridge, ramps curving off it in all directions, like ribbons tied in a series of bows. The Monsignor explained that this bridge was the normal route across the river and that it was linked to highways that traversed the country east-to-west and north-to-south. The old floating bridge was not much used, but preserved as a curiosity because it was apparently the longest floating bridge in the world.

Gerry learned that high-ranking church officials who died were given a special procession to their final resting place: it was traditional that the procession should cross water and process along a route of at least ten miles. They were going to walk along the old coast road, past the Archbishop's cathedral to a special building at Zeelugt, where the final ceremony and the lowering of the casket would take place.

'How can we go past the cathedral?' Gerry asked. 'Is it no longer in Georgetown?'

'The cathedral in Georgetown is the oldest,' the Monsignor replied. 'The Immaculate Conception, but these days there are two other archdioceses in Guyana (on the East and West coasts) and four other dioceses: New Amsterdam, Springlands, Bartica and Mabaruma – making seven Cathedrals in all. Archbishop Henderson, in whose funeral procession we march, was the Cardinal Archbishop of the West Coast.'

'I'm surprised there are enough Catholics to warrant all that,' Gerry said doubtfully.

'Oh, that's something else I should have explained,' said the Monsignor. 'Everybody in the country – in the world – is Catholic. There's only one religion... Between your time and ours there have been many upheavals, some brought about through technological advances, some by social revolutions. There were attempts by rich and powerful nations to bully and exploit the rest of the world and this resulted in so-called terrorist attacks and ill-considered military adventures and attempts at 'world government'. Then there was the period when the Porn Kings took over from the Drug Barons and became the de facto powers in the world through the internet. You've heard of the internet? Computers?'

'I've heard of computers – giant machines for making lengthy calculations – but I've never come across the internet.'

'Well, I suppose 1969 is still a bit early, but I think it's true to say that all of these things will become part of your life by the end of the twentieth century. Anyway, to continue: the Porn Kings ruled for a while and had the world turned onto the most horribly explicit and open sexual gratification. People were fed a diet of continuous sensual titillation and became like zombies. Life was devalued; there was a lot of casual violence and many were killed. The minority who were awake to the dangers and horrors of this situation were driven to desperation. There was another war, perhaps the most recent big conflict, where the Porn Kings were eventually defeated and the internet destroyed. The power vacuum was then filled, opportunistically some say, some say by divine providence, by the church – but not the church as you know it in the twentieth century... but I'll tell you more as we march along.'

* * *

As the procession moved along the West Bank road, Gerry noticed that both sides of the road were paved and built over with homes, shops and offices. There was no sign of any vegetation, only flowers and other plants in large pots and window-boxes.

'Where are the fields?' Gerry asked. 'I take it this country still grows rice and other things?'

'Yes, but not here. Rice is grown on the Essequibo/Pomeroon coast and sugar only in Berbice these days. The yield per acre is several times what it would have been in your time. On this coast they grow market vegetables and fruit, but some distance back from this urban strip. Because the climate can be completely controlled, you can grow anything anywhere: all you need is land area and good soil. Guyana grows most of the food consumed in the Caribbean... Look, there's our first church – Malgré Tout – there's been a Catholic church here for as long as anyone can remember...'

Gerry looked at the large dome ahead. It had a radius of about 50 feet, with a large translucent cross, lit from within, at its top. The dome itself was painted with four horizontal bands of colour: red at the bottom, then orange, yellow and green – the same as the Monsignor's skullcap. It had a short, tunnel-like entrance which made it look like an igloo. Outside was a large statue of a creature with an elephant's head.

'Don't tell me,' Gerry said, 'that that's a statue of Ganesh in front of a Catholic Church?'

'Oh, but it is,' the Monsignor replied. 'As a religious/cultural symbol, Ganesh is older than the cross. All the peoples who now form the new Catholic Church were permitted to bring their own religious symbols with them. We're not as exclusive or self-righteous as the church was in your day. As a matter of fact, the motto of the Guyanese church is taken from one of your early poets: 'All are involved, all are consumed in the fire of the faith.'

'Never heard of it,' said Gerry. 'So there is no more doctrine of one God?'

'Well, there are those who say that there never really was, you know... We had one God, but there were three persons in him... Humans understand and identify with multiplicity and diversity far more easily than with unity and singularity. Of course there *is* one God, but the representations of him are manifold and the modern church, since it is truly universal in embracing all peoples and cultures, welcomes whatever images and symbols inspire devotion and fervour. As I said, you'll find the Catholic church much altered from the church of your day.' The Monsignor smiled. 'On the other hand, you'll still find individual churches in many places in the world, which are the same as they've always been, with traditional altarpieces and images and statues of the saints of the local people...'

As they passed the entrance of the church, the Monsignor made the sign of the cross, and Gerry did the same, wondering at this strange world. He was trying to imagine what the Jesuit masters at the college would say to him when he told them about how the church had evolved over a hundred years...

After they had turned left at Vreed-En-Hoop, the Monsignor took Gerry's arm and steered him to the side of the road. 'This is Den Amstel. Let's pause here for a while, until the archbishop's funeral chariot the catches up with us – it shouldn't be too far behind.' They waited in front of a small blue windowless building, some sort of storage depot or garage. As he observed the people moving along in the procession, it struck Gerry that it was difficult to tell the men from the women. Almost everyone wore the same loose gowns, and even though a sprinkling of children and young people were attired in shirts and trousers, the shirts were large and loose-fitting, and hair-length seemed no indicator of gender. When he asked about this he was informed that differences of dress had no function because the society did not discriminate in any way based on gender. Even in the church, there were women priests and bishops, although no woman had yet been elected pope. Somewhat to his surprise, Gerry found this profoundly disturbing, and to avoid this line of thought, he asked the Monsignor about the smell of electric motors that he'd noticed when he'd first arrived.

'All visitors notice that smell,' the Monsignor said, 'but of course *we* don't smell anything unusual. I suppose that since electromagnetic fields power everything in our civilization, there must be some smell of it to a stranger from a different age... We used to scent the atmosphere with floral fragrances, but people objected that the smell was too intrusive. I'm told that they still introduce a faint whiff of roses into the air through the cooling systems, but I don't think anyone is aware of it any more...'

'I am,' said Gerry, 'and it can be quite distracting.'

'I'm thirsty, are you?' the Monsignor said. 'How about some water?' Gerry saw him beckon a boy on some sort of motorized cart. 'Plain or flavoured?'

'Oh – plain, I guess... Do we have to pay for it?'

'Nobody pays for water!' said his companion, surprised. The boy reached into the cart and produced a clear plastic bag containing about a dozen blue spherical objects rather smaller than ping-pong balls. The Monsignor popped one into his mouth and passed the bag to Gerry.

'Is *this* water?'

'Just pop one into your mouth and chew on it, you'll see.'

Gerry did as directed and the blue sphere softened and released copious amounts of refreshing cold water that tasted no different from the water he was accustomed to. He judged that the volume of water that he'd swallowed was at least fifteen times the volume of the sphere. Not knowing what to do with the residue, he kept it in his mouth like a piece of chewing gum and was surprised to find that within half a minute it had disappeared. 'Put a few in your pocket for later,' the monsignor advised.

By this time they could see the banners and hear the music that indicated that the archbishop's funeral chariot was approaching. The chariot was a large rectangular platform that floated about ten inches above the surface of the road and moved forward at a slow but steady pace. Gerry guessed that there were electromagnetic circuits beneath the surface of the road that caused the levitation and the forward motion. On the chariot, beside the large casket of polished silverballi, inlaid with purpleheart and other forest woods, stood a number of church officials, in their gowns and skullcaps and wearing a bewildering assortment of crosses. Gerry was taken over to meet them. First was Sybil Hanoman-Sanchez, bishop of Mabaruma, who said: 'Ah, the visitor – we'd heard that he'd arrived.' This time Gerry managed the ritual of greeting as though he'd been doing it all his life. In the space of a few minutes he'd jiggled the left cheeks of a dozen ecclesiastical dignitaries.

Suddenly, a strange-looking nun leapt nimbly onto the chariot. She wore an ankle-length iridescent scarlet gown and a matching veil, with a large golden rosary around her neck, which swayed and twitched constantly, because she never stood still. There were heavy golden rings on all of her fingers, and the nails were over an inch long, and curved like claws. 'This,' said one of the churchmen, 'is Sister Iqbal, a dear friend and confidante of the late archbishop, who, as deacon, will lead the wining-down ceremony later on...'

'Welcome visitor, in God's holy name,' Sister Iqbal said. 'God is great! He has sent you to us in fulfilment of our prayer.' And she did a jerky little dance before bowing and leaping down into the crowd, shouting religious slogans. From the evidence of her moustache and gruff voice, Gerry was sure the nun was a man.

'That,' said Monsignor Valdman, leaning close to Gerry's ear, 'is our transvestite deacon. I'm afraid that not all of us are happy with her highly individualistic manner and behaviour, though I'm sure she's a good and devout person in her own way.'

'She – or he – is really weird,' Gerry said, shaking his head.

'Perhaps we should say that her weirdness is more obvious than that of most people,' the Monsignor said, as they stepped off the moving chariot. 'I'm afraid she was a victim of the era of the Porn Kings; from early childhood, she was consumed with lusts and the need to indulge in crude sexual exhibitionism – fires fanned by the internet sites to which she was addicted. Now, however, she's a repentant sinner and an important figure in the local church.'

'You keep saying 'she', but he's a man, isn't he?' asked Gerry.

'We defer to the individual's own perception and description of self. Iqbal thinks of and refers to herself as a woman, and we respect that, despite whatever private reservations we might have. I know it is very different in your time, but in the modern church there is no moral significance attached to such choices as gender or sexual orientation...'

This was a strange church indeed: it's tolerance seemed boundless. It appeared to welcome everyone, regardless of personal beliefs and morals – or the residual doctrines retained from earlier faiths or affiliations. The doctrines with which he was familiar, which were important to the church he knew, appeared to have been abandoned – or simply subsumed within a vast and fuzzy tolerance for *all* views. Questions buzzed in Gerry's head: 'What about transubstantiation? The immaculate conception? The sacrament of penance?' He could already hear these being rationalized beyond recognition in the calm tones of Monsignor Valdman – so decided against voicing any questions of this kind.

As they walked on in silence, Gerry reflected on his encounters and discoveries. He was excited about the scientific advances – the novelty of catching up, in a few hours, with a hundred years of technological progress. But he was also dismayed at the state of this society, and especially, of the 'Catholic' church. He did not consider himself particularly devout, and tended to disagree with certain emphases in the church's teaching, particularly where these appeared to be in conflict with free scientific enquiry and the advancement of knowledge, but he'd never thought that the church should abandon *all* teaching, and he felt that the wide tolerance and inclusiveness of the 2070 church rendered membership almost meaningless.

He began to think that his presence at this occasion was not accidental. Everyone he met not only seemed to have been expecting him (or at least *a* visitor from the past), but also to hint at some specific role he was expected to play in the funeral ceremony. He cast an apprehensive, sideways glance at Monsignor Valdman, whose duty, he felt convinced, was to guard him and prepare him for whatever his role might be. Was the Monsignor's pectoral cross the instrument through which he'd been somehow summoned to this particular time and place? He thought it prudent not to voice his suspicions at that moment.

What he did ask the Monsignor about was the current racial composition of Guyana's population: for it appeared that the country's two main races, Africans and East Indians, had merged into each other – or into a distinct, in-between race. If so, it was extraordinary that this should happen in the space of just one hundred years.

'Oh, but this did not come about naturally or accidentally,' his companion explained. 'Some argue that it is one of the few good things to come out of the era of the Porn Kings. The promiscuity fostered by the internet sites and the sex parlours and other institutions spawned by them, was used by those in government at the time to put an end to the decades of racial conflict and violence that bedevilled this society from before the end of the twentieth century. Promiscuity was permitted and even promoted, and all kinds of rape and sexual violence were excused – once these took place *across* the racial divide, that is, between a Black and an Indian. It was argued that the country was underpopulated and contraception was discouraged. It was even rumoured that the market was flooded with faulty condoms and other devices to ensure that there were as many births as possible. A further rumour had it that babies of so-called 'pure' race were put to death in the hospitals: it would be impossible, I believe, to prove this, but given the times and the government, it is not difficult to imagine. At any rate, the result, which you can see all around you today, is that Guyana is a nation of what you called 'douglas'. It was also decreed that all children should bear names that indicate the mingling of the races – that is, if the surname is identifiably Indian, the first name should not be, and vice versa; hence you commonly get combinations like Adeola Ramsammy and Govinda Bobb-Semple. Our late, beloved archbishop, you will recall, was named Dilip Henderson.'

'You, of course,' the Monsignor continued, 'are of Chinese extraction, and the Chinese, Portuguese and Amerindian minorities at the time tended to leaven and complicate the mixture, adding the fairer complexions, the oriental eyes and the straighter hair that you randomly encounter in today's population...'

Wondering that his informant spoke of such horrors with apparent emotional detachment, Gerry looked at him and said: 'I suppose you consider yourself lucky, Monsignor, that you are Trinidadian, and not part of this awful menagerie?'

'Actually I was born in Dominica,' Monsignor Valdman said, 'although I've lived in Trinidad since my early teens. But no, I don't attach any stigma to the racial hybrids of Guyana: they – we – are all God's children... I'm a hybrid myself: Carib, Black, white...'

They were passing another church, the Cathedral of the late archbishop at Meten-Meer-Zorg. Gerry noted a large sign that proclaimed: 'Cathedral Temple of the Lamb of God of the Seventh Day Catholic Assemblies of Demerara/Essequibo.'

'Seventh Day!' he exclaimed.

The Monsignor chuckled. 'This is proving a hard day for you, isn't it? I told you that the contemporary church contains many elements. This archdiocese and two other dioceses in this country are Seventh-Day – they worship on Saturday instead of Sunday. In the father's house there are many mansions, as the saying goes: everyone will find himself or herself comfortably accommodated.'

Mounted on the roof of the entrance to the Cathedral was a huge propeller, and Gerry recalled there had also been one outside the church at Malgré Tout. Surely ships large enough to carry such propellers couldn't cross the bars of Guyana's rivers?

'Those aren't ship's propellers,' his companion informed him, 'those are the giant turbines that were used to generate electricity in the many hydroelectric stations in the interior. When such stations were no longer necessary and the machinery dismantled, the larger churches mounted them instead of or in addition to crosses, which they resemble with their four blades. One of our young priests has published a brilliant article on the theological significance and symbolism of those turbines...'

'But in my day we're only now dreaming of damming the rivers and building hydroelectric plants – why would they have dismantled them after a few decades?'

'Progress, my boy. Electricity, which now powers everything on this planet, is free all over the world, and that would never have happened if we were still relying on hydroelectric plants and other such means of producing it. One of the greatest discoveries since your time has been the creation and use of superheated plasmas by means of energy fields. There are barren areas of the planet where miniature suns have been created and they're well contained so they have virtually no effect on the surrounding environment. These generate all the power needed on earth. Now, electricity is no longer transmitted through cables, but through a process akin to microwave broadcasting: it is received through dish receptors at distribution and relay stations and re-broadcast to substations or to individual users.

'In the war that destroyed the internet, power was turned off for three weeks. Nothing worked, the planet grew unbearably hot and people were starving. Thousands of porn-site addicts became deranged, there were riots and great loss of life. When the power was turned back on, it was in a different world: no more internet, no more computer screens. Anyone found in possession of an intact screen was shot – and the screens used to be everywhere: on personal computers, on cell-phones, on cameras, various devices worn on the forearm, on the doors of domestic appliances like fridges, ovens, washers, toasters – or just embedded in walls and fences in public places. All had to be smashed, even though the internet itself no longer existed.

'Even now, some of the people who were alive at that time forget that it was all destroyed and you will see them distractedly wave their right hands in front of rectangular plaques and mirrors, hoping that the devices implanted in their wrists will activate the 'screen' and their favourite home pages will appear, with menus and links to their particular delights, from the vilest, crudest depictions of sexual gratification to fuzzy-focused soft porn, sometimes called 'satin sin'. It was the devil's own world before the porn wars – it was only after that world was destroyed that the church could rise again from the ashes...'

'And what a church!' Gerry said, shaking his head.

'Believe me, it is better than what it replaced,' the Monsignor insisted. 'You have to realize that there was no hope for the world, for mankind, while the Porn Kings reigned.'

'OK, I take your word for it.'

There, in the square in front of the Cathedral temple, they ate a meal from packs distributed from hovering carts. Gerry was pleased to discover that food had changed little. He had a wonderful curried chicken with rice and roti and a side dish of spicy okras fried up with onions.

'When we leave here,' the Monsignor said, 'It's only a short walk to the tomb. I'll tell you as we go what will happen there.'

Gerry began to think he'd better have some courses of action mapped out if he didn't like what he heard.

★ ★ ★

The sun was low in the western sky when Gerry first caught sight of the 'tomb'. It was right on a bend in the road, on the 'sea' side, and Gerry was told that it was built on the site of a very old burial ground. He was not surprised to discover that it was another dome, this time painted a brilliant white. As they moved towards it and the sky darkened, he saw that the tunnel entrance emitted a purple glow and he recognized the tunnel of his dream and this rekindled his feeling of foreboding. He wondered whether he should attempt to give the Monsignor the slip, disappear into the crowd until the funeral was over... But he reasoned that his companion had the pectoral cross and this, he felt sure, was his key to returning to his own time. Much as he dreaded the idea of entering the sinister glow of that tunnel, he could think of no fate worse than being stuck in this time among people whose history, experience and values he did not share.

They now rode on the chariot with the senior clergy, family members and special guests. The Monsignor told him there would be music and dance, the casket would be placed in the middle of the floor and mourners would dance around it; when the music rose to a crescendo, a rectangular opening would appear in the floor, just the size of the casket. Gerry, as the visitor from a different age, had to be standing beside the casket at this time. He would be told more as the ceremony approached.

'I've never heard of dancing at a burial and I'm afraid I wouldn't know how to,' he said, 'I've only ever danced at fêtes – parties...'

'*You* aren't supposed to dance, and neither will I,' the Monsignor told him. 'You will wear a special white cape which will identify you as the visitor and...'

131

'But what am I supposed to *do*?' Gerry asked.

'I suppose I can begin to tell you,' his companion said, 'although I'm not really supposed to do so until after we've entered.'

'Aha! So I won't be able to escape!' Gerry said. 'Listen, I have worked out a couple of things for myself. I realized early on that I'm not here as the result of an accident – some flaw in the time-space continuum or anything like that. I believe that the cross you wear is some sort of device that can transport people through time and that you brought me here and can presumably send me back to my rightful time. I want to know a) exactly what I'm supposed to do – so I can decide whether I will do it, and b) at what point will I be transported back to my own home?'

The Monsignor sighed. 'Alright. I'm sorry if everything has seemed sinister and underhand to you, but I've had to allow for the gap in understanding and commitment between ourselves. You have remarked how difficult it is for you to accept our values. The most important thing for you to know is that no harm will come to you. You're right, it is I, as the Pope's representative, who have control – through this cross – over the summoning and returning of the visitor. I promise that you will return to the time and place that you came from. Before that, however...'

Here he stopped because they had reached the entrance to the tomb. Over the entrance tunnel there was a sign which read: 'Zeelugt Community Tomb of Everlasting Peace'. An old woman in a black robe stepped forward and said: 'I take it that this is our Visitor, Monsignor?'

Without waiting for a reply, she draped a long white cloak over Gerry's shoulders and pulled a knitted white skullcap over his head. The monsignor removed his coloured cap and put on the white one he was given and the two entered the tomb. Gerry was amazed at how the misty purple light in the tunnel transformed the colour of his white coat into a brilliant, shimmering lilac – by far the brightest object in the tomb. 'It's important that all should see and identify the visitor,' the Monsignor explained.

Inside the dome seemed to Gerry more like a nightclub or large dance-hall than a place of funerals and death. The purple lighting pulsed in time with the low music: bright purple spikes within the dimmer continuum of light matched the audible peaks in the music. Here was a people who had mastered the art of sensual titillation and Gerry suspected that this probably arose from the pornography-induced hunger for constant stimulation. This civilization might have eradicated the Porn Kings, but it appeared to be ruled by the same aesthetic. There seemed no lull in the sensual bombardment of sound and colour and smell, and he began to wonder about the origins of the ridiculous bum-touching greeting, its inherent vulgarity invisible to those who were still immersed in the values that had tainted all aspects of life, even religious belief and worship.

Just then, as if to confirm his perceptions, Sister Iqbal strode over to where they stood, next to a rectangular patch of floor that was painted black and resisted the shimmer of purple light. Her body twitching and swaying beneath the nun's habit, she directed that the casket be laid precisely within the borders of the black patch. Then she shimmied up to Gerry and the Monsignor, her shoulders dipping in time with the music.

'All set, my people?' she asked, 'I hope our visitor is prepared for his sacred descent?'

'I still have to hear all about that,' Gerry said.

'Well,' Sister Iqbal continued, 'Monsignor will no doubt fill you in; we still have some time before everything is in place. I must go now and prepare for the dance, but remember, young man, don't be afraid.' Then she came very close to Gerry and ran her long-nailed fingers down the side of his face in a gesture of surprising gentleness. She looked into his eyes and said: 'I can see you're afraid, but if you read your book you will see that God asks: "Do you think that we have created you in vain, and that you will not return to us?" Then she turned and shuffled off, shaking her hands at her sides, like a sprinter approaching the starting block.

Gerry protested to Monsignor Valdman that he couldn't recall reading in the bible the passage just quoted by Sister Iqbal.

'I don't think it was the bible she had in mind,' the Monsignor said, 'but let's not pursue that. Don't worry. What will happen is that after the music and dance have reached their final crescendo, and the casket starts to descend beneath the floor, you will get on top of it and ride it down. I will activate the cross and as soon as you dip below the level of the floor, I will press this green button'

133

– he showed Gerry – 'and you will instantly return to where you came from. Now let me explain the thinking behind this...'

'Before that, if you don't mind, can you tell me what happens to the casket after it descends below the floor – and therefore what could happen to me if you don't press that button?'

'I was afraid you'd ask that. The point is that your fate *must not* be that of the casket; that would invalidate the entire ceremony. You're meant to be a guide, accompanying the corpse to the first symbolic signpost, as it were – and that first signpost is the level immediately beneath the floor. At that point you will be returned and the body and soul of the deceased will find its way from there.'

'But what happens to the casket?' Gerry insisted. 'Is it trundled off and buried in some subterranean grave? Is it cremated?'

'If you must know,' the Monsignor said, 'the casket and contents are vaporized. It enters a chamber of superheated plasma and in seconds nothing remains but a small vitrified mass the size of a marble. That will be retrieved and set into the high altar of the Cathedral Temple. But, as I said, that is *not* what will happen to you.'

'Why on earth do *I* have to do this? I don't know anything about this time and all its weird customs. I'm just a little Chinee man from long ago. I'm not familiar with the afterlife; I'd be no help to the dead archbishop in his quest for... for...'

'Your soul is pure... You might have guessed, from all I've been saying, and from your own observations, that we are a people tainted with a terrible spiritual darkness. All of us over the age of forty were involved in the sin of our times. We had abandoned God. The twelve popes in council decreed, years ago, that corpses should be associated with an untainted soul.'

'What about all of your people who are *under* forty? Let one of them ride the casket down...'

'We do – when ordinary people die, but in the case of senior clerics, their rank requires that we be certain of the purity of the one who rides. Hence we use these devices (he touched the cross) to invite a visitor from a less turbulent age.'

'Invite! You mean abduct. I had no choice. In any case, how can you be certain that I have the required purity? I may know nothing about the internet and your computer screens, but in my time there was lots of pornography in the form of books and magazines and films. How do you know that I'm not addicted to that? Or that I'm not an epic fornicator? Or that I don't regularly satisfy an incestuous lust for my own sister? You can't know...'

'Perhaps, but I can believe! And I can exercise my judgment. In the first place, a profile, involving traits of character, age and family background, is programmed into the device that transported you here. Then, our churches have been praying fervently for the purity of the visitor. Finally, it was up to my judgment: you've spent the day with me because I had to give myself time – if I'd judged that you were unsuitable in any way, I'd have returned you and transported someone else. I've done that in the past, sometimes two or three times before finding someone suitable. But in your case, the moment I saw and spoke to you I was confident that you were free from any serious burden of sin and would be suitable to perform the office of Visitor. That impression has strengthened and been confirmed in the course of the day. And here you are,' the Monsignor continued, 'your moment is at hand. Within the hour you will be back in 1969.'

'You must understand that I'm apprehensive. I can't be rational when I'm in a panic. I'm not sure I can trust my life to devices I don't understand, or to people whose beliefs and values I don't share. You'll forgive me for being frankly terrified at the thought that my body might enter this plasma chamber and be vaporized.'

'I understand perfectly, and feel your agony,' the Monsignor said, his eyes bright with tears. 'It is you who must forgive me; but I'm counting on the fact that you would not want to spend any longer than is necessary in this time, where so many things seem offensive to your sensibility.'

Gerry's shoulders suddenly drooped; it seemed there was no way out. 'I will ride your casket,' he said, 'counting on your honesty – that you've been telling me the truth and I will be returned home.'

'Thank you.'

The music swelled and the crowd began to sway and dip as they moved clockwise around the casket. The purple light dimmed and brightened in harmony with the beat.

'Is this the winding down of the archbishop, at last?'

'Yes, but it's wining, not winding,' said the Monsignor, 'as in a wild Caribbean carnival dance: to wine...'

'Oh,' Gerry said. 'I see. Like Satira.'

'Who?'

'Satira. "Satira lif' up she dress and she wine like a Buxton…"'

'You know Satira? You're from the time of Satira?' Sister Iqbal who was gyrating nearby had overheard this. She stood right in front of Gerry, her eyes wild, her face inches from his.

'There is no Satira, Sister; it's a folk song: she's a folk character – a legend – not a real person.'

'No, no! You lie!' Sister Iqbal shouted. 'She really existed in the past. She is – she used to be – my idol. There is – there was – a whole site dedicated to Satira. She was beautiful and brazen and strong – and her body...' Sister Iqbal's eyes flashed with memories that Gerry could not imagine. Then her tone changed and she said simply: 'Well, she was probably before your time, excuse me,' and she resumed her dance.

The tempo of the music picked up and the light flashed more rapidly. Everyone was moving to the music, except Gerry and the Monsignor, who awaited their moment next to the casket. The crowd began to hum and chant. Gerry thought he recognized phrases from the old Latin mass, jazzed up and repeated over and over. Acolytes suddenly appeared around the casket with thuribles belching clouds of incense as they swung them wildly in the dance. The crowd began to sing an up-tempo version of the *Dies Irae*. This was followed by even faster music, and chanting that seemed to be an invocation of the holy spirit, as people flapped their arms like wings. Gerry recognized one of the chants as a version of 'Let the Fire Fall', during which the purple light seemed to become incandescent, as though purple flames danced among the crowd of people. Gerry felt that this was the most amazing spectacle he'd ever witnessed, and wished that he could enjoy it.

Sister Iqbal was in her element: her habit was a vortex of purple and scarlet flame. Her arms pumped the air as at the last jump-up of a calypso fête. She would appear beside the casket and then melt back into the crowd. Then she reappeared minus the habit, wearing only a pair of scarlet bloomers, from which her skinny legs protruded awkwardly as she danced. Her thin, wiry man's body

136

was covered with curly hair. She leapt onto the casket and put down a wine of which her idol, Satira, might have been proud. Her arms were extended and her pelvis was constantly grinding and rotating. The crowd began to chant the name of the archbishop and 'Wine him, wine him down to the Lord...'

The music and the flashing lights got faster. Gerry's heart beat faster and he felt sick in his stomach. These people were barbarians – primitives. He longed for his home and his family and friends – for the Georgetown, the Guyana he knew and had never realized how much he loved.

He became aware that the light no longer flickered and saw the purple light was at its highest intensity. His own gown seemed to be the main source of it, seemed to illuminate the whole tomb. The music had become a single, eternal note. The crowd no longer danced wildly, but swayed, and everyone seemed to be facing him and looking at him. Suddenly light appeared around the casket from below, as the floor opened and the casket hovered there. Monsignor Valdman stood in front of Gerry, adjusted his shining white garment and removed his skull cap. 'It is time,' he said, and embraced him. 'Thank you for being here, for agreeing to all this.' Then he motioned to Gerry to mount the casket.

Gerry was surprised how stable the floating casket felt under his feet. He stood self-consciously on it as the people chanted: 'God bless the Visitor, the Visitor, The Visitor...' Slowly, the casket began to descend. The same purple light came from beneath the casket and it was impossible to see anything below it. When the top of the casket was level with the floor, Gerry looked again into the eyes of the Monsignor, who pointed to his pectoral cross, the coloured lights churning within it, his finger near the green button. Next to him Sister Iqbal swayed in her bloomers, her body covered with perspiration, her face solemn. The chanting grew more hushed and the lights began to dim as the chanting subsided. Gerry's waist was now at floor level and he looked up and attempted a weak smile. His heart pounded and his hands trembled. 'These are a primitive people,' he repeated to himself, 'A primitive, superstitious people.' And he suddenly thought of traditions like *sutee*, or the ritual in some ancient African societies where when the king died his closest attendant had to commit suicide in order to accompany him. All this flashed through Gerry's terrified consciousness. He looked up again at the Monsignor, who stood with his finger poised over the button on the cross. 'Oh God!' Gerry said, 'Oh my God!'

Suddenly, as his head was at floor level, soon to disappear, Gerry lost his nerve; he felt he was a human sacrifice in a barbaric ritual and was descending to his death. Without fully realizing what he was doing, he reached up and caught hold of Monsignor Valdman's robe. His grasp was desperate and tight. Perhaps he intended to pull himself out of the shaft, but instead he pulled the Monsignor in on top of him. In addition, Sister Iqbal, who must have been holding on to the Monsignor to save him, also ended up on top of the casket.

Gerry could hear shouting and raucous consternation above. The Monsignor was screaming at him and he felt Sister Iqbal's nails in the flesh of his neck, but in his mind there was a terrible clarity and only one thought – the cross. As he reached for it he was dimly aware that the floor above their heads had closed and it had become quieter, except for the noise their tangled heap was making. The intense purple light still shone from below and Gerry had the impression that the casket was descending faster. All of this registered in a split second as, with a desperate lunge, he took hold of the cross. As he fumbled for the green button he said, weeping, 'Forgive me Monsignor, Sister... Oh God!' he thought as he began to feel the heat of the plasma chamber. The world went black.

*   *   *

Gerry Fung lay in a trembling heap on the wooden planks of the ferry stelling. He opened his eyes slowly, not knowing at first where he was. An old East Indian couple were looking at him with some concern. 'Is how he fall down so?' he heard the woman ask. Other passengers stopped on their way to board the ferry; then Pompey and Ivan came running up.

'Wha' de ass happen wid you?' Pompey said, concerned, as he pulled Gerry upright and noticed that his body was shaking. Then Ivan noticed the bloody scratches on Gerry's neck. Gerry leant against his friends to steady himself; he touched the wounds on his neck and looked at the blood on his hand. He began to feel an enormous relief. He tried desperately to remember the events in the shaft – but the memory was fading fast.

'I don't know what happened,' he told Pompey and Ivan, 'I must have hit my head when I fell, but I think I'm OK.'

'Well, if you still feel up to the trip, we got to hurry and get on the boat,' Ivan said, and they steadied Gerry as they made for the gangway.

'What happen to you? What you looking at now?' Pompey asked as they stood against the rail of the ferry as it pulled away from the stelling. Gerry had suddenly turned abruptly was looking anxiously up-river.

'It's nothing, I'm OK... I thought I saw a bridge...'

'You must be really hit your head hard,' Pompey said with a chuckle, 'There's no bridge, although they been talking about it for years; latest I hear is that they might buy some old floating bridge and put it up here. I doubt it will happen in our lifetime...'

By the time the ferry was approaching Vreed-En-Hoop stelling, all that remained in Gerry's mind was a vague and gnawing anxiety. God knows what will happen when later in the day he reaches into his pocket and pulls out three miniature, blue ping-pong balls...

STILL LIFE: BOUGAINVILLA AND BODY PARTS

by Geoffrey DeMattis

My dear Saskie,

You said you wanted a detailed account of everything that takes place on this trip – and then I realized that I couldn't really give you that on the phone from Yasmin's apartment, so I'm writing everything down for you so you can read it all like a story when I return. What I have decided is that I'll write these entries at the end of every day that I'm here. Since I'm very comfortable with the idea of writing personal letters to you, they'll take the form of letters, one each day. The letter format will help me to think of you and remind me that I'm writing this to help you understand what's happening here. This, then, is the first of my letters, at the end of the first day: Tuesday 22nd March, 1994.

Actually, it's only 7:15 p.m., but quite dark already. I told Yasmin I was off to see Harpal – on the 'business' that's supposed to be the reason I'm in Toronto. I don't think she bought that story, but we seem to have an unspoken agreement to keep up the pretence. I did go over to Harpal, arriving just as he got in from work, and we had a brief chat over a drink, but he and Zena are off to dinner with some friends, so I wandered around the university campus for a while collecting my thoughts, and ended up here in a carrel in the John M. Kelly Library over at St. Michael's College – you remember: where Paul used to be holed-up working on his thesis, and the two of us and Waveney would go and coax him down into one of the public lounges for a brief chat and a cup of coffee (that was another awkward visit – perhaps Toronto is not a very welcoming place for us, my love). Well, but now I think I know why Paul was so attached to this place – it's wonderfully quiet, almost desolate at this time on the upper floors, and the rather severe carrels lined up against the bleak windows do not permit distractions.

As I told you on the phone last night, the plane actually got in a few minutes early, but of course by the time I arrived at the apartment it was already dark. Augie accepted that I'm here on business for a few days – the way Augie accepts everything – but Yasmin bristled with suspicious curiosity.

'Daddy, I'm OK really, you know,' she said the first time we were alone. 'I told you there's no need to come – I should never have said anything about the painting; you understand 'writer's block'; well this is simply a case of 'painter's block', and I'll get over it...'

Which, of course, is just what we expected her to say. She doesn't know what her brother said when he returned from his visit here last month, and really, so far I see no evidence of anything amiss between them. Augie is just – Augie! We've always known him to be easy-going and somewhat distracted, quite unlike our very focused daughter, but I've always said that's why they get along together. And it's not as though they're married or anything: remember that this is Yasmin's 'experiment' – she's always insisted that she had to live with someone for a year or two before she knew whether she wanted to marry him or not. We tried halfheartedly to object, but she knew – knows – too much about our life before marriage!

The painting in question is on its easel in the solarium, draped with a blue cloth. I'm not – no one is – allowed to look at it (you know how fierce she can get when she's laying down the law! Devin is probably the only person who would dare disobey her – a sibling thing, no doubt). She's taken off the cloth and looked at it on two separate occasions during the day, but hasn't touched it. The two other pieces that are part of her special project are 'over at Spadina' – which I think means in one of the department's studios or storerooms.

I cooked her favourite 'sweet chicken' for dinner and I think she enjoyed it, although Augie ate most of it, picking absent-mindedly and repeatedly at what remained in the dishes long after we'd finished. He's such a large, awkward bear of a man; I always think of him as more absent than present, and if he's spoken more than a dozen sentences since I arrived it hasn't been in my presence. I don't suppose he cares or worries about this – or indeed about anything; he accepts, without any manifestation of emotion, whatever turns up. Perhaps he's the embodiment of 'the strong silent type' – except that Yasmin somehow seems much stronger than he is. I don't know, love, but for me – for us – words and voices have always been central to our relationship. From the beginning, our life together has been one long conversation (and I don't mean only in the eighteenth-century sense!). Our extremes of hurt and pleasure – as well as the dull continuum of everyday existence – have always found expression in words. It seems sad to me that Yasmin should be missing out on that. When she was growing up with us she certainly became a part of it. I can't help thinking these two should talk to each other more; conversations reveal and clarify things – even (as you know only too well) the things we attempt to hide. But how can one argue that silence is a serious problem in a relationship? It can't be really, can it? It's just that when I compare what their relative silence has created in the apartment with our constant verbal engagement, wherever we are, the latter seems so much richer, more full of life.

I can still remember in detail the first time I summoned up the courage to speak to you after school one day.

* * *

Ovid Pearson and Saskia Samlalsingh happen to walk out the school gates at the same time one bright afternoon.

'I discovered where you live,' Ovid said.

'It's no secret', Saskia replied. 'My family has nothing to hide.'

'Oh,' and Ovid wondered whether she was suggesting that his family did. 'Neither does mine,' he said, a little troubled. 'What I meant was I only just found out that you live in Locust Street.'

'And what I meant was that you could have found out any time, if you'd wanted to,' Saskia explained. 'Anyway, where's this conversation going?'

'With you and I, I hope,' Ovid said, looking at her, 'to the environs of number 58 Locust Street.'

Saskia thought for a moment. 'Why are you so indirect?'

'What do you mean?'

'If you want to walk me home, why not just ask me?'

'May I walk you home, my dear Saskia?' Ovid said, bowing and sweeping the air with his right arm.

'It's too late, you've spoiled it – you always spoil everything...'

'What foolishness you talking now, girl? What have I ever spoiled? I've hardly spoken to you before,' Ovid said heatedly.

'I mean in class – you never answer the teacher's question directly, but always in some fanciful, oblique way, trying to be clever. Like the other day when we were doing literature with Miss Meertins – in the end you had to get off your high horse and say in ordinary language that you thought it was wrong to blame Tiger for the way he treated Urmilla, because he was forced into marriage while still a schoolboy, and the only models of manhood he had to imitate were seriously flawed.'

'And all the rest of you agreed with me. Besides, the fact that you remember so well what I said means that it made perfect sense.'

'That's not the point,' Saskia insisted; 'instead of saying that from the beginning, you started with some long rigmarole about 'the child is the father of the man' and the difference between precept and example – the question didn't call for all of that.'

'I was saying the same thing, only much more elegantly.'

'You don't get marks for elegance in the exam – and in any case the 'elegance' only obscured your point. You do it all the time.'

By this time they had entered Locust Street and were approaching Saskia's house.

'Why you want to follow me home, anyway, Ovid Pearson? You and I don't have anything in common and my father is bound to kick up a fuss if he hears about it.'

'I'm beginning to see what your problem is with language,' Ovid said. 'In the first place, I'm not following you home, we're walking side by side; it was you yourself who suggested earlier that I wanted to walk you home.'

'Follow, walk, what's...'

'In the second place, we hardly know each other, and I don't know on what basis you can say we have nothing in common. And finally, I can't imagine why your father would 'kick up a fuss' on hearing that his daughter was walking on a public thoroughfare in the company of someone from her form at school.'

'You can't imagine? Well I don't have any problem explaining in simple language, so let me explain. When I look at the two of us walking up Locust Street through my father's eyes, I see this strange boy following my daughter home – I notice that he is of a different race and immediately I think this could mean pain and embarrassment in the future; so I resolve to let my daughter know that I don't approve of the situation, and that it's not to happen again.'

Ovid laughed. 'Very good,' he said, 'now tell me what you see when you look at the same thing through your own eyes?'

'That's irrelevant – I'm a schoolgirl; it's my father's eyes that count – for the time being. Anyway, this is number 58, in case you hadn't noticed,' Saskia said, stopping at the gate.

'Now what?' Ovid asked.

'Now you continue walking to wherever you're going. Did you think I was going to invite you in for biscuits and lemonade?'

'Not too fond of lemonade,' Ovid said thoughtfully, 'but maybe a glass of mauby…'

'Look, go-long your way!' she said dismissively, tossing her hair and turning towards the gate.

She did not look back, but Ovid knew there was a smile on her face.

* * *

Oh, I enjoyed writing that – though I'm certain you will want, as usual, to dispute my recollection of those events. Anyway, my love, it's getting late and I'm going home to the apartment. I will write again tomorrow.

Your beloved Ovid.

* * *

Wednesday 23rd March, 1994

My dearest Saskie,

Girl, it was really cold walking over here today: one of those dark and windy evenings when the leafless branches of the trees in the park and on the roadside shake themselves audibly at you as you pass by. I feel like a student again, leaning into the wind and making my way towards the library – a refuge from the world and its problems. Except that's not really true: I bring the world's problems with me (or at least our family's), to reflect on and put them down for you in black and white, though like the lingering

144

winter season nothing is ever black and white, only shades of grey: the ageing snow's a dirty grey colour, as is the sidewalk itself. The sky, the buildings, the trees are all different shades of grey.

I think now that Devin was right. Yasmin's problem is not just a temporary 'painter's block' as she calls it, but a more profound dissatisfaction with her situation. I was remembering today how happy she was a few years ago when we all looked at the condo and we (I should perhaps say you) decided to take it. We told her that she was going to be spending at least four years here, far from home, and we'd be happier knowing that she was comfortable and had everything she needed, including that wonderful solarium with its incredible natural light, so perfect for painting. Remember how thankful, how joyful she was? Then – was it a year later? – she wrote that letter telling us that her 'boyfriend' was moving in with her, to save them the hypocrisy, the fatigue, and the expense of maintaining two places and shuttling between them day and night like people with something to hide. 'Her mother's own daughter,' you remarked, though I had to point out that you would never have dared to write such a letter to your parents!

Well, without really approving, we acquiesced in her plan and became accustomed to the idea – if not to Mr. Augie himself, who seemed to us like one of Yasmin's more abstract and experimental canvases – the ones we'd look at and smile politely and comment on the vividness of the colour or the wonders of the technique – and she'd say: 'I know. You hate it. I can tell,' and we'd have to try and convince her otherwise. Curiously, she never required our approval of Augie: his presence in her apartment was something she had chosen and she was happy to accept all responsibility. She never really talked about him, and he of course, in the most inoffensive of ways, never gave any indication of his feelings – about us, the arrangement, or whether he acknowledged any feelings at all...

Well, my love, it seems that Augie 'gave up' his job in the accounting firm sometime before Christmas. He told Yasmin (and she believes him) that he was not fired. He just stopped going to work, and eventually admitted to one of the partners on the phone that he was not coming back. 'It's just the sort of thing Augie would do,' Yasmin told me today. 'He has problems with commitment.' When I asked her how they had been managing financially, she said, 'Oh it doesn't cost anything to support him; the fact is he never spent much of the money he earned: he has a savings account with thousands of dollars in it. As you know, I'm the expensive one.' And she flashed that smile of hers. But it was not quite one of her usual smiles, happy and self-confident; there was an edge of anxiety beneath it, and she knew I had spotted it, because she went on to say: 'Really, that's not the problem, Dad. It's just that... I feel all the awkwardness and... and... shame that he should be feeling, but he isn't bothered in the least. Nothing else about his life has changed, but I don't believe you can give up a job just like that without it meaning something about your life. He says he'll get another job, but seems in no hurry – look at the trouble I had just getting him out of the house and over to the placement office, where he's supposed to have registered. I don't even know that he's really gone there – he may well come home tonight and say that he never actually made it in the end... It wouldn't occur to him to lie about it for the sake of my peace of mind.'

[I should explain that I was there when she was shooing him out of the apartment, advertising the anger she felt by her feeble attempts to conceal it. She felt she had to tell me all about it, once he'd actually left.]

'We quarrel frequently these days – in fact – I take that back, we don't quarrel; I wish we did – it's nothing that you and Mum would recognize as a real quarrel. I remember with great nostalgia the intricate – baroque – arguments that you and Mum had about all sorts of foolishness. In our case I shout at him in impotent rage and he just looks straight at me and endures the onslaught, mumbling some feeble response from time to time, but he has no real inclination to argue, no matter how much I bait him with deliberately unfair statements. And he won't treat me any differently afterwards: my rages are like storms or earthquakes or other natural phenomena that he feels he simply has to endure. He blames no-one for them and just tries to assess when 'life as usual' can resume.

'I'm sorry if my presence has made it worse for you, my love,' I told her, and she flashes me that same smile again.

'You're the catalyst, Dad, your presence enables a certain

146

process, perhaps, but you're not to blame for any of this. I love you.' Then her face crumpled. 'You would never endure my rages; you always raged back...' And the sobs shook her body and the tears came. I hugged her.

When I thought she had finished crying, I said, 'The painting is due on Friday.'

'You don't need to remind me, Dad,' she said, wiping her eyes, a kind of hardness creeping into her voice. 'I will finish it, don't worry.'

Now, in the silence of this library, it is I who am weeping inside for our daughter who is feeling pain and is confronted by difficulties that I can do nothing to solve.

All that happened before midday. After lunch Yasmin took down the painting, wrapped it tightly in cloth, packed a rucksack full of equipment and left. 'I'm going to have to finish this over at Spadina,' she said. 'I won't get anything done here.' When I left the apartment at five o'clock, neither of them had returned. Again I feel that if only Augie would talk, bring himself to life in words, argue with her – things would be better, retrievable. He should talk to her in bed, where the world contains just the two of them. I remember how we used to talk in bed, Saskie, when we lived together in circumstances that were similar... and yet so different.

★   ★   ★

'Ovid.'

'M'hmm.'

'You sleeping?'

'Not really – Hey! Don't touch me there with your cold hands. You know, Saskie, I think there's something wrong with your circulation – your hands are always like ice.'

'Don't exaggerate. Anyway, we know there's nothing wrong with your circulation: something is already beginning to stiffen up.'

'What do you expect if you go pulling at it? Though with those icicle fingers of yours, it's a wonder – Aie! – it's a wonder it doesn't shrink out of reach altogether. Oh God, I love it when you do that!'

'Despite the icicles?'

'They're warming up quite nicely.'

'You ever ask yourself how come we're doing this and my parents back home don't know anything about you?'

147

'Whose fault is that? Who keeps saying "I don't think I'm ready to tell them about us yet"? Hey, what happened, Saskie? You can't stop now!'

'I think we should talk for a while.'

'That's not fair; you get me all aroused and then you want to stop and talk!'

'Well I can't talk with you rubbing up against me, and I need to talk; I was lying here thinking a lot of things.'

'OK, we'll talk for a while, but then promise we'll resume where we left off. Agreed? And try to keep your hands warm.'

'It's just that I feel sad when I think about my parents – especially Ma – not knowing... And if I tell them they'll think that we arranged the whole thing behind their backs – I followed you to Edmonton, or you followed me... The whole thing will seem...'

'Shabby and deceitful. If you remember, those were the words I used when you said we should go ahead and live together without telling your parents...'

'You don't have to rub it in; you don't know how hard it is for me.'

'Oh Saskie, love, don't cry – I understand what you're going through, really, and I only wish I could convince you that it's all so unnecessary. Your parents will be upset at first, of course they will, but they'll calm down and accept it in time. It hurts me to see you torture yourself like this.'

'I'm... I'm their only daughter and Romesh didn't go to university... they're expecting so much of me...'

'And with straight As last semester I don't see any way that you will disappoint them. I'm certain you'll graduate with first-class honours. You won't disappoint them, love, and I won't either, I promise. I don't know why you should be so ashamed of me that you can't tell them.'

'Oh God, don't say that. You know I love you or I wouldn't be here in bed with you naked. My love for you is stronger than parents or everything else. It's just that I'm greedy. I want everything. I want you, I want your love, I want your miserable body that I can't seem to do without. I want to be married to you and to have your children. I want to do well at my studies and I want the love and respect of my parents. I want it all – I've never had to settle for half-measures before...'

'And you won't have to now. Your parents will come round when they know how much we mean to each other. They will have two *children at university to be proud of – though if you keep praising my body and sexual prowess, I might decide to drop out and make my living as a gigolo – but don't worry I'll let you be my manager, or agent, or whatever...'*

'*Fool! Gigolos don't have agents. And be serious: you really think I should just write and tell them? Maybe we should just get married?'*

'*You know I'd jump at the chance to marry you tomorrow, but I think we'd hurt your parents even more if we get married on the sly. Listen, I keep telling you that if we sit down and think through this problem we're bound to find a solution – it's just that you keep refusing to face it sensibly – because it makes you feel sad about your parents. Let's think it over for the rest of this week and make a decision by Monday – and that will be that.'*

'*You're not just saying that?'*

'*Ah, girl, you know I'd say or do anything to get back to that page where it is written: "she reached down with her icicle fingers and began to stroke his..." Hey! I thought you were keeping them warm! Stop! You're going to freeze all our offspring before they get a chance!'*

'*Oh shut up!' she said, burrowing quickly under the covers, like a squirrel in a pile of leaves; then her muffled voice came from somewhere down by his knees: 'How about: "She tries instead her hot, hungry tongue..."?'*

'*O God, yes! Yes! Now we're getting somewhere!'*

★   ★   ★

I think I'll continue to include these 'conversations', Saskie. They cheer me up after all the gloom – both of the weather and of the apartment.

I love you,
Ovid

★   ★   ★

Thursday 24th March, 1994

Dear Saskie,

I'm not in the Kelly library tonight, but home in the den, which as you know converts into my bedroom at night. It is almost midnight and I am the only one at home. There's not much progress to report in the situation here. Your daughter is working hard on her painting – at least I assume that's what she's doing, she has not been home much. She came in around two o'clock this morning, pottered about noisily in the kitchen for half an hour (I had left her a plate of rissoles with coconut rice and spinach balls) and, after she had woken everyone, she crashed on the living room couch and did not get up until after nine. It was clear that she was ignoring poor Augie, who I heard trying to get her to say something – a reversal of roles! He eventually pottered off, telling me (and the walls and the ceiling) he was going to spend some time at the gym and run a few errands; he'd be back in the afternoon.

Yasmin seemed quite bright after he'd gone. She said the painting was coming along nicely, though very slowly and when I asked her she actually told me something of what it's about.

'It's simple, Dad; it's a still life – all three are still lives: the first one distorts colours and light – fooling around with them, you know, experimental... the second does the same with texture and relative scale, kind of surreal... but it's all fairly ordinary stuff. The third is a huge vase of flowers that...'

'Oh, Yasmin, your flowers? Your bougainvillas?'

'What do you think? They're in a big vase on a table with a white cloth, but they needed something to comment on them or to question them somehow, if you know what I mean. So that's what I'm working on at the moment... I'd rather not tell you any more about it now. We all have to hang our work in front of the class and talk about it tomorrow, when it will be graded, so I'm going back there midday to finish it off. I'll probably be late again tonight.' And she is – it's now after midnight.

You remember how obsessed she's always been by bougainvillas? Drawing and painting them since she was in her early teens, when she took all those photographs down in Trinidad that year we spent a few days at Marjorie's place on the way back from Guyana. She can probably paint them in her sleep – but that's not what's giving her the problems, it's this other thing in the painting, whatever it is that interrogates the traditional values and conventions of the still life.

Anyway, to return to my account of the day: I popped out to buy a few grocery items while Yasmin was preparing to leave and returned to find her gone to Spadina and a note: 'Dad, Aunt Waveney called. Please call her before midday.' I called Waveney and agreed to meet her and Paul in the lobby of Paul's office building on Bay Street, and we would go somewhere for lunch. When I arrived Waveney was there and Paul was just getting out of the elevator – and guess who else was there: Aunt Cicely – it was so good to see her, and she looks the same as ever: the woman who never ages. She says Tessa is working on a novel... We walked over to a nice restaurant on Bloor Street. Paul is doing very well, thinking of retiring early – it was good chatting with them and I'll tell you more about that when I return. They all send their love. I should mention, though, that while we were at lunch, overlooking Bloor Street, I saw Augie go past with a bunch of daffodils in a paper and cellophane package. Things must be really serious for Augie to be buying flowers!

When I got back to the apartment it was after three and there was no sign of anyone – and that's the way it has remained. What was in the apartment was the bunch of daffodils, still in its wrapping, lying on the dining table. There's that blue vase that you bought, empty on the coffee table, but it never occurred to Augie to put them in there. That has been my struggle this afternoon: I wanted to rescue the flowers and put them in some water in the vase (you know I like daffodils, despite – or perhaps because of – their Wordsworthian associations and the disapproval of the politically correct Postcolonial brother/sisterhood), but at the same time I don't want to interfere in any way, so the flowers are still where Augie abandoned them.

Is it just my distorted imagination (or my distorted parental emotions) that life is so much more burdensome for today's young people than it was for us? Why is it so painful when I think of Yasmin painting away past midnight, hungry and cold in some attic across campus, knowing that her relationship with Augie is falling apart? And who knows, perhaps Augie's bewildering diffidence is just a learned response to the possibility of pain. Perhaps the truth is that these things should happen away from the observing eyes of a parent. From the moment Yasmin was born – no, conceived – I've had this irrational feeling that I would do or give anything, even my life, to protect her from pain and unhappiness. What a hope! Do you remember the day we first found out that you were pregnant with her?

151

'Saskie.'

'What now?'

'Nothing'

'What's wrong with you, Ovid? Since we left the clinic you've had that silly smile on your face, looking sideways at me all the time – you better pay attention to the road in front of you.'

'Human chorionic gonadotropin.'

'What?'

'That's what they found in the urine sample – that's how they know we're pregnant.'

'We? Look, Ovid, don't make me laugh. Which part of you pregnant?'

'We did it together – it will be our son or daughter – or maybe both, it could be twins...'

'Now look where you gone: a six-week old button of tissue and you seeing twins in matching outfits and lisping for "Da-Da" – I'm sure that's why you have that stupid grin on your face. Well listen, Mister, come down out of the clouds, you hear. All of that is a long way off, and in the mean time I'm the one carrying our baby (singular) and I will have the discomfort and the weariness and the swollen ankles and probably the vomiting in the mornings – like yesterday. Not to mention the labour pains and/or the scar on my belly if it can't be born naturally.'

'I know all that, love, but don't worry, I'll help you in every way. Oh Saskie, Saskie, lean over to my side: I just have to kiss you right now.'

'Ovid! Cut it out! Concentrate on your driving, please, or else you, me and whatever-this-is will end up in the morgue. Don't look at me! Look at the road. Wait, you want me to drive?'

'In your condition? Not a chance. You sit back and relax, I promise I'll keep my eyes on the road.'

'I can see you mean to give me a hard time; I'm not in any 'condition'. I'm six weeks pregnant: I'm not ill, I'm not impaired, there's nothing that I've been doing all along that I can't do now – that includes driving and, before you get any funny ideas, making love.'

'H'mm, I hadn't thought about that. But surely there's no harm in being more careful? In any case it's going to take me a little while to get used to the idea.'

'I like that! I'm the one pregnant and it's going to take you a little while to get used to the idea! God knows good why he gave women the responsibility of bearing children. If he'd given it to men the human race would have disappeared long ago.'

'You're probably right; I'm overreacting – but I can't help being excited, Saskie... and imagine, we found this out on the first anniversary of our marriage – now we have two things to celebrate. I take it we can still go out to dinner tonight?'

'You just try to get out of it, Mister! I'm looking forward to the king crab and the wine.'

'Wine? Are you sure it's OK to drink alcohol?'

'Ovid!'

'OK, OK. You can drink wine.'

'You're right though, Ovid; it's a wonderful anniversary present. I was beginning to wonder if God was punishing us for all our premarital carrying-on.'

'There you go with your guilt thing again. Forget all that, Saskie; our baby will be a perfect child and we'll tell her that she was our first anniversary present from God.'

'I notice you've decided it's a girl. When she's a young child you can tell her anything. What I want to hear is what you're going to say when she's a teenager and asks: "Dad, did you and Mum have sex before you were married?"'

'Only enough, Rebecca dear, to ensure that we had perfected it before we set about conceiving you.'

'Rebecca! Who tell you I would let my daughter be called Rebecca?'

'We can argue about names later, but our daughter, whatever she's called, will be fully informed about us and our past – about sex – about everything, at the appropriate time. I wouldn't want her to go through what you went through – all that guilt for nothing.'

'Whose fault was that? How was I to know that you had written that letter to Pa – all of those letters – and that he knew all about us? You still haven't told me how much he really knew – and I'm not sure if I will ever forgive either of you for the deception.'

'Come on, Saskie, you yourself admitted that it was you who had the problem, who decided that your parents just could not accept a son-in-law who was not Indian; you cried lots of tears before the wedding and asked Pa's forgiveness for misjudging him.'

153

'Perhaps, but before that it was you who got it in your head that I wasn't sure I wanted to marry you, and you and Pa and Romesh stage-managed all that drama when he arrived unexpectedly at the apartment and 'discovered' us living in sin...'

'Oh God, your father is a terrific actor, hear girl; he nearly had me fooled: "And you, Mr. Ovid Pearson, call yourself a man? I give you one week to do the right thing and marry my daughter or else you will find out – painfully – how Indians handle young upstarts who interfere in their family." With those grey eyes flashing and the beard, he looked like Moses smashing the tablets. Although I knew what was happening, I still tremble.'

'Good! I'm glad that you felt something, however minute, of the terror I was going through. I nearly didn't marry you, you hear, when I found out what was really going on.'

'But you couldn't stand the thought of life without me – without this precision instrument of a body on which you so love to play.'

'Fool yourself! Hey! Where are you going, Ovid? Slow down, don't fly past our corner again, like the other night...'

* * *

I was telling Paul today at lunch that I'm writing this for you in nightly instalments, and he said we should keep in touch via computers and went on to tell me about this new 'internet' thing that everyone is talking about. I suppose we should look into it, but it wouldn't be the same: for me, nothing will ever replace the solitary pleasures of pen and paper, of beginning the process with a pen and an empty white page... It's late, love, and I'm turning in.

Yours always,
Ovid.

* * *

Friday 25th March, 1994

My dear Saskie,

It's only mid-afternoon, but so much has happened that I have retreated to my carrel in the library to write this instalment – and to avoid being in the empty flat right now. Yasmin is over at her department showing her paintings and having them assessed. And Augie? Poor Augie is gone for good.

I must have fallen asleep about 1:15 this morning, up to which time, as already reported, no one was home. I was awakened by the phone at about 3:30. It was Yasmin.

'Oh Dad, I'm so sorry, I was hoping Augie would answer; I didn't want to get you out of bed, really.'

'Don't be silly, dear. Is something the matter?'

'No, nothing, honestly – I've only just finished and I'm really quite happy with it, only I'm dead tired and I wanted Augie to come and walk back with me. Could you put him on?'

'Well, I'm not sure that he's here; he wasn't up to a couple hours ago when I turned in. I'll check, but if he isn't, I'll come for you.'

'No, Dad, I couldn't ask you to do that; you don't know where this place is and it isn't that easy to find. Just check Augie for me – he's probably fast asleep.'

And he was – I don't think he'd heard the phone, and he didn't hear when I called him and knocked at the bedroom door; I had to go in and shake him. I went back to bed when he picked up the phone. I heard him stumbling about for five minutes, then he went out the door. Of course I couldn't go back to sleep.

After a much longer time than I expected, I heard the door open and Yasmin whispering loudly: 'Augie, Augie!'

'It's all right, you two; I'm awake, there's no need to whisper,' and I got out of bed and pulled on my robe.

'Not *you two*,' Yasmin said, this time with a touch of exasperation; 'it's only me. Where on earth is Augie?'

'I don't know, dear; he left ages ago to get you.'

'Well, he never turned up. Typical. That man is a dead loss.'

A few minutes later, the man himself appeared at the door and then there actually occurred something resembling a conversation – if a somewhat surreal one.

'Why didn't you wait for me?'

'Where on earth were you?'

'I went to walk you home.'

'And how come I'm home without you? You never showed up.'

'Of course I did, but there was no one there; the building was locked.'

'Augie, you're crazy – I waited in the lobby, I waited on the steps, I waited out on the sidewalk; I kept looking out for you.'

'Well I spent a lot of time looking for you too, but I didn't see anyone.'

'Augie, where did you go, for God's sake? Which building was locked?'

'Your building, the one where you do all the painting and stuff, the one opposite Rick and Kevin's apartment...'

'Rick and Kev? Augie, you are quite mad. Rick and Kevin's apartment is nowhere near the building where I paint – the building on Spadina, with the road going all around it.'

'Spadina? You never said Spadina...'

If it weren't the middle of the night, and the situation was different, it would have been hilarious: Augie certain he'd spent a whole night, some time before Christmas, helping her finish some prints for a deadline the next day – in the very building he'd gone to; Yasmin insisting he was mistaken – that the print studio was in the same building where she had been waiting on him; which was why she'd been certain he would know where to go!

It seemed they would carry on all night. Probably a good thing, I thought, that they were actually arguing for a change, and I went back to bed. I doubted I would sleep, but the next thing I knew it was almost nine o'clock, when I woke to Yasmin's voice. 'My God, they've been arguing all night!' was my first thought, but I learned from Yasmin that this wasn't so. She said that after the argument seemed to be getting nowhere – and more specifically, after he'd tried to appease her with a limp bunch of daffodils – she'd phoned Rick and Kevin's apartment and informed a drowsy Kevin that she was putting Augie out for good and that he was coming over and would they please put him up for a while until he could find a place of his own. Poor Kevin didn't have much choice, really – and neither did Augie, when he finally understood what was happening. He was made to walk through the door at four in the morning like a field slave at the second horn. But when I emerged from the den this morning, there was Augie in the doorway to the apartment, sort of leaning in. Yasmin, in her gown, her hair wild, was shouting, 'For God's sake come inside and close the door!' but Augie insisted on standing his ground.

'I just want to clear up a few things – and you did say, remember, that I was not to set foot in your apartment again.'

'But I know you have to collect your stuff – and anyway, I can't stand here talking to you like this with the door open. You can come in and collect your things, but you can't stand in the doorway indefinitely.'

'I can stand where I want.'

'Yes, and – typically – where you want, and where you always stand, is on the threshold. You're forever teetering on the brink of something or other – some decision or job or lifestyle – you can never commit yourself properly to anything; that's why you can never come back here.'

'See, and you just told me to come in!'

'Augie, for God's sake!'

'OK, but you can't throw me out after fifteen months because I stand in doorways. What is it in one word that you suddenly find so objectionable about me?'

By now Yasmin could probably be heard by anyone waiting down the corridor for the elevators: 'I'll tell you what's wrong with you,' she shouted, 'you're too damned...' She groped for the word and Augie and I waited, not knowing what to expect. 'You're too damned... vestibular!'

'What? What on earth is that supposed to mean?' Augie was so nonplussed by her response that he stepped inside.

'It means,' and Yasmin was now a river in spate, 'that you are unforgivably, horrendously tentative in everything you do; you drift into situations and drift out of them, like flotsam. You haven't a positive, decisive bone in your oversized body; you can't live with me – you can't live with an artist – you don't feel anything with sufficient intensity to care for it, to be able to appreciate form and beauty. Care and appreciation require focused attention. It's clear that you never focus your attention on anything outside yourself and your needs – and it's not just (as most people think) a charming distractedness; from my perspective it's a kind of contempt. Your tentative explorations and hesitations can be exciting in bed, I admit...' – and then she saw him shoot a shocked glance at me – 'Don't worry about offending my father; I'm not the result of immaculate conception, he knows all about sex and, in any case is in no position to object to what I say or do... [Here she seemed like you, Saskie, I couldn't help

157

noticing. Earlier, when she had called him 'vestibular' I realized, with a strange embarrassment, that she sounded like me.] I can't spend my life with someone who cannot commit himself, who cannot decide, who cannot feel.'

'You've always made all the decisions and commitments, love. Anyway, it was Kevin who suggested that I should come over and talk to you, to see if you had changed your mind.'

'I haven't – and I won't.'

'So you're throwing me out into the cold. You know I don't do well on my own; you always said I'd be lost if it weren't for you. Now I'll be at the mercy of all those other bossy women out there.'

I wondered if this was an attempt at humour, but Yasmin was having none of it.

'Yeah, they'll be after you for your bedroom prowess, no doubt. If you're not careful you'll drift indecisively into a socially transmitted disease – although, knowing you, it will probably be diagnosed as 'nonspecific urethritis.' [This I thought was a low blow – again she reminded me of you!]

'I can see it's no use arguing with you in this mood.'

'Listen to me, Augie, this is not a mood; it won't blow over like bad weather – not tomorrow, not next year, not ever. This is the new reality: you cannot live here any more.'

And that was that. He left later with a large suitcase and there's a box with stereo stuff and CDs and tapes that he's to pick up later. About one o'clock Yasmin left for the assessment exercise. The apartment suddenly seemed overheated and oppressive, so I fled to the carrel in the Kelly library – cool and neutral. I miss you, girl, but I'm glad that you were not here for this. I feel guilty somehow, although I did nothing to bring about the split – perhaps my awkward presence pushed things over the edge. Is it for the best? I don't know, and it's not for me to say. Our daughter has always had her own ideas, especially where men are concerned:

★   ★   ★

'Bye Mum, Dad.'
'Yasmin?'
'Yes, Dad.'

'Where are you off to now?'

'I'm going over to school – we're starting rehearsals for the play.'

'And how are you getting there, young lady?'

'Ming is coming to pick me up.'

'Ming? Is he that long-haired Chinese boy?'

'Vietnamese, Dad.'

'Same thing – the one who packs groceries at the market?'

'Yes, he has two part-time jobs: he also delivers pizza three nights a week, that's how he paid for his car and...'

'Yasmin, you know I don't care for that fellow. I thought you said he was just one of the gang – an acquaintance from school?'

'And so he is, Dad, but he's kind of cute, and I think he likes me.'

'See, that's just what I mean, sweetheart; if you encourage him, next thing you know he'll want to take you out on dates. What do we know about this fellow, anyway? His culture, language – everything – is different from our own. Besides...'

'Besides what, Dad? Come on, let's get all the prejudices out in the open.'

'Now, don't you start that with me, Missy. It's not a question of prejudice. I was going to say that the other day at the market he was in one of those sleeveless T-shirts – do you know there's a large tattoo of an animal on his left shoulder? Some kind of lion or dragon or something?'

'It's a horse, Dad, and there's another one on his right hip.'

'What! Saskie, are you listening to this? And just how did you happen to see his right hip, young lady; and tell me, how much more of his body have you been privileged to examine?'

'Don't be silly, Dad, I saw it at the pool – it's a rearing horse and its head and forelegs are above the waistline, as though the horse is trying to leap out of his swim-pants – it's really cool.'

'It's vulgar! I'm sure you're meant to think of something else that's trying to leap out of his swim-pants. You young people are so crude and shameless... Why are you grinning at me like that?'

'I can't help it, Dad. It's Mum there, killing herself laughing.' And mother and daughter both explode with laughter.

'I'm glad you both find it so amusing, and I must say, I'm surprised at you, Saskie.'

'Oh, that must be Ming now, ringing the doorbell; Mum, Dad, I'm *off. Don't ever change, Dad, you're priceless, and I love you. I'll never do anything to make you ashamed of me. I promise.'*

'Well, I hope so. Tell that supermarket stallion to drive carefully and get you home before your curfew – remember it's a weeknight.'

'Oh Ovid, she's right: you are priceless.'

'When you've finished laughing, perhaps you'll consider telling me what's so funny.'

'It's you, love: "It's not a matter of prejudice, young lady". You could have fooled me! You see how it is now, eh? Your own past coming back to haunt you.'

'Perhaps, but I never had tattoos and long hair. This Ming boy is from a different culture – how do we know he's not a member of some Chinese criminal gang? That tattooed horse could be a badge of membership.'

'Now, look where your racial stereotyping has taken you! In any case he's not Chinese, he's Vietnamese – or rather his parents are; he's as Canadian as your daughter. You should listen to yourself, Ovid; the boy is just a high-school kid, like thousands of others in this city – and tattoos are in fashion these days.'

'Fashion? But it's not like some ridiculous garment or hairstyle that you can discard later. Tattoos are a permanent disfiguring of the body.'

'Oh, I don't know about disfiguring – that horse jumping out of the swim-pants sounds quite exciting to me – I wonder if Ming would let me see it.'

'You mean you'd have no objection if I went out and got a tattoo? A fierce jaguar leaping out of the undergrowth of my pubic hair?'

'Now that sounds like a real turn-on. I'd kiss him every day until he becomes as tame as a pussy-cat.'

'By which time I know something else that would be leaping up fiercely – I think I'll do it.'

'Don't get any foolish ideas, Ovid. Leave the tattoos for the kids; I love you just the way you are. Besides, you'd never let anyone with a needle fool around down there!'

'Well, but I still don't see how you can take all this so calmly.'

'Trust. I trust my daughter. It's a secret you taught me a long time ago. You should obey your own precepts sometimes.'

'I suppose; but it's hard to think of Yasmin no longer needing my guidance in making choices and decisions.'

'Don't worry, love; she'll always need that in some form or other. Speaking of guidance, has your son spoken to you yet?'

'Devin? No, why? What's up with him now?'

'I told him to speak to you: he's thinking of having an ear pierced.'

'Oh God, no, not that – I always thought he was such a sensible child.'

⋆   ⋆   ⋆

Tomorrow I will let you know how Yasmin is taking all this – once the project is out of the way and she has a chance to think.

Lots of love

Ovid

⋆   ⋆   ⋆

Saturday 26th March, 1994

Well, my dearest,

I have to report that your daughter seems to have survived her trials and is in good spirits. Too good, I'd thought at first: there seemed to be a touch of the manic when she returned from the assessment exercise – she did quite well, got an A for her project, but more of that later. She took a taxi from Spadina and arrived at the door with all three paintings and a full rucksack on her back. She was in her dark blue coat and beret and had a scarf of vivid blue fleece wound around her neck with one end tossed over her shoulder; springs of black hair protruding from under the beret – and those hazel eyes were flashing. She looked fabulous, the way her mother does on bleak winter days.

That was about four o'clock. She declared that she was too tired for any more show and tell, and she just dumped the paintings in the solarium and promised that we would look at them later.

'So you're going to collapse into bed, I hope.'

'I should, nuh? At least for a couple of hours, but I feel the need for some sort of celebration tonight; I half-arranged with some girls from my class that we would do something tonight.'

'Good idea, get a few hours rest and I'll take you and your friends out to dinner wherever you want to go.'

She was happy with this suggestion and immediately got on

the phone. She disappeared into her bedroom for a while, though I'm not sure that she got much rest. At eight o'clock she emerged all dressed up – you know how she does all that make-up around the eyes, and the weird lip-gloss – I'm sure she was at it for almost an hour. And I'll never know why, because for me she looked much lovelier when she came in the door with the blue scarf and the beret.

I tried to steer them to that 'Brasserie' place that we went to once in Yorkville, but they preferred a little place nearby called Hemmingway's, obviously much beloved by university folk – and it was quite good. The four girls and I had a long, slow, tasty and relaxing meal. Spirits were high; joking about each other's work, gushing about the food and wine, giggling about the people at adjoining tables and generally enjoying themselves. Yasmin was the liveliest of all and did not seem to be missing – or even remembering – Augie. I was worried that she might collapse from exhaustion and emotional fatigue, but she just kept going. I was grateful, however, that when it was mooted that they move on to a club nearby, she used me as an excuse for heading back to the apartment and having an early night. We got home at 11:40 and she was asleep by midnight. I felt that she was in a kind of denial, deliberately refusing to think about her changed circumstances – about Augie.

At breakfast this morning, however, it was clear that she had returned to earth. We sat for over two hours and talked about what had happened. I was impressed with her maturity, Saskie; she knew she was in an unnatural state the night before – 'wired', she called it – and that the immediate future will not be easy. She admits that she still cares for Augie, and misses him, but is adamant that she won't have him back. (Why couldn't he just have been unfaithful, like most men? That would have been easier to deal with.) I reminded her that I'm flying home tomorrow and asked her if she was sure she'd be OK. She claims she won't have time to be otherwise – she has assignments due, exams, her trip and then her summer job: 'So you see, Daddy, if you weren't leaving tomorrow of your own free will, I'd have to kick you out anyway – like Augie.'

Now to the paintings: I should say 'the painting', for while the

162

first two are arresting and quite magnetic in their own way, they are entirely overshadowed by the third, which took my breath away and which, I'm certain, is what earned her the A. It's called 'Still Life: Bougainvilla and Body Parts', and is a terrifying, beautiful, savage work. It's a big thing, four feet by three, so it's more than twice the size of each of the other two. It depicts a table, spread with a white cloth – in fact our white tablecloth, the one that your Aunt Ruby gave us – with the bits cut out in small rectangular patterns, through which you can see the surface of the table underneath – in this case burnt sienna representing the dark wood. In the middle of the table is a large, grey marble vase, almost like a planter, in which are large thorny branches of white bougainvilla, arching over in all directions – at first glance they look like red and white flowers, until you realize that the red is blood! It stains the flowers, the vase and the tablecloth; and even the wall behind the table is lightly spattered with it. What is really striking and effective is the contrast between the bright red and the light colours of the background – the white flowers, the tablecloth, the vase and the wall behind them – which is almost white, with just a touch of umber in it to make it a sort of cream and distinguish it from the other large areas.

The blood comes from the 'body parts', four of them – from left to right: a blue and bloody foot, severed just above the ankle; an ear, looking tiny and forlorn by a small stain of blood, just to the left front of the base of the vase; a severed penis and scrotum on a disproportionately large bloodstain, and finally a human heart, lying on one side with torn vessels and shreds of tissue hanging from it. All the parts are meticulously, grotesquely realistic, sagging and with their shapes distorted by gravity and lifelessness – but clearly identifiable. The whole creates a terrifying and powerful effect. It is somewhat reminiscent of those seventeenth century Flemish still lives (is it Franz De Heem? – I can never remember artists' names) of gutted rabbits and game fowl hanging from hooks and a deer on a table being eviscerated and nearby a silver tray laden with butchered meat and offal. But those scenes are wholly domestic, compared to Yasmin's. Here there's real violence: it's like the scene of a terrible murder, a desecration of the purity of the white flowers, with the profusion of blood – and then there's the way it makes clear that the severed parts were flung with some force onto the table, spattering blood and puckering the tablecloth.

I was fascinated and repelled. I would not have guessed that she was capable of creating – of imagining this. For one awful moment I wondered irrationally if she had chopped up poor Augie! – of course I instantly recalled that he was around after the painting was finished! But that momentary panic does illustrate the power of the painting.

'I know it's wild and violent,' Yasmin said. 'But for me it was also exhilarating, cathartic. And Rob (my prof) really likes it.'

I now understood what the girls meant last night when they kept pretending to be 'scared' of Yasmin – especially when she picked up her steak-knife!

Anyway, love, there you have it. Perhaps the painting is an appropriate conclusion to this whole episode. It reinforces for me the conviction I've always had about the impossibility of really knowing someone and of the absolute mystery of personality and imagination. As I write this, your daughter is off with her friends again. We left the flat together at six o'clock – I for my last walk here to the Kelly library, where I've written all but one of these letters. We will of course talk about all this when I get back tomorrow evening, but we'll also have this rambling and eccentric written account to refer to. I kept my bargain – I hope you won't be disappointed in it.

All my love,
Ovid

164

A LOVESONG FOR MISS LILLIAN
by Jamila Muneshwar

When he received Daphne Shepherd's invitation to 'tea' on the afternoon of Friday next, Raymond Rose's first thought was that he would politely decline. Daphne Shepherd was herself quite pleasant company: a dear old friend of his late mother, she was bent on keeping up the social standards of polite Georgetown society in these much diminished times; but she also cultivated the friendship of a few government ministers as well as that of those eternally gloomy university academics who regularly berated the politicians and their policies in letters to the press. Raymond was not sure he wanted to be caught up in the arguments and recriminations of these two groups. It was true that Alister Shepherd, Daphne's husband, would pounce on the chance to 'rescue' Raymond by proposing a tour of his beloved orchid collection, but an hour's lecture on the fastidious needs and habits of the most recently-blooming phalaenopsis was not Raymond's idea of an exciting way to spend a Friday afternoon...

When Daphne telephoned to find out whether he would be coming on Friday (Raymond having 'put off' the duty required of him by the R.S.V.P.), he hastened to explain, in a suitably apologetic tone, that he was in the middle of some very delicate and stressful negotiations having to do with the firm, and was not sure he could spare the time. Daphne tut-tutted and complained that he was in danger of becoming one of those dull young men whose only concern was their work, insisting that, if humanly possible, he should show up for her 'tea'. Raymond had to promise that he would do his best.

The 'delicate negotiations' were not just an excuse conjured out of nowhere, because Raymond was indeed involved in negotiating the purchase, for himself, of a senior partnership – in fact *the* senior partnership – in what used to be his father's old law firm, Rose, Robinson and Waaldijk. Working mostly on his own since his return from law school six years ago, he had quickly built up both a profitable practice and an enviable reputation, partly because he permitted himself few social or romantic distractions. The gossip was that he lived the life of a monk in the large family home he had inherited. At thirty-one he was still quite young, but everyone had expected great things of the son of Mr. Jefferson Rose, who had died prematurely and tragically of leukaemia at the height of his career, only eighteen months after he had been appointed to the bench. Lawrence Waaldijk, the famous courtroom maverick and the bane of magistrates and judges (he had been censured on several occasions by the Bar Association), had been ailing and in semi-retirement for three years and the firm was being held together by the hard-working Norris Robinson, who was himself past the age of retirement. Apart from these, there were a number of junior partners, youngsters of Raymond's generation. It had always been Robinson's idea that Raymond should be part of the firm, working his way up from the bottom, but Raymond, while agreeing from the beginning to be 'associated' with his father's firm, had decided that what he really wanted (once he'd acquired the money and the experience) was to take over the firm entirely – hence the 'negotiations'.

The deal was concluded on Thursday morning and Raymond was elated. That evening he decided he would go to Daphne's tea the following afternoon, feeling able to take on, in his euphoria, the glib politicians and the dyspeptic academics. So it was that at 5:30 on Friday evening he was seated in the large veranda of the Shepherd home in Bel Air Park, devouring one of Daphne's delicious shrimp patties and sipping her home-made soursop juice which, in his judgment, made the afternoon worthwhile.

'I know you can't resist my soursop punch, Raymond my dear,' Daphne said loudly. 'Your father was just the same, although your mother never could acquire the taste...' Then she leaned closer to him and whispered: 'I have a bottle of it in the fridge for you to take home, but don't let any of the others know.'

Raymond was really glad that he had come, for not only was the food and drink to his liking, but good old Daphne had thought of everything. True the politicians and academics were there (his entrance had interrupted a heated exchange between the minister of health and a professor of sociology well known for his research into prostitution in Georgetown), but he'd noticed at once the presence, in a corner of the veranda, of Mr. Justice Ramcharitar, whom he had known from childhood as Uncle Ram, and whom he admired and respected. He had settled at once into the little wrought-iron chair next to him. As they sat sipping their drinks and munching on Daphne's snacks, Raymond began to tell Uncle Ram about his takeover of the law firm.

'Oh yes, I heard all about it from Norris,' the judge informed him. 'I think you should consider yourself damn lucky. Anyway, Norris is pleased; he thinks the firm is in good hands and he can retire in peace.'

'I think he believes I behaved shabbily at the outset.'

'Oh, you probably did, but you're the son of Jeff Rose and that means that Norris will forgive you anything – short of physical assault. Your father was his idol.'

Raymond was happy to hear this as he worried that he had perhaps been a little too tough and uncompromising in concluding the deal. Just at that point, however, Daphne swept onto the veranda accompanied by a woman of stunning beauty who immediately commanded everyone's attention, including Raymond's, despite the greying hair that signalled that she was at least in her mid-fifties.

'Now let's see, Lillian my dear,' Daphne said, 'whom haven't you met? Does everyone know Lillian de Cunha, my neighbour from down the street?' And the woman went around the small gathering, kissing cheeks or shaking hands with the other guests. She seemed to have brought with her a kind of excitement, a sense of drama that enlivened the atmosphere. Raymond took it that this was because of her striking appearance and her poise. He stood and held out his hand as she approached him.

'Oh, Lillian, this is Raymond, Raymond Rose, the young lawyer who's been winning all his cases and setting the women's hearts afire – not that he pays them any mind...'

'Well, I know about him from reading the papers,' the woman

167

said, taking his hand. 'It's so good to meet you,' and, as she looked into his eyes, Raymond thought he detected a flicker of anxiety – it was there for the briefest of moments and then gone, banished by her smile and what seemed to Raymond an almost professional charm. He was intrigued, not just by the woman and what he imagined he'd seen in her eyes, but also by his own reaction. He had never really been excited by a woman; he'd had several female friends and a few sexual partners over the years, but none of these relationships had become serious nor prolonged, precisely because his feelings always seem to have been engaged only on the surface. There were times when he'd begun to wonder if he was capable of commitment to a serious and lasting relationship – or even capable of falling in love – whatever that meant. The only thing he was certain about was that it had never happened to him.

As he had looked into the eyes of this woman, Raymond had the strange sensation that he was renewing an old and clandestine acquaintance. He felt both a twinge of excitement and the simultaneous conviction that this was quite absurd, since he had never met the woman. She moved on to greet others in the room and Raymond resumed his seat, but did not immediately resume his conversation with Judge Ramcharitar, as he was lost in thought, besieged by unfamiliar emotions.

'You seem quite taken with Miss Lillian, my boy,' the judge said. 'But then you're a man, no different from...'

'Miss Lillian,' Raymond repeated the phrase, as though tasting it in his mouth for the first time in ages. 'You know, I'm sure I've heard that name before, but I can't remember...'

'I'm sure you have, my boy, although you are really a generation too young to be fully aware of what it means. Miss Lillian is what would have been known in a previous age as a 'courtesan'. She was – some say still is – Georgetown's most famous courtesan. She is certainly its most beautiful. I suppose that she now belongs to an era, a world that is fast fading.'

'You mean she's a prostitute?'

'Come, come, my boy, one would never use that term to describe Miss Lillian; she's too beautiful, too refined: her traffic in the pleasures of the flesh is too delicately managed and too intricate and exciting for such a word to describe it justly. A prostitute is what our professor friend over yonder writes about: one of those desperate and brutalized women who pose along certain streets late at night hoping to be picked up by men cruising in their cars – women who are as likely to be repaid for their favours with a beating as with money. Miss Lillian would not be caught dead in such a scenario. No, 'courtesan' is a much better word; she is, after all, a lady...'

Raymond was only half-listening to this, for his eyes followed Miss Lillian around the veranda; he noticed the style with which she moved, greeted people, tossed her head and laughed, inclined her head conspiratorially towards the ear of a smiling politician, as if to impart a tastefully risqué reminder about a shared experience in the past. When she had disappeared inside to visit Daphne's tea-table, Raymond continued to see her in his mind, his frisson of excitement now heightened by what the judge had said. And he could not escape the haunting familiarity of the name, as it repeated itself in his head. He had definitely heard someone say 'Miss Lillian' long ago – perhaps one of his more worldly and knowing high-school classmates, passing on the prurient gossip of the time that fuelled their teenage fantasies.

'Well, boy, I can see you're still most impressed with our courtesan,' the judge said, rising from his chair. 'I'm afraid I have to run: Indra is having a few people over for dinner – that's why she isn't here – and I promised to be home in time to give her a hand. Must go and plead with Daphne to release me.'

As he saw the judge walk through the glass doors in quest of Daphne, Raymond was uncertain what he should do. If he remained in his chair in the corner he would feel isolated and awkward, but as he looked around he did not see a group he cared to join. In his mind swirled the exciting thought of Miss Lillian, but he felt panic at the possibility that she might emerge onto the veranda and choose to sit next to him. As it happened, he soon saw Alister Shepherd, ever the thoughtful host, coming over to keep him company. Noting that it was already quite dark outside, Raymond thought it was safe to ask: 'Well, Alister, how are the orchids doing?'

'Oh, very well, thank you, Raymond. Ramcharitar always thinks that he's in his courtroom and must be the first to leave –

it's a wonder he doesn't require us all to rise! Anyway, seeing you quite abandoned in the corner here, I thought I'd come over and keep you company for a while – or better yet,' he said, suddenly eager, 'come with me, I want to show you something.'

'Not your orchids,' Raymond said with a frown; 'it's too dark outside.'

'No, no – well in fact yes! But it's not what you think – oh, just come, for heaven's sake,' he said, and got up and moved towards the door. Raymond could only follow.

As they got to the sliding doors to the living room, they stood back to let Daphne and Miss Lillian pass onto the veranda, Raymond being again struck by the latter's poise and beauty. Alister Shepherd took Raymond into his study, took a book out of a desk drawer and handed it to him.

'Advanced copy; just got it yesterday. What do you think?'

It was a soft-bound book, very well produced, with a wonderful, glossy cover: *Orchids of Guyana*, by Alister Shepherd and Tony Cole; the front cover below the title was divided into nine squares, each a colour photograph of a flowering orchid.

'This is wonderful, Alister,' Raymond said, 'very handsomely produced. I had no idea that you were working on this.' He turned the book over to read the blurb on the back.

'I'd mentioned to Tony years ago that we should do it,' Alister said, beaming, 'but you know how these things are – neither of us did anything for years; then I met this photographer chap...'

Alister droned on as Raymond read the back cover and flipped through the colour photographs inside. It really was an impressive reference work and Raymond was disposed to revise his opinion of Alister as a pleasant but boring dilettante. He noticed that there were orchids in the book named after him – and after Tony. But when he handed the book back and Alister pulled out a box file and insisted on showing him all the photographs that did *not* make it into the book ('too costly, you know – all of this glossy colour photography'), and went on at great length about the history of its production, Raymond's positive feelings dwindled and he said that he really had to go.

He realized that he had been in Alister's study for over half an hour and when they returned to the veranda about half the guests had already left. Raymond went around saying his goodbyes. When he got to Miss Lillian, she smiled and extended her hand and Raymond found himself doing an extraordinary thing: instead of shaking hands, he took the hand and, bending over, pressed it to his lips.

'It's wonderful to meet you, Miss Lillian,' he heard himself say. As he kissed the hand, a faint whiff of some exquisite perfume reached his nostrils, seeming to convey the promise of sensual delights far beyond his limited experience. Her smile widened, but again Raymond thought he saw a flash of anxiety in her eyes – though nothing disturbed the surface of her charm and self-possession. Raymond thought he had begun to glimpse, for the first time, all that the word 'woman' could mean.

Daphne saw him to the stairs, handing him his bottle of soursop punch, wrapped in a plastic bag. 'Thanks for coming,' she said. 'It wasn't so bad, was it? You should get out more often, Raymond, you can't work all the time.'

When Raymond Rose got home that evening he felt restless. A ripple of disturbance had crept into his calm and carefully ordered life. He had always been self-analytical and keenly aware of his moods and the feelings and the circumstances that influenced them. He wondered how his carefully cultivated sense of security had come to be threatened. It was 'Miss Lillian', he knew, but in what sense? It was absurd to imagine that he was in love with her; she was twice his age; besides, it seemed to him to be something more *personal* than love, though he was not sure what that meant. He reasoned that it couldn't be his perception of her sexual attractiveness and availability. It was true that Judge Ramcharitar's discussion of her was mildly arousing, but Raymond had always prided himself on his resistance to the imperatives of the flesh. He enjoyed sex when it happened. He'd had various 'visiting relationships', but nothing for which he felt he could give up his 'freedom' – his desire to be in control of his life at all times. So it couldn't be that he had just been ambushed by sexual desire or succumbed to a 'feminine mystique' that he had never experienced before, or really believed in.

Some time after midnight he was in bed, but unable to sleep. 'Miss Lillian', he heard someone say inside his head. Suddenly he

171

sat upright in bed; he got up, turned on the light and held his head in his hands. It came back to him in waves, a childhood memory, something that he had not thought about in years. He walked down the dark corridor in his pyjamas to what used to be his parents' room, before he'd remodelled the house five years ago. He stood at the door, transported in memory to his childhood. He pushed the door ajar: the room was quite different now, a guest room with twin beds with identical green, patterned bedspreads; but he could see, in his mind, his parents' double bed against the far wall, with its mosquito net let down around it. His mother sat at her mirrored bureau across from the bed, her hair loosened, her pale blue nightgown almost transparent. His father sat on the edge of the bed in pyjama trousers, the net against his bare back. Now the room was half-lit by a street-lamp out on the road, but then there had been the warm yellow glow of a bedside lamp.

'It's no use, Jeff,' his mother was saying, 'I know all about her.'

His father sighed and said nothing.

'I'll say this for you,' his mother continued, 'you go for the best... nothing but the best. She's beautiful, and dressed in the best of everything... the best there is, but still a *whore!*' She spat out the last word with a venom that had startled the eight-year-old boy at the door, who did not understand all that she was saying, but read infallibly her feelings as she said it.

'It's late,' his father said; 'I'm in court tomorrow; can we discuss this another time?'

'Why, Jeff? Why do you throw me aside for that... that... Miss Lillian? Miss Lillian who makes all the husbands avert their eyes and wink and snicker at the mention of her name – and makes all the wives nervous, imagining, knowing that many of their husbands visit her... Oh Jeff, I thought we were beyond that... Why?'

'Yes, why?' his father had said, his voice rising. 'Ask yourself why. Why on earth would a man with a beautiful wife, a young son, a good home and a promising career go rooting, like a stray dog among the market bins, for scraps of sexual favour? Ask yourself why? – and look good into that mirror as you ask...' Raymond had watched his father get up from the edge of the bed and walk over to the open window. Looking out he had continued: 'One child, *one child!* And sex becomes boring, irrelevant, something to be gratefully transcended... It has served its purpose... That may be how *you* feel, but for me it's different... I'm still a young man, I still smoulder with the desire that you are no longer willing to satisfy... But it's late. I'm in court tomorrow...'

The child Raymond hears his mother's terrible sobs and watches her body shudder on the stool in front the bureau. He starts to scream outside the bedroom door, and feels the scalding urine run down his legs onto the floor. They both rush towards him...

The adult Raymond gently closed the bedroom door, as though closing the covers of a long-lost children's book he had just found and reread, only to be disturbed by a fairytale he had not thought about in years – and he would have laughed at the suggestion that its terrors could still affect him. He went back to his room and back to bed, 'Miss Lillian... Miss Lillian' in his head.

The next morning, after sleeping fitfully, Raymond lay in bed thinking. Another memory awoke. He is eleven; it is the day of his father's funeral. The graveside is full of lawyers and judges, everybody in black, men and women. Raymond himself is in a little black suit: his first suit is a funeral suit, and he only ever wore it once. It is very sad, everybody looks sad; his father died young of a terrible disease. His mother is trying to be strong. She holds onto his hand but he can feel the dry sobs that shake her body. He looks up at her face: it is hard, determined. She has become that terrible thing, a widow. Raymond and his mother are among the last at the graveside. There is a figure in black waiting in the distance, under a tree; she was not at the graveside during the burial, but as the last group is leaving she approaches slowly. His mother's grip tightens on his hand and she drags Raymond to one side so as to pass close to this other figure, walking in the opposite direction. As they pass, Raymond is not looking, but he hears his mother spit. They do not stop. He looks back and sees the other woman stop and take a handkerchief from her purse; she wipes her face without turning around. Raymond has not seen her face. When they get home he overhears Uncle Lawrence say to his mother in the kitchen: 'I know you're upset, dear – and she should never have gone there – but you should not have done it... to demean yourself like that!'

'The nerve of that Miss Lillian!' was all his mother said.

Miss Lillian lived in an extraordinary fever in Raymond's mind for the next few weeks. He went over and over his memories, as though he were preparing a difficult case for trial. He juxtaposed his recent memory of the elegant and stunningly beautiful woman he had met with the dim memory of his father and his mother's sad, hard face. He now discovered that somewhere deep inside he had always admired the woman in black at the graveside for not saying a word, not turning around, just taking out the hanky and wiping the face he could not see. There were times when he felt like laughing wildly, times when he felt like crying. He wondered if this was what had shaped what he had become: serious, driven, self-absorbed (he now realized) – incapable of love?

In the end Raymond decided that he now knew why Miss Lillian had had such a powerful effect on him at Daphne Shepherd's tea party. There was a *personal* reason, after all. He felt very close to the woman from his father's past, which was also, for the first time, his own past, he now realized. He felt closer to his father than he had ever felt before. As a child he was always resentfully aware that he was considered a 'mummy's boy', relying on her for his sense of security; depending on her approval or censure to shape his response to the world. As a fatherless teenager, however, he had rebelled against her, and proceeded to construct what he has always considered his 'own' self. Since he was fifteen he had belonged to nobody.

Now he could discern the unacknowledged hand of his father in the shape of his world. His father had turned to Miss Lillian for passion; he, who had never known passion, felt it beginning to stir within him as he thought of Miss Lillian. Perhaps she might be able to release him from what he now, for the first time, considered to be a self-made prison – as she had done for his father.

Miss Lillian became an obsession. It did not interfere with his work or his routine, but his life – his mental life – expanded to include this new longing. He would meet her again, but not immediately, not until he was ready. He had first to savour her in memory and from afar. Raymond Rose did not stalk Lillian de Cunha; he knew better than that; but he arranged it so that he managed to see her often, in the distance, innocently, without having to go out of his way. Each time he saw her his longing increased. Eventually he started to write her a letter. He started many times, but couldn't get it right. Then, after a sleepless night, he got out of bed early one morning and wrote her a poem:

A LOVESONG FOR MISS LILLIAN

In the pulverized dawn
after sleepless nights
I find at the open window
the morning air charged
with the subtlest fragrances
that are signatures of you.

This is the gift of memory, perhaps,
(mine, and that of another before me)
memory strong enough to spark
the foolish riot of my blood;
and yet, how memory's power slips
and falls when the flesh is sad, needing
the touch of a warm hand, the nape
of a new world against my lips.

So I set forth in this paper boat
stirring the cold spaces between us,
as though paddling towards a star
down a reluctant, unfamiliar reach
of my life's river, hoping to harbour
in the calm certainty of your love.

He reread it every morning for a week, refusing to alter or revise it in any way. Then he typed it, put it in a plain envelope and mailed it to her – anonymously.

★   ★   ★

Like most people in their late fifties who live alone, Liliana de Cunha was keenly aware of the process of ageing. 'I am getting old,' she was always writing in letters to her daughter and the many overseas friends with whom she corresponded. Her constant letter writing, she recognised, was an attempt to devour the drift of time and the pain of distance and loneliness. But Liliana had another recourse: she had long relied on a friend, a professional fortune-teller in the Amazon city of Manaus, to ensure that she was not ambushed by the future and its unexpected terrors. Lenor Araujo, her friend, worked with photographs: her distant clients would send her a recent photograph of themselves (and twenty American dollars) and she would send back, in a week or two, a 'reading' of what the future held – usually in a single typed page.

Every year Liliana de Cunha obtained such a reading of her future. She considered it a prudent and necessary investment to safeguard her from the unexpected. She considered that Lenor had served her well over the years, having forewarned her about a car accident nearly ten years ago – she had not driven since that warning; Lenor had also predicted the acquisition of her home in Bel Air Park, the emigration of her daughter Tara to New York, and the unexpected demise of Sir Eustace Clarke, a leftover expatriate from colonial days who was until then her principal client and source of income. Her fortune-telling friend's only notable lapse was her failure, over five years ago, to predict the burglary of her home. It was her most unpleasant experience in all her years in Georgetown. She woke one night to discover a man in her bedroom, emptying her jewellery-case. He waved a gun at her and said that if she moved or opened her mouth he would kill her. He tied and gagged her before he left with what he wanted. The very next day she had written to Lenor, complaining that she should have been forewarned. She also immediately acquired a golden retriever and had him trained as her watchdog and companion in the house. She called the dog Samson, one of the names of Guyana's president, which she hoped would imbue the creature with sufficient authority and menace to enable it to protect her property and person.

A few days before Liliana turned up in the middle of Daphne Shepherd's tea party, she had received her annual 'reading' from Lenor. As well as translating them from Portuguese, these letters had to be 'interpreted'. She had to make sense of what the fortune-teller wrote in terms of her current circumstances. The letter seemed to contain one specific prognostication that filled her with dismay: her home was going to be burgled again – or at least there was going to be an attempt: '...another man will force his way into your home...' was her translation of the operative sentence from Lenor's letter. At first Liliana wondered if this could be a mistake, but she reasoned that, having made all that fuss about her lapse the first time, Lenor would have been very careful to get it right this time. But would not Samson, who was always in the house, warn her if anyone tried to get in? And what about all her new locks and bolts and wrought-iron protection at the windows?

Here was something else to add to the worries of her old age. She was also worried about money. Her daughter sent her something every month from New York – in addition to the occasional barrel of foodstuffs and other goods – but, although she was grateful, she was not comfortable with the idea of living off her daughter. A few kind gentlemen from her past sent her gifts of cash from time to time, but her major source of income, several thousands of dollars a month, could not be guaranteed for much longer. It came from the last (she told herself) of her big clients, Mr. Matthew Anderson, who had founded a rum-distilling business which he had owned and run for most of his life, until he was persuaded to sell it at the age of seventy.

Never having married, Matteo, as Liliana called him in private, lived in a small apartment beneath the house of his niece, Babsie, who looked after the old man and his finances. Liliana had been for years his only source of carnal pleasure – indeed probably his only source of pleasure. He had arranged her monthly stipend fourteen years ago and had increased it several times over that period to keep pace with the slipping value of the currency. In recent years their assignations had diminished to a sad routine: Babsie would drop him at her house every Tuesday at noon: they would have a meal, with wine, followed by Liliana's famous *crème brûlée* dessert, which he adored. The afternoon of 'lovemaking' that followed had become more and more farcical, as Matteo's aged body now refused to cooperate. Ever the perfect courtesan, Liliana had become gentle and solicitous – where in the past she had been teasing and provocative – and he grew to be quite satisfied with her tender, but inconclusive fondling. Always claiming that he had enjoyed himself immensely ('Just like the old days, my love... just like the old days! God bless you...'), he would have her phone for Babsie at six o'clock.

One Tuesday afternoon, a few months before Liliana had heard from Lenor about the impending burglary, she had left Matteo sitting in the living room as she retreated to the kitchen to put the finishing touches to their meal. For the previous three weeks nothing physical had occurred between them; they just sat close and talked. He would sometimes stroke her hair, or touch the outline of her breast. This Tuesday, however, when she re-entered the living room she found Matteo naked, his clothes scattered about the room, a strange look in his eyes. Samson was eying him enquiringly, his head tilted to one side.

'Oh dear, what have you done, Matteo? You've taken off all your clothes...'

His lips and tongue trembled as they always did these days when he prepared to speak: 'Getting ready,' he said, 'ready to do... the thing. Why don't you undress?'

'But my love, we haven't had lunch yet, aren't you hungry?'

'Lunch was lovely,' he said, puzzled, 'but Babsie will soon be here... We must do it now, or the children will find us... Besides, I'm all pumped up...' and he attempted a mischievous grin.

Liliana glanced down at the limp flag of his withered penis, slumped disconsolately against the inner thigh of his left leg, and could think of nothing to say. As she looked at his face she saw the long string of dribble that hung from his trembling lower lip. She saw, as if for the first time, the profusion of large, dark-brown moles and other discolourations on the light-brown and droop-ing skin of his face and on his fitfully heaving chest. His hands shook as he clutched the handles of the armchair and his right foot twitched, the toenails thick and grey. On his left foot he still wore a fawn-coloured sock, rolled down to the heel. Liliana suddenly glimpsed, as she looked at him, a reflection on her own life to come: its fragility and shame, the graceless attenuation of beauty, of physical capacity, of hope... She wept for her life, for her loneliness, then she called Babsie.

'I will miss the allowance,' she whispered to Babsie, as the two women helped him down the stairs, 'but I don't think you should bring him here any more; it's not fair to him. I blame myself for not realizing it sooner.'

'Don't blame yourself, Miss Lillian,' Babsie said loudly, oblivious to the old man's presence. 'I know you've been very kind to Uncle Matthew. In fact I think you're the only reason he's still alive. These days he doesn't really know Tuesday from Thursday. If he ever asks, I'll say either that Tuesday has just passed or is still a few days away; he won't be any the wiser. As for the money, that's handled by the bank through a debit advise memo, and will probably continue, at least for a while.'

Although she had continued to receive her stipend for the next two months, Liliana prepared anxiously for the day when the cheque would not arrive. And now there was warning of another burglar... She felt that her world was closing in on her. It was in the midst of these concerns that she had looked, on the evening of the tea party, into the face of Raymond Rose as she shook his hand. When she heard the name, and realized who he was, there was a momentary confusion as she saw again the face of his father, the only man that she had ever loved, as she had told herself and several of her closest correspondents – after he had died. She instantly realized how much the son resembled the father. She had also remembered the incident in the cemetery, when she foolishly decided to say her own goodbye to Jeff Rose and couldn't wait until the next day. The boy, of course, would not remember all that.

Although she knew that she could probably still mount a campaign of seduction which would land her some new and rich client who would pay for the privilege and pleasure of her womanhood, Liliana shuddered at the idea. She had reached, she felt, retirement age. Until recently she'd dreamed of settling down with a man she loved to a life where *she* would be the one enjoying all of life's pleasures, instead of anxiously providing them for a fee. Now she felt doomed to the company of the old and decrepit, like Matteo, and she wondered if she should not accept her daughter's invitation to retire to New York and live with her in the new flat. She was accustomed to facing her problems head on; now she felt vulnerable, no longer in control.

She remembered the time, a few years ago, the year before the president died, when the people in the customs department were giving her a hard time. They took to charging her exorbitant amounts for the outfits of clothing and the few luxury items that her daughter sent her in barrels from New York. It was the time of the barrels: everyone received them from relatives abroad – it was the only way life could be made bearable in those days.

When she complained to her friends they had told her: 'You don't know what to do? Just offer the customs man a raise. Is only money they want; that's why they giving you a hard time.'

But Liliana could not bring herself to be involved in bribery. When she could bear it no longer – seeing her friends import all kinds of expensive things without paying duty, while she paid through her nose for the most ordinary of items – she made an appointment to see the president. She had met him socially at cocktail parties and public functions and he seemed to know everything about her. In those days she, and everyone else in Georgetown, it seemed, enjoyed the excitement of her notoriety ('The deadly Miss Lillian: she can afflict your husband's heart – and a spot eighteen inches below it – from fifty paces...'). She was nevertheless surprised at how readily the president agreed to see her.

As she walked into his office, he neither looked up or greeted her or offered her a seat, but continued writing on a pad in front of him.

'I hear you named your dog after me.'

Liliana was taken completely by surprise and it took her a few seconds to recover. 'Samson is also a name in the bible', she said uneasily.

'Of course it is, my dear Miss Lillian,' said the president with a smile as he rose and shook her hand. 'Won't you have a seat and excuse my bad manners – I couldn't resist the temptation to tease you a little.'

Liliana put her hand on her chest and sighed, then she chuckled: 'I wondered if you were going to have me arrested,' she said. 'Forbes is too good a name for a dog and Linden I have never liked, so Samson seemed the least problematic.'

'Is he as handsome as me?' the president asked.

'I wouldn't go that far, although he can be quite intimidating when he wants to be.' She gave him a meaningful look. 'But I don't want to take too much of your time, and I'm here about something else altogether.'

Then she made her complaint about the customs officers, even mentioning the remedy her friends had recommended.

'You're quite right to refuse to break the law by offering bribes to government officers, my dear; you're far more likely to be arrested for that than for naming your dog after the president! But I don't think a woman like you should bother too much about a few sweaty customs clerks – one or two choice phrases from your lips and a withering look would surely put them in their place. Be your magnificent self, Miss Lillian, and don't let them upset you. I offer you Shakespeare's well-known words about another beautiful woman like yourself: Cleopatra. 'Age cannot wither you, my dear, nor the *customs* stale your infinite variety: other women cloy the appetites they feed, but you make hungry where most you satisfy."

'Oh!' Liliana exclaimed, 'I never expected to be so shamelessly flattered by my president! Shakespeare and all... Well! I'm sorry to have bothered you about this, but I do feel better now that I've unburdened myself.'

They chatted a minute or two longer and then he stood behind his desk and shook her hand again. As she was about to go through the door, she heard him say: 'You know, you should have named him Odo!' When she looked back he smiled and waved his hand dismissively to indicate that she need not respond.

At first Liliana doubted that her visit to the president had achieved anything, but every time she received a barrel after that, although it was opened and its contents prodded a bit, she was never charged a cent of duty. Such memories of her resourcefulness and ability to cope in the past she dredged up to buoy her spirit in the bleak present. But she was not always pessimistic and would cling to any positive signs in the world around her and distract herself with the foibles and humorous behaviour of people she met. She was, for instance, in buoyant mood one afternoon as she sat down to write a letter to her daughter, Tara.

My dearest Tara,

I must thank you again for the lovely dressing gown you sent me via Desmond's aunt, who returned on Sunday. She brought me your parcel on Monday night, along with the wonderful news about your new apartment. I'm glad you're doing so well, my dear.

I'm really writing, however, to fill you in on the latest that is happening to me down here. Would you believe that your mother, at her age, has received an anonymous love poem? I have copied it out for you on a separate sheet (enclosed). Isn't it charming? – even if a little obscure in parts. What do you make of it? It's certainly good for a laugh and I've put it up on my little notice-board in the hallway – to cheer me up when I'm feeling down.

The thing is, I think I know who wrote it. As you will remember, Professor Savoury at the university invites me every year to give a talk to her Latin American Literature class on the Brazilian poets. Well, I did it a couple of weeks ago and there was a shy and nervous student – quite cute really – who sat in the back paying rapt attention. When I was finished he was the only one to ask a question and was so nervous about it that I had to help him along. During the coffee after class he came up to me and managed to stammer out that he'd really enjoyed my 'lecture', as he called it. I felt so pleased that he should go to all that trouble to be nice to me that I did what was probably a foolish thing: I kissed him on the forehead. Of course the others 'Oooh-ed' loudly and he was mortified, poor boy, but Professor Savoury told me later that he was quite bright, and a bit of a poet himself, so I have no doubt it was he who wrote me the poem. Whatever, I'm flattered.

Anyway, my dear, I must go and prepare dinner for Samson and myself. Will write again soon...

But two weeks later Liliana found herself in low spirits. It had been raining a lot and she'd been stuck in the house for a few days.

She was not bothered at first; she'd managed to take Samson for a brief walk most nights, using her umbrella. These days she tended to use Courtney, her taxi-man, very sparingly, as she was fearful of his monthly bill. On Thursday night, however, when she'd phoned her friend Alice Jardine to say that she would be thankful for a lift to town on Friday to do her weekly shopping, Alice had informed her that her husband and the two boys were taking the car, early Friday morning, to drive to the Corentyne for the weekend – something about horse-racing at Port Morant. Liliana resigned herself to having to postpone her shopping until the following week. There was enough in the house to feed herself – the only thing was poor Samson. He had eaten the last of his favourite dog food three nights ago and had grown tired of the rice and table scraps she had been feeding him. That Thursday night he had staged a hunger strike in protest. Liliana, fearing that Samson might become too weak to tackle the expected burglar (and this could explain how Lenor's prognostication was going to be fulfilled), decided that, come what may, she would have to get to a shop the following day to buy his bag of dog chow.

On Friday morning she found out by phone that there was a shop not far away, on Sheriff Street, that sold the brand of dog food she needed. She dressed and decided that she would walk over there when the rain eased up a bit, then she would phone Courtney from the shop to come and drive her home with the heavy bag. As it happened, rain fell heavily all morning and into the afternoon, and the only time it had seemed light enough to venture out was when she was in the middle of her lunch. Liliana looked around her spotless home – the dark, polished floor, the expensive drapes from New York, the mahogany dining table with matching chairs upholstered in dark leather, the glass-fronted china cabinet, all the ornaments, carefully dusted and arranged... What did it all mean, she wondered, on the verge of tears, if she could no longer do something as simple as go out to the shop. It looked to her more and more as though she would have to sell everything, as so many people in Georgetown had done, and go to New York and live with Tara.

It was not until four o'clock in the afternoon that she managed to get out of the house. The store was not far, but the rain, though light at that time, was steady, and the afternoon traffic on Sheriff Street was very heavy – she was splashed a few times by passing cars and cursed under her breath in Portuguese.

When she had made her purchase, she asked if she could use the phone to call her lift, but learnt that the phone in the shop did not work when it rained. She had to go upstairs into the owner's home above the shop to use the phone there. Courtney's wife informed her that he'd left twenty minutes ago to take someone to the airport (Why hadn't she let him know that she would need him this afternoon?). She then called Hassan, whom she had used occasionally, but nobody answered. Liliana decided right then that she would emigrate to New York.

Wishing she had bought the smaller bag of chow, she hefted her purchase and made her way onto the street. She had to stop after two minutes to open her umbrella as the drizzle became heavier. With her purse over her shoulder, umbrella in one hand and shopping bag in the other, she moved awkwardly along, comforting herself with the thought of how happy her daughter would be when she received the letter saying that she would join her. It was at this point that Raymond Rose spotted her as he was driving along in the opposite direction in his BMW.

Because of the traffic it took Raymond a few minutes to turn around, but he soon caught up with her, stopping as he drew alongside. By this time it was raining quite hard. Raymond lowered the passenger window and opened the door.

'Please get in, Miss Lillian,' he said. 'We can't have you walking around in the rain like this.'

Before she realized who it was, she was protesting that she was already wet and would make a mess in the car.

'Think nothing of it,' Raymond insisted, and Liliana gratefully climbed in. 'You remember me, I hope,' he said as she closed the door and turned to look at him.

'Oh', she said, 'I hadn't realized – it's Mr. Rose, isn't it?'

'Please call me Raymond,' he said. 'We met a while ago at Daphne Shepherd's tea party.'

'I remember very well,' she said, 'and I'm very grateful for the lift; you've rescued me from a good soaking.' She looked sideways at his profile as he negotiated the heavy traffic. She could not help

184

reflecting wistfully on the youthful male confidence she saw in him, that so sharply contrasted with her own mood and circumstance. She told herself sadly that a man like Raymond was precisely what she had forfeited forever by choosing the life she had... To banish such gloomy regrets, she told Raymond how she came to be walking in the rain.

Raymond reached into his top pocket and took out a business card. 'Look,' he said, 'if you ever need transportation again, or anything else, just give me a call at the numbers on the card; if I'm not there someone will find me and give me the message. You shouldn't be walking the streets in this weather and, I think you should know,' he continued, in what seemed to Lillian a strange excess of kindness, 'there is *nothing* that I would not do for you.'

'Well, thank you very much, but I really couldn't make such a nuisance of myself...'

'I insist, and you must promise me,' he said, turning into her street and slowing as he approached her drive.

'Oh no,' Liliana said, 'you needn't have turned into the driveway...' and she wondered briefly how he knew where she lived. As he stopped in front of the gate and she reached, embarrassed and confused, to open the door, Raymond said, in a tone of authority: 'Stay there, Miss Lillian; it's still raining.'

'But I'm already wet...'

Raymond got out of the car and opened the gate. Somewhere beneath her embarrassed protests, Liliana recognized the possibility of luxuriating in such attention – in such a display of care and protection and mastery. She shook her head, as though to dislodge an unworthy thought, as Raymond drove the car under the house, right next to the enclosed stairway. 'Now', he said, 'we can get out.'

'Oh surely, Mr. Rose, you will permit me to manage on my own from here. You have been very kind and already done more than enough.'

'No, I will take your bag up for you – unless you feel uncomfortable about letting me into your house.'

Liliana felt a light-headed helplessness that made her want to laugh. She had no choice but to let him follow her up the stairs. As she halted on the top landing to fumble for her keys, she could hear his breathing behind her and she felt a sudden thrill of

185

excitement and fear. She dismissed it as a kind of professional reflex, sprung from her years of physical transactions with men. She had become too sensitively attuned to male breath and bravado... As they entered the hallway, Liliana was surprised and horrified to see Samson throw himself playfully upon Raymond, his tail wagging wildly, his forepaws up on Raymond's waist. Raymond dismissed Liliana's profuse apologies and her scolding remarks to her dog. ('Honestly,' she told him, 'he's never done anything like this before.') He chose to take its behaviour as a good omen, although he told Liliana: 'He probably knows that it's a bag of his dog-food I'm carrying...'

Raymond slipped off his shoes and followed Liliana into the kitchen in his socks. Just before he entered the spotless kitchen, he noticed his poem pinned to a small notice-board – another happy omen.

'Well,' Liliana said, when he had deposited the bag on the counter, 'you have done all that you possibly could for me – far exceeding the requirements of kindness and chivalry: I thank you most sincerely and promise that I won't ever allow myself to be such a nuisance again.' She moved as if to see him to the door, but Raymond stood his ground.

'I'm sorry, is something the matter?' she asked nervously, feeling again that premonitory thrill of excitement mingled with fear.

'Aren't you going to invite me to spend the night?' Raymond asked simply.

She caught her breath sharply, refusing to look at him, afraid of what she might see in his face. 'Please,' she said, 'why do you make fun of an old woman. I still have some feelings, you know – and my pride...'

'I never make fun of anyone; least of all a woman like you,' he said, his voice tense.

She turned and looked sharply at him to see if he was mocking her, but on his handsome brown face, so reminiscent of his dear father's, she saw something as familiar as it was unexpected – an intense look of male sexual longing that took her breath away. Her heart pounded with excitement and she felt herself dissolving at the knees.

'Well, are you?' he asked again. Then a note of pleading crept into his voice: 'I know I practically forced my way into your home, but I cannot help the way I feel...'

'Oh,' she said weakly, almost in a whisper, 'do as you like.' As she turned away from him her thoughts were racing. What he had said about forcing his way into her home made her realize that she had misinterpreted Lenor's letter: *this* was what she meant – not another burglary – *this*, that she would never have dreamed of, never dared to hope for – *this*, the solution to all her problems, *this* was her future, and not the confines of a miserable flat in New York. As she thought of being consumed in the youthful energy of his perfect body, a shiver of anticipation seized her and she turned to face him with a smile.

THE BATS OF LOVE

by H. A. L. Seaforth

At the graveside at Lloyd Cadogan's funeral I had hoped to remain on the fringe of the mourners, since I felt awkward about my own role in his life and death; but in the cemetery it quickly became clear that there were two distinct groups in attendance: the small party of Lloyd's family and family friends and a large gathering of the curious, who were attracted by the scandal of the dead man's suicide and rumours of the derangement that led to it. This latter group kept back from the grave in a wide circle. Under the circumstances I felt I had no choice but to attach myself to the smaller group immediately around the grave. Mama, Lloyd's mother, acknowledged me with a nod, her face streaked with tears. It was an especially gloomy occasion, as we were all mourning not so much the death, as the events stretching far into the past that ensured the sad waste of a very promising life.

After the interment no one chose to linger at the graveside and while we were walking back to the cars, Mama came over to me and leant on my arm.

'Ah David,' she said, 'I'm glad you came – glad that you were here at the end, when this happened, since you were so close to him at the beginning...' I said nothing but patted the arm that held onto mine. 'Listen,' she continued, 'you have to come home with us – we're all going there now – just for an hour or so. I know you're busy packing...' and a sob shook her large frame. We stopped and she turned and looked into my eyes: I nodded and we went quickly to the cars.

The house seemed strange, as though the absence of Lloyd was something palpable, something that clung to my skin as soon as

188

I entered. Everything in the living room was as it had always been, since my earliest childhood when I used to come running in with Lloyd from the veranda or off the street, headed for the kitchen or for Lloyd's bedroom, for we weren't allowed to play in the neat and polished living room. The piano stood in its corner, where Mama taught music to generations of students; the walls were hung with photographs, many of Lloyd at various stages of his life: in school uniforms, primary and secondary; in his Sunday-best after church; he and I standing in our scout uniforms on the stelling in front of the M.V. Powis, about to embark on one of our scouting jaunts to the interior; a shot of him as a student on a railway platform in England (self-consciously aware of the un-wonted encumbrance of a dark, heavy coat); and a the studio photo of him in his graduation gown, (a photo which I had insisted he have taken and which came out with him looking much darker than he was in reality – as though it was the policy of the photo-studio in Leeds to avoid offending their black customers by ensuring that they appeared as black as possible). Also on the wall were the framed certificates of O-level and A-level results, of his degree, and the yellowed clipping, from the local newspaper, of the photograph and story that appeared when he won the Guyana scholarship.

But I felt strangely out of place among all these familiar reminders of his life and mine. This was the first time that I'd been in the house without him, and I kept half-expecting him to emerge from his room. Mama and her nieces had prepared lots to eat and drink – black-eyes and rice and stewed chicken and black pudding and souse and heavy coconut bread – but no one seemed to be in a mood to eat much. We nibbled quietly and sipped our ginger beer and talked in hushed tones about the things we remembered in the life of the dead man – the good life, that is, before the first breakdown – the life of incredible brilliance and promise. Mama came over to me and quietly took my hand and said, 'Come.' I followed her down the corridor to the first door to the right, which she opened – Lloyd's room. I saw the neatly-made bed, the shaded light hanging from the roof, the bookshelf, the wardrobe, the desk in front of the window.

'This is where I found him,' Mama was saying, composed and

189

dry-eyed by this time. 'I knew his light had been on all night, which was not unusual, as you would know: he frequently read or worked at his desk until foreday morning, so although I was worried about him, I didn't look in on him when I got up – it was quiet and I thought I would let him sleep. It wasn't till nine-thirty that I tapped on the door and opened it, and then I saw him hanging there...' – she indicated the stout wooden beam that ran across the room beneath the slanting roof – 'and there was like smoke in the room, or maybe not smoke but the smell of burnt paper, and when I look in the waste bin I see ashes and burnt scraps of pages: some of his old essays, I think. One scrap was saying something about love poetry.' On the desk was a large brown envelope which I picked up. 'May I?' She said, 'Of course,' so I reached in and pulled out a dozen or so pages of typescript that had become discoloured with age and handling. I knew what it was before I looked down at the title page: '*The Bats of Love: Poems* by Elena Gutierrez Ramirez. Translated from the Spanish by Jeremiah Lloyd George Cadogan'. This, I thought, he could not bring himself to burn.

'I know that that is something from you all days at university in Leeds,' Mama said. 'I often saw him reading and reading those pages and I knew his mind was back there in those happier times... Would you like to keep that – to remember Lloyd?'

It was clear that she thought I would be happy to have this memento of her son and of our joint past as students in England, so I said, 'Thank you very much, Mama,' and gave her a hug. She could not know how painful a reminder this particular typescript would be for me. On the little notice-board on the wall next to the window was a reminder of more recent pain: the little flyer put out by the University of Guyana announcing the two-week Summer Workshop on 'Critical Writing about Literature and the Arts, conducted by Professor David Adams of the University of the West Indies, Cave Hill', and giving details about dates, cost and registration. That was all over now, I reflected gratefully, but it had turned out to be the final push that had propelled my dear friend over the edge. I hesitated in front of it for an instant, wishing I could tear it down, but I turned instead and followed Mama out of that painful room. When I got back to my hotel

190

room it was dark and I began to pack my suitcase, determined to focus my thoughts on my departure the following day.

The LIAT flight to Barbados departed on time shortly before noon. I had slept badly the night before, staving off the inevitable self-confrontation that Lloyd Cadogan's death made necessary and urgent. As the plane took off and climbed above the brown rivers, I decided that the two-hour flight would be given over to a review of the life and death of Lloyd Cadogan, and my part in these. By the time we landed in Barbados I hoped to have laid some ghosts to rest.

★   ★   ★

I don't remember a time when I didn't know Lloyd Cadogan. From the infant class at Main Street I remember him, tall and silent, his large eyes looking on apprehensively as Sister Brian lashed me on the legs with a tamarind whip. Nothing like that ever happened to him: he was, even from then, a perfect student. Lloyd wrote out his letters and numbers neatly on his slate, recited his Hail Marys and other prayers flawlessly and did not talk in class. I was the unruly one, always in fights, my slate cracked and my slate-pencil lost, my letters and numbers indecipherable, my shirt-tail out of the pants. I remember Lloyd telling me once with genuine concern, when we were in second standard: 'Miss Gill only beats the bad boys, you know; it's not hard to be good – just stay quiet, don't say anything, and do your work,' and I remember really wanting to do as he said, but I could not. I suppose he felt protective of me because I was so hopeless and because my uncle took us both home in his car after school. He would pick us up outside the gate and drop us both off at the top of our street and we would walk down. Lloyd's house came first and I would invariably go in with him, hoping to play till nighttime, but Mama would always send me packing after a few minutes because 'your poor mother must be frantic with worry – it's nearly quarter to five!' And I would walk down the street for what seemed to me like ages, cut across a pasture and arrive home through the side-gate – frequently without my cap or book-bag or some other item, forgotten 'over at Lloyd'.

191

It must have dawned on me at some point that life would be more peaceful if I managed to do at least the minimum amount of class-work and homework necessary to get by, because I did keep up with Lloyd, moving steadily up the school, even skipping third standard, until we both ended up in the scholarship class. It was in the scholarship class that I first got Lloyd into trouble. We were walking home one afternoon after extra lessons and had finished too late for us to catch my uncle. We came upon a laden mango tree in somebody's yard on Lamaha Street. Before Lloyd realized what I was doing, I had picked up a stone and flung it at a bunch of mangoes. Miraculously, and entirely contrary to my expectations, I hit the bunch and about five mangoes fell. Ignoring Lloyd's advice to leave them alone and walk on, I was over the gate in a flash and picking up the mangoes when this lady came up behind me and grabbed my collar. Apparently Lloyd had been shouting, 'Look out, you idiot! Run! Run!' But I hadn't even heard him. The lady carried on for several minutes about how shocked she was to see boys in Main Street uniforms stealing her mangoes, and she ended up by demanding to know my name. Sensing that she might let me go, I told her, but she continued to hold onto my collar and asked for the name of 'your accomplice at the gate, the boy shouting at you to run when he saw me coming.' I had no choice but to give her Lloyd's name as well.

The upshot the next day was that we were hauled before Sister Joseph, the Headmistress, and given six lashes each in front of the whole school. It was a shocking occasion – not because of me: people were surprised that it was the first time I'd been flogged by the Headmistress – but Lloyd Cadogan! Lloyd Cadogan who had *never* been beaten by a teacher since he'd entered the school; that was shocking indeed. Everyone, without having to hear the story, knew immediately that it was 'that wretched David Adams' who was to blame, and even Sister Joseph said as much, going on, as she administered his lashes, about bad company leading him astray! As usual, I was weeping even before the first lash; but what I and everyone else found amazing was the fact that Lloyd did not shed a single tear: his face remained serious and composed throughout. The only thing he said to me about the incident was: 'Next time I'll know better than to hang around and get blamed for your wickedness.' I was relieved to discover that he was still talking to me.

Lloyd won a big Government scholarship and I scraped enough marks to get a lesser award and we ended up at college together. At college it dawned on me that Lloyd was an exceptional student – he immediately found his way to the top of the class in most subjects and quickly attracted the delighted attention of the teachers. I, of course, was at first far too busy enjoying myself with new friends and participating in sports and clubs to pay any serious attention to school work. I was content to drift along somewhere around the middle of the class. In second form I joined the scouts and one afternoon, when I turned up at Lloyd's house in my scout uniform, Mama asked Lloyd if he wanted to be a scout. He said he didn't know, he'd have to think about it, but the following Friday he turned up at scout meeting, and in a couple of weeks, he too was in uniform. Lloyd took scouting very seriously, of course, and in a short time he'd accumulated many badges and was made a patrol leader, and a very good one, too.

A couple of years later, at one camp at some mission in the interior, Roy Sankies and I became aware that several of the younger scouts had a lot of money that their parents had given them for the trip, but there was nowhere to spend it where we were, so one rainy afternoon we cooked up a deal with Bertha, the barefoot teenage girl from the village who swept the school in which we slept. We would charge the young scouts a dollar a time to view and touch Bertha's bubbies. Bertha would get half the takings and Roy and I the other half. We rigged up a groundsheet across one corner of a classroom and Bertha did her thing behind there and the boys lined up and paid their dollars and disappeared one by one behind the sheet – while Roy and I collected the money. God knows how Colin Bishop ('the archbishop', as we called him), our sanctimonious troop leader, got wind of what was going on, but he stormed in and shut down the show, vowing that he would report us to the scoutmaster and have us kicked out of scouts and probably out of college as well. He added for good measure that we would also certainly end up in hell at the end of our days. A couple of the youngsters were in tears. Shortly afterwards Lloyd came looking for me, having heard about the fiasco, and that was the first of several occasions on when he had to lecture me about my behaviour. It's funny because he was only two months older than me and we were in the same class, but my respect for him was so great that I listened in silence. In fact I was very impressed by what he said about responsibility and about whether I ever thought about my parents and the good name of my family when I got involved in these hair-brained schemes. He sounded like an adult and he seemed so genuinely disappointed in me that I remember being thoroughly ashamed and fully repentant. Then he spoke to the youngsters about scout rules and about respect for women and he calmed their fears about ending up in hell. Then he looked at me and said quietly: 'Never let me hear anything like this again; I will have a word with the arch-bishop.' And that was the last any of us heard of the incident.

In the sixth form it was a foregone conclusion that Lloyd Cadogan would win a Guyana scholarship. We were both in the Arts sixth, Lloyd taking Modern Languages and Literature and I doing English Literature, Latin and Ancient History. By this time I was capable of short, but intense bursts of concentration on my work, and I was actually doing quite well, much to my own – and everyone else's – surprise. Over at my house one day Lloyd pointed out to me where my problem lay. He'd been looking over some of my recent essays (at my mother's behest) and he said: 'You see, none of these teachers questions your ability and understanding, only your steadfastness and your will to finish the job properly,' and he pointed out the frequency of such marginal comments as: 'good point, but it needs amplification' and 'interesting argument, but you need to support it with textual quotes and references...' He turned to my mother: 'Everyone's clear the ability is there, Aunt Mavis, he just needs to spend a lot more time on his work and take more care.' So that became my mother's mantra for the next year: 'What do you mean you're finished? Go and read it over and make sure that there is nothing more that you can say...' I was resentful, but I kept getting better marks.

When the exams came Lloyd was a nervous wreck, uncharacteristically unsure of himself and sick to his stomach before each paper. For me, not nearly as much was at stake – I was not going to win a scholarship so, although I studied hard, I took the exams in my stride. When the results came out, Lloyd got his four As and I actually got an A in English Literature, with an B in History and a C in Latin. I was euphoric. We had both applied, long before the exams, to several British universities, and I begged Lloyd to choose one of the three that had accepted me (he was accepted by all). Lloyd, with his scholarship, chose to go to Leeds, and my father said he would pay for me to go there as well, so that Lloyd could keep an eye on me! So in 1970 we both ended up in Leeds, living on different floors of the Mary Morris, a brand new hall of residence for foreign students.

★ ★ ★

I suppose it was inevitable that we would not be as close at university as we had been in school. For me the university, Leeds, England was a whole new world, full of wonderful distractions; for Lloyd it was simply a change of scenery in which he continued to live the one life he knew – that of intense study and scholarly reading and writing. He was like a hermit in his room – when he was not in class or in the library – and emerged only to prepare his meals. Very rarely would I see him in the TV lounge, and when I did he was only there to look at a specific programme, disappearing as soon as it was over: not like many of us who were there not to watch specific programmes, but to watch TV, period – whatever was on. In my case, since there had been no TV in Guyana, I was making up for all those lost years.

Then I met Linda, a Welsh girl, and was amazed to discover that she was interested in me. Before university I'd never sat in the same classroom with a girl and the result was that girls now became a major distraction from my studies. I'd always considered that it was a kind of 'duty' for boys my age to pursue girls in the hope of some kind of sexual favour (in my mind this was unlikely to be sex itself – which couldn't be that easy – but some kind of physical proximity or contact that would fuel my fantasies and longings until I managed to advance a step further, perhaps with another girl), but it never crossed my mind that a girl could/would pursue a boy for the same reason – and it wasn't really the same reason either. Linda's ideas about what we might do together were not along the lines of coy explorations and small advances over time. She was typical of a modern culture that had long decided to short-circuit such time-wasting preliminaries and home in on the big event. But although she kept repeating it as plainly as she could, it took a while for me to realize that she *wanted* to sleep with me. I knew there were men in the residence who had girls in their rooms overnight, but from what I could see, apart from the mature students, these were mostly hot-blooded Turks and Persians, whose oriental aura, I presumed (this was long before I'd heard of 'political correctness'), attracted women the way the musk of gaudy, exotic blooms attracts insects. When the enormity of Linda's suggestion finally came home to me I was in a fever of excitement and apprehension. I consulted a few of my English friends in class as well as some of the other West Indians in the residence, particularly the four Trinidadians who lived on my floor. None of them thought it was any big thing and advised me to go for it. One Trinidadian, whenever we met in the corridor or the kitchen, would sing out: 'Ay-yai-ai, Dave-o, you fix the date yet? Look na, man: any night of the week is a good night for losing your virginity.' I was mortified when others nearby would look at me and laugh. It's strange, but it seemed I needed someone to tell me 'Don't do it, you'll regret it', so I went to see Lloyd in his room and, in his wisdom, he did advise against it. I should think about my parents, he said, and didn't I already have sufficient distractions from my studies...?' It was exactly what I wanted to hear, so I went ahead and happily made the arrangements with Linda and I lost my virginity one overheated Saturday night in my room. It was a very unsatisfactory thing really, but there were other nights and it got better. I was devastated when Linda decided she'd had enough of me and moved on to somebody else, but I quickly got over it...

There were other distractions: I had a couple of cousins down in London and I was frequently down there for weekends, going to the pub or playing dominoes all night in their council flat. I visited all the landmarks I'd heard and read about from child-hood, just to say that I'd seen them. Then I became a football fan, going to most of the Leeds United home matches at Elland Road – and the occasional away match if it wasn't too far – and that was in the days when Leeds was a top team, with Billy Bremner and Jackie Charlton and Eddie Grey and Peter Lorrimer... And when the cricket season came around I would spend lots of time down the road at Headingley and travel to Nottingham and Old Trafford for test matches, even if it wasn't the West Indies playing. I persuaded myself that all of this was a very important part of my education.

But of course my university studies paid the price. When the final year began (so suddenly, it seemed to me), after a wonderful summer of bumming around London, Paris and the south of France with a girl called Abby and a bunch of other happy vagabonds, I realized that I was not ready to take final exams in a matter of months: far better, I thought, to take the year off and travel some more, get the wanderlust out of my system and give myself time to get tired of chasing women and sports teams and then come back the following year and complete my degree... I wrote my parents what I considered a reasoned and reasonable letter outlining all this. They phoned me the night they got the letter. My father was horrified and wanted to know if he had been paying all that money just to have me abandon my studies so close to the end. What, he wanted to know, did I propose to live on during my year of idleness and self-indulgent travel? My mother, on the other hand, couldn't say anything, she only wept into the phone until my father took it from her and hung up. The next day I found out they had phoned Lloyd as well; he came to my room to see what was going on. This became another of the occasions on which he had to lecture me and save me from myself, as he put it.

'What you're running from is the work,' he said, 'the hours of study and reading that will interfere drastically with your wom-anizing and pub-crawling and running down to London; but, whether you do it now, or come back next year or resume your studies years from now, you will still confront the necessity of having to do the work – there is no other way. What I should say to you is: "Do what the hell you want, you're an adult, aren't you?" But your mother phoned me in tears and begged me to speak to you and urge you not to give up your studies at this stage. So I'm doing this for Aunt Mavis, not so much for you, though I will tell you this: I'm convinced you could do it if you wanted – you have a sharp mind and there's enough time. All you lack is the will and determination and the necessary sense of responsibility...'

I found I had no choice and decided that since I was going to do my finals in eight months, I'd better do it properly: I threw myself into my work for the first time and discovered that I enjoyed the reading and studying in the library. I did many assignments, including a long research paper, for which I got an A – fuel for increased effort. Lloyd was not surprised at my effort and apparent success and I was a little put out at how infallibly he had read me. I wondered how many people knew that I was lazy and irresponsible and needed a kick in the ass to accomplish anything worthwhile. 'Ay-yai-ai, Dave-o,' my Trinidadian flat-mate now said, 'you give up the women and you beating book – you ent no Caribbean man for true...' This from someone who was doing brilliantly in his 'AccA' courses at Leeds Polytechnic. I made a point of seeing Lloyd more regularly than before, seeking encouragement and support – or sometimes just information: we would have long discussions about specific authors and literary periods. He always knew so damn much.

The week before finals I was feeling confident: I was thinking that I could, perhaps, scrape second-class honours, but I dared not hope for too much. One night I decided to go to Lloyd's room for a last chat about modern poetry, his speciality. When I knocked on the door there was no answer, so I went back to my room, puzzled that he was out at this time of night a few days before finals. I went to my window and checked for light in his room. I could not see into the room, but the light was on so I went back up and knocked again. I thought I heard movement inside the room and I called his name. 'It's me, David,' I said and waited; after a while I heard the door being unlocked and I turned the handle and went in. I was shocked: Lloyd's room was a disaster, there were books and papers flung everywhere, on floor and bed and dresser – even in the sink. Many of the papers were torn or crumpled, and the desk, bathed in bright light from the desk lamp, was strewn with bunches of pages ripped from books. I looked sharply at Lloyd and received a further shock: he was in tears, his face distorted and his mouth trembling and drooping at the corners.

'What's wrong with you?' I asked in horror.

'The exams!' he shouted, 'I *hate* exams!'

I was astonished by his vehemence and very worried. I wished I had the strength – the words – to help and console this scholarly giant, but every phrase that formed in my mind sounded hollow, I thought, coming from me. Eventually all I could think of to say was: 'Lloyd, don't do this... you're behaving like me.' But this only made things worse, because he began to laugh and cry at the same time and I wondered if he'd gone mad.

'You're right,' he said, throwing himself back onto the bed, 'our roles are reversed,' and he laughed loudly. Then he began to cry again, more quietly. 'I can't face the exams, David; it's tying my stomach in knots; you remember my A-levels – if it weren't for Mama constantly consoling and encouraging me, I could never have taken them. Everybody thought – even I – that because I had done so well in them, I would never suffer these exam doubts again, but they were wrong.'

'But Lloyd, you know everything,' I pleaded; 'the exams will be a breeze.'

'It's not the exams themselves,' he said, after a moment's silence. 'Once I turn over the question paper I'll be OK; it's the days and the hours leading up to that, when I can't eat, I can't sleep, I can't stop trembling, I can't shit...'

This was a revelation to me, discovering this chink in the armour of my hero. I felt as though someone had knocked away one of the main pillars supporting my world. My whole life (I now realized) was predicated on the certainty that there was an invincible, infallible champion who would swoop to my aid or rescue whenever required. It didn't make any sense to me. If I knew as much as he did about the subjects, I would relish the exams; in the period before they began I would luxuriate in the delicious sense of mastery and the confident expectation of success. Yet here was this most able and upright of students reduced to tears and destructive rage, shredding his notes and text books in despair.

'You know David,' he said suddenly, 'you're lucky; you enjoy yourself, you indulge yourself – and I'm not being sarcastic here – and yet you always end up doing what is expected of you...'

199

'Only because of you, Lloyd,' I said. 'I hope you don't think I'm ungrateful.'

He began to sob again: 'It's not that – can't you see – at some point soon you will have a university degree *and* a full and varied and rich experience of life. I will have a university degree, but will scarcely have lived; I may *die* before I experience half of what you have enjoyed over the past three years.'

'Once your studies are over,' I said, 'you will enjoy all that and much more. You will enjoy everything much more than I do because you will be much better prepared.'

'No,' he said, 'I think you're wrong. Marvell was right.'

'Who?'

'Andrew Marvell, the poet: we *don't* have "world enough and time", only the briefest opportunity for pleasure and happiness, and then... nothing: "yonder all before us lie deserts of vast eternity". I will enter those deserts without ever having tasted life – except vicariously: the little bit I've sniffed in books and from knowing you – your activities and experiences...'

'Oh, Lloyd,' I said, 'don't get me scared with that kind of talk, please. No one could be further from being a role-model than me. I beg you, don't destroy your books, your notes. My "wonderful" experience of life is nothing, compared to your brilliance – you *have to* write your exams, for Mama, for yourself – for me. Just tell me what I can do to help; you've always helped me when I've been in trouble.'

He got up, took his face towel and wiped his eyes. Then, without turning to look at me, he said: 'Just stay with me in the room for a while; I just need a human presence,' and he sobbed again, 'to support me in this dark time...'

So I ended up spending the night sitting in his room; we hardly spoke. Near morning he began to clear up the mess and I helped him. At dawn he lay back on the bed and fell asleep. I left quietly. When I checked at midday he was still sleeping. He sat in my room for most of the next night, rereading a long Spanish novel, while I studied. Nothing was more important to me in those few days than Lloyd's health and his peace of mind. I reasoned it was the least I could do for one who had helped me so much in the past. We arrived at the day of the first exam and Lloyd vomited before we left for university, though the only things he had eaten over the preceding twenty-four hours were four nectarines, which he called 'curious peaches'. When he saw the exam paper he was OK – he wrote fluently for three hours and felt good afterwards. The next day he vomited again, but that was the last time. He seemed to be coping, and after the fourth paper, he seemed to be himself again. After the final exam he hugged me and thanked me profusely. The following day I went to a West Indian shop and bought ground vegetables and salt-fish and coconut and cooked and enormous pot of *metagee* and Lloyd and I feasted on it for the next few days. He left for home soon after, but I remained in London for the summer, awaiting results.

★   ★   ★

In late September both Lloyd and I were back in residence at Leeds. He had achieved a first, as expected, and his scholarship had been extended. He was registered as an M.Phil student, writing a thesis on contemporary love poetry and hoping to be upgraded to a Ph.D. candidate. I had got an upper second, which was enough to get me into a one-year coursework M.A. programme. I had decided in the summer (a very tame summer for me: I had no money, so there was lots of reading in libraries and visiting museums and galleries and even writing a bit) that I wanted to do a Ph.D. myself, but I would get there via this M.A. Lloyd brought me a big parcel of goodies from my mother and told me that he had decided to adjust his lifestyle: he planned to go out more, to spend more time with friends in the pub, see something of the rest of the country... 'How about finding yourself a girl?' I asked him, but he said that he wasn't sure that he was quite ready for that yet.

It happened, however, that a girl became interested in him. Towards the end of the first term I became aware of Elena Gutierrez, a graduate student from Peru. She was quite attractive with a smooth brown skin and long black waves of hair lapping against her shoulders. She spoke English with an accent, but quite well, although she would lapse into loud and rapid Spanish when she got excited. I had tried nibbling around the edges to see if she

201

might be interested in me, but although she was friendly, she didn't take my advances seriously at that time. Fair enough, I thought, and went down to London for Christmas. Early in the second term Lloyd gave a seminar paper on two or three Spanish Caribbean poets. It was a polished performance: of course the quotations were read in fluent American Spanish, and he knew so damned much about his subjects. Everyone thought it was a great paper, most of all Elena, who asked several questions in Spanish and Lloyd had responded in Spanish, before translating both question and answer for the rest of us. A few days later Elena came looking for me: 'Lloyd is from your country, isn't he?' she asked, and that was the prelude to so many other questions about him and my relationship to him, that I grew tired of whispering (we were in my carrel in the Brotherton library) and suggested we go to the cafeteria. It was clear that she had a crush on Lloyd, but had the impression that he didn't take her seriously, because he never seemed to have time to chat with her. I explained that he was shy and consumed by his studies, that he was an only child, had attended boys only schools and had no experience with girls. I offered to have a word with him on her behalf, but she immediately said no.

'No, please, David, do not talk to him about me, that would spoil everything because he will think that I am after him.'

'But I thought you were.'

'No – yes, yes of course I am, but it's not good for him to know this from somebody else, believe me.'

'So what are you going to do,' I asked, looking at her across the cafeteria table.

'I don't know yet – nothing – he will like somebody whom he can admire for some achievement, I think...' And we chatted on for some time, ending up talking about her and about Peru and Guyana.

There were many such conversations in the following weeks and I grew quite fond of Elena, and comfortable in her presence. Sometimes we hardly mentioned Lloyd and she sometimes permitted me to indulge in idle flirtations. Then one night she came to the hall with me and I cooked her a meal. As we were sitting to eat in the kitchen, Lloyd passed through, going back to his room from watching the news in the TV lounge – perhaps he'd passed through the flat because he had checked my room to see if I was in – at any rate he stopped and chatted with us for a while, but he declined my invitation to join us for dinner.

After he had left, Elena said, 'You know, he adores all that poetry he reads: he talks about it with such passion. If only I were a poet.'

'Well, aren't you?' I asked.

'What you mean, David? No, no, I'm not a poet, I have never written a poem.'

'Well maybe you should try; it's not that difficult. Write a few poems in Spanish – I'm sure Lloyd would be interested in seeing them.'

'No,' she said with a sigh, 'I can translate literature, but I can't write it.'

'Well,' I said with a mischievous grin, 'you could always settle for second-best.'

'What is second-best?'

'Me.'

And she laughed and said: 'Oh, David, you know I like you: you are the only person who talks to me – no, I mean you are the only person who lets me talk and talk...'

'I'll tell you what,' I said, 'together we can write some love-poems, you can translate them into Spanish and we can present them to Lloyd as yours...'

It was, I see now, another of my 'hair-brained schemes', as Lloyd would have called it, and to tell the truth I didn't really think that she would agree to it. In fact nothing was agreed but that very night we went to my room and fooled around with a few lines from something I had written in the summer.

Without definitely agreeing on anything, we kept meeting in my room and fashioning lines of love poetry – in English first, then she would translate them into Spanish. Before we realized it two things had happened: first, we found ourselves in the middle of this writing project to which we seemed to have become committed; and second, we had drifted, just as inadvertently, into physical intimacy. The two things fed on each other: composing and translating images and poems of love fuelled in us a surprising passion for each other – and vice versa. Our intimacy proceeded in measured steps like a slow dance. She seemed to delight in our mutual exploration of each other's body with our hands (perhaps this is a Latin thing), and by the time we actually went to bed together (weeks later) we were already thoroughly familiar with all the bumps and hollows, the flats and narrows, and knew how to summon into shrill conversation all our eager blood...

It seemed at one time as though we were going to abandon the project of the poems: it had become, after all, just an excuse for us to be together. But such things tend to develop a life and momentum of their own. We grew very fond of our concocted poems and it became necessary to show them off, and who better to judge them than Lloyd? So they were duly typed up: twelve poems on fourteen pages, and Elena had fun doing the title page: *Los murciélagos del amor: poemas. Por Elena Gutierrez Ramirez* – and, near the bottom of the page, the year: 1974. She took the typescript to Lloyd's carrel in the library and told him she had typed up some poems she'd been working on and would be grateful if he would look at them and tell her what he thought. She was not pressing him, but if he had the time she wondered if he might care to translate one or two of them into English, so that her friends in Leeds could read them – she had tried herself, but had found it impossible.

Apparently Lloyd's first comment was: '*The Bats of Love*, what a wonderful title!' And, after flipping a few pages, 'I'd certainly like to read them, and I will let you know what I think. I'm not sure about translating them, though, I might not be able to spare the time; but let me see how things go – and thanks for letting me read them.'

Actually the title had been something of an 'in' joke between Elena and I. The poems had lots of bat imagery, particularly tactile imagery about the skin of bats, because it had emerged in our mutual sexual explorations that Elena considered the scrotum was like a bat – a warm sack of wrinkled skin – and the erect shaft of the penis, like the taut membrane on a bat's open wing to the touch. So she would say: 'Oh David, your bat of love is in full flight tonight,' and I would probably reply: 'Well it's dark, and there is ripe fruit in your low branches...'

204

As it turned out, far from not having the time to translate the poems, Lloyd allowed the little typescript to take over his life entirely. He became obsessed with the poems. He told Elena that he was very excited with her collection: the imagery was startling and original and as love poetry her work was powerful and disturbing. The moment I heard this from Elena, I became apprehensive and wished that we had abandoned the whole idea. Elena was not too worried – in fact she was rather pleased at Lloyd's enthusiastic response and she felt certain he would want to translate them.

'But Elena,' I said, 'they are *already* translations – and while it may be mildly interesting to see how his translations compare with the originals – I don't think it's fair to let him go through all that; he will be taking precious time from his research. The whole thing is a deception, a lie, and we have to let him know before it's too late.'

But she would not hear of it: 'Oh but he has not *said* anything about translating it yet; let him have some fun with the poems, he's obviously very excited by them – we can tell him later that it was all a trick – I mean a joke.'

'Trick or joke, it's very cruel,' I said. 'Lloyd is a formidable scholar, but I've discovered that he's quite frail in certain respects – emotionally – and I don't think we should put him through this.'

'I will take the responsibility; just let him have them for a little while more, please...'

What could I say?

The Sunday morning after this conversation Lloyd came into my room, clutching a sheaf of papers; his eyes were bright with excitement: 'Listen to this image, David,' he said, 'It's from one of Elena's love-poems – give me your honest opinion about it; I think it's fantastic; I will read the passage in Spanish first and then the translation I made. This is from the title poem:

Cuando el sol se pone
el corazón va de caza
como murciélago liberado por la oscuridad
a comer las frutas en tus ramas mojadas...

And in English:

205

The heart goes hunting at dusk
like a bat liberated by darkness
to feast in your damp branches...'

Before I could say anything, he flipped over a page and went on: 'Here's another one, tell me if you can't actually feel the sensation of a bat and the thrill of fear it inspires:

La superficie del amor es suave
al tacto, como una ala desplegada
en la noche, rozando tu mejilla
y llenando tu corazón de miedo y felicidad.

And my translation:

The skin of love is soft
to the touch, like a stretched wing
that brushes your cheek and fills the night
with fear and wonder...'

'Well, I don't think...'

'You see,' he said, not letting me speak; 'it's wonderful stuff, and so fresh, so full of real feeling. She *has* to get this published... I will do the English translations... Perhaps *London Magazine* or some other journal.'

'Look, Lloyd,' I said, raising my hand, 'take it easy – it sounds like fairly ordinary love poetry to me.'

'Ah, but you're not an expert, you're not writing a thesis on precisely this kind of imagery and its cultural provenance and the way it encodes a repressed emotional life... This has to do with a whole world of experience and sensation in a particular geographical and spiritual context – oh, never mind! You will appreciate it when you see it in print. I must get back to work.' And he left as abruptly as he had burst in.

I was devastated. I didn't know whether to laugh or cry. I cursed my short-sightedness in creating yet another monster – and of the very person who had been strong and compassionate enough to slay all my monsters in the past. I wanted to rush up to Lloyd's room with all our drafts and discarded efforts and *make* him see that the poems were a hoax. It had to be done sometime, and it would be more painful the later we left it. But I could not do it; perhaps I lacked the courage. I told myself I needed the guilty support of Elena at that time. I telephoned her, but she could not be located.

Two tense days drifted by and I could not find Elena; a friend thought she might have decided at the last minute to attend a conference on Culture and Translation in Birmingham, and had left on Sunday – if so, she should be back by Wednesday... Late Wednesday night Elena knocked on my door. She was coming from Lloyd's room where he had summoned her 'to help him with the translations'.

'Elena, are you mad!' I shouted. 'Do you know what you're doing?'

'*Yo sé*, I know, David, I know – is problem,' and tears came to her eyes. 'All night I am telling him – I *try* to tell him that I did not write those poems, *pero* he would not listen. He said, "Of course you did not write them, you are the mouthpiece of a whole culture, a way of apprehending and feeling..." David, he does not believe me, he talks and talks about translating and publication, he is *como loco, no?* And I can no longer talk to him...'

We decided to go back up to his room at once and show him the folder of drafts, but he would not open the door. He kept shouting: 'Go away, I don't believe your lies. You, David, have put Elena up to this to cheat me of my first chance of pleasure and prominence in this world. You think I don't know that you two are lovers... I must translate these poems, for her sake and mine.'

We went back to my room and I typed a long letter explaining how the whole deception had come about and apologizing for his pain and wasted time, and put it in the folder. I would make sure he saw it the following day. Elena said she was scared and wanted to spend the night with me, but I called a taxi and sent her home.

Early next morning I went up again to Lloyd's door. 'I'm not speaking to you,' he said from behind the locked door. His voice sounded weary.

'I don't want to speak,' I replied. 'I have something for you.'

He opened the door; I looked past him, afraid the room might be disordered, as on that night before his finals, but everything seemed OK. I pushed past him and flung the folder on the bed:

'Read that, for God's sake,' I said, and walked out of the room shutting the door behind me.

I don't know when he actually read it, because he did not speak to me for ages after that morning. For days I never saw him and then when I did, he made a point of ignoring me. I blamed myself, I considered I deserved his contempt, but my heart grieved for the loss of his friendship. My exams were approaching, however, and I used the fact that I had to prepare for them as a way of hiding from the hurt I felt about Lloyd. Once or twice I would see his sad and drooping figure in the distance and I wondered if he was grieving like me. I consoled myself with the thought that at least this exam time would hold no terrors for him as he did not have to write exams, just work away at his thesis. I tried not to, but I think I blamed Elena for what had happened. I used the excuse of exams to see very little of her and I suppose it was inevitable that we should drift apart.

In the middle of the exams I got a message that Lloyd's supervisor wanted to see me and I turned up at his office just after my penultimate paper.

'Ah, Mr. Adams, isn't it? So good of you to come. This is about your friend Jeremiah.'

'Who? Oh yes, sorry, you mean Lloyd.'

'Mr. Cadogan – isn't his name Jeremiah?'

'Well, he is Jeremiah Lloyd George, but his family and friends call him Lloyd.'

'Good heavens, why would anyone permit himself to be called Lloyd when he has such a wonderful first name as Jeremiah?' He smiled and shook his head. 'I'm just a little disturbed by the fact that I haven't heard from Jeremiah – ah, Lloyd – for quite some time, and I have not been able to get hold of him. I have some work of his that I need to give back and it's about time for him to hand in some more of his draft so that I can recommend his upgrading. He did, though, send me a note, some weeks ago to say that he'd found an exciting new collection of poems – by a Peruvian woman, I think – and he was excited at the prospect of translating it...'

'Well, I'm fairly certain that he has abandoned the translation project, Professor, but I didn't realize that he's not been around.

I don't think he's gone away anywhere. I will try to find him and let him know that you're looking for him.'

'Would you? Excellent. I know you live in the same residence, he's spoken often of you... That's fine, then. As soon as you find out anything, just let me know.'

The next few days I spent looking for Lloyd and worrying about him: he had apparently been seen on his floor up to a few days before I spoke to his professor, but no one had seen him since then. His room, duly opened by the warden of the hall, contained no clue about where he might have gone, but he didn't appear to have taken much with him and his passport was in a desk drawer. The warden informed the police that he was missing. It was the day before my final exam so I had to resume my revision and I spent a troubled day in my library carrel. The exam went quite well and that evening, just as I was rehearsing what I would say to Mama on the phone (for it was time that she were told), word came that Lloyd had been found.

He was discovered, all bearded and dishevelled and his clothes filthy, doing a black-Lear-on-the-heath thing at the ruins of Fountains Abbey, north of Leeds, near Ripon. Apparently for some days tourists at the Abbey had been puzzled and amused by this unkempt black man who was pacing up and down the site reciting poetry in a strange language and gesturing wildly. At times he would laugh loudly; at others, tears ran down his face. He walked off down the road in the evenings and would reappear the following day – God knows where he had been sleeping and eating all this time. The story made the local newspaper and Lloyd was sectioned and taken to the psychiatric ward of St. James's hospital in Leeds for observation. Within weeks he was back home in Guyana. Elena Gutierrez and I had a long, guilt-ridden conversation in a corner of the cafeteria. We deeply regretted what we had done to Lloyd and also, perhaps understandably, what we had done together in those feverish nights of sexual dalliance and poetic composition. We saw very little of each other after that, and when she left Leeds that summer, I never heard from her again.

★ ★ ★

When I returned to Guyana in August of that year, I was very apprehensive about meeting Lloyd. While he was in hospital and preparing to return home, I'd spoken several times to his parents, but I had not told them the whole story. I feared that Lloyd would have told them by now, and that I might no longer be welcome in their home. I was also fearful that the sight of me might upset him, particularly since he'd had to withdraw from his studies. As a consequence I did not go to visit them as soon as I arrived. When I ran into Mama a few days after in Fogarty's, however, she gave me a huge hug and a kiss and seemed hurt that I'd been in the country four days and had not gone to see them. She brushed aside my fear of upsetting Lloyd.

'He isn't in the same state as when he left England, you know; he's recovering very well. He can never complete another degree, but he's back to his old self and he frequently talks about you, though I have the feeling, David, that he's afraid he may have lost you as a friend, since he has not heard from you. I keep asking him if you all had a quarrel, but he wouldn't tell me anything.'

This news brought tears to my eyes and I promised Mama I would visit that very afternoon.

When I arrived at the house, Lloyd certainly seemed to be his old self – in fact I wondered at first whether he remembered what had happened to trigger his breakdown; but later on, when he and I were sitting on the veranda at dusk, he told me that he hoped I didn't think that the business of Elena and the poems was what caused his illness, as it was only one of several factors. I was not sure how he worked this out, but I was grateful for the reprieve, though I told him that I would always feel responsible and apologized (as on so many occasions in the past) for my behaviour.

'Perhaps it's true,' he said with a smile, 'that the behaviour of you two was the last thing I needed at that specific time, but I've learned that mine is a clinical condition that can occur at any time of great stress or anxiety. It's an illness that cannot be cured, though it can be kept in check by carefully avoiding stressful situations and I have medication to help keep me calm. I'm grateful that I understand it much better now, but the doctors tell me that I will never be completely safe from further episodes. It means that my life has to be simple. I have my room and my books, and – from next month – I will have a job: I will be teaching French and Spanish at college...'

All this was wonderful news and I saw a lot of Lloyd for the next month or so, and even gave a talk to his sixth form literature class when he started teaching. After I left to embark on my Doctoral studies – this time at Canterbury instead of Leeds – we corresponded regularly and I was able to send him, from time to time, books and teaching materials from England. Not long after I went to Canterbury, my family migrated to Toronto, and that became the 'home' I visited during the vacations. My contact with Lloyd dwindled to birthday and Christmas cards and the occasional long letter – from him; I was always too busy to write more than a few lines. When I got a job in the English department at Cave Hill in Barbados, I wrote and invited Lloyd over for a holiday, but he never came, and I got married and started a family...

When I first visited Guyana after a long absence and took my family around to meet Lloyd and Mama (his father had died a few years previously, as had mine), it was like old times: Lloyd and Mama were very happy to see me and to meet my family, and I returned at least once a year thereafter, sometimes on holiday, sometimes for conferences or to do something or other at the University of Guyana. It was one such 'working trip' that had culminated with Lloyd's funeral. I was always looking for excuses to get back 'home' (as I still referred to Guyana in my mind), and when Al Creighton asked if I'd like to conduct a summer workshop at UG, I jumped at the chance. This one was a workshop on 'critical writing', as described in the flyer I had seen in Lloyd's room, and would last two weeks, with three-hour morning sessions on Mondays, Wednesdays and Fridays.

When I went around to see Lloyd the evening I arrived, he greeted me with a copy of the flyer announcing the workshop in his hand, and declared that he was going to register. My heart sank at the news: I was concerned about him returning to *any* kind of 'studies', and the course was going to be a fairly intensive one. When I mentioned this to him, he said he wanted to give it a try as it might help him to do reviews and other writing for one of the local newspapers. 'I'm not sure that I can spend the rest of my life in a classroom at college,' he said. 'Besides, I'm not sure that I will

211

attend all of your sessions: I'll just sit in on one or two and see how it goes.' I felt I could hardly deny him that, but I told him not to register and pay for the course – just to come and audit a few sessions when he felt like it: I would have a word with the people at UG.

At first Lloyd was wonderful: he stood out in the group and his contributions to the discussions were excellent. By the Friday session, however (and he had skipped none of them), I detected in what he said the rasp of some powerful emotion – a desperate nostalgia, perhaps, for the days when his intellectual acuity and scholarship were recognized and celebrated. When he did not show up in class the following Monday I was happy, because I thought that he had probably recognized that he was pushing himself too hard. Lloyd phoned me on Monday night, however, and as soon as I heard his voice I realized that something was wrong – his tone was the same as on that Sunday morning, years ago, when he had burst into my room in hall to read and comment on the poems that Elena and I had concocted. There was a kind of driven, manic quality to the flow of sentences and the (now rather outdated) scholarly jargon that came tumbling out of him in that telephone conversation. I tried to suggest that he should take it easy and perhaps give the Wednesday session a miss, but he was most indignant, informing me that he had not felt that good in years and he'd stayed home only to work on his 'assignment' so that he could read it on Wednesday... With sinking heart I put down the phone when he'd finished and immediately called Al Creighton and explained the situation as delicately as I could.

'Well... OK... Do you want me to have him barred from attending the class? We can do that, I think... if you feel he will be disruptive ... I mean... OK.... it's not as if he were a registered participant in the workshop...'

'Oh, I don't know,' I said. 'I'm reluctant to go that far simply because of an impression I received over the phone. How about if we just make arrangements to have you – or security or somebody – intervene if necessary during the session?'

'We could... OK... we could do that... yes... if that's what you prefer. I'll have a word with Agnes Duncan, one of the workshop students – I think you know her – and if there's any trouble...

Well… just signal to her and she will leave the class and come and inform me.'

On Wednesday morning things started off badly. It was still a few minutes before the class started when Lloyd came to the front and announced that he was going to read his assignment and he hoped it would inspire a lively discussion and provide him with valuable feedback. I had to interrupt him and point out that it was not yet time, people were still arriving and settling down, and besides, I wanted to say a few words before any assignments were read. He seemed surprised at this, but returned to his seat. In my preamble I reminded the class that I'd asked them to read *a page or two* from either something they had written in the past about a work of art (poetry, play, painting, sculpture, music), or something that they'd written specifically for the exercise. The idea was to provoke discussion about the aesthetic values or critical perspective evident in the passage read and the appropriateness of the language for conveying these…

'I need to go first,' Lloyd said, 'because I'm not sure I can stay for the whole session.'

I held out my hands in enquiry to the class and they shrugged, so Lloyd came up to the front.

'I'm talking here,' he began, 'about a small collection of poems which I once translated from Spanish. It is called *The Bats of Love*.'

'I'm sorry, Mr. Cadogan,' I interrupted, 'but I don't think that's appropriate here.'

'Please,' he said, in an awful whining voice, 'you *must* let me have my say – I've waited a lifetime…'

I sighed and he continued, but he was not really making sense, except when he read, in impassioned tones, quotations from the Spanish version. Many of the others were squirming uncomfortably in their chairs as he turned over the third page. I reminded him of the page limit but he ignored me and read more quickly and loudly. He got so fast that what he read was incomprehensible, and there was spit flying from his mouth. A feeling of utter desolation, mingled with an ancient guilt swept over me and I looked around for Agnes Duncan – but she was nowhere to be seen. I didn't know what to do. But as it happened Agnes Duncan had already slipped out of the room on her own initiative and now

213

returned with Mr. Creighton and a couple of security officers. It was announced that the fifteen-minute break would be taken immediately and that the class would reconvene in a different room.

Lloyd was quiet by now, his body limp and there were tears in his eyes. I asked Al if he could hold on for me for an hour, as I wanted to take Lloyd home. Lloyd said not a word in the car, he just clutched his papers and sobbed. When we got to the house I went in and explained to Mama what had happened and she immediately phoned for Lloyd's cousin to come and take him to the doctor, whom she also phoned. While we waited for Bernice to arrive, Mama said she thought she had noticed one or two warning signs in Lloyd over the last couple days.

'Oh Mama,' I said, 'I know this has something to do with me. This always happens when I'm around.'

'Nonsense, David. Don't talk like that. You're the person he admires and respects most, when he's himself: he says you are his best friend.'

Then Bernice and her son Victor arrived and took Lloyd to the doctor. I told Mama that I had to get back to my class.

'Don't feel bad, David,' she said. 'I haven't told you yet – in fact I haven't told anybody, not even Lloyd – but the headmaster from college came to see me and he said he was sorry, but he couldn't have Lloyd back as a master in September: he had become rambling and incoherent at times in class; he no longer followed the syllabus and he shouted at the students and upset them...' And Mama started to cry for the son she loved so much. She said she had not yet told him, but I immediately thought that he knew, or at least suspected. Perhaps that's why he had talked of leaving the college and writing for a newspaper...

The class was in no mood, apparently, to continue the workshop after their early break that day, and Al had taken the decision to announce an extra session the following Monday instead. This was OK, as I was not booked to leave until the Wednesday. The Friday class went well, and I was beginning to feel quite buoyant again that evening in the hotel, when the phone rang and it was Mama.

'I didn't want to call you while you were up at university this

214

morning,' she said, choking back tears, 'but I have very bad news. Lloyd is dead. He took his own life this morning…' and she wailed inconsolably into the phone.

All this about our intertwined lives I went over in my mind on that little aeroplane to Barbados. I feel I cannot escape my own culpability for what happened to Lloyd Cadogan's life. He may have had a mental illness, but my own thoughtless and selfish behaviour as his friend had been an unnecessary burden he'd had to bear – and he'd borne it so well out of a sense of loyalty and duty, out of compassion, out of love… It was his misfortune and mine that I had failed to match him in these qualities, as indeed I'd failed to match him in almost everything else. As the plane touched down in Barbados, I prayed for forgiveness…

THE TYRANNY OF INFLUENCE

by Alex Fonseca

The story begins with a painter in his studio standing in front of an empty white canvas...

Several coats of white gesso have been applied and it is stretched on its frame on an easel and everything is ready – tubs of acrylic, cleaned palette, knives and brushes – and yet the painter hesitates: 'A painting is a world; the first brushstroke is the first creative word of God bringing the universe into being,' he had once said to a class and they had shaken their heads and smiled. Now the painter shakes his head as he contemplates the paraphernalia and confusion of his studio and the confusion of ideas and images in his head, the 'ex nihilo' out of which his painting must be created. It was easy for God, the painter thinks, but how to begin a world fashioned out of the gifts and materials of others? For everything in and out of his head was made by somebody else, including the deep morning light that comes in through the high windows smelling of the sea and the blue distance and the dust of an old old world... How to wring the diurnal chaos of his life in somebody else's world into the original grain or fabric of his own vision? How to know truth, let alone paint it? Why did it not help that he had done it before? There are canvases stacked against the walls and a few framed and hung to remind him of 'achievement' – so painfully distant from 'beginning' and 'process'. Some people said painting was just another work, you learnt it and you did it, but the painter's experience was different; there had to be something unknown, something both immaterial and urgent out of which the painting's world is made. The painter likes to think of it as a dream; before every blank canvas he hesitates, waiting to capture the dream, like a thundering white horse to be tamed and broken and ridden through the red mud, across the green savannah, into the black creeks or the flaming sunset. The painter's eyes sweep the cluttered walls of his studio and come to rest on a framed print high on the wall to his left – a gift from his elder brother, an important civil servant who travels with his minister to the world's capitals where he visits museums and galleries and chooses prints to take home for his brother the painter, the dreamer of worlds. This print is from the Prado in Madrid: 'The Dead Christ, Supported by an Angel' by Antonello Da Messina. Other gifts from his brother lie rolled in one of the large drawers in the studio, but a few, like this one, the painter liked and has framed and hung on his walls. He likes this particular one because it speaks to him as a painter, telling him that the forms are built of colour rather than line and shade, that the substance of art is physical, material and yet quite other than reality and no amount of trickery or illusion can bridge the gap between the two... And yet he has framed this print and hung it partly because he recognized the body of Christ as human, less heavenly than the angel, just a dead weight that the angel cannot budge ; there is no ascetic, skeletal beauty in this corpse, no halo, no extravagant evidence of physical abuse and suffering. To the painter, the wounds seem understated, functional, even harshly beautiful; all the pain, the inadequacy, the pale terror belong to the hermaph- roditic little angel, unequal to the demands of the human body in death, let alone in the full bloom and vigour of life. The painter's eyes take in the background, the bleached skulls in the muddy stream, the trees alive and dead, the distant town, the cliff-side at the right edge of the picture, the nothing of the sky... He approaches the picture on the wall, leans close to it, touches it and with only mild surprise, finds himself inside it. He is in the background behind the figures, walking down the slight slope towards the skulls in the river and the surprise comes when he turns to look back at Christ and the angel: it is a large wooden cut-out like a painted billboard, and it's supported by two slanting wooden planks invisible from the front, nailed to pickets in the soft ground. It is a painting within a painting and the painter has no urge to look at the front of it again. He continues to walk down to the river of skulls.

He wades into the stream which is very shallow, touches the

nearest skull with his foot and it rolls over and he sees that there is no lower jaw; he follows the stream off to the right and the landscape changes to the painter's own Guyanese landscape and he is wading in a shallow rocky river somewhere in the rain forest and the skulls are strewn among the rocks and only recognizable by their regularity of size and shape, for they are the same dark colour as the rocks and the river is swift and he is walking against its flow. When he dislodges a skull it rolls and is swept away until it wedges itself against the rocks further downstream. The painter looks around and realizes that he is in a gorge, the steep sides covered with thick tropical vegetation, with large boulders at the water's edge and he has the impression that he's in some earlier historical period, perhaps in Antonello's fifteenth century – but in Guyana. As he continues to wade upstream he notices that some of the skulls have clumps of hair and shreds of flesh still attached to the bone – more recently discarded skulls, perhaps and when he dislodges one of these, the stream tears away some of the remaining tissue, discolouring the clear water. Still further up-river the air became heavy with mist and he hears the roar of a waterfall; clumps of foam float down-river in the churning water and now he has to abandon the swift-flowing stream for the boulder-strewn bank and after a while he does not notice any more skulls. But before long he comes upon a band of naked Amerindians clambering over the boulders ahead of him and he catches up with them and finds that their heads are the same as the skulls down-river – the same shape and size – and he sees one old man clamber down the boulders into the river to be swept away and the mystery of the skulls is solved. Rounding a twist in the river's gorge the painter sees the waterfall; it is still some distance away but he recognises it as Kaiteur Falls from pictures he has seen. The Amerindians do not seem able to see him as he overtakes them, leaping from boulder to boulder recklessly, conscious now that he is leaping ahead in time, to reach the foot of the falls. After a while the Amerindians he encounters are in western clothes, ragged shirts and trousers, and they are carrying baskets and warishees and calabashes hanging at their waists. There are babies strapped to their mothers' backs and several children among them, whereas the earlier groups were older adults only. The painter realizes that he is nearing the present in his journey upstream and eventually he pauses on a flat boulder and looks up at the waterfall: it is enormous and its sound fills the gorge and it is wearing torn shreds of mist and spray like the tattered garments of the Amerindians and there are birds circling in the mist. There is also a small aeroplane which the painter sees but does not hear because it is high above the falls and he is deafened by the roar of the water; it is a tourist plane circling the falls and it disappears for a few minutes, then he sees it again, much lower, flying up the gorge towards him. The band of Amerindians stops to look up at it and it is now faintly audible above the roar; it circles tightly in the gorge and the painter can see the tourists in it as it banks; they are taking photographs and he can see a camera in the hands of one tourist at a window. Suddenly the plane dips and immediately rights itself, but the tourist has let go of the camera and it falls falls falls into the river ahead of the painter. Surprisingly, he sees it bob up to the surface of the water and float on the swift current and he desperately flattens himself on the overhanging boulder and scoops it out. The Amerindians can see him now, for they stand and clap their hands at his achievement and a child comes over to see the camera from close by. The painter takes a picture of the child and her brother comes over and joins her and he takes a picture of them both and soon he is photographing the entire band, with the wall of falling water as background and they tell him they are going up to the top of the falls to follow the river to their village a few days' walk away. The painter joins them and they climb wildly, recklessly, pulling themselves up the steep slope by hanging lianas and dangling roots, finding footholds and handholds on mossy boulders dripping with spray, and the band is joyful, laughing at each other when they lose footing and slide down a rock or a tree-root, but eventually they emerge upon a rocky path where there are a few sprinkles of bright sunlight coming through the leaves, now that they are beyond the cloud and spray. They walk through tunnels formed by overhanging rocks and intertwined vegetation, and there are orchids and bromeliads and tiny, brightly-coloured frogs and slowly it gets brighter and dryer as they ascend, and they are breathing a different air as they emerge into the open on a flat

219

expanse of rock where low tangled grass and a few clumps of shrubs and trees grow, and there is a discernable path which they are following and a mango tree in one of the clumps of bushes to their right and – thank you – they all eat and the children's mouths are yellow and loud with laughter and some of them are singing songs from school, and the painter takes more photographs on the move, then slips the camera around his neck again and the children grin and one of them pokes him with a stick and he chases them headlong along the path, with their parents and the other adults laughing under the weight of their warishees and back-slung babies, and the painter and the children break through a clump of bushes onto the expanse of flat rock beside the lip of the waterfall, and the running and the laughter stop, because there, on a flat stone about fifty yards from the water's edge, is the angel and the dead Christ. The angel is in tears, wings drooping, flight-feathers ruffled, his/her arms supporting the weight of the dead man and this is not a painted wooden cut-out but the real thing, a more desperate and untidy version of the figures in Antonello's painting. The painter is dumb with surprise and sadness and he takes a picture of the angel and the dead Christ and he hears the angel plead 'Help me' and responds 'Certainly sir/ m'am' and he puts down his camera and the arriving Amerindian men put down their burdens and prepare to lift the dead weight of this bearded, beautiful Italian Christ. The angel tells them to take him over to the edge of the water so that (s)he can wash his wounds and the bearers move off and the white loincloth and the blue wrap are dragging on the ground and getting in the way, so one of the Amerindian women snatches them off and bundles them in her arms and the painter and the Amerindian men are carrying the naked *Cristo muerto* down to the edge of the Potaro river near the lip of Kaiteur falls. The corpse is unbelievably heavy and the angel runs on in front, wings folded, looking for a good spot to lay the body. They reach the water's edge, carry their burden up-river for several yards, then the angel points and says 'here' and they rest him gently on a clean stone, smoothed by the running water, with the river lapping against his right arm and leg, and the angel bends down and scoops up the clear cool water in his/her cupped hands and begins to wash the blood from the

220

wound beneath Christ's right nipple. The angel is crying softly and the Amerindians are silent and sad and the children murmur in hushed tones and the painter breathes heavily and watches and the more the angel washes, the larger the wound seems to get and then the painter realizes that the river water is dissolving the flesh of the dead man and soon there is a large hole in his chest, traversed by a few smooth pink ribs, like bars on a prison window and they see that the flesh on the dead man's hands and legs is also disappearing where the river laps against it, and the angel says that this is what must happen and explains that the other body of Christ, the one that will become the flesh and bone of the resurrection, the one that is different from this heavy, awkward mortal mass, is already safely in the tomb and this human body has been brought to this remote time and place to be dissolved in an obscure river to signal the complete disappearance of Christ's mortality. And the painter recognises the intuitive imagination of another painter five hundred years back down the road who had glimpsed the secret angelic operation and produced his painted version of the photograph he had taken minutes ago, with the tearful angel and the massive corpse of the saviour, itself now beyond salvation – and that is some kind of heresy, the painter is certain, the business of splitting up the human and divine, but who is he to question an angel? The dissolution of the flesh continues until soon there is clean bone and skull like the skulls in the river below the falls and in Antonello's painting, and the painter thinks that perhaps this operation will redeem the river and the skulls and perhaps the whole country will be absolved of its historic guilt and continuing sin and sorrow... The painter witnesses the bones loosen and clatter like pebbles in the swift flow of the river, and they disappear towards the edge and then the skull bobs on the water nudging submerged rocks and grating on loose gravel as it trundles towards the lip and the angel hovers above it and watches over it and then he/she returns and says, 'Thank you people...' and unfolds wings and flies away. Some-where in a stone tomb long long ago Christ is waiting for Easter morning and perhaps that is where the angel is headed. The woman who snatched the cloths stands looking at the painter and the painter looks at her for the first time and has to turn towards the river for she is beautiful like a brown Virgin Mary and he sees a rainbow like a halo over the waterfall. He stirs a patch of water with his hand, washes his face and scoops up water and drinks and sees that the sky has begun to grow dark and he wonders where to go from here – anywhere he thinks, except back down into the skull-studded gorge. He looks around for the Amerindians, but only the one woman is left, the others have moved on, presumably up-river. The woman is carefully folding the blue and white cloths on which there is no drop of blood and she seems to be moving deliberately slowly, looking up from time to time at the painter, who notices again how beautiful she is, how strong her limbs appear, how determined the set of her jaw... 'The others have left you,' the painter says. 'Your family, your tribe, the children...' and the woman shrugs. 'I know the way and they will soon stop for the night; I will join them perhaps in the morning – your camera,' and she hands him the camera he had left on the stone where the angel stood supporting the dead Christ; he takes the camera and hangs it over his shoulder. 'Come,' the woman says, and he follows her away from the river, past a few derelict wooden buildings.

It is almost dark when the painter and the woman emerge onto the little airstrip a short walk away from the falls and there is a small plane parked on the grass off the runway and the painter thinks it is the same little Islander from which the camera had fallen into the gorge earlier that day, but it seems that this plane has been abandoned several days or weeks ago as one wheel is flat and there are large cobwebs between the wing struts and the fuselage and undercarriage. The woman opens a door near the back of the plane and tells the painter to get in because 'it will rain soon and this is a good place to spend the night' and she gets in behind him; they are in the last seat at the back of the plane and the other seats are filled with parcels and cardboard boxes. They can feel the plane shaking with their movements and the woman puts the folded cloths on top of one of the parcels in front of them and unwraps a little bundle wrapped with leaves and there is cassava bread and a few strips of dried meat – some kind of bush meat like labba or agouti – and the painter and the woman eat and drink cassiri from a corked calabash she is carrying, tied around

222

her waist. The cassiri is strong and the woman continues to sip from the calabash after the food is all eaten and soon she gets light-headed and begins to make amorous advances towards the painter. The painter rebuffs her and deliberately begins to fill his mind with holy images, like the Virgin in the 'San Cassiano Altar' in her blue mantle and with the child on her left knee with an open bible on *his* left knee and a sad expression on his face... and with images of the saints – 'St. Jerome in his Study', seen through an open archway reading a book – probably his vulgar translation of the scriptures, while his pet peacock is liming on the step outside... and 'St. Sebastian', quite nonchalant with five arrows stuck into him, and this, the painter thinks, is the right image for denying the imperatives of the flesh as Sebastian is not bothered by the arrows or by anything around him – not the polished tree behind him to which he is tied, not the drunk rolling on the floor in the background, not the small groups of people standing around in tasteful poses chatting, not the pairs of women on a kind of balcony who pause from beating the dust out of their carpets to admire the physical beauty of the martyr – never mind that they can only see bits of the backs of his arms and legs because of the tree. It strikes the painter how right Auden was when he wrote 'about suffering they were never wrong, the old masters', the world just goes blindly along, although this 'dreadful martyrdom' is not really dreadful, more like trying to be really beautiful, and it does not take place 'anyhow in a corner', but carefully posed in the middle of a courtyard or a square... and the painter's quibbles about words and images mean that his holy thoughts are fighting a losing battle, because the Amerindian woman, the keeper of the cloths, is giggling and trying to open his fly and he wants to shout and tell her that surely there is world enough and time and that this unseemly haste will only help to unravel the fabric of his imagination, but he doesn't think that she is in any mood to listen to irony or logic and he thinks he will try nonchalance, like Sebastian, but you know where that leads. Very soon he is breathing fast and squirming under her touch and they tear off each other's clothes and make wild and very awkward love in the cramped back seat of the aeroplane, all knees and elbows jammed against windows and ceiling as she straddles him and rhythmically grunts as she thrusts herself onto him, and by this time it is raining outside and there are bright flashes of lightning and explosions of thunder and the little aircraft is dancing about as though flying in severe turbulence, because of their vigorous lovemaking, which goes on for hours because every time the painter reaches a climax she is at him again in a matter of minutes, until she begins to pant with exhaustion and the painter notices that her belly is huge as though at the end of a pregnancy, and it soon becomes clear that not only is she pregnant but in labour, covered in sweat and panting. The painter is alarmed. He feels for the camera and takes a picture just to make sure, in the light of the flash, that this is really happening; the woman screams and grabs the painter's side, digging her nails into his flesh and the windows of the plane, still occasionally illuminated by distant flashes of lightning, are all steamed up and the smell of sweat and bodies is overwhelming in the narrow confines of the plane. 'The baby borning,' the woman says and the painter picks up the camera and is horrified to see in the light of the flash the protruding head, but the woman delivers it herself and its screaming fills the plane and then it stops and he hears sucking noises, and another flash photograph confirms that it's a little boy at its mother's breast – madonna and child – and then it becomes a bigger boy as the baby continues to develop at the same speed as it did inside the womb – it becomes a two-year-old before the painter's flash-assisted gaze of wonder, and then a three-year-old with teeth that bite its mother's breast and the painter wonders if this phenomenon of unnatural growth is not what really happened to the virgin, since she is frequently depicted in icons and paintings with babies of prodigious size and advanced age, sitting knowingly on her knee holding books and scrolls... The woman says to the painter, 'Give him a name, quick, or he will continue growing...' 'What name? You give him a name,' the painter replies, but she insists, 'No! The father must give him a name...' and the baby is now developing rapidly through his fifth year. 'A name... a name...' the painter is thinking wildly. 'Quick,' the mother says, 'name him now...' and the painter names him 'Antonello' and the flash reveals a six-year-old with fat cheeks and a cherubic smile and he repeats his name and seems to be happy. The woman is exhausted and relieved and says, 'Keep him for a while, I'm going out to wash myself...' The painter is dubious but has no choice as the woman opens the door and is gone and a blast of wonderfully cool and fresh air comes into the plane and the painter lets down a couple of windows, for the rain has stopped. The fresh air puts the child to sleep as he leans against his father, who makes a pillow for him out of a bundle of clothing and covers him gently with the blue cloth taken from the body of Christ, and the painter then makes himself more comfortable, leaning against the door, and soon both father and child are fast asleep in the cool air of foreday morning.

When the painter wakes up the plane is flooded with brilliant daylight and he and his son are in the back seat all dressed up: Antonello in a pair of white shorts and a blue shirt that the painter recognizes as having been made out of the cloths his mother had taken from the body of Christ. The plane is airborne and full of people, tourists who are talking loudly over the sound of the engines and the painter shakes his head and wonders how this has come about, what happened to the woman? Who made the child's clothes? How and when? How come they are flying in an abandoned plane with a flat tyre? Then he noticed the camera slung over his neck and he takes a picture of Antonello in his clothes. Someone in the seat ahead of them offers them ham and chicken sandwiches from a plastic container and requests two Banks beers from the cooler wedged in the little space behind their seat and the boy is excited, saying it is his first trip in an aeroplane and the painter asks him if he knows where his mother is, but he says, 'Mother, mother, who is mother?' and the painter, troubled, asks, 'Am I your father?' and the boy says, 'You are Daddy,' and smiles and hugs him around his chest. 'And I am Antonello,' and the painter leans back and looks out at the clear sky and tries to remember all that he has experienced since he followed the woman away from the brink of the falls. Perhaps all this is the work of the angel, he thinks. Perhaps the Amerindian woman with the cloths is another version of the angel, a doppelganger but without wings, a worker of miracles or else a maker of extravagant illusions. He tries to conjure up the woman's face in his mind, but all he can see is the sad face of the angel with a tear frozen on his/her cheek like a bead of glass and then the painter hears a voice in his head: 'Protect me from them fuckin' angels,' and he remembers the wild lovemaking in the plane and the woman's huge belly and the miraculous birth and development of the boy, and then the woman's departure to wash herself, a purification from which she has not returned – or perhaps she *has* returned and cleaned up the plane and dressed himself and the boy while they were under the spell of slumber and forgetfulness that she had woven, then put them in the back seat, removed the plane's disguises and arranged with the pilot to fly them back to town with the tourists... The boy, who has been looking out of the window, turns to the painter and says: 'Look Daddy, all those trees down there...' and the painter looks down at the uneven carpet of the forest canopy below. 'Lots of trees,' the boy says again, 'lots of wood to make lots of crosses, enough for everybody in the whole world to be crucified for ever and ever...' and the painter wonders what manner of child is this, and grows disturbed at the implications of what the boy has said – and yet he looks like an innocent and excited six-year-old out on the first adventure of his life. 'Look Daddy, now there's a big river, for all the baptisms and cleansings and conversions of the fishermen...' and the child bounces up and down on his seat in glee as they cross the wide Essequibo. Later, as they fly over the Demerara and Georgetown can be seen in the distance, and the plane begins to descend towards the strip at Ogle, the child, full of excitement, looks into the painter's eyes and laughs. 'Oh Daddy,' he says, 'you must make me a world just like this one,' and he gestures with his right hand – a wave of goodbye or love or blessing or simply of closure, for at that minute the world disappears...

In his studio in Georgetown, the painter stands before his canvas. In a corner near the bottom he has painted the boy and it is a portrait full of love. There is a smile on the boy's face and his eyes sparkle with excitement and he is wearing the blue and white outfit that the painter remembers so vividly. The painter looks again at the figure in the corner and then at the rest of the canvas. 'Now I will paint your world,' the painter says, 'a lovely world, one without crosses where you can live for ever and ever...'

And the story ends with a painter standing in front of a canvas, slowly filling it with the world he is creating for his only begotten son...

ANTONELLO DA MESSINA
Italian painter, Southern Italian school

The Dead Christ Supported by an Angel
1475-78
Panel, 74 x 51 cm
Museo del Prado, Madrid

San Cassiano Altar
1475-76
Oil on panel

St Sebastian
1476-77
Oil on canvas transferred from panel, 171 x 85,5 cm
Gemäldegalerie, Dresden

St Jerome in his Study
c. 1460
Wood, 46 x 36,5 cm
National Gallery, London

THE CELEBRATION

by Mark McWatt

No one remembered when or where the idea originated that the gang should celebrate the final day of A-level examinations, as well as the month-old independence of Guyana, at the sports club of the Imperial Bank. A few members of the gang, through parents or older siblings, had connections of some kind with the bank, but it was possibly through Alan Dummett that the arrangements were made for what came to be called, infamously, 'the Celebration'. Alan Dummett had been a sixth-former himself, three or four years previously, and was working at the bank, supposedly for just a few years, before going away somewhere to study accounting. He was one of those students who had never really left the sixth-form, always popping in to see what was going on and volunteering his services (arranging tours, fund-raising, helping with transportation) to the current crop of A-level students. At any rate it was Alan Dummett and his fiancée, Aileen Bannister, who led seven of the eleven members of the gang into the sports club that Friday evening in June, 1966. Two of them had arrived in Alan's car and the other five in Val Madramootoo's immaculate Vauxhall 101 Super, his own symbol of independence, which he delighted in driving, filled with classmates, all over Georgetown. The other four members would arrive later on their bikes or motorbikes.

'I know you all say that this is a celebration, but what exactly are we going to *do* at this place?' asked Alex Fonseca, better known as 'Smallie'.

'You will sit quietly and behave yourself, little boy,' said Nunc

DeMattis, 'while we sixth-formers, who have just completed the hard grind of A-levels, relax with a few drinks and some adult conversation – devoid of any reference to school work.'

Everyone liked to tease Smallie, who was not only the most diminutive member of the gang, but the only one who was not a sixth-former at all. He was in the fifth form and still writing O-levels, but because of his wonderful talent as an artist, he'd been permitted to take A-level Art a couple of years early. Another member of the gang, Mark McWatt, was only in the lower sixth and had also done only one A-level that year: Ancient History.

'I'm sorry the club is in mothballs, so to speak,' said Alan, as they climbed the stairs to the bar, 'but as I told you, it's being spruced up.'

'Aren't we supposed to be celebrating Independence tonight, and not just the end of A-levels?' said Jameela Muneshwar, known in the gang as 'Jamoon'. 'Seeing that we were too busy studying for exams at the end of May.'

'Oh, we're celebrating everything there is to celebrate,' Val chimed in. 'Nickie is going up into the bush in a few days and Desi is off to England... we'll have a drink or two for each occasion we can think of.'

'All-you will have the drinks, not me: you know me and alcohol – I don't want to sleep through the whole celebration.' This was from Nickie Calistro, who always fell asleep minutes after drinking even a few sips of alcohol.

'Now remember,' Alan said, as they reached the top of the stairs, 'Sir Rupert Dowding – he's the Manager of the Bank – is bound to be somewhere at the bar for his usual couple of whiskies; he's a pleasant enough fellow, just be polite and avoid any boisterous behaviour until he goes: he'll head home for dinner in twenty minutes or so – he'd better, because if he's late Pippa won't let him forget it.'

'Who the puss is Pippa?' asked Smallie.

'Shhh – Pippa's his wife – and must you be so loud and vulgar? See, that's Sir Rupert at the far end of the bar with Mr. Gonsalves. Come over and say hello... Good night, Sir Rupert,' Alan said, as the man swivelled in his bar-stool at their approach.

'Ah, young Dummett. What have we here? You look like the

Pied Piper; where are you leading that eager band of youngsters? Good heavens! They aren't new employees at the bank, are they?'

'No sir, they're sixth-formers from...'

'Thank God! For a moment there I thought we'd been luring youngsters away from school.'

'Most of them have just finished their A-levels as of today, sir, and if you remember, you agreed that they could use the club, now that it's more-or-less closed down, for a little celebration at the end of their studies, and also in honour of independence.'

'Yes, yes, of course – A-levels, eh? Never did any myself: the only place to learn banking is in a bank, I always say... but things are changing. This independence thing – I suppose we must wax festive – have everything done up spick and span to hand over to you lot... eh Trevor?' he said, turning to his companion at the bar. 'Never mind, I'm just an old leftover from a different time, you know – the world belongs to youngsters like you – but don't just stand there, have something to drink. Dornford, give these young people something to drink – whatever they want – they've just finished their exams... Put it all on my tab.'

'Thank you, Sir Rupert,' said Alan and one or two of the others as the barman began taking their orders. At that point they were joined by Hilary Sutton and Desmond Arthur, and the gang retreated from the bar with their drinks and settled into a cluster of chairs around a low table. To the right of them was a billiard table covered with the painters' canvas – the ceiling had already been painted; the walls, their cracks and blemishes filled and sanded, were awaiting their new coats of paint. To the left of the group were the glass doors to the patio that overlooked the swimming pool. Before too long the last two members of the gang arrived: Hilton (Prince Hal) Seaforth and Terry (Tennis Roll) Wong. Alan took them over to the bar for their drinks. When they rejoined the group they were followed by Sir Rupert.

'Well,' he said, 'must be off now; do enjoy yourselves and stay as long as you like. I'm sorry there's not much to do – this redecoration has shut down most of the facilities, as you see... Everyone got a drink? Good. I say, young man, what is that strange-coloured stuff in your glass? It looks absolutely vile. Surely there's nothing that colour in the bar, is there?'

'It's Vimto, Sir Rupert, mixed with a little soda water,' said Nickie, somewhat embarrassed. 'I'm afraid the hard stuff puts me to sleep...'

'Nonsense!' Sir Rupert exploded, genuinely shocked. 'You can't celebrate anything with Vimto – whatever on earth that is. It's all the beer and bubbly wines and fizzy mixes that get you drunk and put you to sleep – and that awful rum you people like to drink. Not good for you, you know. Have a proper drink and you'll be alright. In fact I'll prove it to you. Dornford – bring a little bit of my special Laphroaig for this young man; mix it with a drop or two of iced water...'

'No really, Sir,' Nickie protested. 'It's just that I can't tolerate ...'

'Just try it, my boy,' insisted Sir Rupert; 'I won't leave until you've taken a sip, you know. Can't have you spoiling the celebration – not to mention going through life with the mistaken idea that a good snort of single-malt will do you harm... Now let me see you take a sip... *Sip*, for God's sake, not sniff. No wonder you fall asleep... Good, now tell me, doesn't it send a lovely shiver down your spine?'

'I suppose so, Sir,' Nickie said dubiously. 'It tastes like alcohol mixed with swamp water.'

'God forbid,' said Sir Rupert, rolling his eyes. 'But I must be off ... Dinner, you know.' And he made for the stairs.

Soon afterwards Alan announced that he and Aileen were also leaving: they had been summoned to dinner by Aileen's unmarried maternal aunt, who wanted to meet 'the young man my niece seems intent on getting involved with'. Alan was not looking forward to the evening and promised to rejoin the group as soon as he could – although he was sure it would be quite late, as Aunt Gladys was a creature of the night, who slept during the day...

Before he had even left the club, Nickie suddenly fell over onto Jamoon, his head on her lap. He was out cold. They all laughed.

'That single-malt stuff is even quicker than rum,' Victor said. 'I've never seen Nickie succumb more rapidly.'

'I hope he's OK,' said Jamoon, as she smoothed his hair. 'He seems quite lifeless...'

'No, that's what always happens with him, I'm afraid. I've seen

230

it several times now – since he came to live in town with us. He'll be out for a few hours.'

'Poor little narcoleptic,' said Desi; 'he'll miss the whole celebration.'

'Yes,' said Mark. 'I wish he'd stood his ground and not let himself be bullied by Sir Rupert into drinking that awful Lafrog stuff.'

'Laphroaig,' corrected Val. 'But if you noticed, he only took one tiny sip while Sir Rupert was here, but he had a few more after he'd left – he needn't have...'

'He was right,' Smallie said, after taking a sip of what remained in Nickie's glass. 'It does taste like swamp-water. That Sir Rupert is a stuffy asshole of an Englishman who must have his way at all costs. I for one will be glad when the government kicks his rass out of the country now that we are independent...'

'Come on, Smallie,' Hilary said, 'Sir Rupert didn't pour it down his throat, you know; and I don't think the government should be kicking out anybody – they need all the expertise they can get to help run this place.'

'Expertise in arrogance? Force-feeding alcohol to minors? We can surely do without that,' Tennis Roll said. The argument continued for some time, until Dornford, who had been following the discussion from the bar, came over.

'I could tell all you things about Sir Rupert, hear. He's not a nice man – don't mind all his fancy talk and always wearing tie and jacket...'

'You see,' Smallie said. 'Who better to judge him than the barman he orders around as if he was a little boy? *Dornford – another drink for this youngster... Dornford, do this, do that...*'

'Well I don't mind that part so much. I accustom to him ordering me about since I was a teenager... You see, I grow up with my family in a little house just outside the fence of the big bank manager's house at Enmore...'

'Really,' asked Hilary, 'is that how come you got the job as barman here?'

'Oh, is a long story,' Dornford replied, and he proceeded to tell them about his family's relationship to the managers of the Imperial Bank over the years. His mother had worked as a maid in the bank manager's home while she was still a girl. When she got involved with a young man from Friendship (Dornford's father), the bank manager at the time, a Mr. Haggard, arranged to employ him as a kind of gardener/caretaker at the house and settled them into the little hut at the back. Shortly after Dornford was born, Mrs. Haggard insisted that his parents get married, and succeeding managers and their families kept up this arrangement and took an interest in the family. By the time Sir Rupert arrived as manager, Dornford was almost seventeen years old and a kind of yard-boy at the house; his father had become ill with diabetes and other complications. When Sir Rupert's daughter, a student at university in England, visited during the summer holidays, she apparently took a shine to Dornford, who was always working around the yard bare-chested. Lady Dowding promptly banished the young Dornford from the yard, noticing, for the first time, that he was always improperly dressed and that, in any case, his work around the house and yard left much to be desired.

His mother had consoled Dornford by pointing out that, come September, the daughter, would be returning to England and he would be able to reclaim his job. But Lady Dowding could not be seen to retract her opinion that Dornford was unsuitable for work around the house. For a time, Dornford's mother supported her sick husband and three children on her meagre wages. When his father died in hospital a year later, Dornford's mother went crying to Sir Rupert, begging him to find a job for her son. Lady Dowding relented, agreed that he might be employed as an assistant caretaker/watchman at the bank's sports club in town. From there he had worked his way up to assistant barman and then barman. But that was not the whole story: a year later Dornford's mother – still quite a young woman – became pregnant for Sir Rupert while his wife was in England for a few months visiting her family.

At this point in Dornford's story, Smallie, who had picked out a few cans of paint from a stack over in the corner, and was sitting against the wall opening them, said, 'You see, and you all quarrel with me for calling him an asshole. The man is a disgrace...'

'You are not even listening to the story,' Hilary countered, 'playing with those cans of paint. What are you doing, anyway?'

'I heard every word that Dornford said,' said Smallie indignantly, 'and don't you bother about what I'm doing.'

'Never mind him,' Desmond said. 'I want to hear the rest of the story... So what happened then, Dornford?'

'Take it easy, I going tell all you, but let me get another round of drinks, nuh?'

'OK,' Victor said, 'but you must mix one for yourself and take a drink with us.'

When they had settled down with their drinks and a bowl of salted peanuts, the barman told them how Sir Rupert, finding out about his maid's pregnancy just a week before his wife's return from England, went into panic, insisting that Dornford's mother have the baby aborted; he would give her lengthy sick leave and pay her handsomely. But Dornford's mother couldn't bring herself to agree. When Lady Dowding returned she soon discovered what was going on. She took the maid's side against her husband; she wouldn't hear of an abortion; she wanted the child to be born and be on hand to remind Sir Rupert of his shameful transgression. Thus Dornford's light-skinned brother, Timothy, was born; a placid and ethereally beautiful child whom everyone instantly loved ('They say children born into that kind of confusion does be given a special gift by God to ease them through life,' Dornford explained). Lady Dowding was completely bowled over by the little boy, and he spent more time in the bank manager's big house than in his mother's little hut at the back. Lady Dowding was not so enchanted, however, that she forgot the power that this situation gave her over her husband: she laid down the law with cruel delight, prescribing what he could and could not do and when and where. He had to be in at the same time for dinner each evening; he could not drink at home, only at the club; she also took control of his salary. The little boy was given the best of everything and was currently, aged twelve, at boarding school in England.

While this narrative was going on, Smallie had found brushes and was painting on the wall, in a bright terra-cotta, the words 'Sir Rupert is a...' in large italic script.

'What do you think you're doing, Fonseca?' asked Hilary. 'Why are you defacing the people's wall?'

'I'm painting a declaration of independence for Dornford,'

Smallie replied. 'I'm recording, for the world to see, how we all feel about Sir Rupert in this country at the time of independence.'

'What foolishness you're talking? I hope you're not going to write anything rude or libellous,' Hilary continued.

'Sir Rupert is... what, Smallie?' Mark asked. 'What words are you going to write next?'

'Oh, I think something succinct, like Sir Rupert is a mother-fucker, will get the message across,' said Smallie, contemplating the space on the wall. There was a general outcry.

'You wouldn't dare ...'

'You don't know him yet? He would...'

'He can't be serious...'

'Listen, you idiot, that wall doesn't belong to you...'

'Since the 26th of May it belongs to a free and independent Guyana, of which I am a full citizen...'

'Don't give me that shit, you know perfectly well...'

'Please, Ladies and Gentlemen, PLEASE...' This was Prince Hal in his most booming and authoritative voice. When he had everyone's attention he stretched out his arms and continued: 'What is wrong with everybody? It's not going to do any good shouting at each other like that. What is the situation? Smallie wants to paint abusive graffiti on the walls of the club because he feels strongly about what he has seen and heard of Sir Rupert. Should he be allowed to do this? The answer is probably 'No', because, independence or not, you can't destroy or deface what doesn't belong to you...'

'Is OK, you know, chief,' Dornford interjected at this point; 'the painters them coming Monday morning to start work up here – they will cover over anything that write on the wall.'

'Don't encourage the little vandal,' Hilary protested. 'It's important that he learns that independence doesn't mean that he can do what he likes with other people's property – not to mention their reputations.'

'How about a compromise,' Prince Hal continued, in his most soothing voice. 'Since the thing will be obliterated on Monday morning by the painters, he can write something, but nothing as objectionable as mother-fucker. It must be some word or words in decent English.'

'As far as I know, mother-fucker is a perfectly good English word, but if you all can come up with a word in so-called decent English that means the same thing and has roughly the same force and effect, I will write it instead... Well...'

'You have to ask yourself,' said Desmond, 'what it is you want to say about Sir Rupert.'

'I already know what I want to say: that he is a mother-fucker; it's you who have to come up with a different word.'

'No, but what does that mean? You don't mean it literally...'

'Don't I? Look what he did to Dornford's mother.'

'He's got a point there.'

'For God's sake stop encouraging him.'

'Look,' Desmond continued, 'if you want to be absolutely literal, all men are mother-fuckers when they make love to a woman who has already had a child – in which case the term loses its meaning and it's so called force. That is not what you want to convey. What exactly is it about Sir Rupert that you object to?'

'I don't know about Smallie,' T. Roll said, 'but look what Sir Rupert did to Nickie: forced him to drink his awful swamp-water and now he's going to sleep through the whole celebration.'

'He should consider himself lucky to be sleeping through this nonsense,' Hilary said.

'Look,' said Val, 'the whole thing about Sir Rupert is that he doesn't realize that he has become irrelevant. His arrogance and condescension are out of place in the new Guyana. From what Dornford said, he's behaving like an old-time plantation overseer – fathering children with his maid, keeping people in his power through unfair employment practices, bullying people into doing what *he* wants, even if it's not good for them... The man is a sad left over from the old colonial days.'

'Perhaps,' Smallie said, 'but there's not enough room on the wall for all of that, and in any case, my word says it much better.'

'You're wrong, Smallie,' Desmond resumed. 'You're ignorant of the power and resources of the English language: you don't have to reach into the gutter to find words that will convey what you mean...'

'Just give me one word, *one word*, that says what Val just said and I'll write it,' Smallie said with a smug grin.

'OK,' said Desi. 'Write: *Sir Rupert is an anachronism.*'

'And who the ass will understand that?' Smallie sneered.

'Probably everyone here except you,' Hilary said. 'You believe that the only real words are four-letter words because your own debased speech is laced with them, but you're only demeaning yourself as well as the language.'

'OK, let's have a vote,' Smallie said. 'All those in favour of mother-fucker,' and he stuck his hand in the air.

'One vote,' said Prince Hal. 'Now all those in favour of anachronism,' and all the other hands went up.

'There, it's unanimous – except for you,' Hilary said.

'Wait, I claim Nickie's vote,' Smallie shouted. 'If he were awake he would have voted with me.'

'In your dreams,' said Jamoon.

'Boy, you would make one hell of a politician,' Victor laughed. 'The mentally incompetent, the dead and the unborn would all be counted as having voted for you. For God's sake, don't wish that kind of slackness on our newly-independent country...'

'OK, OK, how do you spell this word?' Smallie said with a sigh of resignation; and soon the wall was decorated with a beautiful red-brown slogan: *Sir Rupert is an anachronism.*

At that point they were joined by Ramkisoon, the caretaker/watchman, who had heard the commotion of the argument from downstairs and had come up to see what was going on. The whole situation was explained to him after he was provided with a stiff rum-and-water. He smiled broadly at the story, displaying three gold teeth.

'Sir Rupert na bad like he wife, Lady Dowding. Oh Gaad! She does quarrel with everybody, does lef' she own house and yard to come here and quarrel with the gardener and me. Every time she come is nothing but quarrel. All you should write something bout *she* now...'

'Oh no...' groaned half a dozen voices together, but Smallie was instantly enthusiastic and in no time he had added a second line on the wall, this time in white letters: 'and Lady Dowding is a ...'

'Stop right there, Mister,' Prince Hal said. 'What's it going to be this time? Don't you write anything vulgar.'

'I was thinking of *cantankerous old bitch*...'

'Here we go again,' Mark said. 'Quick, somebody, give him another acceptable substitute for his gutter language.'

'You can't say it's gutter language this time,' Smallie countered. 'Cantankerous, old and bitch are all good English words.'

'But what they add up to in this case is not acceptable,' said Desmond. 'And again, there's probably a much better word to express the same thing.'

'Let me hear it.'

'I'm thinking,' Desmond said.

'I know,' said Val. 'Lady Dowding is a termagant.'

'First class,' said Desmond, and the others agreed.

'I never heard such a word, I don't believe there's any such word.'

'Now listen, you half-witted boy,' Hilary said, beginning to get angry again, 'you may be good at drawing and painting, but you don't know language like Desi and Val; just accept your shortcomings (and everything about you is short, it seems) and admit it when you are outclassed.'

'I want to see it in a dictionary.'

'Dictionary deh in the office,' Ramkisoon said, 'Dornford, bring um, nuh.'

When the book arrived Hilary took it and read aloud before passing it to Smallie: 'Termagant: a boisterous, overbearing or quarrelsome woman; a virago, a shrew...' And again Smallie had to acquiesce in the decision of the majority, as he completed his second masterpiece: *and Lady Dowding is a termagant.*

'Good,' Victor said. 'Let's move on from this foolishness, now. Smallie, you've had your fun, asserted or celebrated your independence and realized, I hope, that, whether you're in a gang of eleven or a country of seven hundred thousand, there's no such thing as absolute independence.' But Smallie said nothing; he was outlining the white letters in black and adding refinements and decorations to what he had written, creating shadow-effects for the letters of the first line and thoroughly enjoying himself.

'My legs are numb, I need to get up,' Jamoon said. 'Somebody help me with Nickie, his head weighs a ton.'

'Here, let me take your place,' Desmond said. 'You can rest his head on my lap, and...'

'Nooo,' chorused half a dozed voices, and Smallie had to spell out their objection from over at the wall: 'Nice try, Desmond, but everybody knows that you're a friggin' anti-man and you're always trying to feel-up poor Nickie. One of theses days the buck blood in him going get ignorant and he going drive some lashes in you rass...'

'Shut up, Smallie... I knew that you all were going to say that, I was only teasing... and I was thinking of that Auden poem we did, 'Lay your sleeping head, my love/ human on my faithless arm...'

'Well,' said Mark, 'that might prove that your intentions are somewhat along the lines that Smallie is suggesting: both the reputation of that poem and the sexual orientation of its author point to...'

'Aha, you see, you can't hide it, Desmond,' Smallie laughed; 'everybody know about you...'

'Never mind all of that,' said Jamoon. 'Just help me to put Nickie to lie flat on the settee – but try not to wake him up.'

'Believe me, there's very little chance of that at the moment,' Victor assured them, as they laid him down on the settee.

'Oh, he looks so sweet and innocent in his sleep,' Desmond persisted, in a deliberately cooing tone, looking at the sleeper with his head slanted to one side. 'Let the living creature lie/ Mortal, guilty, but to me...'

'Cut it out, Desi,' Hilary said, and just at that point Nickie turned onto his side, and as he did so he said quite clearly a single word: 'latifundia'.

'Hey, what was that Nickie said?' asked Smallie, walking over to the group with a paintbrush in his hand.

'If you would stop playing with the white people paint and join the gang around the table you would hear everything that's going on,' Nunc told him. 'Nickie said *latifundia*.'

'And what the puss is that?'

'He's probably dreaming about yesterday's Caribbean History exam,' suggested Prince Hal. 'There was a question involving latifundia on the paper – although Nickie told me he didn't do that one.'

But Smallie was none the wiser, and Jamoon had to give him

– and a few of the others – a brief history lesson by way of explanation. Smallie returned to his wall in silence and in a short while he had painted on the wall, in green letters, the word latifundia, in order, he said, to record the only contribution of the sleeping Nickie to the evening's activities.

'Dat little one could paint good-good,' Ramkisoon said in admiration, gazing at the wall. 'When he finish school he can get nuff work painting all kind of signs for rum shop and thing.'

'Perfect,' laughed Hilary. 'That's just how he will end up, I'm sure. I can see it now: *The Eldorado Bar and Brothel*, in large golden letters...'

'Yes, with its twin trades illustrated one on either side,' added Val. 'A bare-breasted woman and a bottle of B.G. rum...'

'*Guyana* rum,' T. Roll corrected him, laughing. 'Anyway, as long as it's not stinking Laphroaig whiskey.' Smallie ignored all of this and continued touching up his lettering on the wall.

'Dornford, anybody else drinks this Laphroaig, or is only Sir Rupert?' asked Nunc.

'Well, we does keep a bottle or two in the bar and one-one body does ask for it every now and then, but Sir Rupert got he own stocks, just for he-one: two cartons at a time, each with twelve bottle. He does bring them himself from home – or somewhere – in the car and get Ramkisoon to bring them up to the bar.'

'So his two cases are behind the bar now?'

'Well right now one case done drink out, and the other got in – must-be ten bottle, besides the one we did using tonight.'

'I vote,' T. Roll said, 'that we dump all Sir Rupert's whiskey in the pool – let him swim in it if he wants: it will be like wading through the swamp.'

'I in that,' said Smallie emphatically, putting down his brush.

'Yes, let's,' said Mark, 'if only in reprisal for what he did to Nickie.'

'Hold on,' said Victor, 'We can't just throw away the man's whiskey; it's probably very expensive.'

'We could tell him we drank it out: we all tasted Nickie's, fell in love with it and decided we had to drink nothing but that all night.'

Whether it was the alcohol consumed, or the resentment of Sir Rupert and sympathy for the oblivious Nickie or perhaps just the anarchic spirit of the place and time, the majority decision was to dump Sir Rupert's Laphroaig into the pool. 'When he hear that all gone, he going only bring more,' Dornford said with a laugh, and that was the turning point of the night: Sir Rupert's whiskey was dumped in the pool, but it didn't stop there – they dumped all the other brands of whiskey in the pool, throwing the empty bottles in as well. Then they decided all the foreign spirits in the bar had to go, anything whose label did not say 'made (or bottled) in Guyana'. Then the gang decided to go downstairs to smell the pool and to luxuriate in the alcoholic stink of the mixed spirits superimposed on the smell of chlorine.

'You could get drunk just by sitting here in the deck and breathing in,' Nunc said. 'You could imagine what it would be like if you went in for a swim...'

'If there was a diving board I would dive in,' said Val.

'And you would burst your head on one of those floating bottles,' Hilary pointed out.

'No, but just to say that I had swam in all that expensive liquor, like those film stars who bathe in champagne, or that ancient queen who used to bathe in milk...'

'The members them did ask for a diving board,' Ramkisoon told them, 'a long time ago now, and Sir Rupert agree and plans get draw up and all, but Lady Dowding say nah, too much money – and to besides, the pool too small for that kind of horseplay.'

'But it wasn't *her* money,' Jamoon pointed out.

'You don't know she,' Dornford interjected. 'She don't like *anybody* to spend money: she mean like cat-shit, and twice as stink.' And many further anecdotes were told about Lady Dowding's parsimony, after which there was a sort of dull lag in the conversation, indicating perhaps that the gang was succumbing to the alcoholic miasma around the pool.

'Look,' Victor said, 'I think we have breathed in enough of these fumes, I'm going back up.'

'Me too; come on everyone. Hey, where's Smallie got to?'

'I don't know... better check that he's not lying at the bottom of the pool.'

'Don't make that kind of joke... I bet he went back up and is writing more stuff on that wall of his,' Mark said.

240

'I'll kill him,' Desi said, bounding up the stairs, closely followed by Hilary. Sure enough, Smallie was at the wall, brush in hand; he had just completed his latest addition to the night's graffiti: an alteration to the line which had read: 'and Lady Dowding is a termagant'. Between 'a' and 'termagant' he had inserted an upside-down 'v', and above the line he had painted, in smaller letters, the word 'tight-assed', so that it now read: *and Lady Dowding is a tight-assed termagant.*

Hilary was angry: 'You need a good beating, Fonseca, you know that? You're just a little own-way prick – determined to put in the kind of abusive language we all *agreed* should not appear on the wall.'

'And who's going to beat me, you? Anyway 'termagant' does not express Lady Dowding's meanness that we were hearing about downstairs, and also I think the alliteration adds something to the line... Besides, you just made my point for me, Miss Self-righteous. You called me 'a little own-way prick' – fair enough, it's expressive, isn't it? No decent English there. Admit it, that kind of language is powerful and very satisfying – not words from the dictionary that haven't been used for two hundred years. I rest my case.'

'Don't bother to argue with him,' Prince Hal said. 'Let him have his fun... it hardly seems to matter any more... Where have those two been?' And all heads turned to see T. Roll and Val out of breath at the top of the stairs.

'What have you two been up to?' Victor asked.

'We just threw... that coffin of red flowers ... into the pool,' Val panted, out of breath, 'signifying the death and burial of Sir Rupert and his type in the New Guyana: Dust to Dust, Laphroaig to Laphroaig – buried at sea, a sea of foreign spirits...'

'Yeah,' added T. Roll, 'we wanted to put him where the spirits would take him back to bonny Scotland, or wherever...' They all rushed out onto the patio, from where the oblong concrete planter, which had been on the pool deck, could be seen at the bottom of the pool, a few clusters of geraniums still in it, though most had floated out and added bright splashes of red and green here and there to the now discoloured water, in which bobbed a few dozen bottles.

'Surreal!' Smallie exclaimed. 'Wonderful! *Now* what else can we do?'

'You keep your tail quiet; I think we've all done enough mischief for the night,' Victor said as they went back in from the balcony. Just as they reached their chairs Nickie stirred on the settee and spoke again, this time a whole sentence. It sounded like: 'Don't pick the blue hibiscus', although Nunc said it sounded to him more like: 'so quick the brew turns viscous', and Jamoon agreed that that was closer to what she heard. There then followed a less than coherent argument or discussion that rambled into the realm of dreams and their interpretations and then into the business of foretelling the future.

'Perhaps Nickie is dreaming about the future of the country after independence,' Desmond speculated. 'Sleepers and dreamers are very important in Amerindian lore, and you know Nickie is half-Amerindian.'

'The truth is,' said Nunc, 'I'm not at all sure about this independence; a lot of people are packing up and leaving the country…'

'I think that's a mistake', said Mark. 'If all the people who can were to leave, that would guarantee the failure of the country, of independence…'

'Look who's talking,' Victor said. 'Your family left for Canada two months ago, and you'll be joining them in a year…'

'That doesn't mean I agree with it; I was against the move and I'm only going up there to study. After university I'll be coming right back here.'

'I bet you don't.'

'How much you want to bet?'

'This argument is foolish, you two,' said Prince Hal. 'I suppose we have to admit that the signs are not good. I think people have the wrong idea about independence; they think it means freedom to be lazy and self-indulgent – like we were tonight. Far from getting rid of the Sir Ruperts, many people seem bent on imitating them…'

'Yes,' added Jamoon. 'It's one thing to be proud of the new flag and the anthem, but these are nothing unless people are going to work together and sweat like pigs to build the country.'

'You know, I disagree,' Smallie said. 'We have to work together, yes, but we don't have to agree on everything and be all lovey-dovey. Look at us this evening – I think that independence also means you have to cuss and destroy and pull down and uproot... I think that is necessary: a purging of the evils of the past before we can build anything. If the country fails it will probably be because everybody wants to be decent and polite and not rock the boat. I say fuck all that. Speak your mind freely and don't be afraid to try something completely new...' As the others turned to look over at him when he began this tirade, they saw that he had written on the wall: *Don't pick the blue hibiscus*; he had decided to accept that version of what Nickie had said, perhaps because it was easier for him to illustrate; as he spoke he was painting a large blue hibiscus flower on the wall.

Suddenly the mood turned lugubrious, and the gang settled into their chairs in a numb silence, as if everything that had happened (both on that evening and in the past) seemed somehow fortuitous and beyond reason. Most felt this as a debilitating tide of anger or disappointment, as though nothing could atone for the ills of the past and, equally, nothing could restore the promise of the future. Only the youngest of them all, Smallie, still toiled with his paint and brushes at the wall, making and remaking the world inside his head. Dornford and Ramkisoon, too, were no longer smiling, and seemed sad and silent. It seemed as though a powerful spell had been cast on the gathering around the low table, and it was only broken when two things happened simultaneously: Nickie stretched and woke up, with a huge smile on his face, and Alan Dummett came running up the stairs, a look of shock and dismay on his. It was three minutes past midnight.

And that is one version of what happened on that night, told by one who was there, and whose reading and narrative of the events is of course suspect. You will have read elsewhere of the 'trial' that ensued from that night's activities, which also can be interpreted in several different ways... It was Alan Dummett and Nickie Calistro, the only two sober and (perhaps) innocent people present, who decided at that midnight hour how to handle the situation: it was they who decided that Dornford and Ramkisoon should allow themselves to be tied to two chairs in the middle of the room, their mouths covered with the painters' masking tape, so that they could not be implicated in what had happened. It was Nickie who said to Alan: 'You drive Mark and Smallie home at once, since they could be kicked out of college for this: we will claim that they left before anything untoward happened. The rest of us have finished school anyway. Then come back here as quickly as you can and call Sir Rupert and/or the police...'

The so-called trial and the suspended sentences it imposed may have haunted the surviving members of the gang for over thirty-five years, but it does not compare in horror to the purgatorial sentence imposed (by its own people – all of us) on the independent country of Guyana – a sentence of indefinite duration which continues to be served and wherein the individual suffering and the social deformity seem to increase year after year. Over the years the country lurches from one calendrical totem of independent nationhood to another – celebrations of emancipation, Mashramani, the hallowed raising of the flag in memory of that first independence midnight – as we continue to bite each other like bugs in a stinking bed where, for years, no warm-blooded body of hope has come to lie...

REMAINDERS

This is an attempt to close this book by bringing any reader who is still interested up-to-date on the lives and fortunes of the members of the 'gang' – the story-tellers. Scattered far and wide, we live our separate lives but keep sporadically in touch, especially when there is news requiring celebration or sorrow. I'm hoping that the publication of this book (at long last) might get us together again...

When **Victor Nunes** disappeared in the Pomeroon he was working in the Ministry of Information and was on an official assignment in his favourite region of Guyana. I feel partly responsible for his knowledge and love of the rivers of the North-West because I think it began when my father was stationed there in the fifties and early sixties and he would spend his school holidays visiting with us. I always liked him, although he was not the kind of person who enjoyed intimate and relaxed friendships: he was something of a loner, a searcher after truth and meaning (aided and abetted in latter years by the writings of Wilson Harris) – as I think his story in this collection suggests. I sometimes wonder if he staged his own disappearance and is living in freedom and anonymity somewhere in the North-West.

Desi Arthur went to England after school and to the universities of Birmingham and then Hull. After his first graduation he wrote me a long letter explaining that England and university life had confirmed for him that he was 'irretrievably' homosexual and he felt that he could never live again in Guyana. We corresponded fairly regularly and sometimes painfully (for me) until about the mid-eighties, when we were deep into our different lives and relationships and our letters became occasional and superficial. In

1994 I asked him to write (or finish) his story, explaining about Victor's death, and he sent me 'Sky' within three months. A year later I got a somewhat altered and expanded (less circumspect) version, which is the one published here. In 1997 I heard from a cousin of his that he was ill and later that he had died of an 'opportunistic' cancer. At one time, when we were in the sixth form, I was fiercely in love with Desi: I admired his knowledge, his wit and what I considered his physical beauty and perfection. I grieved silently and excessively at the news of his death.

Nunc de Mattis won some sort of scholarship to Canada and studied at the University of Alberta in Edmonton. He used to write me in Toronto boasting/complaining about the cold in winter. He married a Guyanese fellow student called Indrani and they have two children. I see them from time to time in Barbados or in Toronto. He is now slim and fit and careful about his health. Versions of the italicized parts of his story were among the materials in the box-folder I inherited from Victor: these were four brief pieces entitled 'Conversations'. I wrote and suggested he expand them or build a story around them, and I love the story he eventually produced, set in places we both know very well. He's a professor of Bio-Chemistry in Edmonton and has published poetry and short fiction from time to time.

Hilary Sutton-Devonish was one of the first to submit her story. She married an Englishman after finishing university at Bristol and she lives somewhere in rural Cheshire. I have not seen her since college days, but when I managed to track down her address she wrote several long and friendly letters. She ended up rewriting her story, seems very happy with her life and says she has no plans to visit Guyana or the Caribbean.

Jamila Muneshwar and **Nickie Calistro** were married during their final year at the University of Toronto. I was Best Man at the wedding. They had three children fairly quickly and seemed happy and settled (as high-school teachers) when I left Toronto, but then they had a 'trial separation' for almost a year some time in the eighties, when Nickie had a breakdown and a lengthy depression. But as he said in a letter to me: ' it didn't work out – we just had to get back together' (despite the fact that he received – as he later whispered to me – a come-live-with-me-and-be-my-love letter from Desi Arthur in England, who'd heard of his separation). They now live in Wisconsin, with the children grown up and scattered in various North American cities. Nickie's story was the first submitted to Victor – before he left Guyana. Jamila apparently had a draft of sorts from early, but only completed it in 1995, when prompted by my letter. Nickie decided he would revise his while Jamila worked on hers, but I had to write and tell him that I much preferred the original story, which is the one published here with only one addition and a few minor revisions. I visited them in Madison two years ago while I was on sabbatical leave. It was then that I collected the final version of 'A Lovesong for Miss Lillian'. They are a lovely couple and I felt completely at home at their place.

Hal Seaforth works for a textbook publishing company just outside London and writes a literary column for a 'black' newspaper. He had taught Literature for years in one of the London Polytechnics (before they all became Universities). I look him up whenever I'm in London and enjoy his wonderful conversations on books, films and music. His Trinidad-born wife died about six years ago and he now lives with a lovely woman of East European origin whose name I can neither remember nor pronounce, but they have visited and stayed with me in Barbados on two occasions, once on their way 'home' to Guyana. Hal sent me his story. 'The Bats of Love' about a year after I'd written telling him of the revival of the project. It is one of my favourites.

Val Madramootoo , I hear, is quite often in Guyana these days, since his divorce two years ago. He officially lives somewhere just north of Miami and runs a Shipping and Export business from there. The family still has businesses in Guyana and I gather that he is quite wealthy. A shorter (and less interesting) version of his bakoo story was in Victor's box-file when I received it. He eagerly accepted the invitation to revise it in 1994 and tinkered with it for another four years before he finally considered it finished. When

I saw him last he had put on some weight and had lost more hair than I had, but his conversation still sparkled with the old humour and mischief and his generosity of spirit was still very much in evidence as we talked about the other members of the gang. He had hopped on a plane and flown to London and visited Desi in Hospital when he learnt about his illness – he also returned for the funeral, and there were tears in his eyes when he told me how bleak and lonely an event it was.

Terrence Wong: it is impossible to keep in regular touch with Tennis Roll. Most members of the gang report that he would storm into their lives after an absence of several years, then after a few months he would disappear again. Certainly my own experience confirms this pattern: he turned up in my office at Cave Hill suddenly one day in October 1985, told me he was on a brief holiday and was working for the Martin Marietta Corporation. He came and had dinner with us that night and the children loved him as he played and joked with them incessantly – 'Uncle Tennis Roll' they called him. Three years later he visited, while we were on sabbatical leave at the University of Warwick. Again the children monopolized him, and we hardly got to talk about anything. In 1991 he turned up in Barbados again, claimed that he was now working on some top-secret electronics and computer stuff for the Pentagon. Two months later he burst into my office, opened up the computer and inserted a little silver box the size of a cigarette pack which he hooked up to the telephone line. All this was before we in Barbados knew anything about e-mail or the internet, but in the mornings my computer screen would be full of messages and greetings and gossip from T. Roll and sometimes I would have a hard time getting rid of them in order to do my word processing which is mostly what I used the computer for in those days.

In a very dramatic phone call six months later he claimed he was 'in deep shit' and that I should remove the little silver box and its connecting wires from my computer and 'deep six' them. I think I did throw the little box into the sea off a cliff in the north of Barbados, so insistent was he that it could get us both into lots of trouble. I never saw him again until 1996 when he came to

Barbados and delivered his story in person. He was relaxed and full of talk about sex with wonderful young girls on beaches in the Far East. He laughed dismissively when I reminded him about his anxious phone call: 'Oh, that turned out to be nothing in the end – sorry if it upset you.'

Last year, over the Christmas and New Year period, while my wife and I and two other couples were touring India, we stayed briefly at the Travancore Heritage Hotel at the Southern tip of the Country, and who should walk into the hotel dining room with a stunningly beautiful girl from Thailand, but T. Roll. There was lots of grey in his hair now and he looked like an oriental sugar-daddy. He seemed not at all surprised to see me and we chatted during a long walk on the beach while the women looked at Pashmina shawls and pictures from the Hindu epics hand-painted on silk... I wonder just when and where he will show up next.

Alex Fonseca in fact became very friendly with Sir Rupert and Pippa, Lady Dowding. Six months after the fiasco in the bank club, Lady Dowding invited to lunch those members of the gang who were still in Guyana – about five of us. She said she wanted to show her gratitude because the incident had made Sir Rupert come to his senses and decide to retire to Scotland ('I'd been telling him for months that independent Guyana was not the place for us, but he insisted that he wanted to live here, travel in the interior and fish for lukanani in the Abary'). I remember her saying at the lunch: 'this tight-assed termagant thanks you from the bottom of her ... whatever. Now I can go home in peace to Edinburgh where I belong.' Before they left, however, she got to know and to love Smallie's paintings, and purchased several at very generous prices. She especially liked 'Madonna of the Koker', a large canvas of an Indian girl with terrified eyes clutching desperately a bawling, naked baby boy, with a forty-foot canal and a koker in the background.

Smallie had visited the Dowdings frequently in Scotland while he was in the seminary there. He is now Father Alex S.J. He still paints, has had several exhibitions in the Caribbean and in Europe and North America and teaches art in Guyana. He handed in his story, 'The Tyranny of Influence', in 1997, claiming, when I asked him, that he'd never heard of the Harold Bloom book. I see him quite often in Guyana and here in Barbados. He still occasionally uses all the known cuss-words, but insists that he's praying about it and trying to control his tongue. He hugged me and wept when I told him of Desi's death.

That leaves only **Mark McWatt,** who left Guyana to attend the University of Toronto and then went over to Leeds to do his doctorate, which he completed in 1975. Since then he has taught English and Caribbean Literature and creative writing at the Cave Hill campus of the University of the West Indies. At Cave Hill he met and married his wife Amparo and they have two children, now adults. He still considers Guyana 'home' (especially the rivers and the interior, where he grew up) and tries to get back there as often as possible. The story of his involvement in this project is told elsewhere. His own 'story' in this collection is something that had been clear in his head for several years, but was not written down until all the other stories had been received. He is relieved that this project is finally completed.

NEW FICTION FROM GUYANA

Jan Lowe Shinebourne
The Godmother and Other Stories
ISBN: 1 900715 87 2; price: £7.99

Covering more than four decades in the lives of Guyanese at home or in Britain and Canada, these stories has an intensive and rewarding inner focus on a character at a point of crisis. Harold is celebrating the victory of the political party he supports whilst confronting a sense of his own powerlessness; Jacob has been sent back to Guyana from Britain after suffering a mental breakdown; Chuni, a worker at the university, is confused by the climate of revolutionary sloganizing which masks the true situation: the rise of a new middle class, elevated by their loyalty to the ruling party. This class, as the maid, Vera, recognises, are simply the old masters with new Black faces.

The stories in the second half of the collection echo the experience of many thousands who fled from the political repression, corruption and social collapse of the 70s and 80s. The awareness of the characters is shot through with Guyanese images, voices and unanswered questions. It is through these that their new experiences of Britain and North America are filtered. One character lies in a hospital in London fighting for her life, but hears the voices of her childhood in Guyana – her mother, African Miss K, the East Indian pandit and the English Anglican priest. Once again, they 'war for the role of guide in her life'. In 'The Godmother' and 'Hopscotch', childhood friends reunite in London. Two have stayed in Guyana, while one has settled in London. The warmth of shared memories and cold feelings of betrayal, difference and loss vie for dominance in their interactions.

These stories crystallize the shifts in Guyana's uncomfortable fortunes in the post-colonial period, and while they are exact and unsparing in their truth-telling, there are always layers of complexity that work through their realistic surfaces: a sensitivity to psychological undertones, the evocative power of memory and a poetic sense of the Guyanese physical space.

Denise Harris
In Remembrance of Her
ISBN: 1 900715 99 6; price: £9.99

Why does the Judge, powerful, wealthy and Black, bring his world crashing down by murdering his son, Baby-Boy? And why was Baby-Boy wearing a dress of feathers, his face painted white? These are the mysteries the Judge's old friend, a private eye, sets out to uncover, though it is not until the very last chapter that the whole story emerges. Until then, the reader is engaged in a journey of twists and turns as complex and surprising as life itself.

A work of gothic splendour, *In Remembrance of Her* has all the complexity, poetry and moral depth of a dark, late, Shakespearean comedy – the wronging and death of a first wife, a lost daughter, and a disturbed and rebellious son – in a world out of joint and crying out for compassion and restorative justice.

Set in Guyana, where colour and class still count for much, it is the Judge's servant, Blanche Steadman, who, though confined to her one-room shack behind the Judge's splendid mansion, is witness to the pain locked deep in the household's secrets. She becomes the warmly sympathetic guide to the novel's unfolding mysteries, along with her friend, the formidable market woman, Irene Gittings, whose role in the novel is one of its surprises.

At the heart of the narrative is the ghostly presence of the Caul Girl who, through the survival of her diaries, becomes the prophetic conscience of both the present and the past.

Denise Harris's first novel, *The Web of Secrets*, was welcomed as "a brilliant cautionary tale… a most complex and aesthetically satisfying web" (Sharon Joseph, *Mango Season*), as a "startling and mesmeric novel" (Chris Searle, *The Morning Star*). More ambitious and daring in its scope, *In Remembrance of Her* is quite simply one of the most remarkably imaginative novels to burst from the Caribbean in recent years.

Ryhaan Shah
A Silent Life
ISBN: 1 84523 002 7; price: £8.99

Aleyah Hassan knows from an early age that some mystery surrounds her grandmother who, besides praying incessantly, spends her days in silence. When Aleyah finally breaks down her mother's reluctance to reveal the family's heart of darkness, she learns that Nani once had a great deal to say, that she was drawn to a vision of revolutionary politics and the desire to speak on behalf of the sugar workers of their village. But in the Guyana of the 1940s, a woman could not play such a role, and Nani was forced to act through her husband, Nazeer. He, lacking his wife's abilities, is destroyed by the villagers' humiliating perception of him as a man ruled by his wife. What has never been clear is the extent to which Nani was directly responsible for his self-destruction.

When Aleyah grows up academically gifted and with the desire to change the world, her family is both proud and concerned, particularly by Aleyah's and Nani's mutual attraction. And later, when Aleyah, following a scholarship to England, has to choose between her work for a radical aid agency and her children and marriage to a charming but lightweight fellow Guyanese, family history appears to be repeating itself.

In a novel that moves easily between the socially realistic and the poetic, *A Silent Life* combines strong social themes with a narrative that explores mythic patterns through elements of the other-worldly.

All Peepal Tree titles are available from our website:
www.peepaltreepress.com

Explore our list of over 160 titles, read sample poems and reviews, discover new authors, established names and access a wealth of information about books, authors and Caribbean writing. Secure credit card ordering, fast delivery throughout the world at cost or less.

You can contact us at:
Peepal Tree Press, 17 King's Avenue, Leeds LS6 1QS, United Kingdom
Tel: +44 (0) 113 2451703 E-mail: hannah@peepaltreepress.com